CANITHROPE

*To Heather
Adventure Awaits!*

VENNESSA ROBERTSON

CANITHROPE

For my wonderful, supportive husband and my two amazing children.
I could not have done this without you.

SBS

And in loving memory of Dingo. He was a very good dog.

CHAPTER ONE

I WAS ENGAGED to a cad; a wealthy cad with a good family name, but a cad nonetheless. If I wished to provide for my parents in their old age, there was nothing to be done about it. That was what was expected of women. They did what must be done, whether they wanted to or not. What was expected of me was to sit in the tea house and rise above my birth. It was no matter that my father was an apothecary and that we served the rich and the poor alike. All that mattered was that I spent my days attending teas, playing cards with my social betters, engaging in gossip, and learning to be pretty and utterly useless for I am to marry, and marry well. I had the blessed fortune of catching the eye of a gentleman of leisure. It was my great misfortune that it was Mr. Byron Goodwin, eldest son of the Goodwins of London in Kensington.

If Papa had known of my misery, he would have prevented the marriage. But Papa would not be strong forever. He did his best for Mama and me, and I would do my best to provide for him in return. It was my fondest wish that, in time, Byron and I should grow to respect one another. Many marriages started with less than love and grew to admiration.

So distracting were these thoughts that I dealt away a perfectly good pair of hearts, which caused my partner to cluck in annoyance. So much for learning to play cards like a lady.

It was late in the afternoon when the bell chimed loudly. The regular visitors of the tea house were too refined to bang the bell into the door frame. I brushed back strands of my dark hair that escaped my careful plait, and glanced over my shoulder, my attention pulled away from my cards.

Calvin walked through the door, staring at the ladies and the occasional gentleman seated among them taking their tea. His usual, stumbling, teenage gawkiness was suddenly gone. His eyes caught me and he was overcome with a sudden need for gallantry. He straightened and an air of determination fell over him the way it might for a boy who professed to one day marry his master's daughter.

Calvin Tabor was the son of Mrs. Tabor, our housekeeper and cook. When she was widowed after the Crimean War, my father took him on as a junior apprentice apothecary. We were grateful for the help but without taking him as an apprentice we would never be able to afford him. Male staff would require my papa to pay an additional tax, and though we sat comfortably in the middle class, we were far from wealthy.

For not being blood, my father still treated him as his own son, and that made Calvin's constant attention feel inappropriate. He was more a brother, in my mind, than a potential suitor. After he has served two years of formal apprenticeship and will be able to open his own apothecary shop, he should have no trouble finding a suitable woman to court. That is, if he manages to grow up first. He was a clumsy nightmare. I couldn't tell you how many batches of cures he'd ruined and bottles broken.

Still, I found no pleasure in seeing him awkwardly shift his weight in the doorway, at a complete loss on how to breathe in polite company, let alone act. He stood there like a new foal; blinking and standing with his mouth slightly agape, watching me take tea with Lady Theodora, Lady Norton, Lady Thornburry, and their friends. He recovered quickly and ripped his cap off his head, exposing hair the color of hay that had cured in the sun, and clasped it behind his back. "I beg your pardon, ladies." He made a short bow. "Madame Theodora?"

Lady Thornburry sniggered.

"Come in please, sir, I will set you a table—is it just yourself this fine afternoon?" Madame Theodora asked, standing from her seat and greeting Calvin. She ran the most prosperous tea house in all of Limehouse.

This seemed to remind Calvin that he was not here to gawk, and he cleared his throat. At least he had the manners to look chagrined. "Madame, a word if you please?"

"Of course. Excuse me, Miss Harper," she said to me, excusing herself and holding open the damask curtain that separated the dining room from the office and, beyond that, the kitchen. He went with her, not even peeking a second look at Lady Norton and her friends.

I immediately felt a stab of pity for him; he did not deserve the mocking that would be coming as soon as he was at the socially acceptable distance for Lady Thornburry's shrewish tongue to begin wagging.

I was sure the trouble was with Byron again. I released a quivering breath and focused on pouring tea. The warm sunlight through the windows made the tea house comfortably warm, even in winter, but I felt a chill snake up my spine. I worried that perhaps there was some tragedy at home and I was needed, but then a deeper worry began gnawing my stomach to knots. My intended came from a prosperous and respected family, but his personal reputation was not well thought of.

"Vivian?" Madame Theodora beckoned. "Mr. Tabor was sent by Mr. Goodwin's valet. You are to attend him immediately at *The Crimson Boar*." She was positively alight with excitement.

I groaned, the gnawing feeling in my stomach confirmed. *The Crimson Boar* was not someplace respectable ladies visited. The smell of tobacco and strong spirits made my eyes water, and the men always seemed to leer which made me uncomfortable.

"Mr. Tabor says he is to be your escort."

I twisted my hands in my skirts. Mr. Goodwin's valet, Hiram, had sent Calvin to fetch me. God, what had Byron done now?

I stood and bid Lady Thornburry and the rest of her little group of friends "good day." I did my best to keep a smile plastered to my face, dreading what they would say when I was gone. They would soon be my friends, I reminded myself, and I knew all too well how they treated their own.

Calvin shifted impatiently from one foot to the next. He looked bored and miserable. It was the look Calvin always had around me since Mr. Goodwin gave me the garnet ring I now wore. The fiancée of a member of *The Crimson Boar* could easily visit her betrothed without her reputation being questioned, but my concern remained. It was fine for the nobility to gamble their fortunes away if they wished but I was not one of them yet. I hated that place, for someone like me, it was a place of vice and sin where the fortunes of lesser men were decided and dealt away like the cards they traded. It was hard to remember in a few short months, I would belong there and no one would be on my doorstep preaching the immorality of drinking and gambling away one's meager wealth. The gambling houses belonged to the world of the wealthy. It was the world of my new fiancé, and the question loomed, what did he do?

I suspect he was drunk and had stayed at the club last night. His father's carriage had been impounded three nights ago after he had run down a poor lamplighter and broke an axle. The ladies at the tea house laughed themselves sick, claiming the chastisement was more for the threat to the fine horse and the damage to the carriage— lamplighters were common as dull pennies. Was this to be my world?

Marriage sometimes civilized wild bachelors. I only hoped this would be the case and my humble, loving influence over the plight of the common man would change his ways. Why, with time, he might even donate to the housing fund. Now, wouldn't that be a sight? Byron Goodwin, a respectable man of the people!

He was drunk. I could smell it before he got close enough to embrace me. Judging from the stubble on his face and the wrinkled suit he wore, he had been at it since the night before— that meant he had been here nearly eighteen hours. Dice or cards, it didn't matter really—he had the skill for neither but the appetite for both.

Byron leapt to his feet as soon as I came in. "Ah there's my darling! Did you bring my purse?"

Calvin was ungraciously waved away by a casual flick of the wrist by one of the men at the card table, gamblers the lot of them, to return home as though he was nothing more than a street urchin.

Byron's valet, Hiram, stood in the corner looking as though he wanted to melt into the plush carpeting. He kept his face blank, but that was more telling to me than any expression.

I liked Hiram. He was quiet and respectful, but quite witty. When I set up our home as Mrs. Vivian Byron Goodwin, I planned to keep him as our butler, Byron's family could well afford it. Hiram's eyes, red-rimmed from the smoke, refused to look at my face, and he declined to move enough to be noticed by anyone but myself. I knew that look at once—he was ashamed. Hiram had sent Calvin to fetch me. Byron had lost and, by the piles of coin and notes in front of the other men at the table, he had lost a lot. I didn't even bother to wonder how much this time. Hiram righted Byron's chair, and stepped back into the corner as two of the men at the table gave him a hard look. He was barely permitted to move. He most certainly had not been allowed to leave and fetch me himself. Byron was in a lot of trouble, and they were holding his servant until he paid.

Byron spoke in a slurred, breathy voice of a drunk who believed himself to be whispering. "You're wearing my ring, good."

"Of course, I am." Why would I not?

"Lord Meyer," Byron said, "I'm sure you know Miss Vivian Harper, my fiancée."

"Of course," one of the men said, smooth as ice. His speech marked him for a nobleman. We had never met before, but his manners were refined. Why couldn't I have managed an engagement to a man with manners like that?

Byron dragged me by the hand to the table. "This ring will more than cover my debts against this round."

I took a deep breath.

"Mr. Goodwin, no. Not even if she came with it," Mr. Bilton, the pawnbroker, said critically.

Byron's pretty, symmetrical mouth twisted into a sneer. I was too stunned to even gasp at the insult. I was going to be sick. Something about his manner made me cold all over.

"I assure you, Lord Meyer, that ring is more than worth my debt to you." He bit the end off of each word. "If your pawnbroker will not give a nice price for it, I have other pieces at my disposal. Her cameo could also be taken as payment."

My hand turned stiff. Surely, I had misheard him. He could pawn the ring, I guess, as it was his gift to his future wife; an adornment to his own property. My cameo, on the other hand, was my mother's, it had been my grandmother's, and it was not his to give. I opened my mouth to protest, but Hiram raised his eyes off the floor, staring at me for just a moment too long. It was a warning.

"But—" My heart hammered in my chest

One look from Hiram in the corner emphasized his fierce warning. He gave an almost imperceptible shake of his head. This was a gentleman's club, it was no place for women. I was only here because my presence here was requested, no, demanded by my fiancé. No, they were holding his servant, my presence here was demanded by the men he owed money to. They would take my jewelry, or they would harm his servant. They would not harm his person, it was not the way things were done. But they could harm my reputation and they could harm my papa's reputation. He was not a part of their world; a simple apothecary was beneath them, these mighty men of wealth and power. The fates and fortunes of the lesser men were nothing to them. Until I married Byron, his name would not protect my family.

I swallowed hard, nearly choking on my tongue.

Hiram looked down at his feet again.

Mr. Bilton examined my cameo carefully, then ran one blunt finger across its warm, polished surface, his touch much too intimate for comfort.

Byron noticed it but said nothing, though the pale blotches on his cheeks grew somewhat. He took something of mine, my own, my person. I was violated and Byron did nothing to stop it. No, he would never be a respectable man.

"Very well, Ms. Harper, I shall take your jewelry to clear your future husband's debts," the pawnbroker said. "Your fiancée's baubles will be held in my store. You have a fortnight to clear the debt or they will be resold. You know the terms, Mr. Goodwin."

"Excellent," Byron clapped with glee and rubbed his hands together briskly to stave off the numb of too much drink. "Another hand of whist, fellows?"

"I believe it is time to head home," Lord Meyer remarked casually. "My wife will be sorely missing my presence." He shot me a sympathetic look.

I could barely breathe. It was all I could do to not vomit.

"Mr. Goodwin," another man at the table said, "I have to close for the day. You should have your man take you home."

"Oh course, you are right." Byron lurched from his chair, almost knocking it over again. "Hiram, where have you gone?"

Hiram appeared at his elbow and carefully guided my fiancé out. I followed, determined not to cry. As we passed the enameled crest on the wall, I observed, not for the first time, that whether inside the establishment or out, the Boar's head was quite ghastly. It looked to be on a field of blood.

"Come, Chuckie!" He called to me as though I was his faithful hound.

Hiram and I struggled to get him into a hansom cab with as much dignity as we could muster. I must admit that I was near useless. Hiram, however, behaved as a proper valet would.

I should have helped but all I could do was follow along behind, my eyes glued to the ground. All I wanted to do was provide for my family, but all I succeeded in doing was make a mess of everything. How could I have believed I could have found happiness with a man like that?

Over the blood pounding in my ears I could hear Hiram placating my fiancé, disarming his drunken anger with profuse apologies and promises to improve his feeble skills as merely a passable valet. I had to smile, it was working. Byron criticized everything from Hiram's keeping of his wardrobe to how he was a horrid companion. Byron had no more attention for me.

I sat next to them in the cab, momentarily forgotten, wondering how a beautiful morning could have turned so sour.

The carriage bumped and splashed along the street. It was times like these that I wished I was more like my mother's friend, the proprietress of the tea shop, Madame Theodora. She was the type of woman that one would call a suffragette, some even to her face, and she always cheerfully agreed. I would give anything to be a woman like that, to have that fortitude. I was not one, but I was beginning to understand how such feelings arose. One could only take so much of being trapped—I had wanted to provide for my parents as I had always been told I should, and a lady did so through a good marriage. A new century was rising. Perhaps a new breed of woman would as well, and suffragettes, like Madame Theodora would not be so uncommon.

I would also give anything to have Mama read the tarot for me, as she did at dinner parties and give me some sort of advice. I would love to see the spread that was to guide what I was about to do now.

Byron Goodwin, in all drunken lordly fashion, was vomiting over the side of the carriage. I reminded myself to thank Hiram at the next opportunity for his foresight to situate Byron near the door. By positioning himself between us, Hiram had also shielded me from most of the foulness. Byron was too drunk to notice the impropriety.

I listened to Byron retch again. This would not be my life. I set my head against the back of the cab and I absently rubbed the bare spot left by my ring. One thing was for certain, I was not marrying Byron Goodwin now.

CHAPTER TWO

PAPA WAS DEALING with a customer when I walked in. He removed his cap and absently wiped his brow. This customer was obviously upsetting him.

The customer, a tall man with blond hair curling slightly at his collar, leaned forward. "I will be needing wolfsbane, aconite, and monk's hood. I'm not sure if there is another name for it."

"I'm sure you are aware, Mr. Cooper, that wolfsbane is not merely a poison for transfiguring and fantastical peoples like werewolves and shape shifters, but also to common, God-fearing peoples like you and me."

"But it harms them more, correct?" Mr. Cooper said, his voice dropped drastically, "Mr. Harper you are known to be a man of discretion, I am sure you support our mission to purge the evils plaguing London."

"Wolfsbane is a poison, fatal to almost everyone—I cannot in good conscious sell you such vast quantities of something that is so toxic to the public," my father answered, turning away from the customer briefly to greet me as I walked by. "Good evening, my dear."

"Papa." I gave him a small curtsy.

"Why don't you go and see about the cat, my dear, while I finish with Mr. Cooper."

I nodded in dutiful daughter fashion. He meant for me to join my mother behind the door that separated the shop from our private landing.

He was very allergic to cats, we have never had a one. The customer must be upsetting father more than I initially thought for him to lie.

Men may very well run the world for now, but the world was rapidly changing and Papa believed we, his wife and daughter, deserved to know what was happening even if other men did not. As soon as I was old enough to understand that I was being trusted with a precious secret, that some men valued the strength of women; I was encouraged to listen to the matters that concerned men for they concerned everyone. We had a great queen, it was only a matter of time before the rest of men recognized the strength in all women.

Mama was waiting for me behind the door in the little alcove. I made sure to close the door and latch it firmly, then I joined her at the panel behind the shop wall where a patch of thin fabric was cunningly painted to match the plastered wall. Mother and I sat quietly by the patch and listened to the rest of father's exchange with the customer.

"Rowen Harper, allow me to be very clear," Mr. Cooper said, "There is a rearrangement of society coming, exploration has revealed all manner of strangeness. The Red Hood society is determined to protect the good citizens of London from unnaturalness. Your cooperation and support would be most appreciated. Especially, when the order comes to protect the citizens from other unnaturalness—like fortune telling, for example."

Mama stiffened beside me.

"Oh pshaw!" Papa said, "No one would think Lilly Harper is dangerous. Everyone knows that her fortune telling is nothing more than a parlor trick. She is just a midwife."

"Ah, but there are many who believe in her readings and her charms. The poor can be so superstitious. We can't be held responsible for the poor acting in an unseemly manner if your shop were to be targeted by vandals because they feared you were an unnatural sympathizer. Or worse, were committing acts of unnatural powers."

There was a long pause.

"I understand your position, Mr. Cooper. I can see if I can find enough Wolfsbane to meet your purposes, and perhaps I can even make a small donation to the good work of The Red Hood society— in the interest of protecting the people of London," Papa said smoothly.

"You are the soul of generosity," Mr. Cooper said. I heard coins clinking. "Oh, and Mr. Harper," Mr. Cooper continued, "Please be sure to warn your women. Suffragettes are not being viewed favorably by those in higher society. After all, we do have order to maintain."

"Of course," Papa replied, "Good day, Mr. Cooper."

"Good Day, Mr. Harper." The door opened, ringing the bell nailed to the frame, and was closed with more force than necessary.

"Now then, Vivian," Mama paused, and looked me over as if she was seeing me for the first time. Her eyes widened in surprise, they were brilliant green—wild and beautiful.

"I wish to hear all about whatever adventure kept you out so late, but first, the cards." She pulled her shawl closer around her shoulders, causing her silver bracelets to chime musically, "You are surrounded by energy, something is happening."

Mama ran her hands over her worn cards. She always had them in a pocket, tucked away in a scrap of green silk with a tattered edge in need of hemming. The pictures were faded and the edges were all worn; every corner was dinged from years of shuffling. This was the deck she used for real readings. Whenever she read for the gentry—for those not interested in the real message the cards held—she used the fancy cards with gilded edges and carefully rendered watercolor images. They were sufficiently mystical looking for mummery. This set was something else entirely. Attuned with real intention, and read with clear purpose, these were the real cards. She closed her eyes and cut the deck one-handed. Nine cards fell into a neat pile on the green silk. She turned them carefully, letting them fall as they wanted which allowed her to tap into the energies of the ley lines of the earth.

"Swords and Pentacles, conflict and money," Mama started.

"That's nothing new. What with all the strangeness, the nobles, and the new factories— this is not surprising." I didn't like the sarcastic way I sounded, but I had something important I wished to discuss with her.

"Shush," Mama admonished. "*Themis*, she says not to worry, all will work out in the end, as it is supposed to." She traced the edge of the Justice card and flipped over the next card. "*Death*, transformation, and change is coming, you know." She turned over the next cards. "*The Hermit*, but in inverse. Over-caution will be your enemy and make it hard to progress and learn what you must. The *Knave of Scepters* crossed by *The Moon* means a good stranger comes your way—but he is ruled by deception—"

"Please stop, I really don't want to hear anymore."

Mama looked at me sharply, annoyed at the interruption, but softened at once upon seeing my eyes hot with tears.

"I'm breaking my engagement with Byron! Mama, I'm sorry." I felt as though I had swallowed something very hot that refused to cool. I had reduced us to beggary. I couldn't bear to say it out loud. It was easy to be brave in the carriage when he was vomiting, it was much harder when the people I may be damning to starvation were before me.

Mama waved her hand, dismissing Byron with a shrug. "Mr. Goodwin is no longer in your spread. You must look to see what you're supposed to see. I wish to hear what troubles you—whatever it is will all resolve as it is meant to—but first, let me finish the reading."

It wasn't that I didn't believe in mother's gift, or value the teachings of the cards, I just had a hard time believing that they were supposed to hold the same amount of weight as social progression. We lived in a time of education, advancement, science—sometimes it was hard to hold faith in something the church itself proclaimed as witchcraft. At least some days I felt this way. Other days I felt the cards calling to me with their exciting forbidden wisdom and I would look through them and ask them, as I did when I was a child, to share their secret knowledge with me. Mama would smile at me and stroke my hair and remind me that all things came with time. While I struggled to believe in them now, concern for my family and our future weighing heavily on me, Mama's concentration comforted me.

I nodded and wiped my eyes. Twenty-five was old for a broken engagement. The scandal could bankrupt the family by making their only daughter unmarriable, at least for the next year or so. It was not unheard of for engaged couples to share a bed before marriage when all was done but the wedding vows. Fortunately, I knew Byron's reputation too well and was never alone with him, but what would the rest of London believe? The worst until a year without a baby passed. I let out a shaky breath. My mother still loved me, surely she would forgive the pawned jewelry, as well.

"There are a lot of cards in inverse; you must adjust your thinking to see your way through this. The *King of Pentacles*, the *Queen of Pentacles,* and the *Ten of Pentacles* all in inverse. A dangerous or maybe deceitful man, a suspicious woman and loss, perhaps robbery. And the *Knave of Swords*, correctly positioned; a spy perhaps or someone who is gathering information for a nefarious purpose. But have courage, my love; the *Five of Wands* means valor and courage. Have strength, my dear." My mother frowned at the cards, "Vivian, what did you get yourself into?"

"Your shell cameo, the one carved like a red fox, Byron sold it to a pawnbroker. He sent for me and when I got there, he was drunk and had been gambling again. He took my jewelry to cover his debts."

"Oh, dear heart!" Mama gathered me up in her arms, rocking me for a moment like when I was a child.

"But I will get it back," I vowed pulling away. "I can take a position cleaning or mending."

"Never mind that," Mama said. "Your father and I will go and speak with the pawnbroker and see if some sort of arrangement can be made."

I nodded, Mama always made me safe, always made it better. But, I was a woman grown now. If I was truly to do all in my power to care for them as they had done for me, I could not be a child forever. Tomorrow morning I would accompany them to negotiate, with Papa's help of course, the terms of the return of my family's jewelry. If Byron wanted his ring back, he could negotiate the terms himself. He was no stranger to the task.

We had set to the morning's business when the door to Papa's apothecary shop was thrown open. Byron walked through the door; he strode as though his very presence was a grace within our establishment. We should be humbled to behold him.

I turned my attention back to the shelves on the rear wall, carefully polishing bottles and setting out stock to be sold.

"Mr. Harper," Byron sat at the table by the front window of our little store front, "Mrs. Harper."

"Good Afternoon, Mr. Goodwin," my mother was cool, but polite.

"Vivian." Byron greeted me informally.

"*Mister* Goodwin." I said, bending over our books. We had several appointments on the books, which were far more interesting to me than Byron. Mama would be attending a lady ready to give birth to see how her contractions were progressing. If she went into labor today, she would bring me along. Midwifery was an excellent trade for me to add to our family's reputation.

"Ah, that's how it is, 'eh dove?" Byron held out his arm, which I refused to take. "Darling, don't fret, I shall get your ring out of pawn by Wednesday at the latest. This is a momentary setback."

"Mr. Goodwin, that ring is mine no longer," I said as calmly as I could. "Our engagement is cancelled. Good day."

"Clearly, she is out of her wits," Byron said, laughing. "Mr. Harper, you must teach her to speak better to her future husband."

"I believe you heard my daughter correctly, Mr. Goodwin. Your engagement to her has ended. I withdraw my permission for you to court her."

Byron paled.

For a moment, and for just a moment, I struggled with keeping from breaking into hysterical laughter. Papa agreed when I said I would wed him, now he said I could cancel the engagement. He accepted both without discussion. He must be as mad as I was.

"This will cause quite the scandal," Byron snapped.

"Her name will be ruined," Byron slammed his chair into the wall, gouging the sill.

"Her name will be no worse for wear. As for scandal, everyone in London society knows already why the engagement is canceled," Papa said.

"You dare spread gossip over my good name?" He was white with fury.

"I have not told a soul, I assure you, Mr. Goodwin," Papa said calmly. "I would prefer you leave my home without further damage. If you will not leave my premises immediately, I shall summon the police."

"Our engagement is already announced in the square. You will be shamed. No one will believe you still a virtuous woman," Byron sneered.

"I will have words with anyone who calls my daughter a whore," Papa said, much less calm this time. "Mr. Goodwin, we will no longer be serving you. How you leave here is your own choice."

"Were you a gentleman, I would challenge you to a duel," Byron jeered.

"Were I a gentleman, I would accept," My father said. "But I am not, and neither are you. Please now, be off."

He shot one last look around the room and stormed out. He slammed the door so hard one of the glass panels in the door cracked and with it, my hopes for a good match. Even though he was a gambler and a drunk, he still carried quite a bit of influence, and provoked animals were dangerous ones. By that token, incensed men were horribly hard on woodwork and glass.

I should not have done that. In my mind's eye, I could see my aged parents begging in the streets as I, an old spinster, took in clothing to be mended, and picked through rubbish bins to keep us fed. I could imagine the cold cutting through us as Calvin struggled to keep the business afloat while it crumbled around him.

No, that's not what would happen. I would be forced to marry Calvin. The prospect would make him giddy. My parents would be fed and I would give him several blond, clumsy children who meant well but would forget their lessons in their earnestness to move along to the next thing. It wasn't the life I imagined, but it would do.

We closed the shop late. Too many customers searching out cures for their health woes— Papa suspected one of the butchers in the borough had been passing around meat that was just past fair for eating. I had to agree. Aside from the expected appointments and house calls, I dispensed quite a bit of ginger, peppermint, and apple cider vinegar for upset stomach and bowel binds. This was now to be my life, not a bad one but not the lavish life I hoped to give my parents in their advanced age.

As I passed through our solar for my wrap, I stared at Mama's cards. Great change indeed—Mr. Goodwin was no longer to be my champion. He had dealt me away like a bad hand, selling me like a mare to cover his debts. Lady Thornburry and all her friends would smirk like kittens in cream at my misfortune. Like rain in the gutter, my prospects had been flushed away and soon would be out of sight.

No, he was never my champion, he had never once treated me properly. He would not shame me! Tomorrow, I would announce the breaking of our engagement. After the appropriate year of waiting, I could be approached to wed again. I just hoped someone would want me. The life I had imagined with Hiram as our butler, announcing our guests, directing our staff to serve dinners, and hosting fancy Christmas balls, faded from sight. A time of change indeed. It was a pity. I really liked Hiram, and I had longed to put my fortuitous marriage in Lady Thornburry's face, but gracefully of course. Lady Thornburry. I dreaded attending tea tomorrow morning. No matter, there was nothing to be done about it now. My father advocated motion, forward motion, at all costs— head up, shoulders back, and move forward. I would make him proud.

The next morning, the tea house was aflutter with news. Thankfully, my own turn of fortune was overshadowed by Mr. Sterling's project for the end of the wharf. It had not been officially announced, but anyone who was in the right circles knew he was about to start a revitalization project. He had already taken over several large blocks of housing and was busy converting them. The construction noise continued long into the night, and workers carried on at all hours making the most unsavory racket, despite the cost of gas lamps and candles.

"That factory is an impressive piece of technology."

"It is that," Miss Rachael Millick said doubtfully, "But the poor workers are forced to work long into the wee hours on those machines so he can have his opening gala next month." She was sitting across from me today, increasing the chances that we would lose whatever card game Lady Thornburry proposed.

Lady Thornburry ignored Rachael. "The factory will make silks, like those from China." She had a disdainful look on her face as she smoothed her skirts. "Papa says I can only get three new silk dresses this season. The rest must be satin or wool."

"But there was another accident last night," Miss Millick insisted.

"There is nothing that links that dead man to Mr. Sterling's marvelous factory."

"But—"

"Nothing!" Lady Thornburry rarely raised her voice, but when she did, she sounded like a gull squawking. She took an exaggerated breath and huffed at Miss Millick.

For a moment, Rachael looked like she was going to cry. She fiddled with the bow at the end of her long red hair.

Of Lady Thornburry's circle, I liked Rachael the most. We had been in school together, and we had been friends. When she fell into Lady Thornburry's inner circle she traded her voice, and at times her very happiness, for the slight social benefit.

She caught my eye.

Sometimes I could still see the girl I had known, more so when Lady Thornburry was so rude to her. I passed her the dish of strawberries at my side. Looking and Rachel, I supposed it could be worse. I could be spending all my time miserable, posing as a friend of a noble lady just to secure a better match as she did. I had at least attracted Mr. Goodwin's offer by my own merit and charm. I excused myself and headed off to the powder room.

The London Times sat folded on the counter. I scanned the headline, "Drowned Man Found in Limehouse Alley." Now why would anyone go through the trouble to drown a person, and then throw the body in the alley? I snagged the paper off the counter as I strolled past.

"Four men found to be drowned in the alleys surrounding the fantastic new factory and plenary being built this month by Mr. Newton Geiger and his financier Mr. Darius Sterling, son of Lord Sterling. All four men, including one that had suffered severe burns and was found lifeless in the river, can trace their most recent employment to Sterling's Factory or the employ of Mr. Geiger, a simple engineer.

According to Mr. Sterling, these accidents are not related, but are quite unfortunate. He claims he will have his engineer, Mr. Geiger, look into them as soon as possible. He also takes the opportunity to ensure the good people of London and Limehouse Borough that his factory and emporium put a great many people to work, ending the unemployment that has plagued Limehouse in the last decade as the essential lime for pottery has been depleted.

Most residents are quite enthusiastic in their welcome of the new factory and the jobs it provides, but one lady states she sees queer happenings in the street, including the river running backwards and flooding her garden and fish flopping in the streets, too far from the wharf to have fallen live from a fisher's barrow."

I tucked the paper into my hand bag, and returned to the bridge game where Miss Millick had left me the second hand. It would take clever and careful defensive playing to keep us from having an embarrassing loss.

"Did you hear Mr. Sterling is attempting to run for a seat in the House of Lords?" Miss Alderton dealt a deck of cards while Miss Millick set up the cribbage board. We still lost, but not embarrassingly so.

"Gracious, doesn't Mister Sterling know he is unable to? At best, he can serve the house of commons." Miss Millick frowned, more at the ladies than the cards.

"That's what's wrong with the world nowadays, the common folk believe they can rise far above their station," Lady Norton said, drawing another card.

"Some believe they can rise far, far above their station. Wouldn't you agree, Miss Harper?" Lady Thornburry said. Her cap was a boat of pale lace atop her fashionably styled auburn curls.

I ignored Lady Thornburry's jab. My mind was on the dead man and the backwards rivers. A puzzle to be sure, rivers only flowed one way, but it was too strange to be dismissed outright. But now that the paper mentioned it, the scent of the wharf had been stronger as of late. I would have to mention it when my parents had a moment.

"But then again, Sterling, the father, was raised to a peer by the Queen herself. He could run, I suppose. A ruling must be made." Lady Norton seemed pleased with her hand.

I forced my attention back to the game.

"The father could run. The father is a lord, the son is not," Miss Millick agreed.

"This does not concern you, Lady Millick," Lady Thornburry teased another of her quartet. "I hear you have no head for politics."

"Mr. Sterling and some lowborn inventor, a Mr. Newton Geiger I believe his name is, plan to open the largest emporium in Limehouse attached to his factory," Lady Norton said, continuing from her earlier thought before she had been rudely interrupted.

"Ah yes, I believe he is calling it *Sterling's Emporium of Uncommon Goods for the Common Man*. The name lacks imagination," Lady Thornburry complained.

"Such a venture, if successful, could increase his fortunes and change his prospects substantially," Miss Alderton said. "And you think *a lady* will marry a man with no class, merely a brand-new name that is not yet his own, and for money?" She made a *tsk* of disdain, then looked over to me. She had the beautiful blue eyes that made all the men sigh. I supposed a lady should be blessed with grace and beauty, even if it was only where others could see it.

"Well, I'm sure he can find someone that would wed him. Tell me Vivian, do you have sisters?"

"I'm sorry Lady Thornburry, were you addressing me with your concerns for matchmaking? I assure you I am fine with my own prospects. Mr. Goodwin could have had his pick of ladies, but he chose me," I said smoothly. "Perhaps he didn't like the taste of his previous offerings." The ladies gasped, and Lady Thornburry looked as though she had just bitten into something sour. I guessed there was some truth to the rumors that my ex-fiancé had courted her for a time before the engagement had been broken. I had a nasty, catty thought—though I had been careful to maintain proper escort while Byron wooed me, it was not rare for women to submit to their future husband's passions. If Byron had sexual knowledge of Lady Thornburry, her reputation would surely be ruined.

She clearly had the same thought; she glared at me. Were we men, I thought, she just might hit me.

"You should call 'Muggins', Miss Millick," I advised, looking over the game board. "Lady Thornburry overlooked nine points."

The look Lady Thornburry gave me could have curdled milk—but then she softened, the mask of courtesy sliding into place, a lady's armor and her sword in the social duel at the tea house. "Perhaps it will solve the issue of beggars and debtors in the streets. There is nothing more vulgar than those unable to find honest work."

They continued chatting like little pigeons on the windowsills, silly creatures with nothing of great importance to discuss; It was an uncharitable thought, quite frankly rude, but I was not feeling charitable in the least to the upper-class and their general uselessness to others in light of my recent business with Byron. At least their useless chatting got me away from Calvin.

CHAPTER THREE

THE CHIPPED, GREEN, dragonfly tea set was my favorite, though I'm not sure why. It might be the gilded rim, the way the thumb groove fit my hand just right, or maybe it's the way the chip in the rim felt against my lip. I've cut myself on it before. I imagine the cup itself was scolding me for being too absorbed in my own thoughts, rather than enjoying the ritual of afternoon tea.

Lady Katherine Thornburry had chipped the pieces; she had slammed the cup against the pot when she and her friends came in after drinking too much gin. Fortunately, she and her hens were elsewhere this afternoon. Since it was already past four, they would be having tea elsewhere.

"You can just take that set home, my dear," Madame Theodora offered.

"You heard about my current situation with Mr. Goodwin, I take it?" I said, raising my eyebrow. Byron always hated when I did that, he said it made me look too intelligent.

"I heard that the pawnbroker has the jewelry you were wearing on Friday." She passed over a small cheese tart. "Now—" Madame Theodora stood and tugged her apron back into place. "Mr. Bowden will be here in a few moments to convert the tea house to his supper club. Mr. Goodwin's dues are paid through the end of the quarter so he will probably be coming by. If you don't want to meet him, I suggest you finish your tea and head home."

She was right. She was always right in an annoying way; she just knew the way people would behave. The bell above the front door chimed. Madame Theodora swept back the curtain separating the serving area from the lounge.

As if she had summoned him, Mr. Isaac Bowden swept in like a spring storm, blustery and energetic. He was wearing a new gold suit with a burgundy vest and green silk cravat. Though well-fitting, it was most definitely not his colors- he looked to be suffering from some sort of fever.

"My darling!" he announced, pulling the cigarette holder from his mouth, displaying his yellowed teeth. Yes, his jacket was a horrible color choice.

"Darling!" Madame Theodora called back. She kissed his cheek in exaggerated motion.

"Miss Harper." He nodded to me. "Please don't get up, enjoy your tea. Then, I would recommend clearing out. Now that you are no longer engaged, I'm sure some of our members will be free to display their interest. Eh?" He gave me an exaggerated wink.

"If they know what's good for them they will maintain their distance for a little while—"

"Oh Pshaw!" Mr. Bowden said, waving his lit cigarette in its holder, narrowly missing the damask drapery. "It's all over town that their engagement is broken. Quite the scandal. Of course, not to your good name, my dear," he said off handedly. "Everyone knows he was a drunk and a gambler and that he pawned your jewelry to pay his debts. His family may be wealthy, but he is working through his income at an alarming rate." Mr. Bowden rushed through the room, motioning for the cook's assistant to pick up the dishes that had not yet been removed from tea service.

Madame Theodora looked around the sparse crowd at the tea house. "I may have to hire some more servers and another assistant to the cook before next week," she observed.

"Why is that? Are they kept too busy as it is?" Mr. Bowden scoffed, pointing at another table that still needed to be cleared.

"You know Sterling's secret project will be revealed next week. Since we are the closest tea house and supper club to High Street and Squire Sterling's mysterious project, we shall be quite busy." Madame Theodora's eyes gleamed at the thought of all the new business.

"What do you assume his emporium will be like, Vivian?" Mr. Bowden asked.

"Hmmm?" I paused, pouring myself the last cup of tea from the pot. I honestly thought they had forgotten about me as they went through the ritual of transforming *Madame Theodora's Tea House* into *The Clockwork Quail Supper Club*. "I am sure I don't know," I said as politely as I could manage. "But I am sure that it will be wondrous." I was absolutely exhausted and in no mood to spend my time sipping cooling tea. But now that I was a single lady, I really should make myself socially visible so the men wouldn't forget that I was eligible to court. I could be just as visible enjoying the last of my tart in the park. I stood and prepared to take my leave when my eye caught sight of something left, discarded, on a nearby table. One of the other patrons left his paper behind, folded and left open to one article framed with his knife and the vase of lilacs:

For the second time in as many weeks, a corpse has been found in the alley behind Cardigan Street. This makes the fourth total occurrence of this strange event. The victim has been identified by London constables as Mister Adolph Grenan, a day laborer from Limehouse. Constable Andrew Paye reports that the man was drowned, leading some to wonder if we are dealing with a maniac that drowns his victims then fishes them from the river. Anyone with information regarding these strange cases is urged to contact Constable Paye. Tips that lead to a person of interest shall be rewarded accordingly.

Madame Theodora and Mr. Bowden chatted on about what they imagined the emporium would be like; it seemed no one wished to discuss the poor dead men. I wrapped the rest of my cheese tart up in a piece of wax paper, and tucked it into my purse. Yes, the park would be a far better alternative. There I could read my book and have a break from being forced into partnering poor card players or making pleasant conversation regarding the deadly emporium.

The park across the square would be my refuge, well that and a barely read copy of *Les Misérables*. I took a nice sunny spot on a bench, and settled back in the world of Mr. Jean Valjean and his experience of redemption. I had just unwrapped my cheese tart when I felt a gentle tugging against my skirts. A small terrier stared at me, licking his lips, whining piteously and begging for morsels. I settled the dog on my lap and offered it a bit of tart when a shadow crossed me, making us both jump.

"The dog—" a man panted, holding out a calloused hand.

"I beg your pardon?" I snapped. I hated being startled.

"I need that dog," he said with forced patience.

I gave him my best cocked-eyebrow and said nothing. I had seen him before, he had been jogging down the street. He left Stanton's kennel with such haste that I thought him a brigand making his escape—that leather long coat of his trailing behind him in a most unfashionable, though oddly intriguing, manner as he dashed off to some unknown errand. He had slammed into me, nearly knocking me into the gutter. He had murmured an apology and then dashed away.

Mr. Stanton himself had come to help me collect myself. "An odd man, that Mr. Valentine. Always looking for his dog. He says a large dog with prick ears and a caramel colored coat. I said I've never seen a dog like that. Then he stares at the dogs in their cages for hours on end, then dashes away."

Odd indeed. He was a man of average height and a lean build—but that of a working man, not a starved waif. He wore a vest of sturdy serge with a cream-colored shirt and stock of the older (and out of fashion) style wound snuggly around his neck and tucked into his vest. He wore a revolver on his hip, barely covered by his leather long coat. His legs were covered in worn brown workman's trousers, and he wore tall thick-soled riding boots. He had no cap on his head of any kind, just dark brown hair that, though short, managed to look chronically untidy. His eyes, a warm amber color, the same as his coat, reflected the sunlight and were darting to and fro looking around like he was searching for something and feeling quite out of place.

"Dog." He was out of breath.

"This is not your dog, this is a sky terrier, not a large dog with prick ears and a caramel coat." I almost laughed at the look on his face: first shock, then that deep impatient look one gives unruly children.

"My Ranger?" He blinked hard. "I know it is not my dog. But I need—" He almost bit his tongue to avoid saying something. "I need it," he finished lamely.

"You know, Mr. Valentine, a little politeness and decorum would greatly advance my willingness to assist you," I said, still holding the terrier in my arms.

He stared at me for a long moment, probably wondering how I knew his name. I had to bite my lip to keep from laughing.

"Nathaniel Valentine, at your service. Now your kind assistance would be greatly appreciated," his voice dripped with sarcasm.

"Thank you kindly, Mr. Valentine, I am—"

"Vivian Harper, the daughter of the apothecary on Exeter Street," he said quickly. "Can I have the dog back? You don't want to keep her, I promise. The police brought her in, she was found by the corpse of the man found in the alley." He put his hand out for the dog again.

I looked at Mr. Valentine. If he was trying to put me off with disturbing details, he obviously didn't know what it meant to be the daughter of an apothecary. I dealt with shockingly horrible conditions daily.

"Why do you want her?"

He was silent for a long moment. His eyes darted to the park behind me as he searched for something to say. Whatever his real reason was he couldn't share it. He had a sad look on his face, his amber eyes somber, his dark hair hanging across his forehead.

"Poor little thing," I said softly, cuddling the dog close. "It must have been awful. I do hope Mr. Stanton can find her a new, loving home."

The little dog licked my nose, then squirmed to get down. I handed her over. Whatever his true reason, I was sure he didn't mean her harm.

"He was dumped there," Mr. Valentine said absently. "He was burned in a fire first, a fire in the factory. The man, not the dog. The dog followed her master."

"The new factory?" I asked, looking up. "Lord Sterling's Emporium?" Yet another grisly death at the construction site. What was going on over there?

Mr. Valentine shrugged. "The new factory by the waterfront. I don't know who owns it." Then he turned and took the dog to the small garden leading to the alley. He stared at the dog like a man possessed, paying me no more mind.

As Mr. Valentine walked away I was disturbed by the interaction. How did he know about the burned man, but not know the factory's owner?

Sterling's new project had been in all the papers, but the dead man's discovery was recent news. The morning's paper only mentioned another drowned and nothing of a burned man, so how was Mr. Valentine privy to such sensitive information? The question that upset me the most, however, was how had he known my name?

§§§

Mama and Papa left for their dinner party at the Martins' home. They would arrive late, but it couldn't be helped. I finished counting out the receipts and delightfully discovered, among the notes promising to pay, there was enough actual coin to reclaim my cameo. I heard Big Ben ring out the hour. It was eight o'clock, and with the evening chimes the fog crept off the wharf, flooding the streets. I hated when the peasoupers started— yellow green—and so thick it was hard to see the lit lamps in the dark street. It drifted through the streets carrying the noxious fumes that caused people to choke and cough. In the morning, people would be at the door seeking my papa's help for irritated throats and lungs. There was something ominous in the air, something more than the poison from the ever-burning coal fires. I considered waiting for a proper escort, but by the time Calvin returned from his errand it would be too late to visit the pawnbroker to reclaim my cameo. I could picture my cameo and Mr. Goodwin's engagement ring in Mr. Bilton's shop. By half-past eight o'clock, I was resolute that Mr. Goodwin's ring would be sitting in the glass case without my cameo for company.

I straightened my skirts, grateful I had chosen my chocolate brown dress tonight. The lace at the sleeves wasn't my favorite, but the warm brocade was perfect for the damp that seeped through the streets in early fall.

Mr. Bilton's shop was only three blocks down, and one over. I turned on the street towards the new square down by the docks, where Mr. Bilton had set up a storefront near the new *Sterling's Plenary Emporium*. I suspected that he was expecting an uptick in business when the emporium opened, and people were suddenly confronted by many wonderful goods. People who were not mindful of their money would be visiting the pawnbroker to sell their possessions for new dresses, shirts and trousers, hats and fans, ceramics, and all sorts of sundries that would be available but entirely frivolous.

By the time I reached the square, I was taken aback by the sheer size of *Sterling's Plenary Emporium*, but the emporium was dwarfed by the factory that stood behind it; looming over it like an angry mountain. As imposing as it was, the small shop beside it held far more importance to me. Disregarding the emporium, I hurried toward the pawnbroker. Mr. Bilton's assistant was putting out the lights, but had not yet locked the doors when I dashed in with as much courtesy as I could muster.

"Ah, Miss Harper." Mr. Bilton was winding the watches in a case.

"Mr. Bilton." I gave a small bow, then politely waited as he wound another watch. He seemed pleased to make me wait.

"You are here to reclaim your property I take it?"

"Yes, sir, a cameo-style pendant bearing a fox and lilies. Mr. Goodwin borrowed sixty pounds against it," I said as politely as I could manage.

"*Mr. Goodwin* borrowed against it, the loan is in his name," Mr. Bilton said simply.

"Yes, but it was not his to pawn," I said as politely as I was able. "That pendant was a gift from my family."

"You are engaged to Mr. Goodwin. He is master of any property you both possess," Mr. Bilton said.

"Mr. Goodwin and I are no longer engaged," I said, trying to remain dispassionate. I felt a tightness in my stomach when his shop girl quickly covered her face, positively alight with new gossip.

"Oh?" Mr. Bilton stopped winding his watches.

"Yes," I said simply. "I do not plan on reclaiming the ring he also pawned, just *my own* pendant." I tried to emphasize 'my own' without sounding too pushy. Either way, Mr. Bilton got the message and raised his eyebrow.

"Fair enough, the note against the pendant is sixty-five and four," he said.

I gasped. "That is quite the sum." I bit my tongue to keep from saying anything else that I might regret.

"Regardless, those are the terms that Mr. Goodwin agreed to. They are the terms to reclaim this jewelry." Mr. Bilton gave me a look of reproach and returned to winding his watches, "Either way, Miss Harper, I must insist you make your payment or leave, my shop is closing."

The shop girl quivered as she cleaned the glass case. She barely contained herself.

"I accept the terms," I said, louder than I meant to. I had hoped to keep a little more coin in my purse, but I was not leaving here without my pendant. I carefully counted out the coins, mortified to find myself resorting to adding up pence to make the bill; sixty-five pounds and four shillings. I was never speaking to Byron Goodwin again.

I scraped the rest of my money off the counter back into my bag, three shillings and nine pence, and tried not to look disgusted. My parents scraped together all we could spare—it cost a small fortune to retrieve, but the chain felt good in my hands and I took a moment to hang it back around my neck. The weight of it was comforting and I felt as though I was finally whole again for the first time in two weeks.

Mr. Bilton escorted me out and shut and locked the door behind me. They put out the other lights, leaving me in the gaslight from the street. It was only then that I realized how late it truly was and how dark the streets were beyond the lamplight glow. I should wait there and send an urchin to fetch my father's apprentice; the trouble was, there were no urchins in the street. That left me no alternative to walking home along the same path that had brought me here.

Sterling's factory loomed angrily in the shadows. I watched it as I walked, I couldn't look away—something about it was so out of place, so menacing, it held my attention.

"Good day, sweet lady," a voice growled.

I turned, then gasped in shock. He was short and stout, no coat, just a vest and soot-stained sleeves. He smiled at me with a smile that promised nothing friendly. The cigar in his mouth glowed in the sick yellow-green glow making his buttons gleam like evil eyes. I froze and felt everything but those little gleaming buttons fade from my vision.

"Hand over that necklace and your purse, now!" His cigar illuminated a round, piggy face, pock marked and topped with straw-colored hair sticking out of a pork pie hat.

I stumbled back a step, right into another man. This one was tall, he wore a black tattered coat such as a chimney sweep might wear. It had been made for a smaller man and stretched across his shoulders. His features were hidden by the shadow cast by his hat and the lamp behind him.

Piggy drew a knife from his vest. "Your finery, pretty lady. Then you'll entertain me and my friend."

I screamed.

The sweep clasped a filthy hand over my mouth. He wrapped an arm around my waist and lifted me off my feet. I kicked backwards, finding only empty air.

Piggy laughed.

I slammed my elbow into Sweep's side, and he dropped me with a surprised grunt. I hit the street hard, losing my breath. Not sparing a moment to regain it, I leapt to my feet and ran.

I must have caught them off guard. I got partially down the block before the stitch in my side had me gasping so hard my vision swam dark and spotty. I turned to duck behind a set of crates. I gasped for breath, realizing to my horror that I couldn't stop making this horrible gasping, sobbing sound. I wanted to stuff the hem of my dress into my mouth to keep from screaming but I needed to pant to catch my breath.

"Sweet lady." Piggy sang as he slowly came closer. "Sweet lady."

I felt like I was going to faint. I couldn't breathe. I couldn't think. I wheeled around to find a place to run, or a place to hide. I desperately needed a policeman on his beat to stroll by. Christ, I wasn't picky, I'd take anyone who didn't wish me harm.

It was then I heard a sound unlike any other I had ever heard. A snarl, but more than just a snarl. A large dog, thick of fur and deep of chest, rumbled a warning like it was a hound from hell itself. Never had my ears heard such a sound, it chilled me and made me tremble.

The dog stood, ears flat, paws wide, hackles raised, teeth bared and slavering. I was going to die. There was nothing to be done now. I wasn't sure if I'd rather feed the fangs or feel the knife. I searched for a stick or a rock but there was nothing nearby to fight with.

I balled up my fists. I was not going to die, at least not without a good fight. Of course, divine intervention, never hurt either. "Hail Mary, mother of God," I whispered. "Save me, Lord, from evildoers; keep me safe from violent people." It was the only verse I could bring to mind, I whispered it reverently feeling hoarse and weak. The snarling grew more terrible. I didn't think it possible, but it was.

"Blimey!" Piggy said. He took a step back.

The dog stalked forward in slow, measured steps. It paid me no mind, moving past me like I wasn't even there. Then it positioned itself between me and the men.

"Stab it!" Sweep hissed.

"Have you seen the size of its teeth?" Piggy snapped at his partner. "I'd shoot it if I had a pistol."

God must have sent this canine to my defense, after all, I had always treated dogs kindly. The lamplight gleamed off the dun colored fur and very white teeth. It might have been a wolf if wolves came in a deep caramel. I had never heard of wolves in London; in fairy tales, yes, but certainly not in this modern age.

"Be seeing you, sweet lady," Piggy said, his voice quivering.

He and Sweep backed off a few steps. The dog lunged forward suddenly, causing Sweep to let out a squawk and sprint away. Piggy swiped at the dog with his knife but came nowhere near the canine. They retreated back into the darkness. The dog turned to me, a slick of drool licked away with a long pink tongue. His ears went pointed up then towards me. It sat and thumped a bushy tail against the barrels. I said a prayer of thanks to the Almighty, clasped my arms tightly around myself, and had a good cry.

I expected the dog to be gone when I finally managed to pull myself together again, but he sat staring at me, amber colored eyes lit by the lamplight. I looked over and he raised a forepaw at me.

"Thank you," I whispered.

The dog lay down on his belly, and pawed invitingly at me again. Suddenly it dawned on me, Mr. Valentine was looking for his dog: a large, brown, densely-coated canine with upright ears, broad head, and amber eyes.

"You're Ranger." I said softly to him.

He flipped on his back and wiggled himself back and forth for a moment, shamelessly asking for a belly rub, tongue lolling out in a canine smile.

"Mr. Valentine will surely be happy to see you!" I said. "Though not nearly as glad as I am."

Ranger rolled back to his feet and shook himself. I was quite sure that this dog, by description, must be Mr. Valentine's canine companion. I should take him by the kennels and find a way to get a message to Mr. Valentine. But then again, according to Mr. Staton, his pattern seemed to be to show up at the kennels to examine the stray dogs after some sort of incident occurred. I wasn't sure if a girl being mugged in the streets counted as the right kind of incident, but it had definitely left an impression on me.

I did not relish the idea of walking ten feet in the dark without an escort, let alone to my own home, several blocks away. Nor the idea to take the dog to the kennel for Mr. Valentine to claim on his next visit. I vowed to take the dog to the kennels first thing in the morning; I would even ask Calvin to escort me for the next little while. He would be pleased, and I would be proper.

Feeling a bit calmer I reached out and offered my knuckles to the canine. Ranger, if it was indeed Mr. Valentine's dog, sniffed my hand then sat obediently at my feet the way any trained lady's companion would. His long, thick tail struck the wet cobble stones, splashing the puddles.

"Are you Mr. Valentine's dog?" I asked him.

He leapt to his back feet for a moment excitedly. On his hind legs he was nearly as tall as me.

"May I take you home? It's only for the night and I will do my best to reunite you with your master on the morrow," I explained as if I expected the dog to understand. Uncannily, it seemed he did. Ranger sat again and barked once.

"Come on then, I'll see if I can get you some meat—I'm sure there's a cold joint in our meat locker. Such a brave and noble beast definitely deserves it."

Ranger fell in step beside me; he pranced right under my hand so if I trailed my fingers they brushed his thick fur. It was a great comfort. Almost as good as a nice glass of port or, barring that, a pot of tea. I wished a pot of tea was in my future when I arrived at home, but I believed my mother and father were staying at the Martins' home after the late dinner party. No matter, I would brew a pot for one. As Ranger and I made our way the few blocks home, I wondered briefly if mother was entertaining them by reading the cards.

As I had promised, the moment we reached home, I slipped down to the kitchen. Calvin was asleep on his pallet by the stove, snoring away. Mrs.

Tabor had her room in the attic, but since Calvin was old enough to apprentice he wasn't going to be sleeping in the same space with his mother. He shifted and muttered something unintelligible when I opened up the meat locker.

The butcher must be coming by tomorrow, as there was nothing there but a bit of bacon for the morning. There was, however, a nice, meaty bone in the trash bin with a bit of gravy and some potato. I set it on a dripping pan and took it up to my room.

The house was dark and silent, the servants had all gone to bed. I would be getting no company until breakfast. The dog lay on the rug in my room. Jenny had set a warming pan in my bed and I carefully undressed and loosened my corset until I could slip it off and exchange my chemise for my winter nightgown, I was too chilled for my chemise to suffice. The dog cracked the bone for the marrow—crunching contentedly.

I wanted tea, or port, or something else that could still my shaking hands and dull my sharpened nerves, but I wasn't sure I could even manage brewing tea with the ay my hands shook. I pressed my blanket to my mouth. A scream was fighting its way to the surface. I had to swallow hard to keep it down. I could see his hands and his knife reaching for my throat. I felt weak and freezing cold despite the warming pan. I pulled my winter wrap tightly around my shoulders. I couldn't stop shaking. Why had I been so foolish? Mr. Bilton would have still had my cameo in the morning. My carelessness could have cost me my beautiful cameo. It could have cost me my life.

My bed shifted and creaked as Ranger climbed on my bed, licking my face, his long pink tongue lapping the tears from my cheeks. I wrapped my arms around his shaggy neck and buried my face in his fur.

He ignored his bone, which he had left on the rug, and let me sob into his fur. I wasn't sure how long, but my lamp was starting to burn low. I wanted my mother more than anything else. Men wreathed in shadow, bound by the moon—rogues, vagabonds, criminals. If I ever had the chance I would have a stern talk with whomever passed along messages through the tarot. Exciting times, indeed.

I wanted to be indignant, but the best I could manage under these circumstances was annoyed that I had been made to be so helpless. I wanted to be strong and independent. I also wanted to have had a man to protect me; women were meant to be protected by the men who loved them, who valued them, and who cherished them above all mortal treasures. I threw my handkerchief down to the carpet in disgust. Damn all men! I thought bitterly. Damn, Byron Goodwin!

It was a horrible feeling. And a confusing one.

The dog watched me, his dark amber eyes boring into me as if asking, "Me too?"

I made myself lay down and invited the dog to cuddle next to me. His presence was even more comforting than the warming pan. I finally fell asleep, stroking his silky ears.

The sun was already up; I could feel it glowing behind my eyelids. I could envision it creeping across the gardens, turning the dew on lavender and mallow and horehound into tiny diamonds, welcoming sleepy bees to visit the flowers. I rolled and stretched. After breakfast, I really should take the dog to the kennel. I would have Calvin escort me— I was leery of going on my own after last night's misadventure.

The shadows in my own room would be retreating across the floor into the corners to hide beneath the chest of drawers, washing table, and the little rug where I had laid the old tea tray and the now well-gnawed bone from the rubbish bin for the dog. I hoped he was not the shedding sort. I could see the shadow of those prick ears against the wall. He must be lying at the far side of the room beneath my window. If it were proper, I would join the dog in the sunny patch on the floor.

In fact, I just might. I leaned over the edge of my bed.

There was a man on my floor. He lay nude and curled on his side, partially obscured by the quilt that always fell from the rail of my brass bed. I froze and lay flat, my heart hammering in my chest. The shadow behind him was that of a dog, not a man.

I breathed out and in slowly several times, doing my very best not to black out. I looked again. The shadow did not change. Neither did the man. He had dark brown hair, disheveled and standing on end like a hedgehog.

There had to be a logical explanation for this. I had to be dreaming. But what if I wasn't? If he was here to attack me, he wouldn't be sleeping on my floor. But if he wasn't a lost drunkard or wayward criminal, he would not be here in my home. Maybe he was just insane. That was not a comforting thought. I grabbed my wrap from my chair. It was no protection if he were a murderer or a vagrant, but I felt better for it.

"Excuse me."

Both man and shadow stirred in sleep.

"Excuse me!"

Though far from an expert in waking sleeping men, for a moment he seemed to wake as one might calmly, then as one might in a panic and his eyes snapped open. He put his hands up to ward me off.

Startled by his movement, I grabbed the warming pan and swung it as hard as I could. It slammed into his shoulder, denting and ringing like a dropped pot. The clasp burst open showering my floor and linens with ash and soot.

"Oww, Damn!"

We both froze, I held the warming pan like a cricket bat ready to wallop him again. He held my good quilt for defense.

Footsteps were galumphing up the stairs. "Vivian?" It was Calvin. "Vivian, are you alright? I heard a crash."

I looked around wildly. It was wistful thinking that the dog might be here somewhere, too, ready to save me again.

"Vivian", Calvin shouted through the door. "Do you need my mother?" He paused, "Shall I come in?"

"N-No." I stammered, "Thank you, Calvin, I was just startled."

"I keep telling my mother, I mean Mrs. Tabor, we need to get a cat, we do Miss. A cat would keep the vermin down." He paused again, "If the master wasn't so allergic that is. It was a mouse right, miss?"

I stared at the man, jaw hanging open. He shifted my quilt to get a better grip. It was the damnable Mr. Valentine; that obnoxious man from the kennel and the park.

"A rat." I called, glaring at Mr. Valentine. "A large one."

"I can call the rat catcher miss," Calvin offered, his voice muffled by the door.

"No thank you, Calvin. Please wait in the hall. I am feeling indisposed. Will you fetch me Jenny?"

"Right away Miss. I believe she is talking to the grocer in the yard," Calvin called

Mr. Valentine took a deep breath and scrubbed a shaking hand through his hair again. He looked as startled as I felt. "I know this looks really, really bad. I'm leaving."

"Wait, my reputation!" I couldn't think of anything else. I felt like an idiot. "If the neighbors see a naked man-"

"No one will see me," He raised a pleading hand.

"Just leave now," I said in a voice that sounded stronger than I felt. He nodded and opened my window to leave. As much as part of me wanted an explanation, I wanted him gone so I could think more.

"Mr. Valentine, I assume you found your canine," I said softly. "He is a good dog. Treat him fairly for wandering off and I will say nothing about this to anyone."

"Good dog." Mr. Valentine repeated, nodding more to himself than to me it seemed. "Yes, I suppose he is."

He turned to leave, and I caught an entirely inappropriate glimpse of shapely male hindquarters as he climbed out the window. I spun around, trying to get my bearings. I was still in my night gown. The remnants of the bones from the dog's supper lay on my carpet. My bedding was covered in ash and soot, bed mussed and disheveled. My cameo, with its beautifully carved lily and fox in cream lines in the coral shell gleamed from my bedside table. Nervous laughter bubbled through me like bubbles in fancy champagne. I shoved my pillow in my mouth to muffle it.

"Miss Vivian?" There was a knock at the door.

I collapsed on my bed sobbing. Jenny burst in, took one look at my room and almost joined me in hysterics. I couldn't tell if it was for all the work ahead of her or my frazzled state.

"Miss Vivian, are you well?" Jenny asked, gently patting my shoulders. "Calvin said you saw a rat." Her eyes darted from one side of the room to the other nervously as though she expected the vermin to pounce on her at any second. She spied the warming pan with its dented lid, "But you gave it a clout with the warming pan you did! Good on you Miss. Now let's get you something a little more fortifying to start your day. Your mother and father sent a note with the Martin's boy. They'll be home mid-afternoon, certainly in time for tea."

I wanted to see my parents and share tea with them, especially after all that had occurred last night, but I was supposed to be meeting the ladies today. Lady Thornburry had secured a catalogue of fashion from Paris and we were all supposed to meet so we could ooh and aah at the catalogue over our tea and cakes. I was tempted to bow out, but then Lady

Thornburry would be insulted and it would take forever to earn back her favor.

"Jenny, help me dress then please make sure that Mrs. Tabor sets me an egg, a coffee, and some bacon. I also require a glass of sherry." I had never asked for spirits from the servants so early in the morning, but if it was unexpected it didn't show on Jenny's face. She went and fetched me a glass of sherry which I sipped as she helped me dress.

I must have dreamed it. It made no sense. I remembered Mr. Cooper's request for a poison to disable and kill werewolves. But werewolves were not real; if they were real, then they would be bloodthirsty monsters like the books. The dog from last night was a dog, not a wolf. Besides, Papa taught me long ago to track the moon phases for harvesting herbs. It was not a full moon.

When I was finally in my new burgundy dress and ready to head down to the solar for breakfast, I was feeling fortified; in my mind, for the moment, Mr. Valentine's intrusion was excusable as a mere illusion.

Except it wasn't a dream. I knew better. Even when I pretended not to. No man cast that shadow.

CHAPTER FOUR

MY LUCK SEEMED to be getting a little ratty around the edges. Last night a mugging and this morning I had to deal with Lady Thornburry in a catty mood. Then, it would seem that fate decided to make my day complete: Mr. Valentine stood at the door to the tea house staring at me holding a bunch of flowers in reds, oranges, and yellows with a bit of white and pink rounding out the haphazard bouquet. Oh no!

He came in and approached the table where we were carefully arranging vases of buds. I pretended not to see him but a blush crept into my cheeks.

"Another suitor in a fortnight?" Lady Thornburry said, shrilly laughing. "First an apothecary's apprentice, now a—well, whatever this is with muddy boots and a bouquet of flowers. What a lucky lady you are. If you play your cards right you might get this one to declare love for you, as well."

"Miss Harper, I need to speak with you." He held out the flowers. I gasped—begonia, teasel, red columbines, carnations, cyclamen, candytuft, and, worst of all, orange lily.

"You came to speak to me here? With this?" I demanded in a whisper, wishing I could sink into the floor.

"I thought if I brought you flowers you'd let me apologize, and explain." Mr. Valentine looked confused.

"What you brought me, Mr. Valentine, is an insult," I said evenly. "Excuse me, ladies."

"But-but they're beautiful," he stammered, looking thoroughly confused as he followed me to the window seat.

"They represent hatred, indifference, mistrust, rejection, and anxiety. And anxiety, I might add, I am filled with when I find you in my presence."

"I just want to explain," Mr. Valentine said, sounding angry.

"I am busy." I brushed past him, trying to be busy but all I had was my wrap, book, and purse.

"I can wait," Mr. Valentine said evenly. He brushed back the tails of his long leather coat and took a table far from the windows, setting a leather pack at his feet.

I sighed heavily. To keep Lady Thornburry and her ladies from exploding with gossip I needed to return to them. I was tempted to inform him that when Mr. Bowden arrived at five o'clock, he would likely demand he leave. That would mean I just had to deal with Mr. Valentine until at least five.

Lady Thornburry and her friends chattered, gossiped, and played cards, but they became bored.

He merely sat, ate, and sipped coffee until Lady Thornburry's party finally left to prepare for their fancy dinner plans, of which I had none.

We were alone. I could hear the cook's pots and pans clank and chime against one another as she worked. If Mr. Valentine attempted anything forward, she would be alerted. It was comforting, but being alone with him reminded me, quite strongly, that I had seen him naked this morning. I blushed, watching him drum his hands on the table. He was working up the nerve to speak to me.

The bell rang, and the only other man I wished to avoid more than Mr. Valentine walked in: Mr. Goodwin.

"Vivian." He swept through the door, letting it *bang* shut. He was terribly hard on woodwork.

Mr. Valentine looked up from his thoughts, startled.

"That's Miss Harper, if you please," I corrected crossly.

"I know you're angry with me Chuckie, but honestly, the breaking of our engagement has not been announced yet. I have come to give you another chance. Apologize to me and for speaking so poorly of me to your father, and all this silliness will be forgotten." He paused, seeming to notice Mr. Valentine for the first time. He stiffened. "Good day, sir. I didn't see you there."

Mr. Valentine politely nodded.

"Women, 'eh?" Byron Goodwin said to Mr. Valentine, taking a seat at his table and helping himself to a pour of cold coffee. "You can't do a thing with them when they're on their courses."

"I am not!" I snapped. "Now this is too much." I stamped a foot on the oriental carpet.

"And now, my good sir, if you can excuse myself and my hysterical fiancée," Byron said, turning his back on Mr. Valentine.

"I am not your fiancée!" I said louder than I intended. Mr. Valentine took a sudden and thorough interest in the dregs of his coffee.

Byron went white, his mouth cut one thin line. "Who do you think you are? I proposed marriage, and your family agreed to my most generous offer. I might add, your father is a practitioner of folk cures, not an accomplished man of medicine. This may have mattered once but we are entering a new age and educated doctors are the new healers. Your kind will be gone soon. Your mother is lucky the Red Hood Society doesn't drag her out in the streets and execute her if for nothing more than to stop her from spreading her influence. She's a provider of charms and reads the unnatural tarot. One might even question if she follows the holy church or the word of something more sinister altogether." He took hold of my arm sharply. I gasped from the pain of it, sure I would have bruises under my gown. "You would do well to remember your place, Miss Harper!" Byron snarled. "Your fortune, and that of your family, can change." He slammed me into the counter.

"Unhand her." Mr. Valentine was on his feet and advanced towards us.

"I am fine," I said having no desire to pull him into this. Byron was grasping at straws by insulting my father, apothecaries were respected, not the same as learned doctors but still respected.

Byron's normally handsome face was twisted in an ugly sneer. "What occurs between a man and his intended is no business of yours, sir."

"The lady said the engagement is broken," Mr. Valentine said evenly. Apparently, he would not be kept from interfering.

"So, you'll ring the police?" Byron let go of me and turned towards Mr. Valentine. He put his hand near his pocket and the revolver he carried. "I am a Lord, you cock-brained fool!"

"I will not ring the police, but I will not leave this lady alone in your presence." Mr. Valentine's voice was clipped. I was sure it was my imagination, but I could see his dark eyes suddenly so similar to the eyes of the canine that defended me so fiercely last night.

It was like watching a dogfight unfold before my very eyes. Dogs froze, sniffing one another out before the fight started, stiff-legged, lips curled waiting for the other to flinch. I shoved my fist to my mouth. It was exactly like a dog fight. Only Byron had no way of knowing that.

My aching arm was suddenly numb, and I could hear my own blood thrumming in my ears. Somewhere beyond my own heartbeat, Byron was still talking.

"Miss Harper, if you insist on this course of action, our engagement shall be broken. But I warn you, by the time you're eligible to wed again you will be an old maid and you will never get a better offer of marriage. I, for one, will not take the responsibility if your reputation is utterly ruined."

I blinked at them, was I really hearing this? They were fighting over me like, well like bloody dogs! Oddly, I found it appropriate from Mr. Valentine.

"Is it her reputation you care for, or your own, sir?" Mr. Valentine asked coolly.

"What is it you imply, sir?" Byron's voice dropped to a dangerous tone. "You dare impugn my honor."

"No," Mr. Valentine laughed. "I'll say to your face that any man who would lay hands on a woman is a poor man indeed. I wish you luck finding another woman to agree to marry you. If you did not have your name and title to barter with, I'd argue you'd find yourself unsuccessful to the end."

"You dare!" Byron spluttered for a moment, overcome. "I shall see you arrested and sent to pillory. The magistrate will deal with you, sir!"

"What's all this then?" Mr. Isaac Bowden said as he brushed through the curtain separating the solar from the kitchens.

I blessed my good fortune that Mr. Bowden had arrived.

"Good day, Lord Goodwin!" He took Byron's arm. "What's all the kerfuffle?" He waved a dismissive hand. "No matter then, please join me in a glass of port. It has been quite a long time since I had the occasion to drink with you, sir."

He moved the curtain aside and started to lead Mr. Goodwin away. "And, you, good sir—if you do not have a membership to *The Clockwork Quail* I'm afraid I have to ask you to leave. Our reservation book is quite full for this evening." He said to Mr. Valentine before he led Mr. Goodwin off.

Overwhelmed, I sat on the nearest chair. It was suddenly so quiet. Mr. Valentine loomed above me. I spied his ill arranged bouquet of flowers and couldn't help myself, I laughed. One kind thing could be said about the flowers he chose, though their meaning was horrid, their aroma was pleasing. I am sure to him that was all that mattered.

"I'm sorry for that," Mr. Valentine said quietly. His leather boots creaked as he shifted. "May I walk you home and explain myself?" Mr. Valentine asked. "I don't like the idea of you walking alone. I hate the idea even more now that I know Mr. Goodwin is so angry." He handed me a tea towel off the counter.

I dabbed my eyes with the tea towel and took a deep breath. "I apologize, Mr. Valentine. I find myself indisposed. The last few days have been tiring."

Mr. Valentine laughed too. He scrubbed a hand through his hair, causing it to stand out on end. "I'm not laughing at you," he corrected quickly.

Mr. Bowden came back in. "Miss Harper, you're still here? I must insist you head home now," he said loudly, then his voice dropped. "Sir, if you would be so good as to escort Miss Harper home, I'd be in your debt."

"Gladly." Mr. Valentine offered me his hand.

Without thinking, I let him help me rise. I jerked my hand free. "I can make it on my own, thank you kindly."

"Good lord, my dear," Mr. Bowden continued, noting the flowers on the counter. "Who received such a horrid bouquet?"

"Maybe whomever sent them thought they were striking," Mr. Valentine said evenly.

Mr. Bowden made a non-committal noise and disappeared into the main dining room.

"Mr. Valentine, I assure you, I did not steal your dog," I said as formally as I could manage.

"What?" He stared at me

I stared back looking as innocent as I could. "That is why you were in my room, correct?" Surely, he must know I was smarter than that.

"Um…" he paused, and looked at me blankly, "I can explain."

"You were reclaiming your property. I understand that, I guess, though why someone would do so naked is beyond me. I do hope you will believe me when I say I happened upon him that very night returning from..." I paused. "A trip to the wharf. I took him home as it was so very late. I planned on taking him to the kennel in the morning, and sending you word."

"I don't believe you were attempting to rob me of my property," he said quietly. His head was gently tilted to the side, rather like a canine hearing a high-pitched whistle.

"Then why are you here?" I crossed my arms.

He chewed his lip, weighing his options. He was caught and he knew it. "I wanted to apologize to you." He rubbed his neck. "And offer some sort of explanation."

"If you don't believe I was robbing you of your property, I'm not sure I want an explanation. I can't imagine any proper reason you would be at my home at such an hour, otherwise." I wheeled to leave.

"I can't let you do that," He followed at my heels, "I promised I would escort you home."

"Really, Mr. Valentine, I can manage." He reached for my hand, but I snatched it out of his reach. "I must insist you let me be."

"I will, after I see you safely to your door. Muggers are one thing, but your ex-fiancé made threatening remarks and I can't in good conscious leave you to your own devices."

I had a sudden chill. What if he was setting me up? But why? He already had had the opportunity to do something terrible this morning. No, if he were evil he would feel fouler. I'd bet my gown he was not out to harm me; he seemed too loyal, too good-natured for that.

The world was swimming and I was suddenly aware that he grabbed for my hand. I was staring at the collar of his coat, a stylish leather, long frock coat— something a member of the Explorer's Society might wear. I swallowed hard, feeling my stomach seize, and the tea I had earlier threaten to come back up. Looking into his eyes I knew without a doubt what I was not ready to rationally accept. I hadn't imagined it, it was not an early morning fantasy like I had hoped. He and Ranger were one in the same.

"Miss Harper?" He actually looked worried. He shifted me slightly and pulled a flask from his coat pocket. It was full of a cheap brandy that stung my throat and made my eyes water, but I took two long pulls.

I handed it back, leaving him to stopper it. "Thank you kindly. Goodnight, Mr. Valentine." I spun on my heel and dashed out the door.

CHAPTER FIVE

MR. VALENTINE FOLLOWED me as I wove inconspicuously as I could through the foot traffic. He should have known better than to follow me. I had no intention of letting him speak. I took the alley behind the tea house. I had no desire to run into any of Mr. Goodwin's friends on their way to the tea house. It wasn't a bad alley, fairly clean as they went, for it opened to a yard where the green grocers sold their wares to cart girls in the mornings. The far side had a nice park with a large, English oak.

I turned the corner and almost ran into someone. Four men stood in crimson capes and cowls by the English oak with a terrified girl standing between two of them with her back to me.

"What's happening?" I asked a laundress beside me.

"Poor lassie has been corrupted. Them Red Hoods are saving her soul."

"What? What do you mean?" I stood on my toes to get a better look, Mr. Valentine entirely forgotten.

It was Theresa Campbell. Her family came in from time to time for a salve to treat a rash the entire family got when they wore metal jewelry against their skin. One of the men in red had the collar of her dress held open, exposing the rash. It was a blistered line of crimson.

"And tell us, Miss Campbell, what piece of jewelry were you wearing when this occurred?"

She was shaking, I could see it from here. She whispered something and the crowd booed.

"Louder, if you please!" the Red Man said.

"My cross," Theresa stammered. "But it's not my fault, my whole family gets it!"

The crowd roared disapproval.

"Her whole family is from the highlands of Scotland," the laundress beside me said. "Poor girl, she's infected with Fae magic and there's only one cure for that."

"What?" I stared. "You can't be serious!" Enough was enough. I could let myself marry a man I didn't love and who did not respect me to ensure my family was provided for as they aged, I could ignore that strange things were happening to the city I loved, I could even turn a blind eye to a system that made sure the rich lived under a different set of rules where women were property and men had all the power, but I would not allow a friend to be harmed before a bloodthirsty mob in the streets.

Theresa needed help, and quickly. I could hear her wail over the crowd's mutterings. I turned to see the Red Man was tying a noose.

I had to get her away from them. There was nothing wrong with her, it was an illness of her skin not possession; it would be the same as with a cross or a ring or a pendant, the shape didn't matter just the metal.

Mr. Valentine had caught up with me.

"Mr. Valentine, you have to help me help her."

He nodded warily. "I'll give you a distraction. You get her out of the square."

I turned back to the crowd. I would need to push to the front to have a chance to get to her in time. When I turned back to check, Mr. Valentine was gone.

The man in the red hood turned to the gathered crowd. He was addressing them, not her, whipping them into a frenzy. "Miss Campbell, is it true that Scotch fairies cannot bear the touch of metal?"

"Iron, yes but—" Theresa stammered

"It blisters them, burns them?" The Red Man continued.

She looked at her feet in despair.

"Answer me Miss Campbell!" Red Man shouted. The crowd echoed him.

"Yes but—"

"Fairies, or 'The Fae,' are cruel to good, God-fearing people. They play tricks, steal babies, sour milk, and kill livestock!" Red Man shouted. "She clearly bears their taint. This holy cross on a beautiful chain burns her skin! She is a corruption upon our fine society!"

The crowd shouted, caught up in his mania.

"She must be purged from us to protect London from her unnaturalness!"

The crowd shouted again, louder this time.

Hurry Mr. Valentine!

"What we do, we do to save her immortal soul!" Red Man screamed to the crowd.

I was close enough to see her sobbing between the two men now. They were not holding her in place, they didn't need to, the crowd would apprehend her if she ran. She was shaking, her eyes scanned the crowd for a savior. Her eyes met mine; they begged for help.

There was an explosion that rocked the square. People screamed and cried out; the air filled with a powder, like finely milled white flour. The powder stung my eyes.

I bolted forward and grabbed Theresa's hand. Her cold, clammy hand clasped mine so tightly I thought she might break my fingers. We bolted behind the tree and through the square.

People screamed, rushing around like a horde of disturbed ants.

The cloaks and cowls of the Red Men were still visible through the haze of powder. They whipped around, searching for their missing captive.

I ran right into Mr. Valentine, knocking him to the ground. Theresa was dragged down, too, shrieking.

He extracted himself from the tangles of limbs and skirts and easily righted her. "Are you unharmed?"

She nodded frantically, tears streaming down her face.

"Get home and get your family out of London," I commanded, my voice hoarse from the soap powder.

She nodded.

"Theresa," I embraced her hard, "If you need help, tell my father, but get out of London— tonight if you can!"

She took off running towards her family.

Mr. Valentine brushed the white powder from his dark serge vest and patched workman's trousers. "Come on." He grabbed my arm and led me up the next alleyway.

"Shall I ask how you managed an explosion?" I asked, dusting off my own skirts as we walked.

"Most sewers will explode if you can find a gurgling pipe," he said.

"And the soap?"

"The laundry had barrels of it, already powdered. I opened the barrels and set them on the drain by the front door. The cloud was a little more energetic then I planned." He dusted out his hair and gave an impish grin, looking quite pleased with himself.

"Do you suppose Theresa will be safe?" I asked.

"No," he said flatly. "I fear no one who is different is safe, despite what Mr. Cooper claims he and his Red Hoods are trying to do."

"Certainly not people like you," I said evenly.

He stumbled a step, then continued on as though he hadn't heard me.

I wasn't fooled. I followed him past the rows of houses until we reached my own home. I froze, scuffing my shoes on the cobblestones.

Our front door had been kicked in, the lock broken, front windows smashed.

Calvin was picking up shards of glass from the stoop.

"Calvin! Where are Mama and Papa?"

"With the police at the station," he said, looking quite relieved.

"What happened here?" I turned in a slow circle, my shoes crunching on broken glass. The air was filled with a sweet, earthy, herbal smell from spilled medicines and scattered herbs.

"Mr. Harper believed the Red Hoods did this."

Months, no years of hard work, and all our income for the season, laid ruined on the floor. The front window alone would cost a small fortune to replace. Cleaning this up would take days, and little would be salvageable. We would lose business to the shady apothecary on the other side of the river.

I was hurt. I was furious! "Who do these Red Men think they are?!"

"They are dedicated to purging London of everything unnatural," Mr. Valentine said quietly.

"Well they surely have their work cut out for them. We live in quite a modern age."

Both Mr. Valentine and Calvin looked grim. They exchanged worried glances.

"Mr. Valentine, you know more than you are sharing—"

"I have to go," he said, turning.

I grabbed his coat. "You will explain yourself now! I am doing my best to provide for those I love and I have had a horrible week and I will not be pushed aside! Calvin, stay here with your mother and Jenny. Tell Mama and Papa when they return that I went out."

Mr. Valentine blinked hard like a dog that had been scolded.

"I have to go," Mr. Valentine said again, turning to leave. He looked pale now.

"Then I am coming with you." I sprinted after him, I wanted to know if I was right in suspecting that he was his dog. Transfiguring peoples? Was it possible?

"You are going to tell me what you know so I can fix it!"

He stared. I must have looked irrational by now. My dress was covered with a fine layer of powdered soap, the lye in the powder had stung my eyes and made them water, and somewhere in all the excitement my ribbon had come loose letting my hair fly freely.

"Fine," he said, resigned. "I will explain what I can on the way."

"The Red Hoods are zealots—they seek out anything they can consider unnatural, and make sure it leaves London."

I cocked an eyebrow at him. "I know that already. Honestly, Mr. Valentine, you must be more help than that."

He gave me the look I had become familiar with from our brief time together: something between supreme annoyance and mild amusement. Clearly, he thought I was daft.

"That includes anything that doesn't fit the traditional London lifestyle that the House of Lords wishes to maintain. That includes anyone displaying uncommon..." he paused, "*skills*, or intelligence, or sympathies."

I grabbed his arm. "What do you mean 'uncommon skills'?" I asked.

He stopped at stared at me. "What?"

"You emphasized 'uncommon skills'."

He was indignant "I did not!"

"You did!" I assured him. "You may not have meant to, but you did. What uncommon skills do you possess that makes you such a prime target?"

He blinked hard. I could tell he was trying to come up with some excuse to avoid the truth.

"You had better worry more about the uncommon skills and sympathies in your own home, Miss Harper."

"What do you mean by that?" I asked.

"Your family is friends with known suffragettes, and your mother reads those devil cards."

"The tarot is a focusing element for divination. They are not 'devil cards,'" I scoffed. I couldn't argue the suffragette point, though.

"Intelligent people know that. The frightened masses don't know any better. Groups like the Red Hoods are taking advantage of that." He led me down the alley across from my home.

"Why are you so concerned? Do you harbor a secret love for suffragettes and tarot cards?"

"No," he said slowly, as if he was speaking to an idiot. "The Red Hoods also hate anything having to do with knowledge coming to light. I was looking into a druid site below London under the orders of the Explorer's Society. I discovered something that the Red Hoods do not wish to be revealed."

"And you now possess some deep, dark secret they will kill you for?" I laughed. "Honestly Mr. Valentine, you really are too much."

He made a face. "Fine. Anyway, I need to consult a scholar I know. He should be able to make sense of what I have discovered."

"That still doesn't explain exactly what you were doing in my room or why my home was broken into," I said. "Unless, were you trying to rob us? Were you looking for something? The same thing they were looking for?"

"Don't be absurd!" Mr. Valentine snapped at me.

"Then why were you in my room?" I asked.

"That's complicated," He said, watching people pass us on the streets.

"I'm a smart girl, explain it," I said seriously.

"Well, that's the trouble, I can't," he said evenly. "But if you really want to know, get me to the docks. I need to get on board the Whispering Wind. It's headed for Calais. It leaves this evening."

"And why do you need my help?"

"Because traveling after dark gets complicated." He sighed.

"Everything about you is complicated." I muttered.

He stepped back out onto the street, blending into a crowd of gentlemen headed home for supper from their work day. I had to hurry if I wanted to catch up.

CHAPTER SIX

I HAD ROTTEN luck as of late. We didn't get more than two blocks towards the docks before we turned a corner and ran right into several of the Red Hoods, all dressed in their fancy capes and hoods with masks that concealed their identities. I suspected by their speech they were just as interested in protecting the population from unnaturalness as they were bored with their status and wealth. In my limited experience with the upper class, they were often in need of distraction and zealotry was hopefully just the flavor of the moment. They turned and immediately started walking towards us.

"Nathaniel Valentine, you are a menace. You and your kind aren't wanted here!" A man called out over the din of London evening streets. His scarlet cowl and cape hid his features, but the voice sounded more familiar than I'd like. He sounded like one of Byron's gambling acquaintances. There were five more men in scarlet cloaks. Three of them were headed straight for us.

I spun to look for the nearest police officer. I tried to swallow, but my heart had lodged itself in my throat. The bodice of my gown felt three sizes too tight.

Nathaniel laughed. I stared at him, trying to figure out what was so funny. This wasn't funny! This was horrible and Nathaniel was taunting him.

"Mr. Cooper, I was wondering when you'd finally be chasing after me. Your mania holds no room for things you can't understand. Though, I guess that's not surprising considering your intelligence."

The one who spoke threw back his hood. He wore a black silk mask but his curly hair, the color of antique gold, matched Mr. Cooper's.

"Red Hoods?" Nathaniel scoffed. "Like big bad wolf hunters from a story? Who do you think you're fooling?"

"We are protecting pure, upstanding human citizens from your unnaturalness," Cooper declared proudly.

"You will come with us, Mr. Valentine," Mr. Cooper informed us coolly. "Or we can put you down like a dog here in the street."

Nathaniel Valentine laughed again. "Quite amusing, and here I thought zealots didn't possess a sense of humor."

I heard a click of a pistol. There was no way I wanted to be shot today. I had seen Papa treat bullet wounds before.

Nathaniel grabbed me by the waist and shoved me behind him. A gallant gesture to be sure, but I was fairly sure that would not offer much protection should they start firing.

Mr. Cooper drew a thin rapier from his cane.

Nathaniel drew a long, wide knife from under his coat.

"Miss Harper, this is no place for the fairer sex—if you'd please excuse us," Mr. Cooper said. He raised his thin sword and saluted as fencers did before a match.

"She's fine where she is, thank you." Nathaniel was suddenly very serious. He pressed me to his back with his left arm.

"Whatever you do, please don't faint," he whispered as we turned in a slow circle.

Though I was thankful for the warmth of his frame and the stink of leather was becoming oddly comforting, I wasn't sure I could accommodate that request. My heart hammered beneath my corset. "I cannot promise you anything."

He was slowly positioning us towards an open square. The sword lashed out—easily batted aside by Mr. Valentine's long knife. I was overbalanced by Mr. Valentine's lunge as he spun away from Mr. Cooper's darting blade, and without his reassuring bulk I was unsteady. It was fall or help. I was tired of being useless.

I used my fall to tackle one of the Red Hoods. We hit the ground hard, I barked my shin on the curb and landed in horse droppings. Fortunately, the Red Hood fell in the same, flipped over me, and landed heavily on his backside. It was a poor victory but my first victory in a fight and was oddly comforting. I lashed out again and kicked him in the head, catching him behind the ear.

He gave a breathy "wuff" and didn't move.

The flurry of action galvanized the men. One wearing a set of expensive rings punched at Nathaniel—he dodged and ducked, his long knife slashing through the air with a hiss. He lashed out, striking the man in the face with the pommel of his knife, laying him out cold.

One of the Red Hoods, a portly fellow I thought closely resembled Mr. McEvoy a local barrister, leveled a silver revolver and fired. Through some act of miraculous fortune, the shot went wide and splintered the edge of a barrel of cod, which splashed and coated us all in distinctly fishy ooze.

Nathaniel threw himself at the man and they grappled, slamming into the barrel, dumping a huge mess of rotting cod into the gutter.

If my dress hadn't already been ruined by horse droppings and gutter filth, it most definitely was now. I battered another Red Man with a piece of the broken barrel lid across his thick back. He yelped at the pain of it.

Mr. Valentine hit McEvoy in the face, leaving him quite senseless, but Mr. Cooper wasn't the only threat with a sword. One of the other men unsheathed a sword from his cane and thrust it under Nathaniel's chin, forcing him to halt his assault on the barrister. Mr. Valentine slowly regained his feet, his knife loose in his hand in what I assumed was supposed to be a submissive gesture.

Mr. Valentine darted forward, ducking faster than I thought he could beneath the sword and grabbed a broom discarded behind the barrels. Nathaniel lashed out with the broom, catching the swordsman in the side of the head. He followed this with a lunge, his knife burying the edge of the blade in the shoulder of his attacker. When he wrenched it free, the coat sleeve was dark with blood.

The broom handle clattered to the street. I grabbed his hand and jerked him away. "This way!"

We jogged down the alley way, the stitch in my side growing steadily worse, but it was nothing compared to the look on Mr. Valentine's face.

Pale and pained, he dragged me onward until we passed a row of apartments. He stopped before an entry, and with one fluid movement kicked in the door. He dragged me inside and slammed the door closed behind us. It was a coal shed for the block to feed the boilers and heat the homes on the proper side of the road. He dropped his pack against the door to keep it from swinging open and ripped off his long coat.

"I hoped to be able to return to the site before the Red Hoods started to put things together. I know a priest across the channel who studies all sorts of fascinating things, aside from merely the word of God. The ship, *Whispering Wind*, leaves port in two hours. If you can get me there, we'll be safe. Get us on board, then you can leave under the ruse of checking on your luggage."

"Merely the word of God?" I stared at him. "Now see here Mr. Valentine, the word of our Lord is absolute. There is nothing *mere* about it and furthermore—"

He spun around, shushing me. He had removed his stock, and was unfastening the buttons of his shirt as swiftly as possible. He looked pained, as though seized with a sudden case of colic.

I froze. I hadn't realized he was in pain. "Mr. Valentine, are you wounded?"

He held up his hand to ward me off. He was winded. "Quietly, please, Miss Harper."

I jerked back, "Mr. Valentine, since I have made your acquaintance, I have been the victim of an attempted mugging, my home has been burgled, my person assaulted, I have been shot at, knocked into the gutter, and my new dress is utterly destroyed." He stared at me, mouth agape. "Whatever trouble follows you is entirely inappropriate to be visited on a respectable young lady such as myself. You have done irreparable damage to my property and my reputation!" I think I was crying now because he reached out, offering me a dingy handkerchief. The other hand gently cupped my shoulder.

"Now you have demanded that I take you with me as my companion, which I might add is improper for a lady!" I was beyond being shushed now. "Then I must imply that I cannot trust my servants to bring my luggage aboard without oversight, what sort of estate does that imply, I ask you? All so I can sneak off the ship and return alone, without escort, to my family home that has been recently burgled by most likely the very Red Hood society that assaulted us in the street. They are unlikely to just forget that I was with you tonight. By the way, their leader, Mr. Cooper, knows my family well, including the fact that I recently broke an engagement to a young man who is heir to quite the fortune. And I am to do this all in a ruined dress. If you think for an instant that I am also going to allow you to also besmirch the reputation of honorable clergy in my presence, well then you have another thing coming!"

I straightened my skirts and took a deep breath. "Now if you are wounded, I demand you inform me immediately for if you are about to fall apart or bleed to death I cannot carry you to my father and I am not equipped to care for a wounded man here. I hardly have a doctoring kit in my dress!"

He stood, stripped to the waist, and cradled me to his chest, letting me sob and rage, despite what I smelled like. I could feel something in him, a deep tremble like a bone-deep tremor of something fighting to get out.

"I'm sorry," he said softly, his voice a soft rumble, barely heard above the boilers. "You're right." He scrubbed his hand through his dark hair. "I can't sneak on board the ship when I'm—well, when I'm not myself. I thought maybe you could get us on board and then return home. I have no right to involve you in this. I will find some way to make it up to you. There's nothing I can do about your reputation but stay here until a maid comes to feed the boilers. You can say I abducted you. From there, go to the police and report your assault by Mr. Cooper and his Red Hoods. Tell them I took you hostage. I will manage somehow until the ship returns from Calais and I will go visit Father Henri Poullain then. He's one of those learned men, a scholar, and he studies old magic. I will send whatever funds I can to repay your kindness, and I will do what I can to ensure your safety."

I didn't know what to say. Just being around him made me safe. It was what I always imagined being around the right people should be; first Papa and Mama, then what I hoped it would be with Byron: respected for being what I am.

He released me from his warm embrace somewhat reluctantly, and ducked behind a coal bin. A moment later, I heard him gasp and groan. He wasn't stabbed, there was no blood. I knew what was happening to him I just don't know how I knew. Everything I thought I knew told me it wasn't possible, yet the evidence was all there. Traveling at night was complicated. He needed me to get on the ship. A curious shadow no man could have. He had been his caramel-colored dog with prick ears that night in my room. He defended me from being mugged. I was ashamed of myself for thinking, even for a moment, that he could have been my attacker.

He was both a man and the dog he had been looking for. Had he really been looking for the dog or information? It was a puzzle to be sure and one he would not be able to answer in his present state. "Mr. Valentine, does transfiguring hurt?" I ventured timidly.

He groaned again and I heard the coal around him shift like little pebbles falling down the riverbank. I wasn't sure how long the actual transformation took, but I didn't want to intrude. Such a shortcoming must be embarrassing, and I wasn't sure if I wanted to see him fully naked again. Though not unpleasant, it was quite unseemly.

Instead, I gathered his shirt and vest and shook them out before folding them and placing them into his bag. It was something to do if nothing else. I put on his long coat. Burying myself in its bulk, then I sat on his bag and waited.

A moment later, Ranger trotted around the coal bin, shaking and stretching in canine delight.

"I suppose you're not going to help me gather his clothes?" I said out loud. "And here I should be married before I am responsible for a man's wardrobe." I stepped around the coal bin, lifting my filthy skirts from habit, not from need, to keep them clean. Any illusions of cleanliness were long dispelled. His trousers, small clothes, boots and belt, and the weapons he had been wearing lay in an untidy pile. I carefully placed his clothes into his pack before sitting on it again.

Ranger sat before me and laid his head in my lap.

Mama's cards were unnervingly accurate, particularly "men ruled by shadow," and "interesting times." I wasn't sure if this counted as deceptive, but I supposed since the cards were often quite literal, deceptive was fitting. Mr. Valentine had to hide his nature, or aspects therein. And his transfiguration seemed ruled by the cyclical nature of day and night—that would make him literally ruled by shadow. I forced a laugh at that.

"This behavior is entirely inappropriate from Mr. Valentine, you know," I said, burying my hands in the thick fur at his neck. Ranger huffed and sniffed at my skirts before returning his head to my lap again. How strange, Ranger caused me no concern. He was instantly a beloved companion, it was the man who caused me anxiety. What a good dog. Were they really so different?

"We'll leave when the lamplighters come," I said to my canine companion. I didn't know if he understood, but it was comforting to speak to him. "I will do my best to get you to the *Whispering Wind*, though I'm not sure what we'll do then. I don't fancy walking the alleys after dark without an escort. You're going to have to protect me."

Ranger gave a quiet *wuff* in assent.

The lamplighters came and went, and the clock tower chimed seven. I waited until they chimed half-past before I took Mr. Valentine's heavy pack on my back and crept out of the coal shed.

Ranger pushed past my legs and out into the damp street. He dashed this way and that across the narrow alley, nose to the ground, occasionally returning to my side.

I squared my shoulders and took a deep breath. With Valentine, or Ranger, at my side, I had nothing to fear. I should be able to avoid molestation if I looked as though I had business at the docks.

We weren't far from the wharf. It was a short walk before Ranger and I turned onto the street where Sterling's Emporium loomed at the end of the wharf. The only building that was larger was the factory where most of the goods it was going to sell would be made. The emporium was brightly lit with fancy electric lights gleaming from the windows dwarfing the small shops in the courtyard of the massive building.

I stopped at the green grocer, across from the pawnbroker that had had my cameo, and bought a few apples which I stuffed into Valentine's bag. If Calvin was any indicator of male eating habits, then Valentine would be ravenous soon.

Ranger nosed the pocket of his coat, searching for something a canine would find eatable. I sighed heavily and crossed the street to where a fish stall dealt portions of fried fish and roasted potato wedges wrapped in dull newspaper. I dug a few coins out of Valentine's pocket and bought two portions. The stall-man looked at me funny, but counted out the change in pennies and we walked back to the park by the green grocer to have supper.

Ranger gulped his down in a few bites, tongue wagging at the heat of it.

He watched me eat mine, licking his chops when I took nibbles, swallowing and shifting when I swallowed. I gave up and tossed him my fish. I put the chips in their paper wrapper into one of his pockets so I could eat them one at a time. Ranger wasn't interested in the apples. He sat at my feet while I ate those without as much as a sniff.

It wasn't long before we could see the docks. I walked slowly, reading the ships' names, trying to locate his ship headed to France. I finally located it and sat down to think. I needed a plan and one I could make on my own; ranger was hardly any help.

I stared at the *Whispering Wind* as it took on cargo, trying to figure out how to get Ranger and Valentine's clothes on board. Perhaps stowing away would be my best bet. I felt like a daring adventurer from one of my novels—unfortunately, I couldn't recall any novels I had read going into great detail on exactly how one would get on board such a ship.

Ranger suddenly leapt to his feet, snarling.

I was so absorbed in my scheming, I didn't notice the crowds milling about. A shadow blocked out the little light the gas lamp was giving and I turned. Derek Cooper was looming, a large length of rope in his hands.

"You gave us the slip on Brewer Street. You almost got away." He snarled at Ranger. "That dog is very dangerous, miss. It will come with us."

Ranger whirled, hackles raised. The growl coming from his throat was nothing I have ever heard before, low and menacing like a demon from hell. No, I had heard it before—Ranger had growled like that when I was attacked in the street.

Cooper waved to another man across the street. Ranger's rumbling snarl didn't cease.

The clock tower chimed the quarter of the hour. People shopped, oblivious to our plight. Despite the warmth of Mr. Valentine's coat, I felt a chill running up my spine.

"Miss Harper, you'll be coming with us. We will need to question you in regards to your acquaintanceship with a Mr. Nathaniel Valentine."

"No, thank you," I stammered. "As you can see I really need to take my dog home."

"You and *that* aren't going anywhere," the other man snarled, drawing a small leather strap from his jacket.

"Ranger, come!" I said, turning on my heel. The soles of my shoes were too slippery for the wet cobblestones and I skidded slightly. We started away, Ranger growled all the while. I heard their boots following, more surefooted than I was on the slick street.

I broke into a run. "Help! Police! Please, someone help me!"

Cooper's friend grabbed my arm and wheeled me around. I looked over just in time to see Cooper twirling the rope he carried around his head. He skillfully threw it, catching Ranger around the neck. He gave a startled yelp and tossed his head violently. Cooper dug in his feet and jerked the rope tightly around Ranger's neck.

Ranger set his paws, trying to back away and pull himself loose.

"Let him go!" I struggled with Cooper's man, but he was taller and much stronger. "Please, Mr. Cooper, let him go!" Tears slid down my cheeks. I punched the man holding me to no effect other than bruising my fists.

Ranger's eyes bulged as he fought, whipping his head back and forth trying to work his way free. He staggered on his paws.

"Please, someone help us!" The strength in my legs was spent and I slumped in the brute's grasp.

Mr. Cooper was reeling Ranger in like a trout. He still fought, but not as vigorously. No help would be coming, the citizens around us stared, but made no move to intervene.

"Help us, please," I implored one last time. Tears blurred my vision. Mr. Cooper was going to kill Valentine and there was nothing I could do to stop it. Or was there?

I stamped down on the brute's feet, hard as I could, but my shoes made little effect. "Easy there missus, you don't want to hurt yourself," he said.

I slammed my heel into his leg as hard as I could. I happened to catch him just under edge of his kneecap. He dropped to the street with a curse. I dove, scrambling into Mr. Cooper. He wasn't expecting a hit from behind, and he struggled to keep his balance.

"Now really, Madame", he grunted as he dragged me along, "Its people like you we are protecting from their unnaturalness."

"I don't care!" I said trying to twist around.

Ranger lay on his belly, gasping in the street. His nose rested on his paws, sides heaving. He gave a pitiful whine. I lunged past Mr. Cooper, one of my better athletic moments actually, and threw myself onto Ranger. I was reasonably sure Mr. Cooper wouldn't harm me with so many witnesses. But then I froze, I was also reasonably sure Mr. Cooper, or one of his brutes, were the party who broke into my father's shop and ransacked it for components for a poison.

Ranger was stiff with tension, panting in my ear. It was then that I heard the gunshots.

They hit in rapid succession, distant, but following one another so quickly that even my non-military trained mind could tell it was from no ordinary revolver. People screamed in panic and glass shattered. I felt pieces of something hit the back of Valentine's long leather coat. I swallowed hard to keep from screaming.

I had the queerest sensation, as if I could feel a revolver pointed between my shoulder blades. The sensation made my skin crawl and I wanted to shake it off, but I was too terrified to move. I wasn't sure I could even manage to breathe. The air had turned thick and sticky sweet. I raised my head, sure I would see Mr. Cooper stabbing Ranger, or even stabbing me.

Mr. Cooper lay in a small cloud of violet tinged smoke. So did many of the people in the street. Broken orbs of gray glass littered the street and violet clouds oozed across the dirty cobbles.

Beneath me, Ranger quivered and sneezed.

I raised my head to see a net, neat as a spider's web, coming at me as if fired from the heavens. I had never heard the priests speak of God's Net before, they always spoke of the hand of God. How strange they got it wrong. Then the world faded to a violet, smoky, sweet haze.

The clock tower rang. My head swam like I'd had too much cream sherry. The bell was too loud. I had the strangest vision that God had decided not to take me, but rather than return me to the square, He merely deposited me in the clock tower where the great bell, Big Ben, resided. How very lazy of Him.

I opened my eyes and screamed. The massive face of the clock could not have been more than a dozen feet from my face. Ranger and I were tangled in an untidy heap in a rough fishing net. The square was a startling ninety meters below. It was my last such view of the Clock Tower as I was hauled like mackerel out of London and into the open sky.

CHAPTER SEVEN

WHEN I OPENED my eyes again, I was lying with my feet propped up on Valentine's pack. By some miracle, I had managed to maintain it in my possession. Mr. Valentine's coat was draped over me like a blanket. I lurched upright, missed the bucket provided for my convenience, and was sick all over the wooden floor.

A woman laughed. "Blimey, what a mess!"

"Water or whiskey, lass?" A rough voice offered.

"Tea," I gasped, my throat raw from being sick.

A female voice laughed. "That settles it, Love. She's definitely not a whore."

"I beg your pardon!" I did my best to sound indignant, but I think all I managed was to sound cranky.

"Well, don't just stand there, Gracie. Put the kettle on."

I cautiously opened my eyes again. I'm not sure what I was hoping for. I already considered myself quite fortunate not to be suspended in the air netted like a trout. Something large and furry pressed against my side. Ranger. He worked his nose under my hand. We were not on the ground; we were being gently rocked. I felt the motion, but not the waves. I couldn't remember feeling this tired before.

I closed my eyes for a moment and opened them to a tall, rawboned woman shaking my shoulder. She wore a man's shirt, a snug leather vest, and a funny hat with shiny lenses that reminded me of spider eyes. She stood, and I instantly looked away. She wore no skirts, no petticoats, she was stood outside of her bed chamber, in full view of God and everybody, in her bloomers. But what beautiful bloomers they were—crafted like men's doeskin breeches. They were tucked into her boots. She wore a leather cartridge box at her waist, and a sash of blue silk that fluttered. I had never seen a woman in such costume. Even when girls dressed as pageboys for costume dramas they didn't look like this.

The woman extended a strong hand. It was a working hand with neat squared nails. "Gracie Morgan. You asked for tea."

I took the offered hand and rose shakily to my feet, following Miss Morgan to the cabin. It stretched before me and was lit with a small gaslight.

She held the cabin door open and I followed her to a table set for five with mismatched china cups and raisin scones with butter.

I felt my mouth water and I swallowed hard. Despite my queasy stomach, I was fairly sure I could manage tea and scones, having had nothing since breakfast.

We were joined shortly by another woman and, judging by their looks, her other two daughters. They all had the same rawboned look, comely, but tall and thin. The youngest, I guessed perhaps seven or eight years my junior, had given an effort at cleaning up but had missed her nails. When she sat at the table, I saw the filth caked beneath them. It was charming in an odd sort of way. The middle girl, closest to me in age, was quite a sight. She had long blond hair, like her sisters and mother, but her face was crisscrossed with deep puckered scars. It was as though someone had tried to peel the flesh from her face. One eye was bright blue, the other a deep stormy gray. I smiled, determined not to stare.

"I am Francis Morgan—my daughters, Grace you met—Molly and Edith. My husband is Captain Zachariah Morgan. You are on board his ship, *The Lightning Aura*."

"Vivian Harper," I said, curtsying the best I could despite my bruises. "I am grateful for your kind rescue..." I paused, looking for the right word. The truth was too fantastical to be believed, but if we were still on board come morning, the situation would become evident. "So is my friend."

"You mean Valentine," Mrs. Morgan said airily.

"Well, yes." Apparently, they were aware of who, and what, Valentine was.

She motioned to one of the passing crewmen, "Mr. McCabe has been following him for the past few weeks. We are aware that some mischief has befallen Mr. Valentine and his beloved canine."

I nodded, relieved that I didn't have to keep such a fantastical thing to myself, at least for a little while.

"Well, let us sit before the tea gets cold. You can tell us all about yourself and we can all become good friends."

I sat at the table and let Mrs. Morgan and her daughters serve themselves before taking a scone and a generous spread of butter.

"Mama, let her eat before you engage the girl," Molly admonished. "Can't you see the poor thing is famished and has obviously been through quite an ordeal!"

Molly might have been my age, or a year younger, but her mothering was welcome. I held the cup in both hands, sipping the scalding liquid. It was a rather nice Indian black tea. Aside from the scones, there was also cheese, some cornmeal crusted kippers, and a sweet pickle relish.

I ate and ate until I thought I would burst, then sat back. Mrs. Morgan and her daughters behaved like rescuing young women and their transfiguring companions was commonplace. They chatted and shared tea.

"Now, my dear," Mrs. Morgan said when I had finished wiping my lips on a worn, but clean, lace-trimmed napkin. "When were you first aware of Mr. Valentine's malady?"

"When I awoke to a naked man in my chamber," I said without thinking.

Edith, the youngest, gasped and blushed giggling into her napkin. The scandal of it all.

"I didn't mean it like that," I said quickly. "I-I'm sorry, I haven't had a chance to talk about it with anyone, even Mr. Valentine, and I hadn't realized just how badly—" I flushed.

"I understand. It's a difficult situation to explain," Grace offered. "He seems to trust you, how much has he confided about his work?"

"Some, he made mention of visiting a scholar—a priest scholar," I mentioned, trying to recall where Valentine had said he was going to travel to. With all the excitement at the docks, I had mostly forgotten.

"Mr. Valentine was heading to Calais to see a priest, one Father Henri Poullain. I understand him to be a scholar in the *Basilica of Notre-Dame de Boulogne*. Mr. Valentine says he was a missionary and was quite interested in the legends of the druids that, at one time, populated London." Grace supplied, filling in the gaps of my memory.

"My husband has had dealings with Father Henri before. He is a scholar and a wondrous source in archeology. He has studied many different cultures from the Egyptians to the Vikings."

"Ah yes, Mr. Valentine did say something about being involved with the Explorer's Guild," I said with a smile. "Do you believe Mr. Valentine—"

"Bit off more than he could chew?" Grace laughed. "Well, that is what Papa thinks. Nathaniel went off on his own, but he had McCabe follow him. I'd bet McCabe could tell us a whole lot more."

"Or we could just ask Mr. Valentine himself in the morning." I sipped my refilled cup. "He'll be back to his old self then." I wondered what he would think of our new surroundings. At least he was on a ship and away from the Red Hoods.

"Valentine became a werewolf?" Molly looked both elated and scandalized.

"No," Francis said. "Nathaniel became something else. There is no full moon tonight and he's not a wolf, he became a dog."

I yawned so wide my eyes watered. I tried to cover it with my hand, but was not very convincing.

"My dear, you have had a trying time," Francis said graciously. "Girls, off to bed, there'll be plenty to do come morning. Molly, please show Miss Harper to the guest cabin."

I bid them goodnight and allowed Molly to lead me down an interior corridor to a small room with a bed that was attached to a wall, and a shelf with a set-in basin. A dented tin ewer sat in a small bin built into the wall beside the basin. As soon as Molly departed and closed the door behind her, I sat down on the bed and promptly fell asleep without even bothering to loosen my stays or remove Valentine's coat.

CHAPTER EIGHT

THE NEXT MORNING when I awoke I wasn't sure what to make of my new situation. The ship creaked, gently rocking me in the berth box. The bed was musty, but clean. I lay watching the sunlight through the cracks in the wall play across the worn leather, long coat. I was most definitely not home and though the prospect was terrifying, it was also very exciting. I had never been more than a few miles away from my home on Exeter Street, let alone London. Now I was traveling across the ocean towards France.

Without luggage. I didn't even have a clean petticoat. I got out of the bed and examined my reflection in a silver mirror hanging on the wall. I combed my hair out with my fingers and tied it back between my shoulders. I washed off the soot, gutter filth, God knows what else, and straightened my skirts.

Mr. Valentine would be a man again. Well, I mean, he would be human again since it was morning. I ought to return his jacket. I hoped that he had already secured his pack so that he wouldn't be running around the ship nude.

I left my quarters and ascended the stairs toward the top deck. The sun was extremely bright, more so than I expected, and I blinked hard in the light. The higher I climbed, the more I was jostled left and right as sailors pushed past, carrying ropes and canisters. They all had the same strange hats Grace had from last night, but now in proper light I could see they were tight fitting glass eye covers, like glasses but cunningly fitted with leather straps to keep them firmly in place. The wind gathered up my hair, freeing locks from my loose tie-back.

I had never been on a ship before. I walked to the side, dodging workers, to look out at the ocean. We were not upon the ocean. My stomach plunged down into my feet and the heavy weight anchored me to the deck. I was going to die right here on the deck of the ship. I never wanted to be home so badly in all my life, but expressing my need to return home would necessitate speaking to the captain. To do so, I would have to open my mouth and if I did that I just may vomit.

A shadow blocked out the bright sun and a comforting hand touched my shoulder. When I opened my eyes, Nathaniel Valentine was crouched before me. His large, amber eyes wide, brow furrowed in concern. "Are you okay?"

I stared at him. "No, I am not okay."

I died, I reasoned. I must be dead—God welcomed me into His kingdom, though with a large rough net not His loving hand. I was going to have words with the first angel I encountered.

Nathaniel was still staring at me. "Can I get you a cup of coffee? Clearly there is a lot to discuss."

I nodded and let him get me to my feet.

He walked me up a set of stairs to a landing where the wide frame of what could only be Captain Morgan, a man with a presence such as that must be the captain— he was every bit what I envisioned one would be. He stood at a ship's wheel, scanning the sky before him. His heavy, leather, long coat shifted in the wind and he had a smoking pipe clamped in his mouth which was fully hidden by a graying black beard. His deep black eyes scanned the ship, then settled upon Mr. Valentine. The pipe shifted as he scowled.

"We be headed to pick up more product, Nate. Your missus is welcome, but The Aura is no place for a lady; she best toughen up or stay below."

He turned and looked me over. "I'm not too sure how ye found yerself in the company of this rogue, my dear, but he left us a bit short-handed. I'll be needing his help."

Nathaniel guided me over to a table set with a steaming pot, wrapped in a knit cozy, and heavy ceramic mugs. Far from dainty china, these had a heft to them, enough to hold a full tankard's worth of beverage and resist chipping by rough handling. They were so heavy, they'd be passable weapons in a pinch.

A man with a tight-fitting leather cap and glass eye coverings took the captain's place, and Captain Morgan joined us at the weathered wooden table.

He poured me a mug of hot, black coffee and motioned to copper creamer and sugar bowls. He did not pour for Mr. Valentine. He pulled up a towel covering a basket of rolls and offered me one. Again, Mr. Valentine was left to his own devices. There was definitely a distinct coolness between them.

"So Miss Harper..." Morgan stirred his coffee with a tarnished, silver spoon. "My wife, Fannie, tells me you met Nate a fortnight ago."

"Yes," I said cautiously. Though I had an immediate like of Zachariah Morgan, something about his demeanor put me on edge.

"Did ye know Nate here was my first mate? He left The Aura last month without explanation. We docked in London, and just like that—" He snapped his fingers. "Nate scurries off without a trace."

I looked at Mr. Valentine. He scowled into his mug.

"You ought to thank me, miss. Had I not sent my man to follow him, I would not have been aware you were in trouble. Those gentlemen in the Red Hoods seemed cultish. They were most definitely up to no good."

I had to agree. When Mr. Valentine shifted I saw the line from the rope left a deep black bruise circling his neck, low by his collar. I blushed when I realized I was staring. He wasn't wearing his shirt fully buttoned, nor was he wearing his cravat— and I definitely remembered recovering it from the coal shed.

"I do thank you for your timely assistance," I said as graciously as I could muster. "Mr. Cooper would have killed Mr. Valentine to be sure. I do not believe that he was too much of a gentleman not to harm me, as well. I suspect he had already ransacked my home for herbs to create a toxin to use against, well, anyone he finds unseemly in our city."

"An herb, you say? What herb does this Red Hood think will be a toxin against unique individuals?"

"He came in trying to buy dangerous quantities of wolfsbane, but my father refused to sell it to him. I suspect he returned and took it for himself." I snorted. "And he dares to work under the premise of being a gentleman. His mannerisms suggest no such decorum."

"Well, Miss Harper, there is a time and place for such 'decorum' as you say. You would probably do better amongst my crew were you to relax your own fancy London mannerisms. I am well aware that etiquette is a lady's shield in society, and a true gentleman's sword as well. Neither will serve you here." He refilled my mug with the strong black coffee and a splash of heavy cream. "Aboard my ship, we don't take with such nonsense. You will be treated with respect, but not as a lady. My own wife is more a man than most on the streets of London, and my daughters are tougher than most men I've met. A 'please' won't serve you here. Sugar?"

I stopped myself before I asked with a please. "Yes, thank you," I said before I could keep the words from passing my lips.

Captain Morgan laughed and slapped his knee. "You're a smart lass, and a bonnie one too. I can see why Nate dragged you along with him. What I can't see is why you'd take up with him?" Morgan cocked an eye at Nathaniel.

"If you have something to say to me, you should say it rather than have your men stalk me around London," Nathaniel growled.

"Have you seen Edith?" Morgan inquired casually.

"No," Nathaniel returned, he was toying with a butter knife from the tea tray.

"Is she the reason you left without explanation?"

He dropped the knife. "I left before there was something to explain."

There was a moment of silence. The two men stared at one another, measuring each other. They were hounds circling, searching for weakness. I expected a snarling, snapping fight to follow.

"You see here, Miss Harper, as I said before…Nate was my first mate, and my Edith was quite taken with him. She still is. Then he ran off like a thief in the night when I docked in London. My poor Edith was beside herself. Locked herself in the girl's cabin for days. We even feared the worst. I had McCabe follow him, to ask him to meet with me like gentlemen so I could be sure there was nothing I had to do to preserve my family's honor. I half expected to have to throw either a wedding or a funeral. Fortunately, my Fannie got to the bottom of it. It seems that though she is quite taken with him, Nate here doesn't share her affections.

Before I could recall Mr. McCabe, it turned out that you both needed my help."

"Speaking of your help—I need you to take us to Calais," Nathaniel said tensely.

"I do not take passengers. I'm not a passenger airship, Nate. I'm a businessman."

"You owe me a debt," Nate said crossly. "I'd consider us squared."

"Correction, I owed you a debt. My debt is paid." Captain Morgan said.

"How so?" Mr. Valentine demanded.

"Your timely rescue in the square. Unless you'd rather I return you and your lady friend to the Red Hood Society of London? They have a privateer's license to protect the citizens of London from all sorts of unnaturalness."

Nate scowled.

"Please, Captain, don't do that. Mr. Cooper would kill Mr. Valentine. I must confess, I am not up to the task of protecting him when he is in his other form," I said. I thought I saw Captain Morgan smile at me.

"I am not headed to Calais this time of year, Miss Harper. Why does he wish to take up residence in France? Quasimodo already rings the bells in Notre-Dame de Paris, I doubt there is room for another in sanctuary there." Morgan laughed at his little joke.

"There is a priest in Calais that studies druidic sites. He might know—"

"How to fix you? How to separate you from your dog?" Morgan guffawed. "I always liked your dog, Nate. I think I like you better as him. Which brings up the question: tonight, over cards, perhaps you'll regale me as to how in the world you managed to become one with that damnable dog of yours?"

Nate gave a glare. I wanted to point out that at night Mr. Valentine wouldn't be able to explain anything. "Ask McCabe, he's been spying on me."

"I was asking you." The men glared at each other. Nate turned away first his jaw clenching. Captain Morgan turned to me. "Now, as I said, we are not headed to France. We are gathering around the Molten Cay."

"You're hunting around the Cay?" Nathaniel sat up straight.

"What Cay?" I asked.

Both men stared at me for a moment.

"Molten Cay," Nathaniel explained, "We hunted there before. In fact, I had to rescue the good captain from the islands," he paused searching for the right word, "*Guardian.*"

"I find myself a man short— my old first mate abandoned his post and left me low on hands." Captain Morgan pulled another roll from the basket and started to slowly smear it with butter and honey. "The Guardian of the Cay surely knows how to cure you of your malady as she is a creature of magic herself. You will serve my crew and I will take you to France, and your lady friend there," He took a large bite," I will return to London. I will only charge you ten thousand pounds."

Nathaniel choked, spitting the coffee across the table, narrowly missing me. "Ten thousand pounds! That's robbery!"

"That is my fee. I plan to retire a wealthy man, someday. But, I am not heartless. You are my best harvester, I will gladly pay you a thousand pounds a year to rejoin my crew."

"And my debt would be paid in ten short years?" Nate's voice had become tense and quiet.

"I have daughters to provide for," Captain Morgan said simply. "I'd suggest you get to work."

Nate stood, shook out his vest, and stomped off.

I wasn't fooled. "Now just a minute!" I stood, "Captain Morgan, you say he was your first mate,"

The captain turned in his chair, amused. "Yes."

"And I couldn't help but notice from your words that you are not wholly opposed to letting your Edith wed him,"

"Not at all," Captain Morgan said with a wide grin.

Men are the soul of madness. "Then why would you charge him, a man you think so highly of, such an exorbitant fee to take him some place you were going anyway?"

"Miss Harper, I like Nate—but there is family, and then there is business. He chose not to be family." He rose to his feet. "Good day, Miss Harper." He gave a short bow, then took back the wheel from his crewman, leaving me to finish the now cold coffee.

I learned in short order that my gown had no place on an airship. My skirts tangled in all the equipment that littered the deck. I stood carefully, positioning myself out of the way by not standing in the shade cast by the enormous balloon suspending us in the air.

"Harper." It took me a moment to realize I was the one being addressed. I turned and saw Grace headed towards me with a large, woven basket. "I took up a collection among the crew to see if we could get you better attired."

I followed her into the cabin and let her make selections from the mismatched cast-off clothing from the crew. She held up trousers and shirts and coats until she was finally satisfied. "Strip down. Hurry up now, I'm needed topside. We're getting to good harvest grounds."

"Grace, what does Captain Morgan deal in?" I asked.

"Lightning, what else?"

"Lightning?" I blinked hard. "How can one harvest lightning?" My mind raced at the problem. "What in the world does one do with it?" They must be joking.

"Whatever you want. It's a fantastic power source. It's mostly in the realm of inventors and scholars for now, but it pays well. We use nets of course—if you dress in time you'll see!" She tossed a pair of glass eye covers on the bench with the clothes and sauntered off.

I undressed slowly and stood in my petticoat and corset looking over the clothes she had picked for me. Dark brown trousers, like the ones she wore. I hoped they weren't so skin tight on me, it was scandalous for women to show off their legs at all but, as wrong as it was, the idea of looking like Grace was also titillating. The shirt was a man's shirt in soft cream linen, open at the neck so I could draw it over my shoulders, but it would show more of my bosom than was proper. She had managed to find leather boots with hard soles. They reminded me of riding boots with a slight heel and square toe. They must have once belonged to one of Captain Morgan's daughters, I couldn't imagine one of his men having feet this small. A leather long coat finished the outfit. The whole crew wore them, the chill in the air demanded something protective and warm.

I started dressing, and immediately noticed a problem. Like all respectable women I wore split drawers under my skirt. There was no room for them in these trousers. Try as I might they would not fit along with my own legs down the legs of the garment. I had to either abandon them or return to my filthy dress. The horse stains, gutter filth, and torn hem made my decision for me. I pulled on the snug brown trousers and shirt. Grace had neglected to provide me with a cravat to hold the shirt closed at the top. I adjusted my corset, untying it and tucking the shirt between it and my chemise. I had to adjust the laces for the bulkier shirt before I bound myself in, mindful of the last day being much more athletic than a tight lacing could accommodate. I left myself plenty of room to breathe. I retied my hair behind my neck, pulling the leather thong tighter this time, before examining myself in the mirror. I wasn't sure what I was expecting, but certainly not this.

The lady looking back at me was quite fetching. There was a decidedly alluring feel to showing off my legs in this manner. It was delightfully scandalous. Byron would have fallen right off his carriage if he saw me now. I felt giddy and giggled.

My mirth disappeared when I saw my dress. Just last week it was brand new, the bodice fit by a professional seamstress. I bought enough fabric to make the skirt myself. Now, it was a broken and dead thing; tattered and dirty, covered in filth. I had been so proud of the color, a burgundy wine— perfect for the coming fall. If I changed the trim on the sleeves it would have been tasteful enough for Christmas. It lay there on the bench like an old chrysalis hanging discarded on a tree branch.

I couldn't bear to leave it lying there. Grace had left a sharp knife on her morning tea tray. I carefully slit the seams at the sleeves, and the stitching that attached the skirts to the bodice in a beautiful box-pleat. I pulled the bodice on over my stays to make a beautiful corset cover like the ones Madame Theodora wore to change her gowns in a moment's notice. The bodice of my dress itself had, thankfully, escaped most of the damage the rest of my dress had sustained. I was amazed at how well the wine set off the deep brown.

I was committed now, without needle and thread there was no going back to my old dress. For good or for ill, I was wearing these scandalously tight-fitting breeches, mannish boots, and shirt.

"Miss Harper, you look quite striking," Captain Morgan said when I rejoined the crew.

"Call me Vivian, if you please, Captain."

"All right then, Vivian. We're headed into a storm; you best get your goggles ready." He motioned to the glass eye coverings in my hand.

I fit them over my face, I was delighted to see they made the sky just a bit darker and much easier to see without squinting. There was a huge gray cloud ahead and we were headed straight towards it. I took a deep breath and gripped the wooden railing.

"Miss Harper—" Nathaniel froze mid step. "You look very..." he paused searching for the right word. I had to bite my cheek to keep from laughing. The resemblance between the look on his face and the look on Ranger's face when he desperately wanted my fried fish was remarkably similar.

"You look different," he finished finally.

"Thank you." I had no skirts with which to curtsy, so I used the sides of my long coat.

"Nate," Morgan bellowed. "Fore cannon!"

He looked like he wanted to say more, but he gave his head a shake and started off towards a huge, bronze cannon with long canisters and pipes. He turned, mid-stride, and beckoned me to follow him with an impish grin on his face.

"Gun powder works differently here," Nate said when I got close. "It's unreliable this high in the air, and useless when it gets wet."

"So, it's not like a cannon?" I had to speak up against the rising wind. Rain droplets started to pelt my coat; it had been treated by something that made it bead and run off.

"It is, but it's a steam cannon," Nathaniel explained. "Get me a cartridge." He motioned with his foot to the bronze tubes piled in a small pyramid pinned in place with wooden stakes.

They were heavy, but I could manage. Through a glass window set in the tube I saw ropes and sand within.

Nathaniel exchanged it for one that the cannon was already holding. The window in this one was full of grey glass orbs that had a violet tint.

"Don't drop it," he cautioned. "You'll knock us all out."

I realized it was full of the glass orbs that pelted the square. "What is it?"

"Aethium." Nathaniel turned one of the large dials on the side of the cannon. There was an audible hiss as steam rushed into a chamber within the cannon, and two gears clicked into place. He slid back a panel and set the sand and rope into the cannon. "Gun one is hot!" He called over his shoulder at the crew, and dug into his pockets for thick wool gloves.

I assumed it was a figure of speech. The wind tossed me into him and my arm hit the cannon. Instantly, my wrist raised an angry red burn where the leather sleeve had ridden up, exposing my bare flesh. I hissed in irritation.

Nathaniel steadied me. "The gun is hot!" He shouted above the wind.

We were headed right for the storm. The ropes holding the ship to the balloon creaked and groaned, but each was made of a complex braid four strands thicker than my thigh and, though I wasn't in a position to check, I assumed the net securing the balloon was the same.

There were several ropes, hanging just below the rail, secured in metal eye bolts and tied into belaying pins every five feet or so. One of the men walked through the crew, handing out harnesses designed to wrap around both legs, the shoulders, and terminate at a woven ring at the waist. Mr. Valentine took one, handed to me, and held it as I stepped through.

"Mind your hands, please," I said against the wind, not sure if he heard me or not. He tied me to a rope closest to his gun and tied himself in in the same fashion. The rain had whipped itself into a frenzy. "Blow, winds, and crack your cheeks! Rage! Blow!" I quoted *King Lear,* grinning to myself.

"What?" Valentine shouted beside me. "Did you say something?"

I waved him off.

The ship bucked and I was thrown off my feet. I slammed painfully into the deck. I expected a hand up, but Mr. Valentine had no attention for me now. I rose to my feet. The air smelled like nothing I had ever experienced. The clean smell of the rain that dampened the soot on land was positively arousing in the air. The rain pelted my coat and soaked my hair, but the goggles kept my vision clear. Like a runaway horse, we could do little more than hang on as the storm tossed us violently through the air. I laughed in maniacal delight; before I was a bird soaring on the winds, now I was a goddess riding through the storm!

When I was a child, Mama and I used to sit in the gardens under the cover of the eaves when the storms rumbled and watch the lightning split the sky. We'd count the seconds between flash and crash and giggle in delight as the plants delighted in the water and everything else took cover. I remember that smell now—the smell right before the lightning hit, like the air itself was readying. The smell hit, distinctive but stronger than I had ever experienced before, hot and itchy and smelling like hot metal.

The crew of *The Lightning Aura* were delighted. No one was afraid and for a moment, I was one of them. It was too exciting to be frightening. The cannon suddenly exploded into a set of dark clouds and the lightning hit its charge. The thunder roared in the same instant so hard and loud I was thrown to the deck again. In the distance, I heard a low and menacing crackle of fire too hot to burn.

I tasted blood. I had a moment of panic. All I could taste was blood, my vision was a mass of gray and my limbs felt like water. For the second time in as many days I was convinced that I had died. I shook my head, spitting blood, and shakily rose to my feet. I was relieved to realize I had only bitten my own tongue. The rope kept me from sliding across the wet deck and into other deck hands.

Valentine and another man were loading another canister into his cannon. They slid panels, turned gears, and crouched at a spyglass waiting for their shot. They fired again. The boom rattled through my core. This time I had wisely stayed on my knees on the deck. I closed my eyes when the blinding light scorched the sky. The very storm itself was hissing in rage.

Grace stood at the back of the ship on another cannon, firing as swiftly as her partner could supply her with fresh canisters. I watched the flurry of activity until the ship passed through the storm.

The mates whooped and cheered, slapping each other on the back and embracing on the wet deck.

Grace embraced a man and held him tightly, then gave him a big kiss. I recognized Francis Morgan in head-to-toe leather, bringing her husband a glass bottle of spirits. He took a healthy swig, then brought it to all his men in turn to toast their good fortune and for many happy returns.

I was an outsider intruding on this strange scene for, as with most things that had occurred since I rose from my bed yesterday, I couldn't fathom what I had witnessed.

They fired cannon shot into the storm, again and again. I could not see that they hit anything, but they were jubilant!

Nathaniel wheeled around and found me on the deck, staring in amazement. Before I could protest, he lifted me into his arms and soundly kissed me.

I'm not sure, but I think I kissed him back.

The crew hooted and hollered.

I froze then, red with shame and flushed from something else. I wheeled and slapped him as hard as I could, every nerve on fire.

The silence was deafening.

Captain Morgan appeared at my side, "Enough. There's work to be done. Vivian, help Gracie and Fannie—get the traps to my lassies below to be harvested. Nate, get that gun cleaned and ready for the next storm."

He turned and addressed the crew. "Quit your lollygagging! Get the boilers filled, reset the cartridges! The rest of you lot, to work!"

CHAPTER NINE

I TURNED ON my heel and stomped away from Nathaniel and Captain Morgan. Grace and the middle Morgan daughter, Molly, were waving me over. They stood at the rail with hooks and pulleys. I was sure she was talking about their trip through the lightning storm. I couldn't think straight. I was wet, cold, bruised and every nerve was zinging.

I took a deep breath, and put Mr. Valentine out of my mind. "How can I help? Captain says we have to harvest?"

Grace nodded and handed me a big lump of sweet, honey-scented bees wax. "Wax the rail."

"I beg your pardon," I stammered.

Molly took the wax and rubbed it into the already-shiny railing of the ship. "We can't have the ropes split."

"Well, above the sea it's just lost product," Grace laughed. "Over land it's a much different thing."

"Lost product?"

"Sure." Grace grunted, and tested the rope against the slick railing. "Reach over and give a feel, the full traps buzz and vibrate."

I put my hand on the rope, and leapt back in alarm. In an instant, my hand felt as one's legs do after a long carriage ride on a horribly maintained road: weak and numb.

Grace exploded with laughter. "I'm sorry, Vivian, the look on your face."

I tried again and got a dizzying look over the rail. My legs felt boneless and I crumpled against the railing, panting. To make my shame complete, Nathaniel was watching as he coiled up ropes. I made myself regain my feet.

"You don't have to look," Molly whispered to me.

"But he's watching me," I protested

Molly gave me a blank look. "You don't have to look over the edge. Just feel the rope, the trap is full."

Feeling like I fool, I took the wax back and rubbed the hard, shiny stuff into the railing where they directed. The girls took the hooks and attached it to the rope and dragged it behind me along the shiny rail. It was hard work at first. It made my arm ache, but the wax eventually softened and the work, combined with the scent, was actually pleasant. I was about to ask how far we were dragging the bundle when I saw, at the back of the ship, a huge wooden, wheel resting partially over the side.

"This pulley will reel in the catch. Come with me below, I'll show you how we harvest," Molly said.

We passed several hammocks nailed into poles and set into the ceiling, and cargo nets securing trunks and barrels to the walls. The walking was slow as we dodged moving targets of wood and netting, but still Molly didn't answer.

"Molly?"

"Lightning is fiddly. It likes it quiet when we harvest, or it throws a completely undignified fit," Molly said, half turning to me, "I have the best hand for it, you just have to be patient and very calm. And quiet."

How in the world did they harvest lightning? It was a force of nature. One might as well try to capture the wind or bottle the pea-soup fogs. But, then again, people gathered the rain in barrels and used sails to move ships and windmills. I just couldn't conceive of it myself. I had heard of airships before, but I had never seen one until just a few days ago. Harvesting lightning. I had never heard of such a thing—but then again, there were dealers of small metal canisters they called batteries that ran all sorts of amazing devices. Madame Theodora herself had a splendid hot pot that boiled water for tea or coffee in an instant with one little press of a button. Zap, and boiling water ready for tea. It was one of the amazing features that made *Madame Theodora's Tea House* one of the most successful and profitable shops in Limehouse, let alone all of London.

I was interrupted from my reflection. Molly stopped so quickly I was hit by a bit of netting hooked to the ceiling that I had pushed aside.

"This is the most dangerous job on the ship," she announced proudly. Her voice dropped to a conspiratorial whisper. "Want to see what I do?"

I felt a lurch in my chest, but squashed it down. "Of course."

She unlocked a huge brass door and let us in. The room was small, and its only adornments were a huge wooden barrel, large enough to bathe several people at once. It had a huge, heavy lid supported with gears and a wooden stool. The far wall was hinged, like the whole side of the room could fall away. I swallowed, hoping she wouldn't open that ominous door. She locked the door behind us, and sure enough, started a crank to lower the wall panel. I held the door latch for support.

"Don't worry, you won't fall out," she assured me quietly.

There were loud whirs and clicks, when the wall lowered a wooden wheel clicked into place, supporting one of the thick ropes. She fished the rope with a huge hook on a long pole, guiding the rope into another set of pulleys by the wooden tub. No, it was a copper tub in a large wooden vessel. There was a huge copper tub within the wooden one, with a small deep-set glass window. It was a giant pot with a sharp wooden spike set in the side.

The machine carefully reeled in the rope. At the end was a huge jagged glass ball, lit from inside with an eerie glow. The glass itself was a beautiful amber color, round like a ball of ice but jagged and imperfect. She guided the glass ball into the copper tub carefully as if it were an egg, but as soon as it was in place she slammed the lid closed and screwed down bolts furiously, as if to keep this golden egg from escaping.

"Sometimes they explode," she said, releasing a deep breath.

I realized I was holding in my breath, too. We panted for a moment, smiling. She looked positively giddy. I was about to be shown some great and dangerous secret.

She gazed through the peephole lovingly, stroking the glass. "Now we have to wait for it to be calm."

She reeled in the other golden orbs and stacked them in nests of old faded quilts. There were eight in all, each the size of a wine barrel—glowing and hot to the touch. A golden warmth filled the room. They produced a heat that soon was similar to a wealthy lady's parlor. I removed my leather, long coat and draped it on a hook on the wall to dry.

Molly stood, transfixed. She watched the orbs with something I would have called lust, but it felt purer. It was more akin to the reverent love a nun has when she takes her orders. Down here, the scars on Molly's face were more pronounced and more beautiful.

"What happened, if I may ask?" I inquired so softly that if she didn't want to tell me, she could pretend she hadn't heard me.

She turned towards me, still bathed in the glow. "I told you already, sometimes they explode."

I should have been afraid. I wasn't.

"Now it's much calmer," Molly whispered. She watched through the deep glass window. The glass orb did seem to have a much more even color. The maniacal flickering had faded to what I could only call a 'hum,' if a glow could indeed hum.

Molly set another device, I thought it was copper and wood, against a small port on the side of the tub. She secured it in place with bolts.

"This will catch the energy when I shatter the trap."

"The trap?"

"How do you think we catch lightning?" Molly asked with a smile.

"I honestly haven't given it much thought," I replied.

"The canisters spray a net and very fine sand. When it strikes the lightning, the force of the electricity turns the sand to glass; melts it and cools it all at once. If we miss, it's just an empty net of rope, like a fishing net."

"You shot one of these at me and Mr. Valentine in the square," I said suddenly. At my loud voice, the orbs flashed, their color erratic shades of blue, yellow, and white rather than the even gold. Molly scowled at me.

"Sorry," I said sheepishly. The spell of the beautiful sunlit parlor shattered and her alluring scars were harsh in this light.

"Gracie shot the net at you, after she and Mother shot aethium into the square to knock everyone out."

"What is aethium?" I asked, remembering the odd, sick-sweet smell of that violet cloud.

"Aether from the air, and powdered opium," she said airily. "It temporarily knocks all sorts of things out. The ropes keep the traps attached to the ship so we can recover them."

The orbs seduced me with their warm golden glow again. "So, these are glass balls full of lightning? I understand now why it would be such a mess to drop one on land, they'd shatter."

"And explode," Molly added. "They release a lightning bolt on land, I'm not sure even an archangel raining holy fire down could cause more destruction." She crossed herself for the mild blasphemy.

"That would happen if one of these would break?" I asked, feeling quite unsettled.

"We wouldn't even live long enough to know. If the one in the collection tub exploded, we would probably both be killed. Or you'd look like me. If one outside the tub exploded, it would set off all the others. The ship would probably explode. Maybe. I've never seen that happen." Molly smiled. "I never want to."

"I quite agree," I said, nodding.

"Quiet and calm," Molly reminded me.

The golden orbs were quite beautiful, gleaming in their hypnotic way. I had no desire to disturb them.

"I release the lightning from the trap when it's calm, and it flows into the canisters so we can sell them." Molly watched the amber light coming from the small window. "Close your eyes, there's a bright flash when I break the trap."

She suddenly slammed the wooden spike into the tub. There was the sound of a thousand china cups shattering at once and a light brighter than a glaring noonday sun pierced the small dark room. The air hummed like thousands of bees. Then it was deafeningly silent.

Molly touched my hand. I had my eyes screwed closed. I released the breath I was holding and opened them. Molly was smiling at me. The row of small copper canisters below the collection device were hot. "We can only reuse them a dozen times or so before they start to melt."

I helped her open the tub. The copper inside was hot to the touch, scorching through the wool gloves. The base was full of gleaming sand and larger pieces of beautiful, amber glass. She swept out the tub and used the pulleys in the ceiling to set another orb into the tub. Then she repeated the process.

"It's amazing," I whispered to her, careful not to disturb the lightning.

Molly pulled out two pieces of glass amber and handed them to me. One was dark but beautiful, the color of burnt toffee, smooth and round like a stone you could skip on a lake. The other was angular and warm, and glowed like a small hot coal. It fit my hand perfectly.

"Sometimes they just form when you break the traps. One this small won't burn hot enough to set anything on fire, but they're nice to hold when it's cold," Molly said. "But don't break it. It's still deadly if released. My father won't mind if you keep it, it's too small to harvest."

I thanked her and put it in the pocket of my long coat.

I left her there harvesting the rest of her very dangerous but very beautiful catch. The lightning stone in my pocket warmed my fingers as I worked my way back up to the main deck. I reached the stairs and was about to go up when I heard singing. Horrible, off-key singing with absolutely no place in a respectable salon, but the voice was happy as a lark. I followed the sound to a small kitchen, no, a galley. After all, when one was on a ship, one should respect the language therein.

The cook, a man whose physical size was only rivaled by Captain Morgan as the largest man I had seen, stood over a small, wood stove sizzling sausages in a pan.

"Missus," he greeted me before going back to his song.

"Good afternoon, sir."

"Hungry, lass?" he asked in a rich, smooth voice.

"Yes," I said with a smile.

"You know, there was a time where I could have banned all women from my galley, but Mrs. Morgan and her daughters, I'll be darned if they haven't grown on me." He motioned for me to sit, and he dished me up a hot sausage from the pan and a hard roll from the pantry.

A moment later, a piece of hard cheese and an apple were plunked on my plate as well. I nodded my thanks and he went back to singing— something more appropriate for a taproom maybe, or soldiers on campaign, but the melody was easy and the chorus repeated. I couldn't help it, in minutes I was singing along.

He gave me a look of surprise but finished the meal he was preparing and sent it off with three men who had stomped down to the galley and took steaming trays to, I assumed, the Captain's table and their shipmates.

"You look quite the cat that had the cream." He dunked a spitting, hissing pan into a rain barrel.

"I guess so," I smiled back. "This is so..." I paused, unsure the correct word to use. "Different."

"From your life below?" He laughed. "Yes, I suppose it is." He turned towards me with a towel in hand and scrubbed the table I was sitting at. "But, then again, the only thing that is constant is change. Take me for example, twenty years ago I was on a ship, a water ship, as a merchant marine with my cousin. Then he goes and gets married and pours all his money into this inventor and his crazy idea." He thumped the wall of the ship. "Now we're sailing the skies bottling lightning to sell."

It was strange, but I understood. A ship was freedom, terrifying but free. We could plummet to our very deaths. I put my hand into the pocket of my borrowed coat where the little live lightning stone warmed my fingers. If this was Nate's life why would he ever leave it? Why wouldn't he marry Edith and remain here forever? I would remain here, but there was Mama and Papa to feed and when my time here was done, I would have to find another man to marry. The thought of doing my duty used to be inconvenient, now it filled me with dread.

CHAPTER TEN

MR. VALENTINE WAS in a small area of the ship overlooking the front, the bow. He was staring at the horizon, watching the setting sun. He had neglected to shave.

"Mr. Valentine? Do you remember things that happen when you change?"

"Some," he said quietly. "It's like a dream, like it all happened, but to someone else."

"How did it happen?" I couldn't help but place my hand on his arm.

"It was only a few weeks ago," Nathaniel said softly, "Some river draggers found this hole in the side of the river bank. They followed it as far as they dared. Finally, they concluded it must be a gateway into the underworld, you know, like in Dante's *Divine Comedy*."

"A gateway to Hell is located in London. Who knew?" I said dryly.

I could tell Nathaniel appreciated the reference. He smiled suddenly, looking quite shy and vulnerable. "Mr. Langton, that's the society head, sent me to go investigate. He thought it was probably just one of the caves cut into the riverbanks from all those underground rivers below London; the perfect investigation quest for a newer member of the society."

"The Explorer's Society?" I clarified.

He nodded. "I had just paid my dues for the quarter that morning. He doubted there was anything to be concerned about, but, then again, stranger things have happened. Were you aware that tombs have been found in the ancient Valley of the Kings in Egypt when the winds blew the sands the right way?"

I didn't know that.

"I took my dog. He's good company. I mean, he was good company," Nathaniel amended.

"I think he is good company," I said. "Better than you at any rate," I added with a smile.

He laughed. I liked that sound. No sarcasm or dark humor this time, just mirth. It made me feel warm and tingly inside.

"There was this huge stone altar carved with knot-work and runes all over. The maps said there was supposed to be a river there. I didn't find a river. Instead I found a lake."

"A lake?"

"Of molten silver. All shiny and flat like some giant had set a huge mirror down and left it there. Ranger ran forward sniffing everything, like we were on a grand adventure. Then he found it."

"It?"

I wasn't sure Nathaniel had heard me. He was staring at some fixed point beyond me, his voice thick with sorrow. "I don't even know what he found. He just started digging at the ground. Then there was this flash. The world smelled like blood. I was knocked out, and when I awoke, Ranger was gone."

"Gone?" I asked.

Nathaniel nodded. "Well, I thought he was gone. I left the cave to go find him. That was the first night it happened." He was drumming his fingers on the rail, absently tracing the wood with his fingers and watching the sun sink lower and lower on the horizon. "Something happened that night. I awoke the next morning like I had way too much to drink. I was under a shrub in an estate just outside of London, and my clothes were gone."

I gasped. "You were naked?"

"As the day I was born." He looked at me again. "I had to steal a shirt and trousers from a clothesline. I found my own clothes near the river. I traded all the money I had to the river dragger who found them. She hadn't gone through the pockets yet. I told her that if she gave my clothes back she could everything in my pockets except my revolver and my knife."

"She agreed?"

"No. I had to steal them from her and run, but I left her my money. I did promise." He laughed.

"You kept looking for Ranger in the kennels."

"Sort of," Nathaniel said. "At first I went in looking for Ranger, but when I looked at the dogs, the queerest sensation came over me. I could hear them. Not just barking, I could hear them, like they were speaking English but they were speaking only to me.

"I could ask them anything. I thought I was going mad." Nathaniel shook his head. "But they had amazing stories and they were just as surprised that I could hear them as I was. I'm not sure dog language has words for what I needed, though. It took some time for me to understand what happened."

"You and Ranger became one." I smiled.

"I suppose so," he said wistfully.

"What's it like to transfigure?"

"Strange," he said. "I can feel it coming on like a body ache...like I'm humming."

"Like the rope on a full trap?"

"Exactly." He nodded. "It's like someone takes a knife to my nose and my ears, gashing them open so they suddenly take in more than they ever intended to, and like someone threw a blinder over my eyes. The world suddenly becomes dull, like a tintype; the lines are sharp, but the color is dull. My bones and muscles are crushed and compacted like I'm under a machine press."

"It hurts," I said softly.

"Yes, but it is fleeting," Nathaniel continued. "Becoming a man again is the opposite; I'm stretched thin, like too little butter over bread, my nose and ears are stuffed with cotton but everything is so bright."

The sun would be setting soon. The clouds had turned pink and violet and orange. It was beautiful—my favorite sight from the ship.

Nathaniel stared out at the horizon again, looking contemplative and quite miserable. What must it be like? To be divided so?

"Do you want to be yourself again?" It was a strangely intimate thing to ask, I only realized it after I asked him. Of course, he would want to be himself again. Who would want to be himself only half the time?

Nate looked over his shoulder, the rest of him was still turned toward the setting sun. He was a man trapped between two very different worlds. "Sometimes. There are many virtues to being the same thing in all hours of the day and night. But, then again, if I am me all the time then I lose Ranger altogether. I don't know that I can—" He shook his head and stared off at the clouds.

I wanted to press him, perhaps talking would help, but he would be transforming soon. More than anything, I wished I could somehow set things right for him. I leaned in and gently kissed his cheek.

He didn't move, his gaze still fixed beyond me, but he gave a crooked smile.

Regretfully, I left him to prepare for his transformation. I went in search of other company. Maybe it would be better if he were a werewolf, he would only be one on a full moon; this seemed to be a permanent nighttime condition. He was so sad, he lost his best friend, he was cursed to become something he could not control, and became hunted by men seeking unnaturalness.

Unnaturalness. Men were drowning on dry land. Fish flopping in the streets, gardens flooding, and a lake of silver under London. They had to be connected, but how?

§§§

Mr. Pierce welcomed me in the kitchen. Apparently, the rules I had read in my books about a woman in the galley were only valid if the ship was actually on the water. I liked to perch on the stool, chatting with him to pass the time as the captain and his crew sailed the air currents, bringing us closer to Molten Cay and the fearsome guardian that resided there.

"Mr. Pierce, have you heard about Molten Cay?"

"Why yes, Miss Harper." Mr. Pierce was busy rolling out dough for biscuits. "When I was cook's assistant aboard *Neptune's Whore*— that's a ship, lass, not an insult."

I smiled.

He grinned back and continued. "We sailed several times by Molten Cay. Landed there a few times too. We once took a rich naturalist there to study the birds— Lord Sutherland sure had a thing for birds, the more colorful the better. He had this pet parrot, a red one with green who would sit on his shoulder and whistle for dates. He also had several of them peacocks in a big, iron cage. He let them loose on the island; he wanted to make a whole flock of them. I think he said they came from India. The boys had these beautiful tails that were all the rage. But then the Guardian of the Cay took a liking to them and got awful offended when he tried to take 'em back."

"You're not the first to mention this Guardian of the Cay. What is it?" I leaned forward on my stool.

Mr. Pierce passed over the biscuit rounds and a bowl of chopped fruit and nuts so I could help him stuff them for tomorrow's breakfast.

"Don't rightly know what it is." Mr. Pierce left me to task and started dinner. "A fearsome creature with the body of a lion and the head and chest of a lady. Quite a pretty one, but queer-like. She had tits like I've never seen before, nor since. I dream of them at times." He looked at me, shocked. "Begging your pardon."

I laughed. Though I couldn't bring myself to be offended by his comments, I was hardly scandalized. It was odd and yet, it wasn't.

"But oh, she's a fearsome creature. She's the only one allowed to hunt on her island. Ye risk her wrath if you poach her birds and beasts. Doesn't seem to mind fishing or taking snakes though. One of me mates killed a huge python. She didn't mind but she was a smart one, used those fancy words to make us feel quite stupid."

"Like a sphinx?" I asked, recalling my education in Greek tales; Oedipus had a sphinx in it. She spoke in riddles and ate men.

"Yes and no. Don't know if that's rightly what she is, but you cross her at your peril. She's got two hands but four lion paws. She asked us for a tribute to set foot on her island. Something of great value."

"What did your lord give her?"

"Money, what else?" Mr. Pierce laughed. "She wanted the thing he valued above anything else. She took the tribute in gold and she ate his parrot."

"I suppose if he loved birds they would be of greatest value," I said.

"Made Lord Sutherland right cross. He had one of his men, a Mr. Plant, kill a peacock for those tail feathers. Poor Tom Plant, she pounced on him in an instant. There was blood everywhere."

"How ghastly," I said, urging him on.

"Then she told us to leave," Mr. Pierce said, his knives making short work of a pile of vegetables for a stew with the joint of lamb. "Lord Sutherland refused."

"Well you don't just dismiss a lord."

"Mayhaps not." Mr. Pierce got a strange look. "But later that night, the moon rose and we could hear this eerie sound, high and mournful like. And sure as I'm before you here, Old Tom Plant stood on the beach before our camp. Dead as a doornail, throat cut from ear to ear, chest torn open, same as the guardian had done for him to do him in. You could hear her voice on the wind like she was a singing. 'Leave this place, Lord Sutherland. Never return.'"

I felt a delicious chill run up my spine, I was told sailors told the best tales. So far, Mr. Pierce didn't disappoint.

"Did he?"

"Oh, aye." Mr. Pierce took the stuffed buns from me and slid them into his small oven, "When the dead give ye orders, ye follow them." He crossed himself. "God grant him peace."

I did the same. "Thank you for the most entertaining tale." I rose to leave and gave him a small bow.

"Miss Harper." He stopped me and I turned back. He squinted at me. "I was not telling no tales. My hand to God, the Guardian of the Cay is nothing to be trifled with. She's a creature of magic, a beast from the old world. If anyone knows how to fix Nate, I'd wager my copper pans she knows how. But I'd not cross her, not for anything in the world." His hand was heavy on my shoulder. "The Guardian of the Cay is not a thing to be trifled with. If you accompany him, be sure you keep your wits about you and do nothing to upset her. I'd hate to hear something terrible had befallen you. I've grown fond of you, lass." He slipped a stuffed bun in my hand from an earlier batch.

I headed back to the deck finding I had no stomach for his wonderful food.

CHAPTER ELEVEN

"MISS HARPER, NATE," Captain Morgan announced, "This be your stop!"

"Very well," I said, watching the island get closer with interest. I had never left London, certainly never left England, and though I was aware in a purely academic fashion that England was an island, it was nothing like the Molten Cay.

The island was a variety of greens, some light, some dark, all melding together like a deep forest in bloom. It was shaped roughly like a crescent, with a white sandy beach surrounding a cove protected by large black boulders where the waves broke and turned back out to the open sea. There was a sea of tents dotting the beach, and a galleon with a blue sail bobbing in the cove. Far below I could see the shiny black shapes of seals darting in and out of the waves. I had seen stuffed, mounted seals before in the Travers' home— where Mama had a regular appointment to read cards while Papa treated a horribly ulcerated wound on the father's leg. His son, Mr. Joseph Travers, was a naturalist of some renown. He had made a fortune creating maps and cataloging rare plants and animals; he was also a member of the Explorer's Society.

I was quite glad I had managed to look at the island without being instantly sick. "I'll gather my things." My things. I had to laugh. Aside from the clothes on my back, all I had was the corset cover I fashioned from the less soiled portions of my old dress, my drawers I couldn't wear under this skin-tight garment, my chemise, and the small pouch I wore on my belt that contained the goggles, my knit gloves, the tin of balm, and the two lightning stones—one live, the other just a pleasing shape. "Don't worry, Captain, it won't take me long."

I felt cross with him. Mr. Valentine and his condition was hardly my fault, yet whenever the sun went down and the moonlight transformed Mr. Valentine into the form of his beloved canine companion, I seemed to be the prime target for Captain Morgan's sourness. He would shake his head in disgust at the way Ranger followed me around.

Though Molly and Grace were quite friendly, the third Morgan girl, Edith, remained distant. I supposed if I loved a man who did not return my attentions, and then he arrived in the company of a woman, I would be upset too. I did try several times to convince her I was just his acquaintance.

I turned at the door that led to the berth that had been my bed the past few nights. Nathaniel was arguing with the Captain over something. Morgan waved a dismissive hand at him, and turned back to his crew.

Someone, most likely Molly, had placed a faded leather backpack on my berth. Its vast emptiness reminded me how much of a pauper I was here.

Francis announced herself with a knock and rushed in, arms full of random goods. "Mr. Pierce packed you some supplies. Bread, meat, and some dried figs. Here's a blanket, don't worry my dear," she added in an offhand way. "We have plenty. It's cold in the air but, then again, I don't need to tell you that." She giggled. "Here's a leather bottle of oil, it will fill this lamp; a flint; and here's a spare knife—I believe it belonged to Mr. McCabe. It would be nice to thank him, dearie," she said turning to me. "It's quite useful. Men have no problems giving to a lady in need, especially things they have no need for—but something of great function is another matter entirely."

I nodded and watched her stuff items into the pack. "Now, Nate will have his own supplies; probably packing rope, a revolver; and many other things he thinks you might need."

The mention of the revolver reminded me of one of the more frightening aspects of Molten Cay, aside from it being a hundred meters below us, of course. "Francis. The Guardian of the Cay, what is it?"

Her voice dropped to a whisper. "A demon. A fierce but beautiful creature, she allows no one to take creatures from her island. The legends say she can make men fall in love with her... then she eats them."

The look on my face made her laugh. "Oh, dearie, it's a fairy story. In truth, I don't know what it is; naturalists from all over the civilized world travel to observe the life there. I'm sure it's just a rumor to protect the island. You'll get more trouble from wild beasts."

She loaded the backpack with the supplies she had brought. "Now hurry, dove. Zachariah shall need his man to fit you for the wings."

"Wings?" I grabbed the backpack and hurried after her. "What do you mean wings?!"

I found Mr. Church strapping Nathaniel into a contraption's harness made of leather and wood with long, folded supports and billowing canvas. He finished as I approached and released Nathaniel with a hearty pat on the shoulder. The ship's engineer beckoned me forward and set the frame against my back. It was lighter than I expected.

"How much do you weigh?" Mr. Church brought the straps around my abdomen and through the buckle under my arm. I thought I felt his hand brush my breast.

"I beg your pardon!" I snapped back. "You do not ask a lady such things."

Eli Church, Captain Morgan's engineer, sat back on his heels. "Miss Harper, if the wings are too large you will not be able to control them and you can be slammed into a mountain or swept out to sea. If they are not large enough, the gears will snap and you will fall to your death."

"Eight and a half stone," I said promptly.

He nodded and took up his tools to adjust gears on the harness I was wearing.

"Mr. Church, how do I carry the backpack full of supplies while I am wearing the wings?"

He sat back on his heels again and gave me quite the rude look. I gathered he didn't enjoy being interrupted while he worked. "The pack's straps are specifically designed to fit around the wings. Miss Edith is quite the accomplished seamstress."

I wished, again, that I could get her to talk to me, but that was highly unlikely as I was sure that she had seen Nathaniel and I kiss, probably both times. If she hadn't seen it she had definitely heard about it.

The object of her affections was arguing with Captain Morgan now, in earnest. He pointed at the island far below and the water around it. Getting a proper look by getting closer to the edge would have given me a much better view, but that was out of the question.

"Wings will allow you to glide to the island. The captain has some more hunting to do here—now, you're gonna want to beware the guardian, miss."

"Pardon?"

Mr. Church clucked his tongue and gave me the look a governess gives her unruly charges. "Were you listening?"

"You said I am to be flying down to the island, like a bird might?"

Mr. Church laughed. "No, Miss Harper. Birds can fly, you will not be flying. You will be gliding. The wings slow your descent enough to make the journey quite pleasurable."

"And why isn't Captain Morgan setting us down on the nice, safe beach?" I felt that tightening of my stomach start again. I would have to get my father to treat me for a peptic ulcer when I got home. Home. The thought of returning home left me conflicted. It was all I had ever known, I thought fondly. It is all I have ever known, I thought spitefully.

"The lightning here is a strong, wild variety. The Guardian of the Cay keeps it so, she's a creature of wild magic, you know." Mr. Church's thoughts drowned out my sudden homesickness.

"Yes, Mr. Pierce told me."

"He's the one to tell of such matters, he's had dealings with her before." Mr. Church said, there was a touch of admiration in his voice. "The captain says the charges here can fill our batteries quicker than anything."

"He does plan to retire a rich man," I said gloomily. Nathaniel— I mean Mr. Valentine— and I would soon be parted; his indentured servitude would begin as soon as he rid himself of his unfortunate and thumb-less nocturnal condition.

"Now as I said, when we get in good range, the captain will open the bay door. You'll glide down. We will be able to pick you up in a week. If you need more time than that, you're on your own."

I nodded, feeling the same tightness and queasy stomach I felt every time I thought about looking over the side, or thought about how high up in the air we were.

But before I faced the wings, I had one more piece of business to attend. Mr. McCabe was polishing the fore steam cannon. He paused and spit on the cannon before resuming rubbing it with a filthy rag. I said a small prayer of thanks that I had never seen him working in the galley. "Mr. McCabe?" He stiffened so I knew he heard me but he returned to his polishing.

"Mr. McCabe, I just wanted to thank you."

He stopped his work and turned towards me, squinted one eye, hawked and spit over the side of the ship. He regarded me coolly, then nodded and turned back around.

"Watch that ye don't cut yourself, miss," he muttered evenly.

"I am grateful for the blade, though I have never handled one like this before." And I hadn't—in fact with the exception of the similar blade Mr. Valentine carried, I doubted this wide, long blade had been used by anyone in the past hundred years. It looked to me more like a shortened version of the swords ancient knights carried into battle. "I wished to thank you on another matter."

Mr. McCabe turned once more, giving off the air of a thoroughly annoyed bulldog. I cleared my throat. "I wanted to offer my thanks for our timely rescue. Had you not been following Mr. Valentine, I shudder to think what would have befallen us. I am certain that Mr. Valentine would have been murdered by Mr. Cooper and his fanatic Red Hoods. I do not even wish to speculate on what would have been my fate."

Mr. McCabe gave a crooked smile, revealing many missing teeth. He pulled a pipe out of his pocket and set to scraping it out and refilling it. "Certainly, no help would have come— I doubt a lady was waiting to send her man in to intervene like you did for that witch."

"You don't really believe she was a witch, do you?" I scoffed.

Mr. McCabe lit his pipe with a match from his coat, puffed for a moment thoughtfully. "No, I know she was. Not a dangerous witch— more one like your mother, but a witch none the less. They would have burned her to save her mortal soul, then collected their fee from the magistrate and expected the family to thank them for their action."

I went cold. "How do you know my mother?"

"She's a witch, miss, everyone knows that. She's a wise one to be sure. She deals with charms and reads cards in the salons of fancy ladies, but people talk. She has the true sight with those cards. It's no secret."

I stared at him. He turned back and resumed puffing on his pipe. I turned to leave but he spoke again, "Never you fear. I believe in my heart that your mother is safe."

"Did she read for you?" I asked in a hushed tone.

"Aye, she did," Mr. McCabe said softly, he had a wistful look on his face. "More than once."

I didn't think my mother just read for anyone. Such a thing was dangerous for this very reason. "How do you know her, sir?" I asked quietly.

Mr. McCabe ignored me and returned to his work.

"Mr. McCabe, how do you know my mother?" I demanded louder.

"The world is bigger than just you, Miss Harper." Mr. McCabe said with a sigh, "And your mother wasn't always a missus."

My Mama wasn't always a missus. Well of course she wasn't always a married woman, but what did that mean exactly? She had always loved my father so Mr. McCabe could hardly be a lover, but she was well-liked and had many family friends. I narrowed my eyes at him, ready to demand an explanation, but he had already turned and set to smoking his pipe. How dare he. How did he know my mother? What did he mean by that? My mind was racing.

Before I could puzzle against it any more, I was rudely told, apparently for the fourth and final time, that I needed to leave now.

CHAPTER TWELVE

"YOU CAN'T OPEN the wings until you jump off the back of the ship," Nathaniel reminded me. He stared out into the open sky.

Molly had opened the back of the ship, just as she did to admit the lightning traps. Molten Cay loomed below me at least thirty meters. How comforting that Captain Morgan brought us closer to the ground for what was to be my maiden flight. I felt like I was going to be sick.

"You are serious about me leaping from a perfectly serviceable airship," I verified.

He nodded, I couldn't see his eyes for the goggles strapped on his face, but the huge grin on his face was easily the look of a madman.

"We do this all the time," Nathaniel said, as though that would reassure me.

"You are not a bird," I reminded him. I edged closer and could feel the wind tugging at my clothes. The wings strapped to my back strained against their straps. I must be the only thing in the room that didn't wish to fly.

"No, but it's a pity," Nathaniel called over the wind. "I would make a smashing bird."

"Smashing is what I am afraid of," I yelled back.

Molly was at my side. "You will be okay," She whispered.

I turned to look at her, she barely spoke but when she did, it was a strong, sure sound. "Eli Church and I designed them. All the crewmen have used them. When you step off, spread your arms, the wings will catch you. Remember to try to keep your legs up, it will make the ride smoother."

"I will fall." I looked over the edge.

Nathaniel couldn't wait anymore. He leapt out, somersaulted in the air and spread his wings. The wind caught him gently. He started to glide to the ground, graceful as a bird. I heard him whooping like a gleeful child.

There was a time to be afraid and a time to accept what was happing around you. Being rescued from a pack of privateer zealots who would murder Valentine and myself was a time for accepting the rescue and thank God for the good fortune they intervened, even though rescue meant an airship, but this was a time for soul-crushing madness.

I had come to realize that, though I had no love for the heights, the airship had not fallen from the sky so I had no reason to believe it would now. Therefore, leaping out of a perfectly good flying machine could only be an act of madness. It was madness Nate was all too ready to embrace. Clearly, he was not merely a man cursed with the form of his dog when the sun went down, he was also mad as a hatter.

I took one look over the edge and my knees buckled. It was only a blessing of fate that let me fall on my backside, rather than forward and into the sky. I crab-walked away from the hole as quickly as I was able. I could only get as far away as the far wall. The damnable wall was in the way.

I took a deep breath and wiped the sweat from my brow that had plastered the loose hairs to my face. Whoever expected me to leap out of a perfectly good airship was clearly out of their mind. I was going to have to have a talk with Captain Morgan. He might even respond if I begged.

Molly's commanding voice cut through my thoughts. "You will not fall. You are a strong woman. Let him see that now."

I stared at her for a moment. She gave me a knowing nod.

I swallowed hard and stepped off the edge.

For one brief moment, I was sure the wings were failing and I was plunging to my death far below. Then I realized my arms were clasped tightly to my chest. I straightened my arms, locking the ratcheting gears in place. The wings gracefully caught me as they gathered the warm air coming off the island.

I forced my eyes to open. The ground was still frighteningly far away, but it was approaching at a manageable speed. Below me I could see

Nathaniel and his leather, long coat billowing in the wind like the tail of a magnificent bird.

With the wings locked open, I didn't have to fight to keep them spread and myself aloft. A slight tug on one let me steer. I passed over the green forest and headed towards the beach, following Nathaniel to the ground. I envisioned making a wonderful entrance and impressing him with my gliding prowess. Instead, I ended up nearly drowning myself as I overshot the beach and landed in water up to my knees.

I choked and sputtered, gasping on the sea water while the wings, once light but now heavy and soaked, tried to drag me under.

I flailed and fought trying to free myself from the yards of wet cloth, metal gears, and wood supports. I was so absorbed in my panic to free myself I wasn't aware I was in no danger of drowning until Nathaniel was practically screaming in my ear.

He had shucked his glider and waded into the surf. He still had his hands wrapped in the leather straps. He must have used them to drag me out of the sea; there were drag marks made by my heels.

I flushed bright red.

To his credit, Nathaniel seemed not to notice. "You did well, for your first flight."

I muttered my thanks and finished extricating myself from my sodden wings. Nathaniel expertly folded them back up and stashed them under a large tree with a canopy of wide, flat leaves.

It was not hard to locate the rows of tents that dotted the beach on the west side of the island. It did, however, take most of the morning and my stomach was rebelling at the thought of missing tea again. I considered setting the packs down and tearing into the supplies Mr. Pierce and Mrs. Morgan set aside for us, but then we came out of the heavy jungle.

I had never seen any place so fine in all my life. My boots sunk into the white sand up to the ankle. I turned in a wide circle, taking in cool, blue waters and the lush green of the jungle. Birds, the likes of which I had only seen in books, flew by in massive flocks calling to each other. They eyed us as though we were the oddity. The air held a warm salty tang and the scent of a thousand beautiful flowers in colors I had never seen back home. There was so much color here; so different from the drab dirty gray of London. This was the perfect place to holiday...barring monstrous guardians, of course.

It was hard to see how any sort of danger could lurk in such a beautiful place. I wondered if the monster the crew warned me about was a sort of ruse against the poor, foolish little London girl.

Up ahead, at the small city of tents, men froze in their work. Some were consulting books, others, obviously laborers, stood with their mouths agape. There was a French flag snapping away in the light breeze atop the largest tent. Clearly, they were unprepared to see a woman in trousers come strolling out of the deserted jungle and walk right into their camp.

I couldn't help but stroll like a lady presented to the queen. I did have to bite the inside of my cheeks to keep from laughing. Mr. Valentine was not suffering under the illusion of such manners. He was walking a few steps behind me, the way a servant would, and I heard him snickering.

"Do I honestly look that ridiculous?" I asked, trying not to blush under the intense scrutiny.

"You most definitely do not look ridiculous," He assured me. He sounded much more sure than was necessary. I turned to give him a look.

"That's the Rothechild crest," he said. "They're a rich banking family in France."

"Have you had dealings with them before?" I asked.

"Lord Rothechild, yes. His wife, not so much. I did some research for him in Cape of Good Hope on the railroads. Vivian, when I say they are rich, I mean rich!"

"Is this a favorable contact of yours?"

"I'm offended you would ask me that," Nathaniel scoffed.

"Don't be," I said evenly, "Your last contact turned out to be inclined to help us based solely on clarifying your relationship with his youngest daughter. Then he only helped us upon the terms of offering you a tenure of servitude."

Nathaniel went white at that. I shouldn't have reminded him that he would have to serve ten years at the mast. I turned to apologize, but he strode past me to where a sailor was standing with a rifle, acting as sentry.

"Nathaniel Valentine and Miss Vivian Harper to see Lord Rothechild," he announced.

A man dressed in a fine dark suit came up, sweating in the sun and his layers of wool. "I am Hugo, Lord Rothechild's *majordomo*." He had a heavy French accent. "Lord Rothechild is off with his naturalist friend, Lucas

Verany; they are seeking out samples for their conservatory in France. But, I am sure Lady Rothechild would be happy to entertain you while you wait."

"We appreciate your kindness," I said formally in French.

He beamed at me and offered me his arm so I could cross the sand in relative ease.

Nathaniel fell in step behind us.

The butler led me to the largest tent. A tea table had been set in the center of an expensive oriental carpet. At the table sat two ladies in fine day dresses done in the French style, with light colors and fancy lace. They turned at our entrance.

"Madame," he said formally. "Miss Vivian Harper and Mr. Nathaniel Valentine from England."

"Goodness! Society, even here. You see Sarah, there is society everywhere." The elder of the two sisters stood and took my hand in both of hers, then embraced me like a long-lost friend, kissing my cheeks in formal French greeting. "I am the Lady Marie-Laure Rothechild. My sister, Sarah, the Lady AuClair."

"You will join us please for tea," Sarah said in halting English.

"I am pleased to make your acquaintance," I said in my best French.

"English please, we shall use this as an opportunity to practice our English," Marie said, releasing me from her embrace.

"If you insist," I said, with as much courtesy as I could manage. Tea— a real, formal, high tea. I hadn't sat for a formal tea in quite a while, and my mouth was positively watering at the thought of all the wondrous things to eat.

"Yvonne." Lady Rothechild commanded the room. "Another chair, please, for Miss Harper."

"Will your servant be joining us?" Sarah asked, motioning to where Mr. Valentine stood by the entrance to the tent.

"Oh, he's not my servant," I said quickly. "Mr. Valentine is a member of the Explorer's Society, I believe he and Lord Rothechild are acquaintances."

He bowed at the waist, too formal for this setting, but the effect it had on the women was worth the social misstep. "Nathaniel Valentine, at your service."

He flashed them a grin displaying his beautiful teeth. He looked roguish in his long coat, knife and revolver, unshaven jaw, and dancing amber eyes. I found myself momentarily charmed by him.

"Regretfully, I shall see if I can meet up with Lord Rothechild." He turned and left.

"Oh my," Lady Rothechild said with a wide grin. "You will have to tell us the nature of the relationship between yourself and that Mr. Valentine."

"Indeed," Sarah giggled.

I could still see his shadow outside the tent door, no doubt he had heard them.

I blinked hard, trying to come up with something both appropriate and clever, but my mind was drawing a blank.

"See how she blushes," Sarah teased.

"Never mind, my dear," Lady Rothechild laughed and motioned for her maid to set me a place at the table. "As soon as tea is done we shall all be like old friends. Then you will want to tell us all your secrets." Lady Rothechild said, indicating to me the freshly set seat and for her maid to pour me some tea from a beautiful teapot.

I noticed the maid didn't pour milk in first, so it must be a new or meticulously kept tea pot. In the older tea pots, you poured the milk first so the hot tea wouldn't crack the cup. And what a beautiful set it was, too: Fleur-De-lis with a pattern of French lilac and gilded rims. The maid passed me a small matching tea plate. I placed a small salmon puff on the plate and inhaled the wonderful aroma of Darjeeling tea.

"Thank you kindly, Lady Rothechild," I said with a smile. I had missed tea more than I thought.

"Think nothing of it, my dear. Now tell me, what is the news from London?"

I took a small sip, where to start? I figured the political issues might be best, followed by anything I knew socially. "The queen is still in mourning. She must have loved her Albert very much."

"It has been seven long years. I believe she is setting a record," Lady Rothechild said, not unkindly. "Sarah just finished her second mourning; her husband was killed in a skirmish just outside of Belfort."

"I am sorry for your loss," I said softly, appropriately lowering my eyes for a moment.

"You are kind to say so," Sarah said with a small smile. "I loved Jacques well. My sister suggested my son and I join her on this holiday to ease our pain."

"You look beautiful in your colors, I hope that you find love and move on soon," I said politely.

Sarah nodded and motioned for me to continue. She clearly didn't wish to discuss her late husband.

I went on. "The Earl of Derby resigned from Prime Minster. His health was failing him. He is succeeded by a man named Benjamin Disraeli, he is another conservative, so the common folk shouldn't see much change, though I suppose foreign policy might be amended."

"Oh dear, that is ill news, my husband did truly like Lord Derby. We shall have to pay him a visit when we are in London next," Lady Rothechild murmured.

"The Fenian bomber, a chap named Barrett, was hanged outside Newgate Prison. Even though his crimes were great, he is to be the last man publicly executed—an amendment to the Capital Punishment Act was ratified." I was running out of proper society talk.

Lady Rothechild clicked her tongue. "I myself am of two minds on the subject, violence is the only thing a violent despot will understand. France still has public executions but I often wonder how effective they are as we continue to have so many of them. Very well, enough of the politics of the day," Lady Rothechild laughed. "Though I find the topic highly stimulating, it is hardly a subject for tea."

She took another cucumber sandwich from the plate and ate it in one neat bite. "Tell me, is this—" She motioned to my clothes. "Now all the rage in London?"

I laughed. I had quite forgotten until this moment that I was wearing scandalously snug trousers and a man's shirt under my corset. "No, Lady Rothechild, it isn't. I assure you, fashion has not changed much, though I believe the season is trending towards reds and golds for the autumn."

"Ah, I do tire of brown. Last fall, brown was the color for day dresses. What I wouldn't give to have a nice, vibrant green be the color of the day. Just the thing to liven up dreary London. You must tell me how you found yourself in such a fetching ensemble."

I laughed and proceeded to tell her about being rescued by *The Lightning Aura*, the harvest, and the crew. I glossed over any parts that would reveal

Mr. Valentine's true nature— that was hardly my tale to tell, and I was sure that Lady Rothechild would ask how Mr. Valentine found himself in that condition.

We worked our way through the sweets and savories and three full pots of tea until I was feeling a bit giddy. We had eaten through plates of sandwiches including: pear and stilton, cucumber, smoked salmon and dill, a salad of cold lobster with radish, watercress and herb, and a rather nice roast beef. I wish it had been proper to set some aside for Ranger. Her maids brought three types of flaky, crumbly scones with clotted cream, lemon curd, and strawberry preserves served in cut crystal, and platters of tartlets, shortbread, and fairy cakes. There were even tiny, chocolate sponge cakes with raspberry cream.

"Now, you must tell us about your Mr. Valentine," Lady Rothechild said, setting her tea cup down and motioning for yet another pot of tea and the cream cake.

I was stuffed. I wasn't sure I could manage another bite, but when the pudding was set before me I found a new vigor. "Mr. Valentine is a member of the Explorer's Society. I myself am seeking membership." I felt bad lying to them, but it would go a long way to protect my reputation and explain my odd dress. "We flew here on an airship."

"Oh my word!" Sarah gasped. "My son, Clément, wishes to see one of them. Perhaps we could see your ship before you leave?"

"With regret, it is not mine to show. Mr. Valentine and I are seeking an ancient temple on the Cay. The airship that brought us here will be circling back for us in a week. Hopefully, that will be enough time for us to investigate and explore the temple."

"How exciting!" Lady Rothechild said. "I am sure that my husband would love to see this temple. Perhaps we shall accompany you."

I chewed cream cake slowly, trying to find a way to ward them off. "Perhaps, though it is a hard journey. I thought Lord Rothechild was collecting samples for his conservatory."

"Either way, we shall discuss it further this evening. You will have to join us for dinner."

I nodded, thinking frantically. How in the world would I excuse us from this? The problem was solved for me less than an hour later as we sat in the tent listening to Sarah play the piano.

Mr. Valentine came sprinting right up to the tent. He was out of breath. He appeared moments after we heard the French sailors calling for him to stop, or they would be forced to shoot him. I leapt to my feet to see what the ruckus was only to have him barrel into me as he came through the tent door.

"We have to leave!"

"Ouch! Unhand me!" I snapped, quite unwilling to deal with his brutish ways. For one brief moment, I was reminded of just how vexing Mr. Valentine could be. He was ruining the wonderful illusion of high society cast by the Rothechilds. "Mr. Valentine, this may serve with your friends in the Explorer's Society, but one does not rush about and take hold of ladies!"

The muscle in his jaw twitched. "My apologies, ladies," he said through clenched teeth. "You need to leave now. Get on your ship and return to France, do not come back here."

"Mr. Valentine, whatever are you going on about? We are staying here until the end of the month." Lady Rothechild dismissed him with a flick of her hand.

"One of your men killed a deer," He panted.

"A deer?" Lady Rothechild laughed. "Good for him! A bit of fresh meat would be welcome at the table."

One look at Mr. Valentine's face told me this was no game. Though he was not used to how upper society operated, he was hardly trying to be obnoxious— though, I assume, I was driving him mad. As pleasant as this was, we were far from the parties of London. There was very real danger here. Mr. Pierce had warned me about this. Tom Plant had killed a peacock, and the Guardian of the Cay's vengeance was swift and fierce. I had no desire to see such violence first hand. We were not in a secure French villa, we were in a flimsy, canvas-walled tent at the mercy of anything Molten Cay chose to set loose upon us. I owed Nate an apology, and my help.

"Lady Rothechild, if one of your men did kill an animal on this island, then you all are in terrible danger. This island is protected by a fearsome guardian."

Mr. Valentine glanced at the table where the remains of our lunch sat. I saw a glimmer of longing, but he quickly refocused. He looked anxiously over his shoulder. Tea had begun at four. Now, the sun was sitting low and preparing to sink into the sea.

"Mr. Valentine, can you please make sure the dog is not tied up so he may find himself food and water? I doubt he'll wander off. After that, can you please see if you can make yourself useful to the crew?"

The look he gave me was full disbelief. He almost opened his mouth, probably to tell me exactly where I should go if I believed myself in charge of him...then he realized what I was really saying, what I couldn't say here. He nodded. "I will send the dog in your direction."

"Thank you."

CHAPTER THIRTEEN

RANGER CAME LOPING back to me less than a quarter of an hour later. Perhaps some things remained in the forefront of his mind when he transfigured, for he walked with his tail low. He looked as I felt.

I had made no headway in trying to convince the Rothechilds to leave. A dread filled me, the likes of which I had never felt before.

"My dear Vivian, you must calm down," Lady Rothechild said. "People eat deer. That is the natural order of things. Why, it's the reason the deer exist!"

"Yes, but there is a magical beast on this island," I tried to explain for the dozenth time. "She is quite offended when people poach."

"Oh fuff!" Lady Rothechild waved me away. "One deer on an island that is not owned by either England or France is hardly poaching!"

Maybe she was right. I was feeling quite strange. Oddly calm, like I didn't have to get away. I felt like I was being lulled to sleep, rocked gently in Mama's arms when I was a child. The queer feeling broke in waves over me like opium fumes, battering down my senses in waves.

The deer. The monster. They were all parts of a fairy tale.

Clément and his nurse, a timid lass by the name of Eloise, came in to sit with his mother, Sarah. Such a beautiful little boy—rather than be dressed in the gown that was common for little boys, he wore knee breeches, a shirt, and vest. His little leather shoes were a perfect version of what a man would wear, in miniature. He sat on the oriental carpet by his mother's feet and started playing with tin soldiers crammed into the pockets of his vest.

His nurse produced a wooden horse and cannon. I watched the little boy play and felt a pang of regret. By the time I was eligible to be courted again, I would be considered an old maid—children wouldn't be impossible, but a man would have to consider that they might be.

I shrugged away the pain of regret. Ranger sensed my melancholy mood and laid his head in my lap, his tall ears flicking from side to side. Ranger displayed no urgency; perhaps the tale was nothing more than a mere tale.

Lady Rothechild set down her tea cup. She was slumping as though it were very late and she had consumed too much drink. "Come sit over here by us and tell us of this monster, I heard a tale before we left. I thought it was a fairy tale, mind you," By the tone of her voice, she was very used to having her own way.

I could hear music of a flute on the wind, far off and haunting. Somewhere from long ago and far away, I could remember a tale of this place and a tale of a great fearsome monster.

Clément's eyes opened wide. "A monster?" He set the soldiers aside and turned, spinning on his little bottom to face me. Little boys loved a good story.

"I don't know much about it," I confessed and the little boy pouted. His nurse went to gather him up and take him back to whatever tent served as a nursery. I didn't want to see him leave. "But I can tell you how I heard the tale. It was from a ship's cook."

Clément cheered immediately. "A sailor? Sailors have the best stories," He told the ladies sagely. I nodded, agreeing. I loved the little boy already.

"Yes, but not just any sailor, he served on board *The Lightning Aura*, an airship that flies through the air, hunting and capturing lightning."

The little boy stared at me, tin soldiers left ignored in his lap. Clément was absently petting Ranger, who was looking quite amused. I told them a tale of a naturalist who loved birds and planned to set peacocks loose on an enchanted island, but the island had a monster who lived there and loved all animals. The monster hated the naturalist for hunting and killing the animals on her island and so demanded treasure as payment for their wicked deeds. The naturalist offered gold but the monster was crafty and stole his parrot instead.

I had just gotten to the part about the peacocks growing to enormous size when a cold wind kicked up and the flaps of the tent began to shake and blow. Wind off the cove was supposed to be warm and salty, but it blew icy cold and brought the scent of rot and decay, and with it the queerest music. It sent me trembling in a way that had nothing to do with the cold.

The shivering made me suddenly very aware of the tent and its low-burning, sputtering oil lamps, the lumpy sand beneath the carpets, and the hissing, moaning wind. Ranger leapt to his feet and was pacing by the tent door whining. The music was back, eerie and moaning like the wind crying in torment. Ranger shook his head, whipping his ears back and forth. The music hurt him.

"Shush!" The nurse scolded. "Bad dog!"

"I think he's a wonderful dog," the little boy said reaching out to grab for Ranger's tail.

"Clément." Sarah took the little boy's hand and snatched him back as though she expected Ranger to rip the child's arm off at the shoulder.

"I assure you, he is quite friendly," I said, "Most of the time." My head felt strange again as though a thick cloud of opium was in use again. As if to prove me right, he laid down on his stomach and thumped his tail on the carpet covered sand. He was up again in a moment, shaking himself then circling and whining.

It was then that I heard the first gunshot. I leapt to my feet. That music! That awful, wonderful music! Why was I telling stories? We had to get away from here! I snapped my fingers.

Ranger sprang from the tent, going right under the nearest wall rather than using the door.

I would not have fit the exit he took, so I ran to the tent door and threw it back.

Men were staring dumbly out at the jungle. A horrible chill was sneaking up my back. I turned back to warn Lady Rothechild, Sarah, Clément, and the servants inside the tent. I saw the warm ocean rippling against the wind and waves. Something was coming ashore. I prayed, for all I was worth, for turtles or fish or some sort of marine animal gone mad. Without knowing how, I knew something awful was coming— and it was worse than merely mad sea life.

Heads, human heads, appeared on the waves; then shoulders and torsos, half missing, rotted and gnawed upon. Men walked up from the sea floor, covered in barnacles and growths, fish falling from their wounds and crabs falling from their flesh. They did not stop to wipe the water from their eyes or pull seaweed from their clothes. They stumbled and shambled along. The men were dead. Animated, just as Mr. Pierce had warned. They were the army of the Guardian of the Cay, and they were coming for us all.

Ranger growled, the hackles on the back of his neck sticking out on end. That sound turned my blood to ice. My throat felt tight. I forced myself to breathe.

I threw open the flap to the tent. "Mr. Valentine was right! We have to go now!" He had not left because of me. I needed to remedy that now.

Lady Rothechild looked up at me. The look on my face must have convinced her. "Sarah, Eloise, get Clément and find Mr. Marchel. He's our master-at-arms," she said to me. She stood and flipped open a chest that had been hidden under a beautiful lace tablecloth, a silver and glass oil lamp, and a small painting of a lady on a fine mount dressed for a hunt. The glass top of the lamp shattered onto the carpet. Lady Rothechild pulled a pair of revolvers out of the chest. She handed one to me and took up the other.

I wanted my hands free, so I tucked the revolver into my belt. Outside I could hear shouting, a gun barked again, releasing the scent of burnt gunpowder in the air.

I dashed out of the tent. Ranger had held his ground with that vicious snarl. It gave something for my frazzled nerves to hold on to. Nothing could harm me if Ranger was around.

"Madame." A man armed with a long gun and a cavalry sword dashed up to us, panting. Mr. Marchel, I supposed. "We must get you to the boat, madame."

"No!" I said. "Not a boat!"

"Stupid English girl!" Mr. Marchel snarled, checking his pistols.

"Listen here you oaf!" I was in no mood to be treated as such. I squared my shoulders and drew myself to my full height, almost to his shoulder. "They're in the sea as well as the land. On land we can run. If we get into a boat all they have to do is capsize the boat and drag us under."

Sarah was shaking. Clément had large tears glinting on his cheeks.

I swallowed my own fear down like a sour tonic. "Hey there, brave soldier. I need you to help protect us fine ladies, eh?" It would not do to have everyone panic. He nodded through his tears. I gave Sarah a sharp look. I needed her to get ahold of herself.

Behind us the men were firing on the shambling forms coming from the jungle. I turned— the dead men bucked and spun from the bullets, but they didn't slow. I wondered briefly if I would be able to pick out Mr. Plant.

We had to move. High ground—that seemed the best place. The beach had a large set of boulders over by the boats. Trapped on the rocks was infinitely preferable to trapped on the beach with these creatures.

The music on the wind was louder. It was hauntingly beautiful, and for a moment it made me feel stupid and sleepy again. I slapped my cheeks, and grabbed Lady Rothechild's hand to drag her and Sarah along. Ranger spun and faced the coming threat, hackles raised. He was covering our flight.

We had just reached the rocks when I heard the first scream. High and thin, followed by a gurgling. Men had been shooting, stabbing, fighting; now men were dying. The lowest boulder was just above my shoulders. I made a stirrup with my hands and helped Lady Rothechild up. Sarah screamed. Ranger snarled. One of the shamblers was close, close enough to see his face. Bloated flesh that seemed to slide off the bones like the icing of a cream cake on a warm June day. The pudding I had eaten earlier rose up in my throat.

Ranger leapt at the drowned man. Clément shrieked. I grabbed Clément and tossed him up into Lady Rothechild's waiting arms. Sarah was trembling, and making small sobbing sounds around the skirts she had shoved into her mouth.

Ranger had his teeth on the dead man's throat. He whipped back and forth until I heard a snap. The dead man fell. Ranger got to his feet and shook his head. He gave a little whine.

I turned back to Sarah, and sent her up into Lady Rothechild's arms. She sat and wrapped her child in her arms.

Ranger yelped. The dead man I thought he had dispatched rolled back over and latched onto Ranger's leg with one filthy hand. His head hung limply to one side. Ranger broke the hold, then sprinted off into the sand. He stopped after a few steps, turned, and then barked and bounded in the sand from side to side.

"Ranger no!" I screamed, he was luring the creature away. I wheeled in the sand and followed. Somehow, a tent had caught fire—I suspected an unattended lamp. I seized one of the tent poles, an impressive piece of hard wood, longer than I was tall, one end on fire. I swung it as hard as I could. The flaming end struck the drowned man and knocked him back. Ranger turned and looked at me for a long moment. Then he howled—a sound that pierced the night air and for an instant, cut through the awful music on the wind like a saber.

Several of the creatures turned. With cold dead eyes, they started shambling. Drowned men were before me and dead men, dry from the land, stood behind. They shuffled past me, intent on their new target. Ranger sprinted away, turning and barking every so often to taunt his pursuers.

All around me I could hear the screams of the dead and dying as they battled foes unable to die. Blood I could have handled. I had seen blood before. This was something else entirely. There was no blood, merely gaping holes in human flesh that should, my mind assured me, bleed. But, then again, dead things do not bleed. As they shambled along, the gaping holes in their flesh moved, opening and closing like toothless mouths; ever hungry and ever gasping, seeking something they would never find.

The light from my torch gleamed on the silver buttons of a man I had mistaken for a wounded member of Lord Rothechild's party. He shambled towards me. His throat had been torn open, but that was far from all—he wore a frock coat, the color long rotted away. As he moved, the tails of his coat shifted and rocked. He was missing much of the flesh on his right side. I could see his ribs. I could see his spine.

I slammed my elbow into him but it grated into his chest. He had no breath to lose. I ducked. He lashed out at me. His bones creaked, the flesh squished. I hit him hard with my fist. His skin was cold like a fish. Striking a dead thing was useless.

I pulled the borrowed knife and jabbed it hilt deep into the dead man. He didn't flinch. How do you fight a dead thing? And there were so many of them. The men on the beach were firing again and again but what good were bullets against dead things that just kept coming? The dead things seemed mindlessly clubbing and pounding at the living, overwhelming them as I watched. But in watching the horror of the men fight the dead, I nearly lost track of my own peril.

The dead man lurched for me, reaching for my hair. I spun out of his reach but he caught some of it and tore it out, sending tears to my eyes. His other arm clubbed me in the side of the head and I landed heavily in the sand. I tried to regain my feet, then felt one heavy arm slam across my throat. Pain exploded through my head. I tried to breathe, but the pressure against my throat was too great. The dead man grabbed my head with one hand, his other arm still pressed against my throat. I could see little white explosions of light behind my eyes. My God! The dead man was trying to break my neck.

I fumbled for the revolver in my belt. I managed to get the revolver under its chin, and fired. The top of its head exploded like a rotting gourd, spraying a soupy mass across the sand.

The pressure stopped. I rolled across the sand and regained my feet. I ran without being able to see clearly, the white spots were fading, but still obscured too much. I heard women screaming. I heard a boy sobbing.

I blinked hard to clear my vision. The dead man was now struggling to stand, half his head missing. His face sagged to one side. I shoved the revolver into my belt, barely registering it was hot against my hand.

Two others were standing at the boulders, reaching for Sarah, Clément, and Lady Rothechild. One of the creatures, he must have been quite tall in life, had a hold of Clément's wrist and was trying to drag the boy down. Sarah and Lady Rothechild were engaged with it in a deadly game of tug-of-war; poor Clément was jerked around like an old rag doll.

I was not sure I could shoot the creature without hitting the boy, but the tent pole was still on fire. I scooped up the end of my burning lance as I ran for them. Then I struck the tall creature in the back. As he spun, he slammed his other arm into the boy. I heard something *snap*, and the boy shrieked in pain.

The tall, dead man turned with the tent pole sticking out of his back. In any other situation it would have been comical. The dead man stumbled and grabbed at the burning pole in a grotesque fashion. I made sure the revolver was still in my belt and searched for another weapon. There was an oar not far off. I would have to get closer to the sea to reach where it lay on the sand. I couldn't see any movement near the longboat. I took a steadying breath, and then sprinted off for the oar.

The oar had a long, wide blade. It was planted in the sand and leaned against the boulder. I had just enough extra height to clamber on top of the boulders to join Lady Rothechild, her sister, and Clément.

I leaned down and grabbed the oar, nearly falling off the rock, and hauled it up. I was thankful again for the leggings and boots, I would not have managed this feat in dress shoes and skirts.

My movement had attracted attention to our high, and relatively safe, perch. Three of the dead men shambled over to us. They couldn't reach us if we stayed at the center of the rocks. I positioned Sarah with Clément in her lap in the center. Lady Rothechild and I drew our revolvers.

My pulse was pounding in my ears. I prayed Ranger was able to evade his pursuers. I couldn't bear to think of him as Mr. Valentine right now. If he were to die, would he remain a dog or would we be able to bury a man? I could have slapped myself at the thought. I did my best to distance myself from the sight. Papa had taught me when treating a patient to treat the critical symptoms first, to see the person as parts of a whole rather than an entire being. It allowed one to look past the suffering, to take it in as chunks.

There was nothing to be done for the dead. Giving in to the gut-wrenching terror that had snaked its way through my belly and coiled around my spine like a cobra ready to strike would keep me from helping those I was still able to help; namely Lady Rothechild, her sister, and Clement.

If any of the dead men came too close, I hit them with the blade of the oar. The drowned men were the worst; the oar would stick in them and it would be hard to pull it out. They were soft like old melons. Twice I was almost pulled off the rock by their falling bodies. I would say corpses, but I'm not sure if that is the correct descriptor or not; I had never before seen dead men move.

Sarah had dissolved into a fit of hysterics; she wept and cradled Clément in her arms. Aside from an obviously fractured arm, he was in good spirits. He kept sneaking looks at our situation from beneath his mother's arm.

A few hours after the brutal attack began, it suddenly stopped. The wind died down and with it the horrible, beautiful lilting music. The creatures followed it, fading back into the water or into the jungle from whence they came.

Lady Rothechild sat holding her sister in the darkness, speaking to her gently in French. I was too fatigued to translate, but they were words of comfort. I kept searching the beach for a dark, brown canine with tan markings and erect ears. I was still searching when the sun rose.

"Darling!" Lord Rothechild came running up, surrounded by several of his men. He held out his arms and she leapt down into them, weeping for the first time since the awful night had begun.

They jabbered at each other in French so quickly and so heavily mixed with slang that I couldn't follow. After a long while, she handed him her revolver and together they helped me lower Clément and his catatonic mother to the sand.

I burst into tears when I finally spied a man staggering across the sand, long knife in one hand. He exchanged exhausted greetings and salutes with the other men, their weapons still their hands. I lay half-crouched on the rock, vitality gone, sobbing and thanking God for all I was worth that he had survived the horrible night.

Mr. Valentine's face was stained with dried blood. It was absent from his hastily donned clothing, but no one seemed to notice except me. He carried that wide-bladed knife— I have come to think was something akin to a short sword— openly in his hand, he made no move to sheath it.

I slid off the top of the rock with the oar. I hit the ground with quite the undignified *thump* on my backside.

Mr. Valentine was at my side in a moment. He offered me his hand and drew me into his embrace. "I have never been so happy to see anyone," he whispered.

"If you lick my cheek I will brain you with this oar," I whispered back. "I can tolerate that from Ranger, not from you."

He laughed, a warm throaty sound that assured me I was not dreaming. Despite the blood and offal smell that clung to him like a whore's perfume, I held on tightly, letting him spin me around. I would not have slapped him if he kissed me this time.

"Mr. Valentine, I must say you missed all the action," Lord Rothechild said, there was a touch of hurt in his voice. Then he seemed to see Nate for the first time. "Good God, man, I take that back, you must have been upon our parameter."

Nathaniel gave an exhausted nod. He let go of me only long enough to return the blade to the scabbard at his back and take Lord Rothechild's offered hand. His arm was around me again. I was not sure who was more comforted by it. Did he fight them as a dog, as a man, both? The lullaby sedated us more than laudanum could have.

I stared at my hands, blistered and covered in black blood and slime. I would have to dig a splinter from one. A tremor had started somewhere in my knees. I was thankful it took its time reaching me and did not happen during our battle. I thought I could scream until my lungs burst, or collapse, or cry, or maybe even all three. I threaded my fingers into Nate's belt. At least he gave me something solid to anchor to.

"It's good to see you again, Valentine." Mr. Rothechild said.

"So you two do have a history," I said. What an awful place for a reunion, this graveyard. He had quite the interesting list of contacts.

"Yes, I believe I hired Mr. Valentine through the Explorer's Society to recover artifacts for me from an Egyptian king."

"Pharaoh," Mr. Valentine corrected. "I never even got to see Egypt, the artifacts were in a private collection in Cape Good Hope."

"Ah yes, of course. We were searching out investment opportunities in the new railroad," Lord Rothechild said absently. "Hugo, I want a double guard placed. We will be leaving this place as soon as we are able. Have all other able-bodied men begin loading my ships."

He turned to his wife. "I apologize, my dear, there are things more important to me than new plants for our conservatory. Leaving this island alive comes immediately to mind."

Lady Rothechild said grimly, "Yes, I agree."

Mr. Valentine was absently crushing the life out of me, and seemed disinclined to be letting go anytime soon.

"Thanks to you my nephew is alive," she said, there were tears in her eyes.

Lord Rothechild turned back to his butler, and another man so well-armed he resembled a human porcupine. "Have the men work in four-hour shifts, the best eyes need to guard the perimeter. We need men well-rested and able to defend us should this happen again," Lord Rothechild continued.

Hugo bowed. "At once, my Lord Rothechild. May I suggest you order me to hand out extra food to the men and the servants? It would increase their morale and there would be less to load on the ship."

Lord Rothechild stood with his hands on his hips watching his men leap to carry out his orders. Though I suspected it had taken the better part of a week to set up their tent city, I was sure it would be dismantled in much less time. "Make it so, Hugo."

Nathaniel informed me that he had passed several tents set as makeshift hospitals as he searched for me. The man I saw stabbed by the rotting sailor was dead, another two lay dying from belly wounds; there was nothing I could do for them. They had a resident physician. He was busy doing everything he could for those wounded by last night's attack. The men must be in poor condition indeed if the physician had put off treating the Rothechild's nephew's broken arm. Doctor Albert Forrest was doing his best to keep them comfortable with large amounts of laudanum. For once, I was sure my father and the physician were in agreement in how to best treat a patient. Making them senseless was a kindness, and all that could be done to improve their condition.

"I'd like to provide care for Clément," I offered, stifling a yawn and extricating myself from Valentine's embrace.

"Good Lord, you are a lady, not a physician," Lord Rothechild said.

"Any physician would suggest bleeding him or leaching him first, for shock," I explained. "My father is a well-respected apothecary. I have assisted in setting many bones in my life. Your nephew needs to have the broken bone realigned and bound. Bleeding him in this state will make him quite senseless. He does not need to be weakened, he needs proper care."

I followed him back into the ladies' tent. Amazingly, it was still standing. Lord Rothechild turned to consult his wife. She nodded furiously. Clearly, I had earned some of her respect from my actions last night.

"Very well, what do you suggest for my sister-in-law?" Rothechild asked.

I regarded Sarah for a long moment. She was in shock from the events. She would need time to recover her wits, nothing else would help her much. She sat there, staring, holding tightly to her son like he was the only thing tethering her to this plain. "Sarah needs time to recover, my Lord. Time and brandy."

Rothechild nodded and turned to pull a cut crystal decanter from a chest in the tent. He poured her a healthy amount. I had him pour a bit for Clément too—though the break didn't look as complicated as I had seen, it was already a few hours old and he was definitely feeling the pain.

Thankfully it was a simple break. I set and splinted without any real difficulty. Within the hour, Sarah was singing softly in French. I watched Clément as he lay in his mother's arms, his arm heavily bandaged.

Valentine returned to the tent, then, and I was relieved to see Mr. Valentine free of the blood and gore, looking none the worse for wear. He must have rinsed off in the sea but I had the mad desire to strip his clothes off him, not for lustful exercise, but to further examine him for wounds. After all, he managed to draw several of them away and keep them from attacking the crew. It was hard for me to believe he could do this without sustaining any injury.

"I said, my dear, you must take an opportunity to rest while the men load the ship and the maids finish cleaning your clothes. Then when the ship is fully loaded you must return with us. We are headed directly to France, but we will certainly put you on the next passenger ship to London, you and Mr. Valentine both."

I glanced at Nate.

"Regretfully, I cannot," I said. "I mean we cannot," I amended hastily. "Mr. Valentine and I are contracted to explore the ruins for Mr. Horace Stanton of London through the Explorer's Society. We must complete the task at hand." I surprised myself at how well I lied.

Nathaniel's eyes narrowed at the mention of the kennel master's name and my casual, blatant lie, but said nothing.

Lady Rothechild fixed me with a look. To my credit I do not believe I blinked. "Very well. Then I insist you and Mr. Valentine take a rest before venturing into that jungle. I would be most distressed to find something awful had befallen you."

"You are most kind," I said, "But no." I had my fill of society.

"Then we shall miss you, and I will pray for your safety. Please send word, if you are able, to let me know you are safe." She embraced me as family. There was nothing formal now, no friendly meeting in it, only true love between us. "There is nothing else I can do for you but insist that you will be rewarded for the bravery and fidelity you displayed last night. If it weren't for you, my sister, my nephew, and myself would all be dead."

I bowed, unsure of what to say.

"Rothechilds always pay their debts," she said simply. "Vivian Harper, I owe you greatly."

"Think nothing of it, Lady Rothechild," I returned. "See that Clément doesn't move his arm much for at least six weeks. Try to make sure Sarah gets plenty of sleep."

Mr. Valentine had already been rewarded. He stood with the reins of a cream-colored gelding in his hands, pack on his back. Lord Rothechild and his naturalist adviser were able to provide more than just the horse. They had caught a glimpse of some sort of crumbling ancient temple on the top of a large hill made of bronze sandstone and were able to direct us to it with some surety.

For a moment, I wanted to stay with the Rothechilds and to take Lady Rothechild up on her offer, but I also wanted to remain with Mr. Valentine— if for nothing else than to see this through to the end. I turned towards him and he led the gelding into the jungle in the direction the dead men had taken the night before.

"If the Guardian of the Cay knows how to cure me, I doubt she'll give that information willingly," Mr. Valentine explained, trudging forward, the gelding followed amicably along.

"We have done nothing wrong," I said. "We are not with the Rothechild party and we didn't partake in the poached deer. That would be like the queen punishing all of London for one drunkard. Surely she has some decency."

"Decency?" He snorted. "There was nothing decent about last night."

I had to agree with him. "Well, we were with them when she attacked. Now they are leaving. With luck, we will escape her notice until we ask for an audience."

"You are the eternal optimist, aren't you?" Mr. Valentine made a face.

"Stiff upper lip. Being down doesn't get you anywhere," I said, feigning cheerfulness. "So, this horse is a gift?"

"More like an offering," he said grimly.

"What's the difference?"

Mr. Valentine patted the horse's long neck. "Well, we still don't know exactly what she does with the animals here. She may love them, she may obsessively hoard them. She may believe she has the exclusive right to hunt them. I'd guess she'll either turn it loose on the island, or eat it."

He said that so matter-of-factly I expected the horse to pull free and bolt for the ship, determined to swim to France if need be. The horse followed placidly, being led to its fate. I fell in step behind, feeling very much like a sacrifice myself.

CHAPTER FOURTEEN

WE SPENT THE AFTERNOON hiking up a steep, winding path. The climate, though wonderfully warm and tropical, was less than desirable for a march leading a horse. We paused at a small, well spring just before the final approach to water the horse and rest. I was filled with a nameless dread looking at the temple before us. I wanted to turn around and go back to the beach and pretend we were just on a holiday in the sun.

I couldn't ask Nathaniel to turn away from his quest when we had come so far, but it was more than that. Nathaniel was my friend. I needed to see this through, for him, for me. In truth, I had to be more than the gelding led to slaughter, sacrificed to whomever wants it. I needed this adventure before being given away to whomever would support my family in their old age. If this is all the freedom I ever got, then I needed to make the most of it before I was to meet my fate. True, Papa didn't sell me to Byron, I did it to myself, but I did so with them in mind. No, I needed to do this for me. I needed to see this to the end, to be poached or set free. I had to see it end.

The gelding stopped at the tiles in the antechamber of the temple and would go no further no matter what Nathaniel tried. Finally, he gave a resigned sigh and pressed his forehead against the horse's flat broad head. The horse nickered at him and didn't pull away. He pulled a spare shirt from his bag and used it to blindfold the horse. Thus impaired, the horse hesitantly followed him inside the darkened temple.

We left our packs at the entrance of the temple. It wasn't dedicated to any particular deity I could identify. The statue upon the altar had been smashed beyond recognition. All I could make out of the statue was a pair of bare feet on a wide base decorated with flowers.

She watched us enter with a lazy predatory gaze as she lay reclined in the shadows. I wasn't fooled, it was the way a cat watches a mouse; the cat feigns disinterest until the mouse is too far from its hidey-hole to return to safety. She knew we were coming.

Mr. Pierce had been right; the guardian was unlike anything I had seen before. She was a lady, quite a beautiful one at that. From the head to the waist, that is. She had long auburn hair that fell unbound in waves down her bare back. Her ears were pointed like an old fairy painting, and she had brilliant, green eyes, almond shaped and compelling. She wore no clothing, no adornment. Her breasts were scandalously bare. I was quite impressed by Mr. Valentine's restraint, he didn't stare. Though, I would guess he had seen a nude woman before, he made a point not to leer.

She was well-muscled, much like a dancer, not plump like a true lady. She had graceful shoulders and arms and carefully shaped nails. Her stomach terminated into the body of a lion. Her pale flesh melded into tawny fur and four strong legs, each ending in a strong, wide paw with sharp, black nails. She rose from her nest of pelts and stretched, scoring the tiles with her claws. She was terrifying. She was beauty. She was grace. She was death.

I understood immediately what Mr. Pierce had said. Well, not about her tits. Though far from an expert, I would guess they were what men looked for, but she was perfection. There was something about her that filled me with a nameless longing. I wanted to be her, wanted to be possessed by her even though she scared me to the very depths of myself. I realized that there was nothing I would not do for her if she promised not to harm me. I wondered if it was because of her beauty, or her magic, or something else altogether.

"You are the Guardian of the Cay," I said.

"I am," she replied.

"What are you?" I asked, for the moment she was too fascinating to fear, though in the back of my mind I knew I should be terrified.

She threw her head back and laughed. She had long, sharp, feline teeth. "The Guardian of the Cay."

"That's fair," I said with a small smile. Ah, there was the fear in the very core of my being I was supposed to be feeling. It started low in the pit of my stomach and coiled around my spine like I had swallowed a whole nest of snakes. She was no less beautiful, but was now appropriately terrifying. "What is the Guardian of the Cay?"

She gave a small bow.

"It's a Lamia," Nate said softly.

She looked at him and hissed, eyes narrowed.

"Knowing a thing's name gives power over it. Knowing what to call it is a start," Nathaniel whispered, his eyes never leaving it. "This is our offering. We seek an answer."

She stalked over to the horse and pulled Nathaniel's shirt away from its face. The gelding screamed and reared. She reached out and touched its neck. He instantly quieted.

I was both startled by her magic and sorry for the horse. I couldn't shake the feeling that something awful was about to befall it.

The offering dealt with, she turned her attention to Nathaniel. The Lamia raised her head and sniffed the air. "You've been touched by magic. Your human stink pollutes good, clean magic." She stalked back and forth, tail lashing.

"I want it cured," he said loudly.

"You don't cure magic, manling," she scoffed. "Magic changes you; and you change it, use it, mold it." As she spoke she dragged her fingers up her stomach and toyed with her breasts. It was obscene. It was fascinating. She was slowly stepping closer and closer to Nathaniel. "It becomes a part of you, runs in your veins like blood."

He stood, a man transfixed as the Lamia drew closer and closer.

"We didn't hunt on your island!" I yelled.

Nate turned towards me, his attention broken. He realized how close she was and took a few hasty steps back.

"But men did." Her tail lashed in impatience. "You were with them."

"We didn't eat that deer. The men who did are all dead." I didn't have any weapons on my person, I thought it might make her angry. I had left Mr. McCabe's knife in my pack with the rest of our supplies at the entrance of the temple, but from my experiences with the dead attacking the Rothechild's party on the beach tents, I wasn't sure that even Nathaniel's revolver would stop her.

She gave an amused *purr*, tracing her lips with one well-manicured finger. She closed the gap between us faster than I thought possible and slammed into me. She knocked the wind out of me and I slid across the old, cracked temple floor tiles. Then I fell. And fell.

"Vivian!" Nathaniel called out to me.

Everything was black. I bounced against hard and soft surfaces. The smell was positively horrid. My hands, wet and slimy, grasped and tore at my surroundings, searching for purchase.

I landed on my side, legs twisted up above me like I had fallen in a refuse pile. There was something digging painfully into my hip. I shifted, grateful nothing had been broken in the fall. My knee throbbed and my back had been painfully wrenched. I carefully righted myself.

The lightning stones were still in my pocket. My fall must have damaged the one that had the small bit of live lightning; it was once only comfortingly warm, but was now hot to the touch. It was also brighter. I raised it in my palm.

I wished it wasn't so bright. It was worse than a refuse pile. Much, much worse. I was sitting by a huge pile of bones; some were animal, but some were terrifyingly human. I was quite familiar with the sight after last night's adventure. I gasped and turned away from the site, but there was more and more. Everywhere I looked I could see bones and bodies, all in various states of decay. I wanted to scream and strip my soaked, slimy clothes off. I was sitting in a pool of sludge that used to be other humans. The smell. The smell of it was enough to turn me off meat for the rest of my life. I threw my arm over my face to try to hide from the scent of rot and putrification that seeped from the air into the very core of me. Then there was the cold. It was enough to suck the air straight from my lungs. Nothing on a tropical island should be this cold. Nothing in the world should be this cold.

My eyes were screwed closed, but I could only picture a skipping disc on a phonograph repeating the same phrase again and again: *dead; they were all dead.*

I took a few slow, deep breaths. My whole body quivered and my stomach took a queer turn. I pressed my fist against my mouth hard enough to cause pain. The sharp pressure of it gave my thoughts focus. I took several deep breaths before I could see clearly again.

I had dropped the lightning stone in the sludge. I bent to recover it and saw that there was more than just dead things in the hole. There was a glimmer and a gleam in the sludge. I fished around the sludge at my feet, hoping for some sort of weapon. Surely one of these corpses had died with a knife. Something flat and articulated slid through my fingers.

I couldn't hear anything from above, but I figured this was a good thing. I assumed that Mr. Valentine was stubborn enough to not be murdered by a mystical creature without a fight. I figured it was safe to search a moment longer.

It was a necklace, gleaming in the ooze, made of several set stones in flat oval settings that were linked together with rings. Each stone was the size of a robin's egg, except the central piece, which was easily twice the size of the others, and its setting had small dangling gems. I wiped the gore off of it the best I could and tucked it into my pouch. If it were precious to the Lamia, she might appreciate its return.

As I straightened, I saw something else that stood out—it was a dome, shaped like a head. I mentally slapped myself. I was doing my best to not think of wading through something that was somewhere between a charnel pit and a refuse bin. The thought made my breath short. I crouched, panting, forcing my breathing to be more even. The gleam from the lightning stone helped somewhat to focus myself.

I thought of Nathaniel's eyes, as man or canine they were the same. The mental image was oddly calming.

I had to climb up the pile of bodies that I had tumbled down. I really didn't want to do this. The domed object reflected off the light again. I set the arduous climb aside and crouched. It was a bird cage with three bird sculptures set on the branches in the base. From what I could tell, one was red, one yellow, and one blue. I had seen something like this before in high-end stores, it was a beautiful music box. I picked it up. The key to wind it was still plugged into the bottom and attached to the key was a thin gold chain. Perhaps the Lamia would appreciate it and the necklace being returned to her. After all, she appreciated Nathaniel's gift of that beautiful cream-colored gelding.

There was another surprise hiding under the bird cage: another necklace. It was a collar made of fine gold set with a dozen dark stones. It closed by a small chain at the back, but it was cunningly weighted so it would always keep the chain at the back and give the illusion of a fine, golden collar. Several small rings sat there, as well. Surely this was no accident. These jewels must be tossed out intentionally, but why? A huge pile of gold and silver and gems sat by her bed of hides.

I gathered up the rings, nine in all, set with various stones and in various designs, and another pendant on a gold chain. I set it all in my pouch except the large bird cage. I held that in one hand and started the ghastly climb out of the charnel pit. It was easier if I didn't think of what I was climbing on, so I tried to put it out of mind. I had to set my feet against the dead. I was sure I set my feet on shoulders, on heads. I shuddered to think on it.

A gunshot went off above. I heard the sounds of fighting. I redoubled my efforts.

The Lamia had Nathaniel backed into a wide corner. She was tearing through the gelding that lay on the floor between them, making an unholy mess of blood and offal on the beautiful tiles. Nathaniel saw me emerge from the hole. He flashed me a broad grin that quickly returned to worry. He tried to motion me back down into the hole. I ignored him.

"Welcome back. You are not a part of my army, yet, but you will be soon. I give you credit for suffering his company, female," she said with a *purr*. She wiped her bloody mouth on the back of her hands. "Your manling is exhausting. He must be very difficult to travel with, all he does is talk, talk, talk. Then shoot and punch. He doesn't entertain me any longer. I think I shall eat him."

"I'd prefer you didn't," I said.

The Lamia laughed. "Whatever remains will be added to my pit. They serve me well."

Her meaning dawned on me, and I felt as though I might vomit. "They are the army that attacked the Rothechild's party last night."

"They are. Your Rothechilds violated the sanctity of my home, now they join my army and answer my call."

"You mean to do the same to him?" I clarified, more angry than afraid.

"It is a small matter," She laughed. "Though magic taints his mortality. I do not know how it will work, he may become useless after death. Magics don't always work well with one another."

"The magic from the ley line corrupts your spell," I thought quickly. "Then why do you not just let him go? We mean you no harm, we just seek a way to cure him."

"Cure him?" Her eyes narrowed to green slits. "There is no cure for magic; those touched are always touched."

"Can we alter it?" I asked. I was sure this creature would tell us what we wanted to know if we could ask the right question. Greek mythology said magical creatures had to answer questions honestly if you asked the right question. I wasn't sure this creature was Greek, but it was all I could bring to mind. If I could make her talk, she was not murdering us.

"Magic can always be altered. Once it is a part of you it remains until you pass from this world." She turned on all four feet to face me, then shot a glare over her shoulder at Nathaniel. "Fire that at me one more time, manling, and I will kill you just for the pleasure of rolling in your blood. Mortal weapons do me no harm. Though touched by magic, *you* are mortal still."

Nate froze where he stood.

"I will trade you," I shouted. "I will return this music box and jewelry I found in the pit for the knowledge to control his magical affliction." I held up the birdcage music box.

The Lamia laughed. "Annoying creatures! They make impure music. Their false singing is an affront to my ears." She stalked towards me. "Return it to my trash heap or take it with you. I care not. I will suffer you no longer."

So anything down there wasn't of interest to her. I couldn't barter for any knowledge she might have for anything I had picked up from the pit. I was fairly sure that would also mean I couldn't barter for our lives. The fear, lying dormant in my mind, settled in my stomach again. I was starting to hate the feeling.

"Female, you may leave. I change my mind, if you want him so much he must be something you value greatly. He is loyal and he cares for you. It is quaint. Your manling amuses me. I will keep him."

"Now hold on just a moment, he amuses me too!" I said indignantly, "I am not leaving him here."

"It is not your choice, mortal. He will live as long as he amuses me." She turned, lashing her tail. "We were conversing over dinner." She motioned to the dead horse.

"Mr. Valentine is a poor dinner guest," I said suddenly. "No manners, why he doesn't even know how to assemble a proper gift of flowers."

Nathaniel scowled at me. He chose the oddest times to be offended. Didn't he realize I was trying to get him away from the Lamia before she turned him into a mindless, undead servant?

"I did offer him some of the wonderful meal I'm having." She turned back to me and tossed her head, causing her long hair to cascade down her back. "You are female. You battle with your words while males punch and shoot and demand. Males are stupid and loud. Perhaps I will eat him and keep you instead."

"You will find me a poor captive," I said, unsure how we both were going to get out of this alive. But, if she was talking, she was using those fangs for something other than burying them into our flesh. I had to keep her talking.

"You like to talk. You argue for him, but are you intelligent? "I will ask you riddles. Should you best me, I will reveal the path to controlling his malady and let you leave my island. However, if you fail, you will stay and serve me and I will eat your manling," she motioned to him.

I took it as permission so I walked toward Nate slowly.

She made no move to stop me. She moved over and sat on her pile of furs. She took up a long, white flute and blew a few notes. "The cuckoo and the gowk, the laverock and the lark. The twire-snipe, the weather-bleak. How many birds is that?"

Nate had been counting on his fingers. Six. He motioned with six fingers.

"Three," I said shaking my head at him, "for the second name in each line is a synonym. The cuckoo is called a gowk in the North of England; the lark, a laverock; and the twire-snipe and weather-bleak, or weather-bleater, are the same birds." I was thankful I was a voracious reader. Riddles were also something done at parties, though not around the tea table. I was glad I was not born to the high society of Lady Thornburry and her lady hens which would have prevented me from attending such parties.

"Most clever. Manling, I was not speaking to you. Do not interfere or I shall tear your throat," the Lamia said, her eyes narrowing. She ran her tongue over the edge of the flute again and blew a few notes. Something about them made me shiver; it was more than their eerie beauty, it felt like my boots themselves were quivering slightly.

"Of flesh and blood sprung am I ever; but blood in me that find ye never. Many great lords bear me proudly, with sharp knives cutting me loudly. Many I've graced right honorably, rich ones many I've humble made; many within their grave I've laid!"

Nathaniel blinked.

"Not so clever now, manling," she taunted softly. "You don't know?"

Nathaniel put his hands over his ears. The haunting melody clearly didn't just affect me.

I could still think, and I had the feeling I had heard this one before. "A quill pen."

The Lamia nodded, green eyes boring into me. "Below this temple is an older site still. What you seek is a mirror, a magic mirror that is able to put things right. But mirrors also reveal things meant to be concealed. What you want is to become the man you were, but the taint of magic will never leave you— it is a part of you."

I felt so sleepy, I heard her voice whispering as if she was right beside me.

"It is in you as well."

I had closed my eyes. They snapped open.

The Lamia closed the distance between us, and that terrible music was still in the air like an echo from that flute. She licked my arm. She was terrifyingly beautiful, her skin, pale and smooth and flawless, her soft silky hair brushed my shoulder. She had a warm animal smell, but then something else, earthy and spicy sweet...but beneath the pleasing scent was the smell of blood, old rotting blood like the alley behind the butcher's shop. Her eyes were too large for her face, they had vertical slits like those of a snake.

I wanted to touch her. I wanted to kiss her. I wanted her to touch me, in ways I had only dreamed of men touching me.

"What magic lies in you?" she whispered, licking my arm again.

She bit me! I felt a sharp pain in my arm. The pain made the music end. No longer beautiful, she glared up at me, her sharp feline teeth pressed to her lip as she hissed. I jerked my arm back, clasping it to my chest.

Nathaniel heard me gasp. He leveled his revolver and fired.

The bullet struck her shoulder. She bucked and whipped around. His gun reported again, this time striking her above her left breast. She snarled and pounced.

She threw him into the wall beside me. The plaster panel cracked and he slid down the wall. If he had been knocked senseless, it didn't last long. He slowly regained his feet, positioned himself between the Lamia and myself. His revolver lay on the floor by her feet, very much outside our reach.

He drew the long knife he carried.

The Lamia licked her hand, still wet with my blood. "Foolish manling. Mortal weapons cannot kill me."

"Vivian. Leave," Nathaniel whispered.

"What?" I said. "Absolutely out of the question."

"I'm going to keep her busy," he said. "Run."

"And I already told you, that's out of the question," I whispered back.

The Lamia sauntered over to her flute from where it had fallen to the floor. She ran her tongue over her lips, licked off my blood, and blew a tune.

My boots quivered again. I felt it clearer this time. The soles of my boots were quaking. I felt it around my knees and backside and my shoulders—all places that had been dunked in the ooze in the human charnel pit. Nathaniel felt something as well; he whipped around, looking for the source of the rumbling that seemed to becoming up from the floor.

A hand, missing too much flesh to be living, slapped up from the trash heap in the floor. A corpse was dragging itself out from the hole. There was a roaring in the air, like the wind. I had heard this before, on the beach. The night that the Rothechild's camp was attacked that sound was in the air.

"My God, Nathaniel, it's the flute!"

Thankfully, for once, he didn't argue or ask questions. Nathaniel dove into action, wheeling to one side and cutting through one of the corpses coming up from the hole in the floor.

My hands were shaking. I wanted to scream.

There were more of them now, surrounding Nathaniel. He spun and ducked under their clumsy swipes, using his knife to a devastating effect. He severed limbs and shattered bones, sending bits flying. Still they came; crawling out of the hole, dismembered limbs creeping across the floor.

Nathaniel stumbled over a broken hand and slid to one knee but he was up quickly, swinging the blade in a wide arc. He was closer to the Lamia.

She played the flute like she was in a trance: eyes half closed, swaying to the music.

Nathaniel wheeled, his blade shattering the flute, spraying blood into the air. His swipe had caught her chest, too.

All around us the dead men crumbled, soggy, sodden masses of flesh and dried husks and piles of bones crumbled falling as dead men should and lay still.

She screamed her rage, a sound that was something between a roar and a shriek. She reared up on her back paws and leapt for him. Her arms and front paws wrapped around his chest, she dug her back feet into his chest, raking him with her rear claws.

Nathaniel grunted in pain, his blade spinning out of his reach. He tried to roll away from her but she held fast and punched him hard in the face. He raised his arms up to protect his head and neck like a bare-knuckle boxer.

She slammed a flurry of heavy blows into his chest. I heard him grunt as each blow hit home. She was going to kill him. The Lamia screamed in rage.

I grabbed and threw the first thing I could lay my hands on. It was hot and fit my fist perfectly.

The lightning stone struck the Lamia and exploded. She screamed again, this time a sound that made my blood turn to ice. Something in it was different. The Lamia was wounded. The air smelled hot and sharp like in the lightning storm. I felt something slam into me and knock me to the ground. I screwed my eyes closed. It would be parts of the countless dead that littered the floor. I prayed I was not anywhere near the hole again.

I was lying on my back and I was being dragged awkwardly across the floor. God please, not the Lamia. I slowly opened my eyes. Nathaniel was cradling me in his lap.

His coat, vest, and shirt were torn. Blood ran down his chest from where the creature had ripped into his skin. From this angle, I could still see the bruises on his throat from Cooper's rope six nights ago. Had it really been less than a week that I had followed him to the docks after he refused to leave *Madame Theodora's Tea House*? After I found him naked near my bed the morning after I had almost been mugged in the street? Just shy of three weeks since I broke my engagement to Mr. Byron Goodwin?

I started laughing, silently at first.

Nathaniel glanced down at me. His nose had been shattered, his eyes were dark from bruising. He had several days of beard growth he had not had a chance to attend to.

I laughed and laughed. I laughed until I cried.

Nathaniel took me into his arms. He was too tired to try to stop me from crying. He just held me.

I'm not sure how much time passed as Nathaniel sat holding me against him and I dissolved into hysterics. His long knife and his revolver were at our side. I didn't remember him reclaiming them. He was staring at nothing, looking how I felt—exhausted and shocked into disbelief.

"How did you know the lightning stone would explode?" he asked quietly.

"Molly told me," I said.

He nodded, still staring off into the distance. "How did you know it wouldn't kill me?"

I gave him a blank look. He looked funny from this angle, I had never seen him from upside-down and backwards. "I didn't."

"Oh." He nodded again. There was a long silence between us. "I'm glad it didn't."

"Me too." I meant it.

"Nathaniel—Nate?" I said. "Do you think the Lamia is dead?"

"No." He took a deep breath. From the look on his face, it hurt. I shouldn't wonder, his shirt was soaked with blood. "From my experience, nothing is dead until you have its body," he gave a dry chuckle. "Of course, now I'm going to have to revisit that assessment."

"Where is she?"

He shrugged looking as stunned as I felt. "It was too bright for me to see. She's not here now."

"Did you know she was going to slaughter the horse?" I asked hesitantly.

"Yes." He sounded wretched. "I knew the moment it refused to enter."

I slowly sat up. The air in the temple smelled burnt like the lightning storms, and somewhat heavy and smoky. All around us lay the bodies of the dead men that attacked us. Paintings of ancient battlefields never accurately captured the look of it. In paintings the people lay supine, some bloody, but always at peace. These were shells of men, some brutally broken, some puppets with cut strings, heaps of man flesh on the beautiful mosaic floor. Most of the bodies had been blown clear to the walls from the explosion of the lightning stone.

Nathaniel stood and groaned. He cleaned his blade on the edge of his long coat. He pulled bullets out of his pockets to refill the chambers of his gun, then holstered it. For him, it was an absent action done a thousand times before. Re-armed, he offered me his hand. I let him help me up.

My legs would barely support me no matter how I mentally cursed them. My knees felt like jelly. Nathaniel just handed me his flask full of cheap, strong liquor. I think it was supposed to be cognac. It burned my throat just by virtue of raw spirit. I choked and coughed but kept sucking it down. When I handed it back, Nathaniel clapped me on the shoulder and took a few pulls himself.

"Honestly, we just survived a fight with a Lamia. You can't afford anything better?" My voice echoed in an entirely inappropriate manner in the room.

Nathaniel proved his lack of social consciousness again, he laughed. He gripped his chest and laughed like a mad man, snickering and hissing through his teeth. I must have looked that way before, and he bore it without outward panic. I must do the same for him.

I left his side for a moment, picking my way across the corpse-strewn floor to the pile of furs on a dais where the Lamia had played her awful flute. It lay broken into two pieces, each almost the length of my forearm. I picked it up and I could immediately see it wasn't made of wood. Though no expert in human anatomy, I had a basic, recently acquired knowledge of bones. I was reasonably sure the flute was one bone— a femur of a man. It was polished smooth and soft from use. How many men had she killed with this awful music?

I returned to where Mr. Valentine was composing himself and surveyed the damage done to his torso from her raking back feet. I pulled the long knife from its sheath at the small of his back. He didn't try to stop me. I took it over to the bone flute.

Mr. Pierce's Tom Plant, Maurice DuPuy, George Langston, Yvonne and Annette from the Rothechild's party, all the men whose names I didn't know who died on the beach last night, the boy, Clément; by God, how could I forget the poor boy? All dead or wounded by the terrible music this flute made. How many others? The ground was littered by dead men. Their rotting blood stained my trousers and the soles of my boots. How many were killed by that demon?

I brought the long knife down on the flute again and again with all my strength. Pieces of it cracked free and spun across the tile floor, others seemed to shift from under the thick blade and I struck tile again and again. I pounded away at it until I was breathless.

"Vivian?" Nathaniel was calling my name. I stopped, panting for breath.

I turned. His face, always so expressive, his eyes, always the same whether he was Ranger or as himself, now looked upon me with sorrow and with pity. I returned to him and wrapped my arms around him. I felt his blood seep through the corset and soak my shirt. I was beyond tears now. He just stood and held me.

There was no place to go but forward. I meant to see this through to the end. I wondered what Mama would say when I finally returned home. If I ever got home.

"Well, Mr. Valentine." I finally straightened. "If that demon was telling us the truth, there is a mirror somewhere here that will restore you to man form both day and night. There is no mirror in the floor directly below, I can assure you that."

He nodded. Thankfully, he didn't ask me to elaborate. He took his blade from me but carried it in his hands. I'm not sure if he remembered what happened during the attack when he was Ranger, or the battle on the beach by the dead men at our feet, but he seemed in no hurry to put the blade away now.

I didn't want to let go of his hand, either. He graciously let me hold it. We stopped only for a moment so I could pick up the beautiful music box with the singing mechanical birds. It was wrong to leave such a beautiful thing here. It was my hard-earned trophy.

We returned to the entrance of the temple where my pack and the blade from Mr. McCabe waited for us. I immediately pounced on the blade and carried it in my hand. I attached the music box to the straps and we returned, by unspoken agreement, to the spring we had passed that morning. I had seen some St. John's Wort growing there, it would be helpful to Nathaniel's wounds. There wasn't time to properly press the flowers into a usable balm nor time to boil them into a tincture, but I was reasonably sure that mangled and mashed until their juices flowed would serve better than nothing.

He drank at the spring while I gathered the herbs. I also found something that by sight, smell, and taste, I was fairly certain was aloe. It was very hard to come by in London, being a foreign plant from the tropics, but my father bought it whenever he had opportunity and believed it to be a medical marvel, nearly as useful to heal wounds as willow bark was to help with pain.

The way he shifted to drink the water made my own flesh ache and I desperately wished I had willow bark to brew for him now. "Mr. Valentine,

I hope you will allow me to treat those wounds," I said as formally as I could manage.

He stared at me as though I had suggested something scandalous. "Miss Harper, with all we have been through together I will ask you one last time to call me Nate, or Nathaniel if you feel the need to be so damn proper!"

"Mr. Valentine..." I began.

"Nate!" he snapped back.

"Mr. Valentine!"

"Damnit, Vivian, you've seen me naked for God's sake!" He scrubbed his hand through his hair. "We've kissed! Twice! We fought a demon together. If that doesn't make our relationship less formal, I don't know what will!"

He must have thought he startled me. He came over and took both my hands in his, he stared at me for a moment. He looked as if he was about to kiss me. I wished he would. "You are my friend, Miss Harper— Vivian." He looked as though he wanted to say something more, his mouth formed a word but no sound came out. Finally, he added, "If you'll allow it."

I nodded. I felt breathless and had to pull my hand away from his. I pulled my drawers out of my backpack and tore them into long strips. It was only fitting, I guess. I could not wear them with my leggings and I had no skirts to cover them. They were light flannel, designed for the fall chill in London, and were perfect for bandages.

Nathaniel didn't say a thing as I helped him remove his leather coat and vest. Fortunately, the leather and thicker serge had taken most of the blow from her claws. His shirt was soaked with blood but the cuts were shallow. It seemed they had bled mostly from being aggravated by movement than from severity. I treated them carefully and bound the mashed and mangled St. John's Wort and aloe pulp directly to the skin. The bruise on his throat from Mr. Cooper's noose must have still pained him—it was ugly purple and green, swollen slightly. I treated that with the very last of my comfrey balm.

"Mr. — um, Nathaniel?"

He cocked an eyebrow at me.

"Nathaniel, do you remember what happened when you are Ranger?"

"Some. It's fuzzy and very far away. Like it happens, but it doesn't really matter in the grand scheme of things."

"And when you're Ranger, do you remember things that happened to you as a man? And things from being a man while you're a dog?" I asked, biting my lip. I was fairly sure this cut was deeper than the others and would leave him with a most impressive and manly scar.

"Different things are impressed upon me when I am a dog," he said. "Smells and sounds are more important, sights are less so. Are you asking if I remember what you looked like changing in your room that night?"

I flushed. He laughed. "Honestly, I have a dim memory of you moving around and giving me the most impressive meaty bone."

"Ranger is a good dog," I said softly.

"Yes, he was. He was my best friend; or is my best friend. I'm not sure how that works now."

"Was there anything between you and Miss Edith Morgan?" I pulled out a few hard rolls and apples from my bag. I also had a bag of dried dates and a hard cheese, but thought I'd save that for later.

"No." He accepted the fruit and bread. He always ate quickly, man or dog they shared that trait. "For my part, no. Gracie is married to Fred, that's Alfred Ellis, the crewman," he paused, chewing. "Molly seems to have no taste for anything but lightning. Edith wanted to marry a man she sailed with."

"And first mate was a good choice," I teased.

"I have other virtues, too," he sounded mildly offended. "Good shot, not too bad to look at, good at cards, strong hand at—"

"Modest," I interrupted.

"A grace I lack," he said with a smile. "Morgan probably would have allowed it, too. We're like family."

"He's charging you 10,000 pounds for this little venture, that's hardly family," I said, shocked.

"He's a businessman first, a family man second— unless his daughters are concerned, then he lives for them," Nathaniel explained. "He's hurt I left, I'm sure this will eventually blow over."

"I doubt it," I said. "We could offer him the Lamia's treasure."

"Vivian Harper," he said, fixing me with an even stare. "I am not setting foot in that temple again. Even if the mirror is in her dead men pit. I shall just have to ask you to feed me and let me lay on your feet for the rest of my nights. I doubt another sensible woman would deal as well with my nocturnal malady."

"I'd have to hire you as a groom then, when I wed," I said airily.

He scowled. "I suppose so."

"And you'd best be gone when the sun rose lest my husband find you there and murder us both," I teased.

"Without even letting us explain," he had to laugh at that.

"Let us revisit that later, we still have three days before Captain Morgan returns for us," I said sensibly. "I'm sure we can find your mirror by then." I stood, hands on my hips, his wounds were dressed to the best of my ability. I prayed no infection or fever would set in.

"Now, I must ask you, on your honor as a gentleman, to leave me be. I cannot stand to be so befouled a moment longer."

"My honor as a gentleman?" He snorted rudely. "I have no such thing." He stood and stretched. "I will scout some and leave you to your own devices, Miss Harper." He gave me a small bow. "If we don't find the mirror by nightfall, you'll have to deal with me as a dog again."

"I much prefer you that way at night, Mr. Valentine," I said curtseying with exaggerated courtesy. "You are warm and furry to lay with." I was instantly glad he didn't see my blush.

"I'm not leaving earshot," he warned, suddenly serious. "If you see anything, give a shout."

I nodded and watched him leave, the green swallowing him up. I wanted to call him back, but I also desperately needed a bath. The water was cool, and clear. I washed myself and my hair. I would look like an angry cat as it dried. I had to brush it dry to make it look proper, but lacking brush and fire I would have to just tie it back wet and hope for the best.

I washed my clothes as best I could, then put them back on. I still had the other shirt in my bag, so I changed into that. I was cold, but clean. Nathaniel was still scouting so I took a moment to wash the jewelry I had taken, as well. The gold and jewels gleamed in the sun. A few of these pieces would make me richer than most ladies at the tea house. Altogether, the lot would elevate my family to high society. More importantly, this would provide for my parents and perhaps keep me from having to accept the next proposal of marriage as soon as I returned home. I turned the gems in around my hand in the light. 10,000 pounds. This necklace was easily worth more than that—I wasn't sure how much more, but I was sure it was enough to purchase a man's freedom.

I tucked it away with the others and turned my attention to the bird cage. I wasn't sure, in truth, why I had kept hold of it. My mother would definitely find a place to display it. The one I had seen in the shop in Kensington hadn't been this nice, but would have cost our entire annual rent. I took the small key on its gold chain and hung it around my neck as I cleaned it, lest the key be lost in the well spring forever. There were words on the bottom of the cage. They had been written on a card that was sealed with a clear resin to the bottom of the gilded cage. The wording was spotty, it had gotten wet before the resin applied, or perhaps the seal was failing. It looked like Latin. I hoped the birds still sang and the piece hadn't been too damaged. I set the key to the keyhole and carefully wound the box.

There was a switch on the side. I pressed the lever forward. The birds sprang to life. Beautiful figurines made of cloisonné flapped their mechanical wings and opened their beaks. They chirped and sang and cocked their little heads like they were watching me. I was utterly enchanted. I watched them for a long moment. Other than a faint ticking like the whispering of a watch, the birds were easy to mistake for the real thing carved from jewels. They chirped and sang and hopped all along their branches, flying within their cage like real finches in a hutch.

"Can I come back now?" Nathaniel stood at the edge of the clearing with one hand clasped over his eyes in exaggerated mock-blindness.

I laughed, he looked absurd. "Yes, Nate, come and see these birds. Have you ever seen anything so cunningly built?"

He watched them for a moment. "They are beautiful," he admitted. He hesitated. "Vivian, I found a steep path leading down. I'm not sure, but I think it leads to the other side of the beach from where the Rothechild party was camped."

"Is it below the Lamia's lair?" I asked, carefully shutting off the birds. They froze, mid-chirp, on their little metal branches. I packed it carefully away in my backpack with my blanket, long coat, and the rest of our provisions.

"I believe so, the path winds down to where I cannot see." He busied himself filling the leather bottles with water from the spring and packed them away.

"Well, we've come this far," I said cheerily.

"Vivian, you are the most remarkable woman," Nathaniel said with a grin. "Does anything dampen your spirits?"

"Another Lamia might," I said in all seriousness. "Let us be off now, Nate."

He gallantly offered his arm. I took it, and we stepped carefully into the unknown.

CHAPTER FIFTEEN

WE LOCATED THE TRAILHEAD he found earlier with ease. It wound steeply around the side of the large black mountain, then became a steep path of sand and loose dirt. I heard an odd squawk and found we were being watched by a few peacocks. At least they looked like peacocks, but larger than I had ever thought they could be. They stood almost to my shoulder, their tails extended high above my head. Lord Sutherland's birds had done quite well here, indeed. I made a note to tell Mr. Pierce when I saw him again.

It was a slow, steep trek. I could not properly enjoy the view as I followed Nathaniel; the walk took just enough concentration to require my attention, but wasn't hard enough to keep my mind from wandering. He had insisted he lead the way after I had one innocent, little, misstep that sent me sprawling in the sand.

The sun was low on the horizon and I sincerely hoped we found the mirror before he turned to a canine again. The dressings I had carefully applied to his wounds would most certainly not remain in place when he transfigured into Ranger.

"I think the birds turned back on," Nathaniel said after we had been walking a while in the shadow of the mountain. It was much cooler there and grew quite dark.

"Hmm?" I asked

"The music box, I've been hearing it for about twenty minutes now."

He was right. If I focused, I could hear the chirping from my pack. I stopped and pulled it from my pack. I watched the mechanical birds while they sang and twittered, moving from one branch to another. I flipped it over and fished out the key to wind it again. The music was pleasing.

I noticed the card in Latin again, something about the words caught my attention. "*Incendium, Reperio Aquae, Aureus Lux.*" At the sound of my voice the birds froze and stared at me. I swore they were listening with their little beaks half open, heads cocked to the side.

I cleared my throat. "I believe *'Aureus Lux'* means 'Golden light'."

The red bird and the blue fell silent, but the yellow cloisonné bird started to glow. At first, I thought it was just a glint from the sun, but soon the bird took on a warm glow. It continued watching me.

I opened the cage door and the mechanical bird stepped onto my hand. Its tiny, metal feet clamped around my finger securely.

"That's amazing!" Nathaniel said with a smile.

"Even with the lightning stone gone, we won't hurt for light," I said with a smile. "Now I wonder what these birds do, one of the words means water, the other means fire."

"Please refrain from commanding any of them to burst into flames," Nathaniel said dryly.

I nodded and we followed the path to where it disappeared into a dark cave. My hand grew heavy, but when I went to lower the light bird it merely took flight off of my finger, flying slowly beside us. I laughed and clapped my hands. "This is truly an amazing device, Nathaniel, have you ever see anything like this before?"

"You mean a glowing magic bird you wind like a watch? No, never." He drank from one of the bottles. "The sun will go down soon. I can feel night coming. Do you want to press on or wait here until morning?"

"How long do we have?" I asked, not wanting to have to deal with raw, open wounds on Ranger. Though a good-natured dog, even good dogs snapped when in pain.

The bird was becoming dim. It chirped slowly, then fell to the ground at my feet. Nathaniel picked it up and set it in my hand with a sad smile. It was hard to remember the bird wasn't alive. It was truly an amazing little clockwork masterpiece. I set the little bird back in the cage. The other two birds righted it and stood it up on one of the mechanical branches. They resumed singing rather than mourn their worn-out friend.

calm. I was aware that I was no longer underneath the quicksilver mirror lake. I was lying at the edge, lying in the shallowest part of the mirror. I rose, feeling both exhausted and yet more alive than I had ever been.

My skin felt moist and tingly, like I had emerged from a hot bath but my hair and clothes were dry. I thrust my arm before me. Though I swore I could feel the tender lines of tattooing, there was no mark on my skin. I rose, shaking. My pack sat by the trail, the yellow bird lying on its side next to it.

Valentine! I felt on the edge of panic. I looked wildly around, searching for him. The quicksilver lake was wide and glowing brightly; in the center, I saw the full moon, high in the sky, reflected in the waters.

I ran to my bag. Even running didn't disturb the waters or dampen my boots. I pulled the bird cage out of my bag and shoved the yellow bird back inside. I pulled the key from under my shirt and jammed it into the hole scratching my neck with the chain when I wasn't quite close enough. I wound it feverishly. I needed light, now!

"Find him," I commanded the bird. They chirped excitedly around the cage. "*Aureus Lux*, find Valentine please!" I pulled the bird from the cage and it came out of my hand, flying off a few feet ahead of me.

The lake was huge. I wasn't sure I could cover the entire shoreline in any reasonable amount of time, and my steps felt so heavy. What if I had gone the wrong way around the lake? What if Nate, or Ranger, lay just beyond my sight on the side opposite the one I headed out in? What if he was in the middle of the lake? Or even worse…what if he wasn't?

"Nate!" I called as loudly as I could. I suddenly imagined Nathaniel Valentine lying dead at the feet of the Lamia we managed to harm but not kill. If she followed him down here, she could easily kill him. She wouldn't hesitate. She would rip his throat clean through.

I flew here on wings of canvas and wood. We fought a demon who raised men from the dead. I was starting to believe there was nothing I could not face, but now, as the light from the mechanical bird began to fade, my courage dimmed with it. I was not about to let the shadows of this place and the other me strip my courage away. In this wondrous place, this womb of the earth I was reborn. I was so much more than I had ever been before and I was not about to stop now.

I set my teeth and squinted in the dim silvery light. There was something in the shadows, it may be a rock or the Lamia, but it could also be Nate.

The Lamia could very well be lying in wait, but if it was Nate he was not moving. He would need me. I dug my nails into my palm and strode forward. There was no returning now, not to my old life. Not to the old me.

It was Nate, He was lying in the mirror from the waist down. He looked as though he had exhausted himself trying to crawl free of the lake and had fallen short. I broke into a run, my boots crunching in the gravel shore.

"Nate!"

He wasn't moving. From this distance, he didn't appear to be breathing. The golden bird flew around his head, its brilliant light nearly spent. I skidded to a stop, my boots kicking up loose rock.

He definitely wasn't breathing.

I grabbed his shoulder and tried rolled him over. He was dead weight in my arms. Through the neck of his shirt I saw the marks from the rope and my bandages. I tugged his shoulder until I rolled him onto his side. The quicksilver leaked drunkenly from his mouth.

"Nate!" I shook him and shoved my ear to his chest. His heart was beating, I felt it thud reassuringly in his chest.

He gave a slight choking sound. I tried to pull him over to his back, but he lolled disjointedly in my arms.

I heard rumbles, rattles…something else in the cave was moving. I saw the tattooed me coming closer in my mind's eye, ready to drag us both back under the mirror. The moon's reflection was dulling, a cloud was passing over the light. The little golden bird was winding down. If it went out, I couldn't help him.

I could imagine the Lamia, battered and burned, dragging herself after us, intent on finishing the job she started. I saw her tearing Nathaniel open with her teeth and claws. I had no doubt she would find me in the dark.

I wasn't sure how I would find the bird when it went dark, or my pack and the cage to rewind it. I should have taken the time to wind it further.

We were going to die here.

"Nate," I whispered. "Please, don't die. Please don't leave me here alone."

He choked and struggled in my arms.

When I was a little girl, a poor family brought a young man to my father's door. They couldn't afford one of the fancy physicians on High Street. The young man had been crushed and dragged under a wheel, while working in a sawmill.

He choked and bubbled like Valentine did now, except the workman had choked blood, Nathaniel was choking on the liquid silver. My father couldn't save him. He choked to death on his own blood, struggling for breath after feeble breath on our wooden counter while his family looked on, helpless.

I felt this way now, unable to assist him, unable to ease his pain.

A young woman had come with them as they brought the workman in. She held him, brother or lover, it hadn't really mattered. She held him close and told him she loved him. I stopped and forced myself to be calm, to focus on my breathing, on his heart beating—on my own heart.

I held Nate to my chest. The liquid silver had stopped flowing; either it was all expelled, or he lacked the strength to cough it out. I bent and kissed him.

"I choose her," he spoke so softly I barely heard him. His eyelids fluttered and for a moment he looked at me in dim recognition. "I love you."

The cloud cleared, bathing us again in reflected moonlight. I froze. My first thought was that he spoke, therefore he must be alive.

He lay in my arms, bathed in the silver; bathed in the moonlight. He was a man, not a dog.

Then a horrible thought dawned on me. What if he was Ranger in Nate's body? After all, Ranger was much more affectionate to me than Nate was.

"Nate?" I shook his shoulder. "Is that you?" I remembered the odd, feral, foreign look he had given me earlier and swallowed hard.

He slowly opened his eyes and sat up. I marveled again at the silver lake, for though he had been lying half in and half out of the liquid mirror, his clothing and hair were completely dry.

"Of course, it's me," he said, sounding a little unsure.

"I-I feel the same way," I whispered.

Nate let out a strangled gasp and flushed bright red. He got to his feet, albeit a little shakily, stumbling on the gravel, and started off to the mouth of the cave. I scrambled to my feet to follow him, scooping up the little, dark, yellow cloisonné bird as I went.

He reclaimed his pack, coat, and vest, scooping them up almost as an afterthought. He strode into the moonlight. He stared at his arms and his hands, turning them this way and that in the faint glow of the moon.

My shoulders and hips ached. I grabbed my pack and the bird cage and followed.

He took off in a long-legged stride into the jungle. I heard his snarling under his breath. I had no idea who he was calling an idiot. I followed as quickly as I could, ignoring the branches that whipped past or the roots that snagged my feet. In a moment it was clear, I had lost him.

"Nathaniel," I whispered. I didn't expect him to hear me, I didn't expect him to care. I hurt, more than a muscle ache, more than the weariness of my bones, more than overwork and lack of good food or sleep. I remembered him whispering 'I love you,' and I was heart sick.

CHAPTER SIXTEEN

THE ROTHECHILD CAMP should have been relatively easy to find. I just had to hike back up the path by the spring and then south, back to the beach. Since they had planned on staying until the end of the month they had set up a city of tents, some of which should still be there, at least in part, as they had packed hastily to leave. But, going back meant getting close to the Lamia's temple.

I nibbled at my fingernail, weighing my options. I wasn't sure I could find the Rothechild's camp by going another way, but there was nothing in the world that made me want to set eyes on that temple again. I picked my way back up to the path that led steeply up the mountain side. I was horrified that I was crying. I sniffed and wiped my eyes on my sleeve. How could he leave me out here? What kind of a man tells a person he loves her, and then leaves her behind? What kind of a person takes a woman with him to transform him from a dog back to a man, then just walks away?

I angrily pushed aside a branch. I heard rustling in the bushes off to my side. If it was Mr. Valentine, he could just go have a good pout elsewhere. Then, I had a horrible thought—he didn't think the Lamia was dead. I didn't either. Every step I took brought me closer and closer to her lair, and the mass grave of all the men she murdered and then forced into her service.

It also stood to reason that there were probably lions or tigers or some other sort of man-eating beast out here. My mind wandered from vicious snakes to huge spiders to wolves and great cats. I wasn't sure, but I thought even a gorilla might eat a lady if it got the chance. My steps became markedly less bold.

I found the spring. Right where I left it, I joked to ease the tension. I filled the water bottle Mr. Valentine had left me and paused for a rest. At least the full moon gave me enough light to travel by.

Captain Morgan and his crew would be returning for us in three days. I wondered if they would pick up just me or if they would leave me here if I were not joined by Mr. Valentine. No, the necklace in my pouch assured me that he would take me back to London.

I splashed the water on my face and opened my pack to take stock. As far as provisions went, I had the water bottle, a pouch of dried dates, three apples, some bread, and hard cheese. If I was careful, it would easily last me three days. I wasn't sure what Nathaniel had left.

"Mr. Valentine will be just fine," I snapped at myself. "He has his revolver and his pack. After all, he left me behind. He will be fine! If not, that's on him."

I wanted to be angry. I rested my chin on my knees and watched the water flow by. It drifted down from the underground source and down a little spillway, past a clump of St. John's Wort. Why had he left like he did?

I stood, repacked my bag, and slung it back on my shoulders. I trudged onward. I was tired of being dragged along on this adventure. I wanted a hot pot of tea—the dragonfly pot with the matching cup and chipped rim. I wanted a cucumber sandwich and little tartlets made with strawberries. I wanted currant scones and honey. For one moment, I even wanted to be sitting by Byron Goodwin's side as he drank too much and made bawdy jokes to his business associates in the company of their wives. I wanted to see him gloat over a good hand of whist. I wanted my mother. She could read for me, tell me that something better was coming, something worthwhile was on the horizon; all I had to do was endure to see it to the end. I wanted my father to gather me up in his arms and take me out back where the lavender grew and the sweet peas climbed their vines between bushes of cat mint and rosemary. I wanted to watch the flowers dance and the bees hum as they gathered their nectar.

More than anything, I wanted someone wiser than me to assure me that I would be okay.

CHAPTER SEVENTEEN

I HEARD THE RUSTLING in the shrubs and it was unnerving. I *knew* there was nothing to be afraid of. It was probably a deer, or birds, or rabbits, or squirrels, or one of the peacocks, or some other harmless creature. Or it could be the Lamia. I couldn't shake the feeling of being watched. It felt like some unknown gun was targeting the back of my neck. Of course, it could have been Mr. Valentine returning to apologize for abandoning me by the quicksilver lake.

I shivered. I thought again about the quicksilver; naked me, tattooed with short hair, which had enveloped me and dragged be beneath the surface. I looked at my arms again; no tattoos, though I was sure I could feel the burn of the lines on my skin. I rubbed my hands briskly down my arms to rid myself of the feeling.

What did it mean? The symbols that the quicksilver lake had drawn on my skin were definitely related to my mother's tarot gift. My grandmother had the gift as well—in fact, my father used to tell me stories of the family being blessed with the gift. He believed in it so greatly that Harper wasn't even his own name, he took my mother's family name. They wed in the country, away from the reading of the banns in churches. I wasn't even sure what my father's first surname had been. Everyone called him Mr. Harper, I had never met anyone who believed him to be any different. Mama just refused to discuss it in society. When the question of her own pedigree came up, she would just smile and change the subject. It caused her some mild scandal when she was younger, but it was finally just accepted that she must have left her own family in shame. That was the one benefit to being comfortably well off but not rich; we were eccentric, but not enough to raise eyebrows.

I suddenly longed to touch her cards. I wanted to touch the real cards, not the two decks she used for readings. Beautiful, but faded from generations of handling, most of the edges were tattered and frayed.

One day the magistrate's daughter came in for a reading and a charm that could make the boy she was desperately in love with to think of her and none other. That evening, the magistrate came to the store demanding to know if my mother was in league with some dark force. She and father laughed it off—all she had given was a folk cure with a pleasant smell to make her feel better about the whole situation. Reading the cards was an elaborate ruse, like a drama or an entertainment. There was nothing sinister at work. Papa further smoothed things over by offering him some of his headache tonic— the single father of a headstrong teen-aged girl would eventually need it, he explained. Though doubtful, Magistrate Wyer thanked us and left, but not before warning my mother to use care. A warning she echoed to me over dinner.

"There are more things in heaven and earth, Horatio, than are dreamt of in your philosophy," my father had said, quoting Shakespeare.

I smiled. How I missed them! Mama would know what the symbols meant. I would explain that silver lake and Mr. Valentine's queer transformation as soon as I got the chance. She might even wish to read for him, to use the cards to gain insight on his odd condition.

If I ever saw him again. I wasn't even sure I wanted to. Except that I really, really wanted to.

The sun was rising. I didn't want to be this close to the Lamia's temple, but I was having a hard time putting one foot in front of the other. The green-gray of the forest at dawn was beautiful, but also disorienting on such little sleep. I desperately needed sleep, but I was also mortally afraid the Lamia would come for me while I was sleeping.

Perhaps I could be safer in the trees. There was still the risk of falling out, but I was reasonably sure that I could just stay put. I climbed into a tree with, I dare say, much more difficulty than the average little boy. The boots and lack of skirts did help immensely. I wedged myself into the "y" created by a set of branches, and promptly fell asleep.

"Where is your manling?" A voice hissed.

My eyes snapped open. I was sure I imagined it in my sleep-deprived state. Then, I remembered I was perched in a tree. I was barely hanging from my heels and my underarms in the "Y" of the tree, quite undignified, if I do say so myself. I righted myself, glad Mr. Valentine wasn't around to see me.

There was a rumbling giggle below me. "Where is your manling, little female?"

That voice. Oh God! The Lamia!

I bolted upright, smacking my head on a branch. I pulled my legs up tight and wrapped my arms around the tree.

"Come down, female," she purred, lashing her tail with great impatience. "Come down so I can eat you."

"No thank you, I'd rather stay here," I said evenly. I wasn't sure I could get much higher without falling. My heart was drumming in my ears, making me feel dizzy. It was already afternoon.

"Then I shall climb up to get you!" She snarled.

The Lamia turned. One side of her body was covered in singed fur and a bloody mass of burned, blistered flesh. I saw the muscle in her flank ripple as she gathered herself to spring.

Her fingernails were long and sharp, she gnashed her white, knife-like fangs. Clearly it hurt to move. At that moment, I would have traded everything I had for another active lightning stone.

She narrowed her eyes and sprang for the branch I was on. Her back claws dug into the wood. I felt the tree shudder. I pressed my forehead against the rough bark.

One strong, sharp nailed hand grasped the branch I was resting on. I lashed out as hard as I could, driving my booted heel into her fingers with a crunch. She let out a roar that deafened me.

I kicked at her again, this time she caught my boot and gave my leg a hard jerk. My knee wrenched painfully, and I let out a screech.

"I will make you beg, female!" she snarled.

I tried to pull my leg in close to my body, but my thighs ached from this awkward crouch and my knee wouldn't hold me.

"I will rip you apart slowly," she taunted, springing for me again. She caught the tails of my leather coat and jerked. I fell, the ground rushing up to meet me. I prayed the fall would knock me out so I wouldn't feel her fangs. I hit hard, knocking the wind out of my lungs.

There was a low snarl as she crouched, lashing her tail in satisfaction. Then there was another sound, something unlike anything I had ever heard before.

The hair on my arms stood out. I covered my head in my hands, still gasping for air.

The ground seemed to tremble as something threw the Lamia into the tree. I could hear the meaty impact of flesh on flesh.

A spray of dirt and soil was thrown into me. In my panic, it seemed like spittle showering the back of my neck. I glanced up from beneath my elbow. The Lamia let out a scream of rage. She was being pummeled by a mass of dark colored fur. The new creature was straddling her, hitting her with raking claws sending up a spray of blood, hitting her so hard they both were rocked back and forth with the motion.

I couldn't scream. I couldn't cry. I could barely gasp as I scuttled on my hands and knees to a small outcropping of rocks where I had left my pack and the blade. I wedged myself into the crack between two rocks, grasped the blade in my hand, and crouched.

I heard the battle rage on, and, despite myself, I had to peek out. I had to know what would be coming for me. The new beast was larger than a man, heavier in build and thicker in the shoulder. It loped after the Lamia, using one forepaw to assist its movement. It spun on a foreleg and pounced on the Lamia. She was now fighting desperately to get away.

She wheeled and slammed into the beast, rocking its head back. It had the head of a wolf with a large slavering jaw, dripping saliva and blood. Her slash caught its jaw, clamping it shut with a snap. The creature wheeled and kicked with back feet. They weren't clawed, but still powerful and built to walk on toes the way a dog did.

They battled and rolled, snarling and hissing, barking and snapping; sometimes the Lamia got the upper hand, but mostly this new creature dominated the battle, tearing with long, sharp fore-claws and rending with teeth. Finally, it managed to pin the Lamia's arms to her sides and bend her legs beneath her. It sunk its teeth into her throat with a twist and a tear.

The Lamia's scream was cut short with a gurgle and a crunch. Blood sprayed hot and thick into the air, and the new monster stepped away, letting the Lamia hang in its arms. The creature dropped the Lamia in a heap and raised its head, staring at me. It backed up a step and pivoted to turn on me. Sweat snaked down my back, my breath cut short. The blade I held would not stop trembling.

Then the monster took one step forward and collapsed to the forest floor.

CHAPTER EIGHTEEN

I SHOULD RUN while the beast lay wounded and senseless. I should run before the smell of the dead Lamia or the wounded beast attracted an even larger predator, ready to finish it off. I lay wedged in the crack in the rocks, blade quivering before me, my breath coming in gasps. I vowed to never complain about having a plain existence again. Part of my frazzled brain thought the coloring of the beast was very similar to Ranger: the deep, walnut color overall, the cream streaks on the face, the lighter underbelly.

It *was* Ranger.

Something had happened to him. The larger question now was the nature of the beast before me. I had seen Nate at night, he was a man as he was in the day. If the quicksilver managed to separate them then it had turned Ranger into a violent slavering beast.

I wanted to run for the beach. I wanted to run my hands through Ranger's silky, thick fur again. I desperately wanted to find Nate.

The beast was moving. It stirred, gathering its arms under itself in an effort to rise. Ranger made a pathetic pained whine.

I extricated myself from the crack in the rock, and creeped toward Ranger. If he was dying, I at least owed him my thanks.

Ranger opened one bloody eye and regarded me with that same canine adoration I had seen so many times. His cheek had been torn open, nearly to the jaw. His face twitched. He licked his bloody chops and then issued a soul-weary whine. I reached out with my right arm. Somewhere in the back of my head I realized I still had the naked blade in my left. His warm amber eyes watched me. He gave a deep sigh, blowing hot air over my hand. He tried to stir again.

"Shhh," I whispered, throwing caution out like cold tea and laid my hand on his broad furred head.

I closed my eyes, I wasn't sure how I could even roll this mammoth of a beast over let alone treat his wounds without proper supplies.

I felt him move again under my hand. His body was shaking, shifting. He gave a deep groan—a very human groan. The long, wide muzzle started to move in and back, contorting like it was being compressed into an impossibly tiny place. The thick dark fur started to melt and slough off against my hand.

I drew back in alarm.

He shifted and hissed in pain—he was compacting and shrinking and shifting.

Nathaniel Valentine lay covered in mud and blood, his cheek cut open, throat scratched, sides and back scored by the Lamia's claws. I whipped off my leather coat and draped it over him. The clawed forearm slowly shrank and acquired four fingers and a thumb. His hand clasped onto mine, trapping dark fur between our hands.

He said one word: "Vivian."

I needed to stay with him. I needed my father and his medicines and supplies used to treat anything from a burn to a large open wound. I needed needle and thread to sew up those terrible wounds. He would have to make due for the moment with water from my bottle.

Nate seemed unable to do anything but watch me, opening one eye from time to time and cocking it at me before lapsing senseless again. It only dimly registered to me that he was nude—clothing didn't seem to make it through this transformation either. I had only one damp shirt I could use to bandage him up this time. Finding his pack and his clothes would give me much more to work with.

I thought longingly of my father's yards and yards of clean bandages and collections of herbs in neat little rows along the back shelves. And honey, he swore by the proper application of honey into wounds to help them heal. Looking at Nathaniel, he could use quite a quantity of honey to get himself right again. But lamenting what I didn't have would not solve the problem now. I needed to figure out exactly how damaged Nate was, to do that I would have to get him up and arranged better and ignore the fact that he was naked.

I took up my leather pack. I would have to commend Edith for her excellent sewing skills; so far this pack had put up with an extreme amount of abuse. My blanket was neatly folded at the bottom. I had to set the birdcage aside. As I unpacked on the rough, uneven ground it fell to the side with a clatter. It must have switched on, for the birds made an indignant chirp.

I set my long coat on the ground for him to lay on and started to awkwardly tug on his shoulder to roll him over. It is hard to move a man larger than myself and keep him adequately covered at the same time, so I uttered a very unladylike curse and decided to pointedly ignore his nakedness. After all, if nurses could, I most certainly could do the same.

The damage wasn't quite as bad as I assumed upon first sight. The only conclusion I could manage was that the thick fur of the beast bore the brunt of the damage, much like his leather coat and serge vest during his first battle with the Lamia. Though he bled, the amount of blood was not troubling and most definitely didn't look fatal.

Nathaniel had rallied enough to help me get him secured in my blanket and upon my leather coat. When I shared the observation that he wouldn't likely bleed to death, he met me with a snort of laughter before becoming senseless again.

I needed herbs, water, and his pack. I returned to my own for the empty water bottle. The birdcage was lying on its side. I could read the card on the bottom, though it was partially upside down. One of the birds made light when so commanded. The word "Aureus Lux" was Latin for golden light. The remaining birds, blue and red, must relate to the remaining command words. Logically, I could assume the red bird was related to fire, the blue one to water. Though my Latin was no longer perfect, I was fairly sure that "*Aquae*" meant "water" and "*Reperio*" meant "to find or to locate."

I wound up the birds tightly until I felt resistance. I pulled out the blue bird. Its dark eye regarded me with interest. In a loud, clear voice I said, "*Reperio Aquae.*"

The blue bird took off from my hand and headed into the trees. I followed, taking care that I could find my way back. The blue bird took me through the trees to a small clearing where a little stream ran clear over light-colored rocks. The bird perched on one of the rocks, just clear of the spray, and sang in a loud clear voice.

"You are amazing!" I clapped my hands for the little bird. I filled the bottle and turned to take in my surroundings. Growing by the stream in groves grew something that looked a lot like garlic. It was unlikely to be the same variety that I was used to in London, but the juice of garlic was almost as good as honey for treating wounds. I dug the bulbs up with my fingers, tearing my nails, and gathered up as many as my hands could hold, then I tucked more into my collar.

But for now, I had been gone longer than I cared to be, I picked up the little, chirping, blue bird and carried it in my hand back to where Nathaniel Valentine lay on a bed made of a leather coat and wool blanket. He hadn't moved much, if at all.

"Nate?" I shook his shoulder gently. "I need your pack; do you remember where you left it?" When we had left *The Lightning Aura*, Nate's pack had contained a tin, cook pot. I now wanted it desperately so I could cook the garlic down into a paste to cover his wounds.

It took a few tries to get him to answer. I found his pack and clothes in an outcropping of rock. His long blades were horribly unwieldy for the fine work of pealing and crushing garlic and working it into a paste, but it gave me something to focus on. I always did better if I had something to do instead of just sit and wait. I gathered wood for a fire, I couldn't help but glance back every few moments to where the corpse of the Lamia lay by the resting form of the wounded, and exhausted, Mr. Valentine.

I found flint and steel in the bottom of my bag. For the moment, I was glad Mr. Valentine was senseless. He would have laughed himself sick to see me struggle with it. I had seen flint used before to start a fire, however I was disappointed to realize theoretical knowledge didn't translate into something usable. I did, however, have one final tool at my disposal. I wound the birds tightly and lifted the cage up to my face.

"All right, *'Incendium'*, my limited Latin remembers this as "to burn."" They chirped and hopped excitedly. The red bird stared at me, curiously. I carefully opened the cage and offered my finger as a perch and said, *"Incendium."* The little, red bird squatted down on my finger and started shaking. His little talons became uncomfortably warm.

I ran him over to the little pile of kindling I had been battling and set him down on the edge of it. The little red bird started chirping louder and louder, faster and faster. He was glowing hot, a much different red than his cloisonné covering. Oh lord, what have I done?

I rushed back to Nate's side and grabbed his leather coat to smother the fire pit. There was a hiss and an audible bang. The red bird exploded, sending bits and pieces flying; I felt one bounce off my boot.

The birds in the cage chirped in avian mania. I couldn't blame them, I had murdered their little friend. I dissolved into tears. The little birds kept up their frenzied hopping and chirping— if I were them, I'd want to get away from me as well. I opened the cage door and they sprang out of the cage like real birds. It took a moment for me to realize they were gathering up the little bits of their demolished friend. They collected up the bits like they were readying for a nest, bringing them bit by bit back into the cage. Blue and yellow hunted down the pieces, then landed close to the fire, peering in, little shiny heads cocked to the side, dark eyes watching the flames. I took up a stick and fished out the burned red bird. It still resembled a bird, though one very old and made out of rusty tarnished metal. It seemed the bird had simply blown the cloisonné covering off. They broke it into several smaller pieces and carried it back to the cage. If I was lucky, I would be able to find someone to reassemble the little, red bird. I left the birds to mourn their friend and went to add wood to the fire. Though the birds were not alive, it was hard to not feel saddened by their ruin. At least the yellow bird and blue bird still sang in their cage.

I knelt to make the garlic into a paste I could apply to Nate's wounds after cleaning them, and then I could bind them with the last of the clothing in his pack.

The birds were still moving. I thought it a trick of the light from the fire, or the sun that was preparing to set, but upon careful observation, I found the yellow and blue birds were hopping to and fro, taking pieces from their pile and adding them back to the charred mess that was the little red bird.

"Well aren't you clever little things?" I sat back on my heels, hands on my hips. These happy little industrialists were reassembling the red bird. I left the cage door propped open so they could fetch any pieces they had overlooked. I thought it very unlikely, but their song was reassuring to my heart while I prepared to treat Nate's wounds.

The garlic paste was ready around sunset. With a little prodding, I managed to get him awake enough to sit up and help me. We cleaned out the scratches with clean, cool water and then dressed them with the garlic paste. He sat, exhausted, and looked in need of several stiff drinks.

A few of the wounds were deep and full of dirt from how he lay, I hesitated cleaning them out. It would cause him a lot of pain, but without a good way to clean and close the wounds, I worried that a fatal infection might set in. He still had a bit in his flask. I didn't relish the thought of dressing the wounds with raw spirits, but then again, I never was one to shirk from a healer's task, no matter how unpleasant. I hoped that maybe he was numb enough not to care. As it turned out, he wasn't. By the time I was finished, I had been called things I had never heard before; things *certainly* not appropriate to say to a lady. He lay flat on his back on my blanket, panting in the twilight.

We had managed to get him partially dressed, and though we had to use his blanket to pad his gashes, I considered the evening's work a success. He must have too, for even though he snarled and cursed as we worked, now he lay smiling at me. I passed him the last drink in the flask. He gulped it down, though I thought his enthusiasm was less from needing the fortification and more from wanting to remove it from my arsenal as a wound treatment option.

"You did all that?" He motioned to the fire, the last of the garlic paste, and the full leather bottles of water.

"Yes," I said feeling a little offended. "Do you see me as a helpless little lady, unable to do anything beyond plan dinner parties and choose dresses?"

He laughed at that. "No, you're just unlike any *lady* I have ever met."

"Well, I apologize for not being the lady you expected," I said. "Aren't you glad I'm not just a lady?"

"Yes." He was suddenly very serious.

"I must ask, how in the world did you manage…this?" Lost for words, I motioned to him in one, broad sweeping motion.

He laughed, wrapping his arms around himself to support his damaged torso. "I have no idea." He sighed heavily and looked up at the moon. "I needed to become something strong enough to protect you from her."

"You wanted to protect me from her?" I was quite pleased. I turned toward the bird cage to hide my smile. The yellow and blue bird had almost completed the repairs on their friend.

"I *needed* to protect you from her." He sounded like he wanted to say more. He was quiet for a long moment, feeding twigs into the fire with a stunned look on his face. "The mirror told me the form I chose was the one I would be able to keep." Nate lapsed into staring off into the fire.

I took the opportunity to go off and gather some more wood. I wasn't sure how to tell how much we would need to last the night, I gathered several arm loads, falling easily into the rhythm of the work.

We had two more days, after tonight, before Captain Morgan and his crew were supposed to be headed back to Molten Cay. Two days before help was coming, and that was if Captain Morgan decided to return for us at all. I didn't put it past him to decide that the lightning harvest was better in one direction or the other and assume we could last for several more days. The food in my pack would soon run out, leaving us without provisions.

I added "more provisions" to the running mental list of items I planned on taking with me upon my next grand adventure. I froze at the thought— my next grand adventure. My God, first I had to focus on finishing the adventure I was on. Perhaps, Mr. Valentine had the right idea in joining the shadowy Explorer's Society. His penchant for adventure was contagious.

As far as polite society was concerned, that particular guild was enmeshed in grand adventures: exploring jungles, deserts, and mountain ranges seeking out long, lost treasures. Suitable only for the restless, the vagabonds, and those consumed with wanderlust. Some members were quite wealthy and they bought their way into London society, but I assumed those who had made a true fortune were few and far between. I was fairly sure that most of them had little wealth, and merely used the Society as a way to exercise their roving natures.

Perhaps I could see if Mr. Valentine would sponsor me for membership—now wouldn't that put Mr. Goodwin and Lady Thornburry into fits? I laughed at the thought and returned with my load of wood.

I could see myself dressed as I was now, ignoring the idea of polite society and afternoon teas, instead riding a camel across the desert or feeding an elephant a melon in a jungle.

But my poor parents would need someone to help care for them in their advanced age. Calvin Tabor was a passable apprentice, but if he never managed to outgrow his awkwardness and learn to settle and focus his mind he would never be as prosperous as my mother and father. No, they would need me to return and find myself a good match with money and means so they could retire to a quiet life with teas and holidays by the sea.

I made myself stop thinking about an adventure with Mr. Valentine and focused, instead, on the list of eligible men I knew who might be willing to consider me as a wife, and how I might go about getting their attention.

Mr. Valentine was rifling through our packs when I returned. He moved like one pained, sliding things aside and pulling out the food. He laid out our provisions before him. Aside from the rolls, hard cheese, three apples, and the dried dates, he had a small folded bit of parchment full of salted dried fish, a few onions, and a loaf of bread that had seen better days.

I seized the bread, fish, and onions from him—I could stew them together and serve them with the rolls and cheese for our supper, saving the apples and dates for the morning. Then we would be out of the food we had packed and at the mercy of whatever we could scavenge. Oh well, there was nothing to be done for it. I figured Mr. Valentine was the sort that would rather starve all at once rather than by degrees.

We ate all of the simple fish stew, heavily flavored with garlic, mopping up the last of it with the bits of bread. We also ended up eating the apples and dates. Though familiar with male eating habits, Mr. Valentine seemed to be putting away food at a rate even Calvin would be hard-pressed to match. We finished our provisions, and he rooted through his bag again like a hopeful child. He gave a disappointed sigh, and finally accepted we had run out of food.

"I don't suppose those birds of yours would be of any help?" he suggested hopefully.

I smiled. "They are quite helpful, but I'd guess not for that task."

I watched him by firelight, shifting on his battered body, trying to get comfortable. I sat, wrapped in his leather coat as mine was still underneath him. He was wrapped in my blanket since I had ended up using his for bandages. The wind swirled around us, sending sparks up from our campfire. I shivered.

"You're cold," he observed without really looking at me.

"Some," I agreed.

"Come over here to me, Miss Harper. I assure you, your virtue is safe with me tonight. Though you are a rare beauty, I am in no shape to entertain a lady."

I wanted to say something clever to him, but I found myself on the edge of fatigue myself. The last time I had slept so close to him to share his warmth he was Ranger. I had fallen asleep stroking his ears trying to calm the quiver in my bones from being assaulted in the streets.

"You are nothing but trouble, Mr. Valentine," I grumbled. " I seem to find myself so close to you only after some terrible, awful happenstance has befallen me."

"Then we shall have to work on that," he said softly, nearly asleep.

I slipped close to him, cocooning us in our leather long coats, the wool blankets, and the warmth of a man. This was his first night in a long while as fully, just a man.

I was not sure when we finally awoke the next day. I was quite aware that something was watching me.

Mr. Valentine lay propped up on an elbow, watching me sleep. The gash on his cheek had bled again in the night, leaving the crusty black of an irritated wound.

I had shifted in the night so I was laying on his other arm, pinning him to my side. I gave him a sheepish grin and sat up, allowing him to reclaim his limb. I should probably have attempted to clean myself up a bit. God only knew how horrible I looked.

He watched me as long as I stayed in the bounds of the camp. I finally lost his gaze when I stepped into the trees to relieve myself and wash my face in the stream. My reflection in the water wasn't as horrific as I feared. I made my toilet as best as I could, combing my hair with my fingers and washing in the cool, clear water. I looked better than he did, at any rate.

When I returned to the camp, he was attempting to dress in what remained of his shirt and vest, covering the bandages crossing his back and chest and the mess of bruises. I felt a stab of sympathy, he must feel awful. Today, I vowed to make a serious effort in locating willow or feverfew for pain relief.

We broke camp quickly. There was little to pack. We trudged through the jungle towards the beach. I wished that the Rothechild party would still be in residence in their rows of neat tents there—for company, tea, and the use of their physician, if nothing else. But I knew it was unlikely that they would be. If we were lucky, they might have left some supplies in their haste to depart. The slow walk didn't reveal anything in the willow family I was comfortable in brewing into tea for Nate.

As we came over the ridge to find the bare beach, I noted with disappointment that the Rothechild's party wasn't there. For a moment, I hoped that we were at the wrong place, but then I saw fire pits and huge sections of torn-up earth from the battle with the dead. I sniffed hard, and fought back the tears. Society would have been nice, but frankly, I was exhausted. I had been harboring the fantasy of falling into a nice soft, clean bed and letting someone else be responsible for keeping watch while I slept for a day or two.

Nate had the same thought. "No matter. Morgan will be back. We have two days, I won't let you starve, Miss Harper." He took off his leather coat and unpacked our remaining blanket. "We are not far from water, and I am sure I can find us something to eat."

I found a little place to sit in a copse of trees, out of the direct sun and out of the wind.

I started to pick up drift wood. Hopefully, Nate could make a fire. Suddenly, it was all I could do to put one foot in front of the other. I could not remember being so tired.

"Vivian." He was suddenly at my side, his voice husky and tired as my own. He took my hand and the pile of driftwood from my arms. He steered me to the trees, where he had dropped the remaining blanket and his coat. I dropped into the blanket and let the sound of the waves washing up on the beach lull me to sleep.

SGS

It was near dusk when I awoke again. I smelled meat cooking and heard a fire merrily popping along.

He was in profile, partially lit by the fire and the setting sun. The play of light and shadow made the bruises and shadow of unattended beard stand out on his skin. He was cooking something in a spit over his fire, crouching as an animal might, rather than resting on his seat.

"More rest will do you wonders," he said.

The meat he was cooking was in long, thin strips. It was some sort of snake. The head and the skin were on the sand next to him. Nate broke a large piece off for me and handed it over. It was still steaming on the stick.

I was amazed to find it had the hearty taste of chicken, but flaked like fish. "Good show, Nate!" I felt instantly cheered. "You are quite capable. I'm not sure even Hiram could have done better."

"Hiram?"

"Yes, he is Mr. Byron Goodwin's Valet. He's quite handy, manly, and of good cheer, but I doubt he could have done better." I ate around the little bones. "You know, that is one thing I dare say I will miss. I was so looking forward to having Hiram in my home."

Nate handed me another piece, "Why would you think of him?"

Why had I? The life I thought I had waiting for me had nothing to do with this one. They were nothing alike. "I don't know. He was the one good thing I thought was waiting for me in the life I had in London. There's no reason to think he could catch and cook a snake, but men should be able to do such things."

Nate had a queer look on his face, maybe it was being compared to a valet, or to a lord, or just to another man. "And Mr. Goodwin could not?"

I laughed, "He wouldn't dirty his hands."

Nate gave me a strange look, "So it was the valet you wanted, not the man."

I didn't like his tone, but it was only because there was so much truth in it. Hiram was nearly old enough to be my father. He looked out for me on every outing I attended with his master as an unofficial escort, of sorts. He was really under the employ of the Goodwin family, not Byron. Perhaps together we would have worn the rough edges off Byron and made a good man of him, in time.

"You might get the opportunity," Nate said slowly. "Hiram doesn't work for Goodwins anymore."

I breathed around hot, roasted snake. "What?"

"Goodwin fired him with prejudice," Nate explained. "It'll probably be hard for him to find another good position."

"Whatever for?" I exclaimed.

"For you," Nate said simply. "Hiram told him he was an idiot to treat you so poorly."

"Hiram called Byron an idiot?"

"Not in so many words, but that's what he meant. Goodwin knew it, too," Nate amended.

"How do you know?"

"Ranger followed him, the night after we met." Nate carefully picked out little snake bones. "I couldn't help it, Goodwin rubs me the wrong way. Ranger wanted to bite him."

"I guess that is Ranger's idea of gallantry?" I said with a smile.

"His idea," Nate said, grinning back, then wincing as it made the cut in his cheek move and pull. "I just wanted to punch him."

"So, Hiram is unemployed," I mused. I felt sorry for him, released with prejudice was a horrible state. It often made it impossible to get another respectable position.

"Goodwin better start being more careful," Nate continued moodily. "Everyone knows his business and the way he is with women." He snuck a look at me from the corner of his eyes. "And his habits."

"What exactly do you mean by that?" I demanded, hands on my hips. I knew exactly what he meant.

"Nothing," he said, quickly putting his hands up.

"You're asking if I was affectionate with him since we were engaged," I snapped.

"I am not," Nate said quickly.

"Then you're assuming that I was, knowing the common reputation of landed gentlemen," I returned.

"No, it just…" he paused, "Well, it's not unusual for women, if there is a marriage looming, to, um—"

I cut him off. "You are asking if I submitted to his desires even though we weren't actually, officially, married yet! Well I can tell you one thing, *Mr. Valentine*—"

"There she goes again," he muttered under his breath. "You only call me that when you're incensed."

I continued, undeterred. "I am not the sort of lady to allow such impropriety. I know Mr. Goodwin has been engaged three times, and all three times the rumor was that he broke the engagement after he exercised his pending rights. I assure you that is not the case here. How simple do you think I am?"

"Not at all." He was grinning now. Infuriating man! "So, you don't love him?" He said, his grin wider.

"No," I said evenly. I stabbed the fire with a stick.

"Then why would you agree to marry him?" Nate asked quietly.

"That's a highly personal question."

"Whom am I going to tell?" Nate asked, reasonably.

I sighed. Why *had* I agreed to marry Byron Goodwin? The answer was actually pretty pathetic. "My parents."

"Your parents liked him?"

"Not in the slightest," I laughed. "My parents are getting older. My father runs a sound business now, but soon the physicians will seek to put apothecaries out of business. And, if my mother hasn't been denounced as a witch by the Red Hoods yet, she soon will. A good marriage to a wealthy man will ensure they can retire in relative comfort. I am a woman, there isn't much I can do, personally, to ensure they are well off, but I can marry well."

"Well, that sounds like a poor solution to me." Nate said careful not to look at me.

I wanted to be offended but he was right. My papa was right. I was in a cage of my own making. I made my engagement, I broke it, now I was gallivanting across a tropical island fighting demons and dead men. Imagine what else I could do.

We sat in silence for a moment. Saying it out loud reminded me that, while I was out on this grand adventure, there were no courting offers coming. I had the Lamia's treasure so we would have money, but no husband. And, to be fair, I should offer half the treasure to Nate. He earned it. No, the best way I could provide for my family permanently would be to trade myself away. I sat, staring into the fire.

After a long moment, Nate spoke. "But you don't love him. You shouldn't marry someone you don't love. You definitely shouldn't marry someone who doesn't respect you."

"No." I let out a deep breath. "But, in time, I might have grown to love him. Peers don't marry for love. He was the best match I could manage, and perhaps we could grow to at least respect one another. I would happily bear his children, just to know my children and my parents are well cared for."

"Happily?" he repeated.

"Well, maybe not happily," I clarified. "But stiff upper lip and all."

Nate made a non-committal noise like a snort and added a bit of driftwood to the fire.

Luckily, though I was without current offers for a husband, the jewelry in my pouch might go a long way with assisting my parents in their advanced age. I pulled out a ring. Five sapphires set in platinum.

"Is that your engagement ring?" Nate asked, aghast.

"No," I laughed. "Mr. Goodwin was on his fourth engagement, I sincerely doubt he would have ever purchased something so fine for me. I'm not even sure he could have afforded it. I found it in the Lamia's charnel pit. A few others, too." I handed it over.

"I've been an explorer for quite a while, and though I have unearthed some treasures, nothing this fine." Nate polished it on his vest, then handed it back. "Maybe you should wear it when you get back. It would drive Goodwin mad if he thought you were engaged to such a wealthy man."

"And scare off any other perspectives." The rings provided my family income and would offer independence, but would they make me a spinster? Men needed to be needed. Could I return to my life in London and await the right man? Should I attempt to purchase Nate's contract with all the jewelry I possessed and hope it was enough to take Nate with me? Then I would have a man who was becoming very dear to me and who, in a moment of senselessness, professed love— but was it even Nate who spoke, or Ranger?

Nate was watching me. He looked like he wanted to say more. I willed him to say something, anything, but whatever he was thinking he kept to himself. His smile disappeared and he finished the rest of the snake in silence.

CHAPTER NINETEEN

THE NEXT MORNING was warm and clear. Bad weather for lightning hunting, but perfect for our impending rescue by Captain Morgan and his crew. Nate was sharpening his blade with long, ringing strokes against a bit of stone from one of his coat's many pockets. It was a wonder he could move as fast as he did while wearing the coat. When I had put it on I had been surprised at the sheer weight of it. I wasn't sure how many pockets it had, he always seemed to fish something he needed out of a pocket I had never noticed. Now, he pulled a small grimy piece of cloth out and polished the sharpened blade until it gleamed in the sun. There were waves and swirl patterned in the metal; such a beautiful and odd weapon.

A man such as Mr. Nathaniel Valentine would have no place in the life I led back home. Unless I had gone looking for it, I would never have known anything about the Explorer's Society, other than their penchant for a distinctive and utilitarian, yet grossly outdated, style. I never would have even heard of a Lamia, and chances were even better that I would have never been able to see such wondrous sights like a floating airship or a tropical island. I certainly would never have met such a wonderful companion.

I must have been staring, Nate suddenly looked uncomfortable. He tucked his gleaming blade back where it rested, almost invisible under his coat at the small of his back.

"It's called a Seax," he explained. "It's somewhere between a sword and a knife. The guild was quite impressed with the shape and style when they were discovered in the wilds of Scandinavia," He paused and climbed to his feet. "You were pretty impressive the night the dead attacked the beach."

I shrugged, certain he was teasing me. I was not a warrior by any means.

"Why didn't you just shoot them?" he asked. "Lady Rothechild handed you a revolver."

He hadn't seen me shoot the dead men. "Well, I did, when it was loaded, but when it ran out I couldn't shoot anymore." It was strange, I had been able to fight them then, I didn't have to think about it. I didn't have time to think about it. Now, I shivered at the memory of impaling the dead man with the burning tent pole and the way the blows reverberated up my arms when I caved in skulls with the oar. Not only was I not a warrior, I detested violence. Before this trip, I had never struck anyone. I never enjoyed the barbarism of duels. It just made more work for physicians and apothecaries to repair the damages. I also had absolutely no interest in watching pugilism with Mr. Goodwin. He was quite enamored with the sport. Watching two grown men beat each other senseless frankly churned my stomach. I wrapped my arms around myself, feeling a chill despite the warm beach.

To his credit, Nate wasn't laughing at me. "The world is a violent place, Vivian," he said softly. "And from what I've seen, it just gets worse from here. Not everyone respects women enough to protect them."

"Then I am fortunate to be traveling with you, Nate. It seems you are willing."

"I'd defend you from anything," he said, very serious. He was close. His eyes were the color of dark sherry, a warm reddish brown, still sharply intelligent yet possessing a great kindness. I had never seen eyes like that before, at least not on a man. I was certain, though, that it would be very fitting on a caramel colored dog with prick ears.

"But you can't depend on me to be there to protect you from everything. Did your father teach you to shoot?" he asked.

"No," I said. "He is not a fan of violence either. He has seen too many injuries from guns."

"Well, a fan or not, you need to know how to protect yourself," he said matter-of-factly.

Well, in for the penny, in for the pound. I handed the Seax back and dusted off my hands. "So, teach me."

"Me?" For a moment he was dumbstruck. Then, he smiled "Of course, for what would you have done if the Lamia actually got a hold of you?"

"I would have died," I returned. "Your gun seemed to do little more than annoy her. I do not have another lightning stone, so I expect I would have died."

He spent the better part of the afternoon schooling me in the use of a revolver. I shot it half-a-dozen times and was surprised at the way it made my hand tired and numb from the strength it took to hold it. My forearm shook from bullet after bullet that I shot. My ears rang and I was sure the birds were laying scrambled eggs at this point, they were so stressed from the repeated racket from the gun and would probably never return to this side of the island.

We shot through half the bullets Nate carried with him. My shoulder hurt so badly that even my stomach ached, but finally I could load the revolver and hit the place on the tree we were aiming for. Even more wonderful than the ache in my shoulders and my core was the warmth spreading through me as Nate would place his hands on my hips to adjust the way I stood or moved my shoulders to provide a better stance from which to shoot.

I shyly took the revolver he reloaded and tucked it away. "If we get attacked by a fearsome beast again, you can protect me by turning into…well, whatever that was you turned into to kill the Lamia." I meant to be coy, but I failed. He sucked in a deep breath.

"I'm not sure I can do that again," Nate said. "I'm not sure I want to."

He had a strange look on his face. He was lying. I had seen that look before. We used cocaine as a way to dull pain in open wounds. My father treated a man who preferred to inhale the cocaine powder. It made him frighteningly strange, he seemed to do everything quickly and seemed immune to pain. He was jumpy, and he refused to eat or sleep. Finally, Papa had to lock away all the cocaine and prescribe him large doses of laudanum to help him get some much-needed sleep.

Nathaniel had the same look now: jumpy and twitchy. The power of that beast must be immense, indeed. There was something in him that should have scared me. Maybe before I came to know him, before the mirror lake, it would have. I didn't need him to protect me anymore; certainly not from him.

I heard the sailors before I saw them. I was about to ask Nate how in the world we were going to get back to the ship, when I realized it was getting larger and larger on the horizon. The airship blocked out the sun as it prepared to land. Sailors shouted, bellows hissed, and wood creaked as the airship set itself down in the crescent cove.

Captain Morgan shouted at his crew who were battling the tide to bring a longboat to shore. "Put yer backs into it, lads!"

"Captain Morgan." Nate stood at attention.

"Mr. Valentine," Captain Morgan growled. "I hope we shall find your condition much improved."

"Aye sir," Nate said.

"Then get yourself to work," Captain Morgan said. "Fresh provisions, water and food, and anything else worthwhile on this wretched island! But be quick about it! That demon is around here somewhere, so stay together."

His men leapt to obey. The flurry of movement was disorienting. I should tell him Nate killed it, but would it then make him more valuable to Captain Morgan? Would he raise the cost of his contract? Would he ever let him go? I chewed my lip. Knowing the monster was gone would set the men at ease, I should tell them.

Nathaniel wearily took my arm, walked me to the longboat, and helped load the recovered gliding wings inside, his expression blank. Then he returned to the island with the men, bent on fulfilling his captain's orders.

I let Mr. McCabe row me, and several barrels of water, back to the ship. I felt the space between us open up like a great wound. It was almost more than I could bear. I had grown accustomed to having him close. I only hoped that Captain Morgan was a business man, and an honorable one.

Molly was standing on the deck of the *Aura* as it sat resting on the sea, rocking in the gentle surf in the protected cove. She had her hands clasped tightly to the rail, though not out of fear. In the bright sunlight, the scars crossing her beautiful, delicate features gleamed, making her look both beautiful and grotesque.

"Why aren't you on the beach or heading off into the jungle with the others?" I ventured softly.

"I don't leave the ship," she whispered.

"Why not?"

Molly turned and looked at me. "I never have." She turned back to look at the shore. There was no sense of longing in her face, it was just as if she was telling me the winds blew and the ocean was blue. "I was born on the *Aura* and I have never left it."

"You have never set foot on land?" I joined her at the rail and looked at her out the corner of my eyes. "Don't you want to? Does your father forbid it?"

Molly laughed. "No, I have no desire to ever leave the ship. My father encourages it, but I have never wished it."

"Surely when you wish to wed or have children—" I stopped myself. The Morgan women had other goals. They were not bound to the convention of making good social matches and securing their position with wealth and prosperity.

Molly turned to me. "I will never wed, nor have children, but I understand your meaning. I am not sad. I love my life as it is. Here is where I belong." She gave me a little bow. She turned and went below.

I followed her example and went to lay down in my berth. I tried to rest, but found my mind racing as I recalled the events of the past few days.

I was still trying to make sense of things when I heard a flurry of activity on the deck. The crew had returned with their supplies. I heard Captain Morgan's voice ring out. "Be careful with them peacock eggs—if Molly can get them to hatch, those birds will be worth a small fortune."

A business man indeed.

CHAPTER TWENTY

BACK ON BOARD *The Lightning Aura*, the crewmen worked like a very excited anthill, scuttling about and working humongous bellows, pumping air from large canisters into the balloon that supported the ship as it flew. I watched Nate, he was in his shirt sleeves, rolled past the elbow, working hard—though I saw him grimace in pain every so often. The ship began to creak as the thick, metal cables, which held the balloon, started to become taut and rise.

Captain Morgan gave the huge eggs to Molly and her warm lightning den care for. Molly nestled the precious cargo in her little den where the harvester loomed like a sleeping, powerful monster— the mama of the rookery. I told Molly about our battle with the Lamia, thanking her for the gift of the lightning stones as we made a little nest of blankets on top of a base of warm lightning stones. I left out the part where Nate managed to transfigure into, well, whatever that was. Molly was no fool, she knew I left something out, but she didn't press the issue.

I harbored no ill will against Captain Morgan, but he made a huge distinction between business and family. Though I was sure he wouldn't betray his family for anything in the world, I was also just as certain he would not pause to advance his business at any other cost. In fact, I was betting on it.

Captain Morgan was going over a map, sextant in hand, squinting in the bright sun. He and his navigator were planning their next destination. Perfect.

"Captain Morgan, may I have a word?" I called out clearly.

"Of course, lass." He motioned me up to his helm. The resupply, and the wondrous find of the gigantic peacock eggs, had set him in a pleasant mood.

I squared my shoulders and stood my ground before this mountain of a man. "You are a business man, correct?"

"Aye, lass." Captain Morgan gave me a once over.

"I propose to hire your ship and crew, and to purchase Mr. Valentine's contract, as well," I said evenly.

"And just how do you propose to do this?" he asked with a slight smile.

I pulled the gold and amethyst collar from the pouch at my side. "I wish to trade you this."

The egg-sized gems gleamed in the sun. He took up the necklace, thick fingers stroking the jewels. I could practically see his mind tallying up his latest score. His eyes were alight with the fortune in his fingers. So, he was a privateer at heart. "Your servant, Miss Harper. Where would you like to go?"

"Calais. We need to find the priestly scholar Nate spoke of. He may be the only one who knows how to seal the ley well. I am sure that there will be storms to harvest crossing the channel. I only ask a small detour. Captain Morgan, you will be able to retire a gentleman much sooner than you first thought, and you may well be helping save the world."

"God's wounds lass, you do know how to talk to an old pirate like me." He handed the necklace off to Francis. She smiled at me.

Captain Morgan turned back to his ship's wheel. I hoped he was plotting the new course. "Would you like paperwork on Mr. Valentine's contract or is my word on the matter good enough?"

My mind was racing. I never hired a servant, indentured or otherwise. "I wasn't aware there was paperwork on the matter?"

The captain laughed, I flushed, he had been teasing me. "No matter, Nate is a man of his word. He will honor his contract. Or I will enforce it same as I would here?"

I did not like the implied threat. "And how is that?"

"Violence," he said simply

I stamped my foot, "You will not! I will not allow it." How was I to deal with this? Nate was hardly property and this was not how I envisioned this going. I wanted him to be free to do whatever he wished. I did not wish to discuss him as though he was a horse, or a book, or a trinket. The man I had come to know was honorable, not a villain to be punished by threat of servitude or transportation. "Please, captain. All I want is your honor appeased and any debt between you settled."

"Miss Harper," he gave me a short bow and cleared his throat. "You know where your cabin is." He clasped Nate's shoulder as he passed by. "Mr. Harper!" The crew broke into peals of laughter. Mr. Valentine flushed red.

I retreated to my cabin and shut the door. I couldn't look at Nate now. That was *not* what I had intended. He was not just some indentured servant whose contract could be bought and sold. I wondered how much teasing he would have to endure thanks to me. Yet the thought of him sailing on with Captain Morgan, not because he wanted to, but because he was indebted to him, was more than I could bear. Regardless, Mr. Valentine was now a free man.

There seemed to be a debate among the crew as to whether Nate had allowed a London lassie to unman him, or if he was in love. There was also speculation that he had merely sold himself to the highest bidder and he had suddenly become an accomplished buccaneer. To his credit, I never saw him react with anger to their teasing. He seemed to join in, making fun of himself with such skill and unabashed shaming that they just lost interest.

I spent my time helping Molly tend the eggs and socializing with Mrs. Morgan, who insisted I call her Fannie, but I found myself no longer content to just sit, take tea, and be what passed for a social lady on the ship. I set myself to being useful and patched laundry, not a task too different from sewing up wounded men.

Edith Morgan sat on the deck with a mending basket before her. She sat in the best light available, working from sun up to sun down, repositioning as the sun moved across the sky.

"Edith?" I ventured. She squinted up at me. "May I join you?"

"Of course." She motioned to her side and gave the deck a friendly pat. She was clearly no longer cross with me. "Would you like to help?"

I was glad she was speaking to me. "Of course." I happily took up a shirt from the basket and grabbed a needle and thread.

A shadow blocked out our sewing light. It was one of the younger sailors on the Aura. "Edith?"

She gave a huge grin as she leapt to her feet and took his hands.

I lowered my eyes and tried to hide my grin. So, this explained everything. She had found a new, and more suitable, suitor.

The new man made a big show of presenting her with oranges from the Cay. Edith gave a squeal of delight and thrust the mending at me, heedless if I actually caught it or not. She and her new paramour linked arms and sauntered off to the bow of the ship together. I was genuinely happy for them, and hoped it turned out as she wished.

Nate was waiting for her to leave before he joined me.

"I'm glad she and Mark are getting along so well." Nate sat beside me.

I couldn't keep from smirking. "Really? You're not the least bit upset to no longer be the object of a young girl's affections?"

"I suppose that depends on the girl," he said with a small smile.

"Ha!" I told him. "I'm no girl, sir."

"I'm very aware of that." The look on his face betrayed him. He had that crooked grin again.

"It seems you were too old for her," I told him, doing my best not to laugh.

Nate looked genuinely offended at that. "I am hardly old." He stood, dusted off his trousers and offered me a hand.

I gave a gusty, theatrical sigh, and set the mending back in the basket before letting him haul me to my feet. "Where are we going?"

"I want to show you something." He led me to the rail.

I immediately did my best imitation of a mule and dug in my heels. "I can't look over, the heights!"

"Still?" He scratched his neck. "You're telling me you can fight a man-eating Lamia, explore a magical lake, face down an army of undead, and nurse a monster back to health, but you can't look over the railing?"

His argument stopped me cold. I stared at him for a long moment. Yes, it must sound completely ridiculous. "It's not the height per se that bothers me, Mr. Valentine, it's the fall and the sudden and quite messy stop at the bottom."

He made that dismissive noise of his. "Then don't fall off the ship."

Before I could protest any further, he grabbed me by the waist and heaved me onto his shoulder like I was a sack of grain or a water barrel. I squeaked in protest, but that drew attention to us, and the assembled sailors started hooting and cheering like a pack of excited gibbons.

Nate ignored them and brought me over to the railing where he set me down. "We'll be over the coast of France tomorrow, mid-morning. Morgan is going to contact one of his buyers for the electro-ion storage matrices Molly filled from the latest hunting expedition."

He had shaved for the first time in weeks, he now ran a hand absently across his jaw. Though the look would not pass for society in London, I was growing quite fond of the rakish look. "The men are beginning to think of you as a good luck charm."

"Oh?"

"Captain Morgan is a good captain, he gives out shares of all income. That includes those eggs and that necklace. Combine that with the electro-ion haul and this trip has become quite the profitable venture for them."

I leaned in to whisper against the wind. "Then we should be careful to never mention the Lamia's treasure hoard in their hearing."

He shuddered. "They would wish to recover all the treasures within. I, for one, am happy never thinking of that place again— no matter the riches inside."

I couldn't agree more. There was nothing in the world that could make me set foot in her temple again.

"Anyway, lucky charm..." he said, positioning himself behind me, against the rail to lend me his support. "This is what I wanted to show you."

I looked over. The sea's gentle waves and rolls were disturbed by what I thought was a large piece of rock sticking up from the sea. Then it raised one massive arm and slammed it into the water, sending spray up high enough to reach us. It had several long arms, a gaping toothy beak, and eyes with vertical slits like a snake.

"My god, what is it?"

"A kraken. Damn fierce creatures, but its blood is worth a fortune to chemists, alchemists, and occult hunters."

The kraken flailed its massive arms in the waves at the fish surrounding it.

"Are those dolphins?" I asked, suddenly grasping the size of this beast.
"Yes."

"Shouldn't we help them?" I asked. I could have slapped myself; if he said yes, I had no idea how we would help.

"Naw," Nate didn't seem worried for the dolphins in the least. "They're playing with it."

Mr. McCabe was coiling up a recently spliced rope near us and glanced over the side. "Fierce sense of humor, dolphins have. Krakens can take slow things—like boats—but they're too big and ungainly to catch anything quick and crafty like a dolphin." He squinted at Nate and me, then gave a small nod of approval. "They probably want to drive it back down into the black where it belongs." He gave Nate a pointed look. "Watch that you don't let that lass catch her death out in the wind without a proper coat. Miss Harper, Mr. Harper."

Nate gave a snort, and though he was standing behind me, I was certain his snort was accompanied by a rolling of the eyes.

"I'm sorry for that," I said softly. I wasn't sure if I wanted him to hear me. I wasn't sure he wanted to discuss it. I wasn't sure *I* wanted to discuss it.

"For purchasing my contract when Morgan was looking to keep me as an indentured servant for the next ten years in service to the ship and the crew?"

"Well, yes, that." I bit my lip. Why was it I couldn't talk to him now?

Nate gave a bark of laughter. "I am your man, Vivian Harper, bought and paid for. Perhaps you would be willing to inform me of my duties someday soon."

A wild madness gripped me and I felt the blood rush to my cheeks. I suddenly wanted to tell him exactly how he could serve me—he could start by kissing me again. But good ladies *did not* think like that.

I took a shuddering breath. "You are my man in name only. When we get to a port you can take your leave. You are not bound to me." I wished I was better at reading people. Was he disappointed, or merely unsure of what I was saying? "Though I would hope that you would accompany me safely back to London."

He smiled at that, at least. "I seem to remember promising Mr. Bowden that I would see you safely home. I didn't anticipate such a long detour."

We both laughed at that, and just for the comfort of it, I leaned back against him while we watched the kraken finally yield to the dolphin's harassment and sink back under the waves.

Captain Morgan was calling for me. "Miss Harper?" I had just emerged from the hold where Edith, Fannie, Molly, and I had been doing laundry.

The ship had quite an ingenious system for such. It cunningly directed and sluiced water from the cables that held the great balloon into water collection tanks so we always had more than enough water for food and drinking. I had even managed a warm bath from one of Molly's inventions—her electro-ion powered hydro-thermo-generator. It managed to heat water to a toe-curling, almost scalding, heat. If I were a true lady of wealth and means, I would hire her in an instant to install one of her boilers into my home for hot water on demand.

Now we were using her hydro-thermo-generator to boil shirts and small clothes in one vat, and darker clothes like vests and trousers in another. After being properly agitated and scrubbed, we ran them through manglers, then exposed them to tiny lightning stones that were cracked in a large kettle with a brass tipped wooden pole that took them from wringing wet to damp in an instant.

My arms ached from the work, but I was grateful for the distraction.

I came up on the deck, blinking in the bright light. Below me I heard the girls open drains that were plumbed to the side of the airship and loosed the water into the air below us.

I approached the captain.

"Calais will be below us within the hour," he said formally. He was polite to me since I had made him a wealthy man.

"Thank you kindly, captain."

"We tie to a watch tower called the _Tour du Guet_. We have a client to see there. I trust you can complete your business within the span of two days?"

"I believe so," I said.

"We will be leaving the morning of the third day. The wind currents are much like the tides, they wait on no man. Or lady," he hastily added.

"I understand, captain. Thank you."

"Several of the men will be off the ship to provision her, or accompany us to the client, but do not fear that the ship can be taken. My best will remain behind quite well-armed."

"Several of your best, and Molly," I said.

"Molly, yes." Captain Morgan sighed and his bushy eyebrows went up, softened with fatherly concern. "I do wish that she will chose to leave the ship, if only to feel the solid land beneath her feet."

I nodded and turned away. If we were going to be among civilization again, I should at least attempt to make myself presentable.

Nate's worldliness was amazing and infuriating all at once. He clearly had been to France before. He surveyed the horizon and approached landing with his usual, self-assured and unimpressed manner. We tethered at the *Tour du Guet* just before tea time and started down to the ground in a large basket that was lowered by a pulley to the square.

"Why couldn't we have reached the Cay like this? We had to use those damnable wings," I demanded, feeling the fool.

"We couldn't use the basket because there is nothing to tether to on the Cay," Mr. Church explained, patiently. I always felt like he was lecturing me like a professor when he used that tone. "The basket would have spun in the wind and knocked you senseless, then thrown you out."

I shut my mouth and smoothed the short bustle I was wearing over my trousers, it matched the corset cover as I'd made it from my burgundy dress, too. I wasn't sure it was fitting for meeting a priest, but it would have to do. It was all I possessed.

CHAPTER TWENTY-ONE

THE MONASTERY WAS a beautiful but incomplete monument of stone sitting upon a field of green not far from the village that housed the mighty lighthouse where *The Lightning Aura* sat tethered, like a dolphin dancing on the waves of the sky. We were lowered by a winch in a basket to the ground. The crew must not be strangers here, our appearance caused no great kerfuffle.

Nate and I were offered the services of a small donkey cart and driver, several others headed off with their precious cargo in a different wagon to meet their benefactor. I meant to watch their wagon as it faded from view as Paris would be off in that direction, perhaps if I squinted I might be able to see it, but then Nate cleared his throat, offhanded in a great manly fashion, and my interest in the city of lights was lost.

The donkey's hooves clopped on the crushed stone. Like all proper holy sites, it was laid out in a cross pattern but though unfinished, the gardens were well-tended and overflowing with herbs. The wind brought the spicy sweet scent to me and I was suddenly home again in my Papa's little gardens where we grew what herbs and medicines we could. I was homesick. I was a woman and a child. How strange to be all and neither; to be so far from where I had come.

The donkey tossed his head, his long ears flicking as we came to a stop. There was no howling wind, just a warmth and a peace here. This must be the peace the priests sought. I could see why. I could not wait to help my Papa and Mama retire to a quiet holiday.

Nate climbed down and offered me his hand.

"How will he know we're here?" I asked.

Nate looked around in mock suspicion, "He already knows. He always knows."

A gray-haired priest dressed in dark brown robes was coming to meet the cart. He offered the donkey a carrot that the animal happily accepted. It chewed thoughtfully, rolling the treat around its mouth, letting the priest rub his knuckles up and down the long furry nose. "It is a priest's prerogative to watch the sky, Nathaniel. We are quite fond of the chief resident of the kingdom of heaven."

They shared a chuckle. Nate turned to me to offer a hasty introduction. "Miss Vivian Harper, may I introduce Father Henri Poullain."

Father Henri took both my hands within his. They were oak trees, gnarled but still strong and warm. I liked him immediately. "It is a pleasure, my dear. Welcome to Basilica of Notre-Dame de Boulogne."

I wasn't sure what I had expected a scholar-turned-priest to be like, but Father Henri Poullain was not it. He walked without a cane, his back straight and strong. His blue eyes, greatly magnified by his glasses, displayed an interested, curious gaze, and they twinkled with the look of a man quite happy with his advanced age. Some men detested aging, some fought it, some railed against it; but those that accepted that it was merely part of the grand adventure of life, were happiest. I was pleased to see Nate's friend was one of those.

"Well, what brings you here, Nathaniel?" Father Henri asked as the cart driver bid us good-day with a wave and left. "I doubt it was a social call."

"Adventure and we need the advice of a learned man, a man with learning of ancient mythology and how it may relate to possible magic." Nate said mysteriously

Father Henri offered me his arm. "Very well, my interest is piqued. Ah to be young. Come along then. Let us hear about this grand adventure you are on."

"How long have you known Nathaniel?" I asked as we walked to the Basilica. "You seem to have quite a history."

"Nathaniel and his brother, Trevor, were left in the care of the church when they were young boys. I have a good friend at Bishop Webster's

Industrial School for Boys. I was visiting when the boys were left, and I spent a few years as a guardian for them and the other children left in our care."

I didn't know what to say. Behind us, Nate was deafeningly silent. I was just trying to be friendly, I never meant to stumble upon something I wasn't supposed to know. "I'm sorry, I didn't know he was orphaned."

"I'm not," Nate said firmly from behind us.

"He's not," Father Henri confirmed. "His father is a soldier in the king's army, fighting in the Americas. His mother..." Father Henri paused. "His mother was not able to care for them. She grew quite ill."

"I'm sorry, what were her symptoms? Perhaps my family can help."

"You can't help," Nate said firmly.

I opened my mouth to protest, but Father Henri gave me a small shake of his head. The hand tucking my hand into his elbow tightened. So, it was not a conventional illness. Perhaps she was mad. Regardless, neither one wanted to discuss it. I thought of my family at home, in our small townhouse, with Jenny and Mrs. Tabor and Calvin, and felt a pang of sympathy. Family was everything, and he had none.

We sat in a warm little room, off the kitchen where beer brewed. The yeasty, earthy scent filled the room. Several stoneware bowls sat covered with cloths. I took a peek, it was bread rising. Tiny specks of flour hung in the air dancing in the sunlight filling the world. All was harmony and good smells and happiness here. Whatever transgressions I committed against Nate by bringing up that he had no family were forgiven. Whatever worries I had were gone; I didn't have to be strong, I just existed and here, that was enough. This was a tiny island of peace.

Father Henri listened carefully as Nate told him of the ley well beneath London, and his exploration that lead us to our journey to seek out the ley well on Molten Cay. Father Henri took out a quill and a piece of paper and started a list. He paused from time to time—setting the quill between his teeth. Nate waited with a patience I had not seen in him before. He didn't look annoyed or anxious at all. Finally, Father Henri handed him the list. "Find these titles in my quarters and the library. Please find them all and crate them. They are necessary resources to solve the problem you have placed before me."

Nate nodded and headed off. Clearly, he had been here before.

"I would like for you to hear my confession," I said as soon as we were alone.

"Ahhh, I assumed you needed something like that." Father Henri gave a small smile, his eyes twinkling. "Something weighs heavily on your mind. People who wish to speak with a priest in private often have a look." He glanced at me, weighing something in his mind. Finally, he nodded again. "Just to be sure, you are Angelican? You are British, correct?"

I wondered if he would be offended. Being French, he was most assuredly Catholic. Catholics and the Church of England did not have a history of always seeing eye to eye. "I am."

Father "What is the aphorism held by the Church of England?"

My Papa said it from time to time. It was one of the observations of men he liked. "All may confess their sins, none must, but some should."

Father Henri smiled, "Ah yes, that is the one. I can see why Nathaniel likes you. Let me get my stole, and I will be happy to ease your mind."

He moved quickly for an old man. He led me through the kitchens again, where monks were tending a stew pot and kneading bread. He stopped to greet them each in turn and inquire about their health.

"Brother Elmer, are you warm enough in our kitchen? Brother Edward, your cold seems much improved." I struggled to keep up as we moved from one room to the other.

He led us through the long hallways and out through the ante chambers where the monastery would have seen hundreds of visitors. Finally, he turned back to me. "At one point, there was a statue here called *Notre-Dame de la Mer,* the lady of the sea, where pilgrims came to seek miracles of God. This is where we are laboring to rebuild the rotunda. It is set to be just over 100 meters high when it is finished."

The scaffolding was staggeringly, nauseatingly, high in places with long boards holding the structure from collapsing in on itself and burying the cathedral under tons of stone. Huge gothic arches held most of the dome in place but the very center was open and uneven as it was unfinished and the broken edges of it made it appear as though it could collapse upon us at any moment. "I am awestruck" I said quietly. I didn't like the way my voice echoed in the cathedral.

"It is impressive," Father Henri said. "At first, the plan was merely the large dome, but we kept getting funded by wealthy patrons who wished to see the majesty of this Basilica restored. This site has existed in some form or another ever since the 4th century. It made it a natural place for me to retire to my life of study and purpose. I love old things." He gave me a conspiratorial wink. "As one ages one gains an appreciation for older things. Perhaps it is merely a desire to stand the ravages of time with similar grace."

He motioned to the confessionals against the far wall.

"Do you still wish to give a confession?" he asked, opening the door for me.

He struck me a man with more learning than most, and quite a bit of sense. I hoped I was not wrong. "I do. Bless me father, for I have sinned. It has been three weeks since my last confession." It was the traditional beginning.

"Goodness." Father Henri laughed from the other side of the confessional. "You must be a wicked creature to come up with sin in such short order."

Though he was joking, I burst into tears. How to explain myself? In truth, I hardly recognized myself now. It was only weeks ago that I was ready to barter myself to the man who had essentially become the highest bidder, to provide for my family. I had been so short-sighted to think I could operate within society and be happy. Now I was not sure where I fit, the only thing I was sure of was that I wanted Nate to be a part of it.

I heard the other side of the confessional open. Father Henri joined me on my side and sat beside me in companionable silence. He patted my shoulder in his comforting, grandfatherly manner until I could continue.

"I'm not sure where to begin." I wiped my nose on my sleeve. I knew it was horribly uncouth, but I lacked a handkerchief, and did not wish to look at him so ill-composed.

"Begin where your heart demands." He patted my hands, heedless of the mess. "That is where the pains that weigh the heaviest lie, and that will be most eased by speaking."

I nodded. Nate and I had told him of our adventure starting at the point of being on the run in the street from Mr. Cooper's Red Hood Society. I assumed he started there to protect any reputation I had left, which I imagined was already quite tarnished from showing up, as I did, in the company of the roguish Mr. Nathaniel Valentine.

I told him of Byron, and how, in my rage, I broke my engagement, stripping my family of position and financial stability for my parents' advanced age. I told him of how I had seen Nate naked several times, and how I had been developing lustful feelings for him, clothed or no. Why I refer to him as Nate, instead of Mr. Valentine. We had told him, together, of how Nate was now able to transfigure into that demon monster, but I confessed that after the initial shock wore off, I wasn't afraid of him, though any respectable person would be. I told Father Henri about the run from the Red Hoods and how my parents must feel dishonored, as I have made no move to contact them and assure them of my well-being. Instead, they must be beset with worry and scandal.

I took a shaking breath. Then I told him of the mirror lake and the creature wearing my skin that came out of the waters to claim me. I told him of my mother's gift with the cards, and that I didn't possess it, but this strange force had enveloped me and tried to drown me in the mirror.

Father Henri didn't say much other than to ask the occasional question to clarify. Finally, he nodded. "The mirror lake is a ley well. A place where magical energy collects when ley lines in the earth are disturbed." He offered me his hand and helped me rise, then led me out to walk in the garden. I followed him, feeling very confused.

"The confessional is for sinners my dear. You are not one," he said by way of explanation. "This world is changing, and changing quickly. You broke an engagement of marriage to a man who treated you poorly, without love or even basic respect. You were right to terminate your relationship with him. You are fortunate that you discovered this now rather than later, when divorce is a sin. I believe you and Mr. Valentine are bound together by something stronger than merely acquaintanceship. I have known him for quite some time, both as a boy and now as a man. Both he and his brother are quite secretive of themselves, and do not offer their true self to just anyone. Nathaniel is particularly restless. That he has found comfort with you says quite a bit about you, Miss Harper."

He stopped to sit on a peaceful bench. The garden was in full bloom.

"Your parents will worry about you, but they believe in you. They allow you your own mind, I am sure because they trust you. They raised a strong daughter, and they know it. Now, as to the ley well's magic and how it affected you both: ley-magic is from the earth, not merely the aid of some demon or devil. The magic contained in you can be viewed as a magic to be feared and purged, or as a blessing from God. Jesus was able to walk upon water, heal the sick, and transform water to wine. He was able to feed the masses with what little he had, making it multiply in a prosperous miracle. We accept these as blessings now, and not as impure magic."

He stretched and plucked a bit of mint from the garden. "We can accept and use what we are given, or we can turn it away. Peppermint: I believe it a gift from God to help settle my stomach, rather than a temptation from the devil." He munched down the plant. "I would like to believe that if you were not conflicted at all, then it would be more likely that your gifts were from a darker power. The devil likes to make things easy until he exacts his toll. You say Nathaniel was quite fatigued after he transfigured back to a man from the beast?"

"Yes, exhausted and nearly starved," I said earnestly. "He slept for nearly a full day and night, waking only to take food and water. He could barely move when I was treating his wounds, though I could tell it hurt him."

"God makes us understand the balance by asking us to work for what we want though hard work or prayer or suffering. Nathaniel was blessed with the power to battle a demon. He paid for it dearly. That sounds like a gift from God, not a boon from the devil. That is why you don't fear him."

I could smell peppermint faintly on his breath.

"Now," he continued. "You came to me for confession. Confession is only accepted as saving you from your sins if you are truly repentant, and I can see you are repentant for the pain you have caused others. Confession is also only accepted if you complete appropriate penance. Are you ready for the penance I am assigning you?"

I nodded, sure I would be on my knees in prayer all the way back to London.

"Live, Miss Harper."

"Pardon?" I was sure I hadn't heard him correctly.

"Live. Live the life you are meant to live in a world that isn't changing quickly enough to provide for those with true vision. Live in a world where your worth is measured by what you wear and the social position and wealth of your spouse. Live in this world, and live being true to your heart in a world where people still believe women to be inferior. Live as a forward woman in a backwards world. Do not merely survive this world, Vivian, live in it."

His answer was both too simple and too complex. "I was hoping for a thousand 'Hail Marys,'" I said.

"I know." He patted my hand, and then reached out to me so I could help him stand. "That would be too easy. Rest assured that God loves you and holds you in his heart. Now, live according to yours." He gave me a sympathetic nod. "Ahh, here comes Nathaniel now."

He was right. Nate came towards us, his long coat trailing out behind him. Father Henri took my arm so I was suddenly supporting him. He gave me a little wink.

"I found all the books on your list, except for one," Nate puffed.

"Such a good boy," Father Henri said with a smile. "Was the book you couldn't find *Fantastical Tales of the Magical Kingdoms*?"

"Yes, that's the one," Nate said, "Did you loan it out?"

"No, it doesn't exist, though I do plan on writing it soon," Father Henri said. "I wished to have a little time alone with Miss Harper, and you are quite the industrious lad when the mood takes you."

Nate shut his mouth with a snap.

"Go on now, Nathaniel, I will finish my walk with this good lady. You can inform the brothers that you and she will be staying with us for supper, and to prepare you both chambers for the night. We need to discuss this druidic temple and how to handle it. This I will not do on an empty stomach."

The brothers of the monastery provided a wonderful dinner of a rich, creamy seafood chowder and biscuits. It was simple peasant fare, but more comforting than the most impressive eight course dinner. I ate until I was stuffed, then sat back, sipping a glass of sweet white wine. The monks had provided enough of the vintage to get quite drunk if I so chose.

I listened to Nate and Father Henri jabber away in French while I sat, sleepy and comfortable in the light from the small fire in the hall. They pored over ancient texts and made a list of notes.

"I do believe we have lost her, Nathaniel," I distantly heard Father Poullain say.

Nate gently took my hand and dutifully escorted me to the room the monks had set aside for me down the south wing.

"Until tomorrow, Vivian," he said softly.

I turned so I was facing him. My head swam with excellent French wine.

"You have the most beautiful eyes, Nate," I heard myself say.

He flushed. He actually flushed bright red. I couldn't help but laugh. "No one has told you that before?"

He ignored that and tried to gently guide me through the door. I planted my feet and squared my shoulders, like he had taught me.

We were almost equal in height. I smelled him, a warm earthy scent mixed with the stew from dinner and fresh bread, old musty books from Father Henri's quarters, and warm polished wood from the tables in the quiet, cramped dining hall, and something else uniquely him. I felt the sturdy serge of his vest under my fingertips, and his soft dark hair, ends curling at his collar.

Then I was kissing him— and he was kissing me back. I tasted the cognac he sipped after dinner—stronger than wine, it sent my senses reeling and I was sinking into an intoxicating haze. He had one hand on my back pressing me close and his other on my waist, pushing me away. While I was relaxing into his kiss I could feel him tensing. After a moment he pulled away.

"Mr. Valentine, you surprise me. For all the times you kissed me, now you don't wish for me to kiss you?" I gave him my best coy look.

If he bit his lip any harder he would have cut straight through it. "You have consumed far too much wine, Miss Harper." He disentangled my arms from him and tried to help me through the door.

I resisted, so he picked me up and carried me through the narrow doorway and set me down on the bed with an undignified thump. "You think I'm drunk, do you?" I snapped. "Did it ever occur to you that I wanted to kiss you?"

"Miss Harper, you have no idea the restraint I am exercising at the moment. We can discuss this in the morning. For now, I am thinking only of your reputation!" He closed the door with more force than was necessary.

My blood was too hot in my veins. It was thrumming through my veins, racing through me like horses tearing across an open field. Why wouldn't he kiss me? In the ley well, the me covered with tarot markings had the major arcana covering her, I mean my, torso. Above my heart, the Lovers held hands and gazed adoringly upon their future together. If I were a new, enlightened, free woman I should just be able to take him as my lover and damn the consequences.

Father Henri said my penance was to live my life in a world that was changing too slowly for a strong, enlightened woman. But I was learning to be strong. What I was not willing to do was to face this life without Nate knowing I wanted him by my side.

I lay in my bed the next morning, crippled by a horrific headache. It served me right for drinking so much. I wish I could have had Jenny fetch me a tray of coffee and sweet biscuits and maybe even an egg, but no bacon—just the thought of greasy, fatty bacon made my stomach flip. I wish I could have had my mother make up a tonic for my head. I rolled and found the edge of a narrow bed beneath my cheek.

The light from a small window illuminated a beautiful cross hanging on the wall. I was in the dormitories of the Basilica of Notre-Dame de Boulogne.

I combed out my hair with my fingers and splashed water over my face from an ewer and basin made of simple ceramic. Every bit of light was agony, and I dreaded rejoining Nathaniel and Father Henri. I straightened my clothing and ventured out to see what damage I had done to my friendship with Nathaniel.

Father Henri was sitting in the same hall from the night before, pouring over tomes and carefully eating a soft-boiled egg with toast points over a napkin. I was glad to see Nate was not with him, but I would need to talk to him again soon.

"Good morning, my dear," He greeted me without looking up. He stared at the book in the poor light through his thick rimmed glasses.

"Good morning, Father," I said.

"If you'll forgive me for saying so, you surely have that poor boy quite perplexed." He looked up from his notes.

"Pardon?"

One of the brothers brought me a simple, wooden plate with bread and eggs and thinly sliced pears with a light sweet sauce.

"Nathaniel doesn't know what to do with you, my dear."

I looked away, but he laughed merrily. "It's actually quite gratifying to see. Both he and his brother are quite well assured of themselves. It is wonderful to see him disarmed so thoroughly. I'm not sure the Lord would be pleased by my mirth, but it does my heart well to see it."

"Disarmed?" I blinked at my plate, feeling quite stupid. A brother returned with a pint of dark beer, which I gratefully accepted.

He closed his book and gave me a long look. "Well then, this settles it," he tapped his notes. "I shall accompany you back to London to see this ley well for myself."

"You are?" It was the first good thing I had heard since he had absolved me of my sins by ordering me to live. Of course, I did try that last night—apparently kissing Nate was part of the plan for living my life as a forward woman in a backwards world. "Did you two decide this?"

"No, I decided this. I shall have at least one more adventure, maybe more. I am not too old yet." Father Henri pulled off his reading glasses and polished them on his robe. "From what Nathaniel tells me, the druidic site he was exploring used to be held in check by an underground river. I am given to understand these are quite common in England."

I nodded.

"The water washing over the site kept the ley line, that is a magic line in the earth, sealed. When the water was diverted..." He paused searching for the right word.

"The seal cracked," I finished for him.

"The ley line will spill magic into the earth, eventually creating a ley well, if you will, where the magic will gather."

"Then London could become the home to creatures like the Lamia?" I shuddered at the thought.

"Well, creatures of a magical and otherworldly nature are attracted to ley wells. That sounds quite fascinating," he said.

"And terrifying." I said. "We have to seal it before it attracts something awful."

"Quite right, I fear that without intervention, unnatural things may start to occur. The damage done could be, well, pardon the term my dear, Biblical." He snickered at his own joke.

I smiled back politely, but inside I felt as though I had swallowed a nest of snakes. When I left London, Sterling's Emporium and factory were using water diverted from an underground river to power his machines and create power. Men ended up burned in rivers and drowned on dry land. Things that shouldn't happen had, in fact, happened. Men and dogs had been fused into one form dependent on the sun or moon. Unnatural things indeed.

"Nathaniel informs me that you come from a respected family of apothecaries. In that vein, I assume that our gardens might be of some use in preparing remedies. I do fear that we may have need of a skilled apothecary before we are done."

"I will do my best, Father," I said, making a list in my head of supplies I wished for. Pain medication was at the top of the list.

"Brother Andre has had some training as well. I am sure he would share some of his recipes and simples with you."

"Thank you." I finished the last of my beer and snagged a piece of toast to stuff in my mouth in an unladylike fashion.

"Nathaniel is packing me some items for our journey. He has informed me that the airship is leaving on the morrow and we need to be there as the captain will not wait. Is it true? Does the ship float, placing us closer to God?"

I smiled. "I remember having quite the similar feeling when caught in the net like an eel and hauled up to the ship. Yes, the ship floats on air as if it were the ocean. Closer to God, you must judge for yourself."

He nodded and turned back to his book. His hand tightened on the rosary at his neck.

Brother Andre was a round and joyful fellow. He reminded me of Friar Tuck from the Robin Hood stories. He scuttled through the gardens, sniffling and snuffling like a large hedgehog. He dug out little weeds here and there, setting worms aside so they wouldn't be cut in half by his trowel. At his side he had a basket he was filling. I spied rosemary, fennel, garlic, and dill. He paused when he heard my footfalls. "Good morning, Miss Vivian."

"How did you know it was me?"

Brother Andre sat back on his heels and wiped his forehead on his sleeve. "There are only two people wearing riding boots at the monastery today. Mr. Valentine has a heavier step. You are the only lady here."

"Father Henri said you would be willing to share some of your simples and herbs with me."

"Ah, yes. First, I prepared this for you." He handed me a mug covered with a cloth. "Willow bark tea with turmeric and honey, helps after too much wine."

I should have felt annoyed that he seemed to know my business, but it was kindly meant. I sipped it down and knelt by his side in collegial respect as we picked herbs and talked about their uses.

It was past noon when one of the brothers came up to us with a basket of rolls baked with nuts on top, and a soft cheese tart. We happily took the basket inside to a little warm room where Brother Andre and I spent the afternoon preparing salves and balms and tinctures for the monastery. He graciously let me pick from some of his preparations to take with us on the journey back to London. It was a pleasant distraction, and for a little while I didn't have to think of Nate. Though on occasion I still did.

The little warm storeroom was crammed with bottles and jars of wonderful ointments and salves and medicines. Dried herbs filled the air with an earthy, spicy, sweet aroma like the store that was the drawing room of the house I grew up in, like the storeroom off the basement and the workroom in the attic. It was the scent of my mother's dresses and my father's sleeves.

I wanted to be home more than anything else in the world. Nate and Father Henri would be able to seal this ley well without my help— truthfully, I hadn't been much help as of yet. It was Nate that found the ley well on Molten Cay. It was Nate that killed the Lamia. Lady Rothechild and her sister, Sarah, were safe, though I wasn't sure that was my doing. Anyone would have had the sense to move to high ground, out of reach of the dead men.

I carefully packed the bottles and vials into a small wooden box after wrapping them in scraps of cloth. He also gifted me with a huge quantity of clean sterile bandages. Clearly, he had read the most recent work on germ theory as well. The most precious gift was a vial of carbonic acid to be used as a disinfectant. I happily traded him some of my family's most successful remedies for fever, treating infected wounds, and for a stomach tonic.

Nate knocked on the door frame. My heart leapt in my chest and I felt a smile hit me with such a rush it stole my breath. So, I hadn't ruined things entirely last night. But he wasn't smiling. In fact, his face was as blank as slate. He was not happy to see me.

"Father Henri is ready to take the carriage back to the ship," Nate said hesitantly.

"I think when we reach London, I am headed home," I said.

"Oh."

'Oh' was all he had to say. I swallowed hard, my voice feeling suddenly strangled. "You don't really need me, anyway."

Nate looked like he was going to say something. I stared at him, begging him to say something else, anything else. He stared at me.

One of us had to break the tension. "Would you have kissed Edith?" I hadn't meant to open with that, but it just slipped out when I opened my mouth.

"What?" He blinked hard.

"Answer the question, please." If I was going to start down this line of questioning I may as well see it to the end.

"No."

"'No' you wouldn't have kissed her or 'no' you won't answer the question?" Why couldn't he just give me a straight answer?

"Exactly."

"Is it because I'm not a liberated woman, sailing the skies and shooting guns and hunting down lightning and krakens and monsters?" I demanded.

"You're insane!" he snapped, heading out into the gardens.

"Just tell me. Last night, would you have stayed if I were Edith?" I leapt in his path and drew myself to my full height. It worked earlier with Captain Morgan.

"I don't know, maybe." Nate moved to get around me.

I stepped in his path again, hands on my hips. "Maybe? Maybe!?" How could he say that to me?

"Of course not, Vivian. Let this go." He stepped around me.

"You would have kissed Edith but not me?!" I almost screamed.

"Okay fine, yes—happy now?" He was louder too. Father Henri was sitting on a bench in the garden pointedly reading his bible and not looking at us. He would have been more convincing if he had been wearing his glasses.

"Absolutely not! Why would you have kissed her but not me?" I demanded.

"Because I don't care about her!" Nate snapped.

"What?" I said softly.

"I care about you. You were drunk. When I kiss you, I want to be sure you know who is kissing you. And every time I do, I don't want to stop." He traced my shoulder softly in a distracted manner.

I fell silent, chewing my lip. It was the answer I was hoping for, but not the one I expected. All my boldness, all my willingness to fight with him, melted away. He reached out and took my chin in his hand and lifted my lips to his.

"I don't want you to stop." I was ridiculously shy again.

"You shouldn't let me do this," he whispered.

"Why ever not?"

"Your reputation."

"Damn my reputation! That's for securing a suitor. Clearly, I don't have any better options here." I went to kiss him but he pulled back.

"Better options?" he repeated dully.

"That's not what I meant," I said quickly. "I meant that no one is going to be beating down my door since I broke my engagement to Byron."

"So, you'd best settle for whatever you can get?" The little muscle in his jaw twitched. He dropped his hand back to his side. "Well then, I best get you home so you can be available for other suitors to come to call."

Damn all men! They are so moody! I didn't mean I wanted to settle for him. I adore him. I hate him. Nate frustrated me in ways I hadn't been aware existed. That idiotic man melted my heart to warm pudding. The little spot he had so gently stroked a moment ago was on fire, but the heat was burning away too quickly leaving me chilled. I wanted it back. In fact, I have never wanted anything more. He makes me miserable. Oh my god, I do believe I'm in love.

Stamping my feet on the stone in the Basilica was ineffectual, but made a satisfying sound in riding boots, much more satisfying than the slippers a lady wore, anyway. Girls pouted; it was what Lady Thornburry would be doing. It felt silly and childish now. Besides, if I put up any more fuss I might upset morning prayers, so I abandoned the effort. With as much dignity as I could scrape together, I grabbed the medicine chest to take it to the hall. We would have to return to the ship today.

Father Henri was waiting patiently for us in the dining hall with a chest of books, a carpet bag, and a leather satchel. I added the wooden box of medicines to our little pile of luggage. There would be a donkey cart to take us to the ship and then the ship would take us to London. He and Nate would close the Ley well and I would return to my old life, or whatever I could salvage of my old life knowing that I once had something more. I would not be the same woman who left London, and I would go on. The jewelry from the Lamia's lair would secure my family's future for a time. All I ever wanted, since I was a little girl, was to be a good girl and care for my parents as they cared for me. But now that I had all that I had ever wanted, I would trade it for the one person with whom I had been free to be myself.

My voice sounded halting and stiff. "Father Henri, thank you kindly for your hospitality."

"Are you ready, Father?" Nate seemed focused entirely on the task at hand of getting the items to the small coach. *The Lightning Aura* was waiting at the lighthouse. I was ready to return to my home and away from damnable, dark-haired men with amber- sherry eyes.

"You are quiet, my dear," Father Henri said as we pulled away from the monastery.

"I am homesick, Father," I said simply.

"Ahh, that is always the way of it. We long for simpler times when our lives suddenly become complicated." He gave me a knowing wink.

Nate snorted rudely, staring out the window.

We loaded Father Henri's luggage into the bottom of the basket, along with my jars of medicines and potions, and climbed inside. I was amazed at how well Nate could avoid me in such a cramped space. He turned a crank attached to a wheel and pulley. Slowly but surely, the basket began to rise the fifty or so meters to the waiting airship.

Looking up, I saw someone peering down with a spyglass. I waved.

The winch used to haul the lightning traps was now used to haul us over the edge and onto the deck of the ship. So long as I didn't look over the side, I was fine gently swaying in the basket. I watched Nate's biceps and forearms work through his thin shirt. I had to remember I was cross with him.

When we were safely on board, I went to my little cabin and sat down, burying my face in a nearby pillow. I would have loved to watch the crew prepare for the journey, but I now just wished it was over. I longed for the safety of my parent's house on Exeter Street. My life had been quite wonderful and fulfilling until it was invaded by a man who stared moodily at dogs and made me accompany him to strange lands full of magic and terror. Damn him! I ripped the pillow off my bed and hurled it at the wall.

Almost immediately there was a knock. I waited, but it was followed by silence. Not Fannie then, probably not her daughters either. It must be Father Henri. I rose and crossed the cabin in four steps, opening the door. It was Nate.

"Yes, Mr. Valentine?"

He made a little face at that. Hurt perhaps, annoyance? I bit my lip and decided not to care.

"This is yours." He held the small wooden box from the monastery.

"Ah, yes, thank you. See that you don't give me occasion to be using it." I motioned for him to place it on the bed. He did.

"Vivian..." he started, then seemed to think better of it. He turned and hurried out.

I slammed the door behind him. It was easier to be angry than to be hurt. He should have at least been hurt that I was trying to be indifferent. I went to the little cage of mechanical birds and wound them. The sweet music felt mournful.

Within the hour I knew Captain Morgan was back on board. The whole energy changed from dogged earnest work to a frantic buzz of activity. By the demeanor of the crew, his quest to sell his electro-ion batteries was successful. The crew would be quite wealthy from this particular voyage. I switched the birds off and left my cabin to witness what was very likely my last view of France. I had no desire for Nate to see me moping about the ship.

Molly was happy to provide me with distraction, we played backgammon late into the afternoon.

"Ahh, Miss Harper," Captain Morgan said. "Our good luck charm!"

I gave him a small curtsy.

"Father Henri was begging our help. He is quite amazed by my ship, you see."

"Naturally," I said.

"He wishes to know exactly how much weight it can hold."

"A grand amount I imagine," I said laughing. He was baiting me like a trout and I found myself caught by his enthusiasm.

"Father Henri says they have been unsuccessful in setting the key stones for the rotunda of their great Basilica. They managed to set them in place, but in the night, they fail and do not hold. The force pressing on them before they set is much too great and they end up falling loose, sending the stone of this holy site crashing to the floor." Captain Morgan said.

"Unthinkable," I said smiling, sure his theatrical nature would eventually let him tell me we were offering the ship to help set their stone.

"Yes, the workers are losing faith, they are building the mighty church for the glory of God and yet it seems that God is testing their resolve."

"Such hopeless men, if only a brave, strong captain of a marvelous ship could step in and help them." I clapped my hands and feigned a swoon.

Captain Morgan gave me a gentle pat. "Exactly my thinking."

"Do you know of one?" I teased. The crew watching our theatrics exploded in laughter. Captain Morgan feigned a look of hurt.

"Oh lass, you wound me so." He clutched his heart.

"Never fear, Captain, I do believe you, the God-fearing soul of generosity that you are, can aid them in their time of need," I said.

"Quite true lass, quite true," Captain Morgan assured me. "And it's a clear afternoon, we should be able to see the shadows of Paris on the horizon."

"Paris?" Never in my wildest fantasies had I imagined I would see Paris.

"Aye," Fannie said, stretching out her arm towards Paris. "If only we had more time before we had to head home, I would love to see Paris again."

"You'll have to tell me all about it," I said hopefully. If I would never set foot in the city, then hearing about it from someone who had actually been there would be the next best thing. "We shall have the entire journey back to London."

She gave me a look. "I would assume you would be spending time with Valentine."

"You assume wrong." I tried to sound nonchalant.

"Oh, Vivian." She took my hand and tucked in firmly in the crook of her elbow. "Men are such brutes. They have no idea what is good for them. Now, don't you worry, if he is being a bully I will see to it that my husband gives him a great wallop in the head to make him heed his heart."

I smiled at the thought of Captain Morgan smacking Nate like an unruly child, but then thought better of it. No, it was hardly his fault. I made it clear to everyone that Nathaniel Valentine was his own man. Well, everyone but myself. A part of me wished he would remain with me. I know it was irrational but if I could turn myself into a dog, I think I would bite Nate right now.

The Airship cast a large, deep shadow across the French countryside as we flew overhead. More than anything, I was struck by the beauty of it all. My family had taken a holiday into the country a few summers ago, though still in London we were on the very edge, far from the gray stone and suffocating smoke. Up until now, the carriage ride out of the city proper was the most beautiful thing I had ever seen.

Now, far below, black and white cows grazed in the fields and vines of beautiful lush purple grapes sat in neat rows, looked after by crofters in their fields. I had never seen something so peaceful and so inviting. Maybe I could open an apothecary shop in the country.

Calvin always showed interest in courting me. In truth he wasn't an awful prospect. He's kind hearted, he was quite well-trained in the business, had boyish charm, and was utterly, well, utterly boring. No, he would never do. My family would live on the Lamia's jewels. Then we would make do with something else.

Nate was sitting with the other crewmen passing around a stone bottle of beer and laughing. He caught me looking and the smile on his face faded. The rotunda was just ahead. I shaded my eyes with my hand and peered off to the east. Sure enough, I could see the dark shadows cast by the huge city in the distance.

CHAPTER TWENTY-TWO

WE TIED TO the rotunda and Captain Morgan ordered for the sails to be lowered and the propellers to be at full stop. Matt Hines and Eli Church lowered rope ladders to the scaffolding and scrambled down them like little spiders descending their silk lines. Out of the corner of my eye, Edith was clapping her hands and cheering at the skills of her athletic paramour to Gracie, who rolled her eyes.

It was no use for me to watch the men deep in discussion as to how the airship could assist them in their most holy work, since that would involve staring at them easily thirty meters below me; a less daunting distance than the ground but, my fluttering stomach reminded me, no less deadly of a fall.

Nate and Mr. McCabe were working with one of the thick steel cables, checking it for damage and winding it upon a huge spool and spoked wheel the men could use to wind the cable. I had been informed that morning it was called a capstan. Apparently, my creative explanations of ship parts while I was trying to get my ideas across left something to be desired. Molly had spent the better part of the last two hours teaching me the name of items on the ship.

The crew set a large stone into the spare metal mesh netting that held the balloon to the ship and hauled it high above the ground with the capstan and metal cable. The ship quivered slightly with the effort. The workers below carefully aligned the stones in place for the keystone to hold them in place.

They labored hard into the morning, shouting commands back and forth. Finally, the moment of truth came and they set the keystone to drop into place and slide the remaining tiles in to make the dome. With a loud chink the heavy stone fell into place. The workers cheered and several of them leapt on top of the dome of the rotunda and danced in their joy. Father Henri closed his eyes in prayer.

Above them, the clouds that had been steadfastly watching for the past hour suddenly sprouted several dark spots. Birds. But they didn't quite move like birds. Large and ungainly, they had more mass than birds. Maybe they were men on gliding wings; that could fit that shape and size.

"Captain!" I shouted and waved my arms to get his attention. Finally, he and the other men ceased their revelry and looked to where I was pointing.

"*Gargoyles! My God!*" one of the workers cried in French.

"Gargoyles!" Mr. Church echoed them in English.

The crews, airship crew and construction crew alike, leapt to action. The men readied themselves to do battle. I turned, trying to catch up as the mood exploded around me, changing from jubilant celebration as a monument to God was finally completed, to a battle to demons loomed. It was as though someone had disturbed a great, bloody ant nest. Men shouted, weapons were drawn, and bloated gray bodies on bat wings came creaking and swooping out of the sky.

I had seen stone gargoyles on buildings back in London, these were similar, but there was a grotesquery to them that the motionless, inanimate sculptures could not match. These creatures, with their knobby heads, spiny horns, and sharp teeth were the stuff of nightmares. As they drew closer, I expected them to have red eyes and to have drooling mouths, but their eyes were full of hate. They were bent on one thing: murder. There was no other conclusion that could be drawn by the way the men prepared themselves for battle.

Here I nearly thought they were angels, descending upon the rotunda to bless it now that the *Basilica of Notre-Dame de Boulogne*'s great dome was finally complete.

Mr. Hines grabbed the end of the rope ladder and started hauling himself up to the ship. Mr. Church was only a step behind. One of the gargoyles grabbed a worker and threw him off the top of the rotunda. He hit the ground with a sickening *crunch*.

"My God!" Father Henri breathed. "I am not a warrior, I believe I am better suited for prayer. I am going below."

"Good idea Father," Nate said, grabbing a harpoon gun. He cranked it back, ratcheting the clockwork mechanism on the top. He raised the weapon and followed his target, a gargoyle that was swooping down to take another of the workers.

"They've come to ruin God's work!" Captain Morgan's voice cut through the growing chaos between the sailors. "Give'em hell, boys!"

Nate leveled his harpoon and squinted in the bright sunlight. His shot took the gargoyle in the abdomen, shattering it and sending chunks of stone raining down on the rotunda and the grass. Far below, brothers and visitors to the church ran for cover.

Edith was calling for Matt to hurry his climb. The gargoyles' wings caused the rope ladders twist and turn, heaving in the air.

"Arm yourself, Miss, or get below!" Mr. McCabe warned over his shoulder. He picked up a large maul the men had been using to set belaying pins into the capstan.

I bolted for my cabin. My Seax was lying in the small box-topped table. I wasn't sure what a knife would do against stone, but it was all I had. I grabbed it from the sheath and headed back out to the deck. I wasn't sure what use I would be in the fight, I was much better after the fight when men needed to be patched up and wounds needed tending, but Nate would not run from the fight and they would need everyone on their side they could have.

The deck rumbled as a gargoyle landed between me and the door I had just come through. Its gray, stone face was spotted with pale green lichen, and dark moss covered its shoulders.

It snarled at me, gnashing sharp stone fangs. It was growling something, though I had no idea what it was saying. I swung the Seax at it in the chopping motion Nate had shown me. The blade struck the creature between the wing and shoulder, sending up sparks and sticking fast in the crack that formed the joint. The gargoyle whipped to one side, taking me and my firm grip on the handle with it. I stumbled and was thrown down and slid across the deck as the airship lurched.

A gargoyle was tearing at the balloon with his sharp claws, aiming to pop the balloon and send us crashing to the ground below. The gargoyle before me tore the Seax out of his body and slashed at me. I threw my arm up before my face. The claws tore into me.

I gagged at the pain. It made the world spin alarmingly; though in fairness, I wasn't sure if that was the ship being battered or the wound I had just sustained. I held my injured arm to my chest and ran, trying to get away from my stone assailant.

"Vivian!" It was Nate, in the bow of the ship. I saw his face contort. He dropped the harpoon gun and ripped off his vest. I lost sight of him for a moment as he moved beyond stacks of barrels and brass deck-mounted guns.

A grunt turned into a growl of rage as Nate, now wearing the skin of that canine beast, dashed across the deck, dodging people and equipment, completely focused on his prey.

I heard the massive brass steam guns firing, sending the silver purple orbs at their attackers. A thought dawned on me. Gargoyles are creatures without slaver, I doubted they had breath, why would opium and aether knock them out?

Then a hulking, brown blur sprinted through my vision and leapt onto a gargoyle, knocking it to the rail. The gargoyle hissed in irritation, spread stone wings and leapt into the sky. Nate, huge and in the form of that massive beast, now climbed up on the rails and watched, sides heaving, snarling his anger. The gargoyle glided around to the other side of the ship, taking a thermal draft to land on the balloon.

Gracie turned toward the terrifying beast that Nate had transfigured into. She must have believed him to be with the gargoyles. She readied her steam cannon, with one well-placed shot she could hit them both. She took careful aim as she did earlier at the lightning storm, her face screwed up in fierce determination.

I couldn't move quickly enough. I felt like I was running through a swamp. There would be no way to close the gap in time. She fired a capture canister. The sand sprayed, disorienting Nathaniel. The coiled-up ropes and net hit him in the chest and knocked him overboard.

"Nate!" I screamed, rushing across the deck. I threw myself at the rail, heedless for the first time of the reminder of how high we were in the air.

He was howling, snarling. The sounds coming out of him were nothing human. The rope went taut, swinging beneath the ship. Gracie and her amazing aim—my god, she had caught him.

I heard the rope rending and tearing. He was going to fall to the earth, thirty meters below. My breath caught in my throat. I grabbed for the rope. Then the rope went slack. I barely had time to gasp before the sound of splintering wood and shattering glass came from below. Nate came bounding up the stairs on three legs, using that front paw to help balance and gallop. He slammed into the gargoyle at the wheel that was ripping the helm apart.

Gracie grabbed a harpoon gun.

"Don't shoot him," I screamed. "Don't shoot him! It's Nate! For the love of God, please don't shoot him!" She gave me a strange look but recovered quickly. She took aim at a gargoyle and fired. The spring-loaded clockwork harpoon gun fired the bolt so hard and fast it shattered the gargoyle's head, spraying bits of granite across the deck.

Nate spared me a glance. Our eyes locked. Not the eyes of an animal or a demon, but the eyes of a man bent on defending his ship and the people he loved. Then the moment was over. It left me shaking.

Gracie sprinted to me with the harpoon gun in her hands. She stood over me, protecting me as I examined the wound on my arm.

There was blood all over the deck. Gargoyles didn't bleed, so it must be mine. I was oddly aware of it as my own blood. It was all I could even see. I slid my sleeve up. My forearm had been laid open to the bone. I saw the slick muscle and the thin layer of fat beneath the skin.

"Oh my," I said. My mind was racing to the bandages in my cabin. I needed one, maybe I needed several. Gracie pulled a kerchief out of the neck of her shirt and bound my arm tightly. It was only then that I felt intense pain.

Nate was climbing up the metal rigging with his massive arms and legs. He moved faster than I would have thought possible. He leapt onto the netting that held the balloon and crawled across it. He grabbed hold of the gargoyle—it was so focused on destroying the balloon he didn't see Nate coming. They wrestled for a moment, then Nate jerked the creature off his feet and the two of them went crashing to the deck below. The gargoyle hit the deck first, shattering into tiny shards. Nate lay there covered in dust and, for a moment, was stunned. Then he leapt to his feet and shook his head to clear it. He grabbed another gargoyle who was staring at his broken kin. The gargoyle tried to twist out of his grip. Nate bit down on the creature's wing and punched it in the back. With a crack, the wing broke off. Nate spit bits of stone and blood to the deck and hurled the one-winged gargoyle over the edge. It twirled like a tree seed in small circles towards the ground.

Around us, the battle was winding down. The crew had managed to kill several of the creatures, taking them apart with bullets. They themselves were covered in small wounds from the shattered bits of stone that exploded back at them.

Nate lowered himself back down to three legs, one arm tucked up against his body like a dog passively returning to his master, unsure of the reception he was likely to get. He had his head down, muzzle almost touching the floor. He crept up to me, stopping at my feet and the huge puddle of blood there.

He laid his head against my shin. I was suddenly aware that everyone else on the ship was staring. He was huffing and panting, giving a pitiful whine—begging forgiveness. He seemed to shudder and let loose a breathy groan that turned to a very human cry of pain. He seemed to shrink slightly, then the dense brown coat fell off him all at once, dense fur piling on the deck then evaporating into the air. He remained crouched in position for a moment before collapsing.

I wanted something to cover him, but not just because he was lying nude on the deck. I wanted to shelter him, to protect him just as he had protected me. I went to remove my coat to cover him, but them my hand brushed my gashed arm and the world went foggy white and I collapsed onto Nate on the deck.

I don't believe I was senseless for very long. When I opened my eyes, Fannie was supporting me and directing Mr. McCabe and Mr. Hines to carry Nate to her cabin. They had draped him in a bit of sail cloth. I saw all the blood beneath him and panicked. Someone said it wasn't his blood. Fannie helped me to my room. Edith, and her skill with a needle, waited for me. Fortunately, they had quite a quantity of good, French brandy on hand. I sipped the tumbler I was handed to help fortify my nerves.

"You should gulp that down," Edith advised as she washed her hands with the harsh lye soap I demanded she use before I would let her touch me.

"Someone has to treat the men," I said reasonably.

Fannie shrugged and passed the needle and thread through the brandy. I suppose she figured it was easier to do as I demanded than to argue with me. After all, if they refused, I had already threatened to sew my arm up myself. It was a hollow threat. I could barely see the wound, let alone stitch it with any neatness. I was familiar with all the work on germ theory and I had seen wounds turn septic. I had seen men die from them. I knew what had to happen. The wound had to be cleaned, then stitched, then carefully wrapped to prevent infection and speed healing. Knowing what was going to happen and actually living through it were entirely different issues. Thankfully, the blade had been quite sharp and had only chipped in two places when I struck the gargoyle. The edges of the wound lined up well. The first stitch wasn't too bad, but as the needle flashed in and out of my flesh I found myself quite nauseous and longing for the bottle of brandy just out of reach. Actually, at that point I would have been even happier to have a healthy dose of laudanum.

It suddenly dawned on me. I remembered the men in Limehouse square by the docks. "The aethium. Get aethium."

Edith rushed to bring it to me. Molly appeared with her sister a few moments later, holding a glass flask wrapped in leather. She splashed a few drops of the black liquid from the flask onto a cloth and motioned for me to hold it to my face.

"If you pass out, the cloth will fall away; if you need more, breathe deeper," she said with a gentle hand on my shoulder for support. My eyes drifted closed.

The aethium made the process much more bearable, though I felt horridly sick later. It also caused the most remarkable dreams...

SES

I was in London. Kensington to be exact, attending a wedding in a beautiful, and quite familiar, burgundy dress.

My mother came to me with her cards in hand. "It is time."

"Time?"

"It is time for you to wed. Your bridegroom is waiting," she explained quietly.

It was the wedding I was planning to Byron. Before I left London. Before I broke the engagement. I recognized the flowers I spent so much time choosing to decorate the hall.

On the chaise beside me sat a bundle of ferns, forget-me-nots, and red roses; ready for me to take in hand and walk down the aisle. "But I broke the engagement. I am not marrying Byron."

My mother had a sad smile on her face. She cut the deck revealing the card—the hanged man. "Vivian, love, you have to let go."

"I'm not marrying him!" *I said, stomping my foot encased in a dainty satin slipper.* "Mama, I am not."

She ignored me and tucked my hand into the crook of her elbow, dragging me down the aisle where a man stood waiting for me with a priest.

I couldn't see his head. The beautiful arch was decorated with ivy and flowers. It cast shadows over him and the priest at his side.

Her grip was iron. I tried to pull away but I couldn't. She dragged me towards Byron and my fate. The guests stood and started to whisper behind their hands. They realized something was wrong. I was making a scene. I was creating a scandal. I squared my shoulders and let her lead me.

The sun shifted, the priest was Father Henri. "Live, my dear."

I came closer to my bridegroom. It wasn't Byron, it was Nate. Nate in a fancy expensive suit wearing an Arbutus Blosseum flower in his button-hole lapel. "I trust this is a better bloom?"

"Vivian, do you take this man?" *Father Henri asked me.*

I nodded dumbly. Yes, I would take him. For the rest of his life and for the rest of mine.

"Forever?" *Nate asked me, a look of doubt on his face.*

He turned towards me and took my hands in his. They turned to long clawed paws, his expanding forearms splitting his suit. He was splitting his very skin. His skin tore like a stuffed sausage casing, and beneath his human skin was the skin and fur, muscle and bone of the monster he could become. His face rended along his jawline and temple revealed the elongating snout and long sharp teeth, his spine curved and lengthened, ripping his suit and his flesh as the beast emerged, not merely transfiguration but the beast was within him, coming out from inside him. It was a part of him now and forevermore.

It crouched before me, letting out a breathy whine. The transformation must hurt him. He raised his head to look at me—the eyes, the eyes were still the same. Intelligent and familiar, but in this form the kindness and humor were gone and replaced with a fierce love.

"Forever," I said. "In either form."

He seemed to melt back into a man, dark fur evaporating into the sunlight, his arms and legs twisted back into strong straight human limbs, well-muscled and appropriately formed. He stood there awaiting my answer in a fine dark suit. I leaned in to kiss him.

S§S

Molly was dabbing the wound with creosote and wrapping it with one of the clean dry bandages from my box. The rag, damp with aethium, lay on the floor. I had the queerest feeling in my stomach. Molly caught my look and passed me a basin, where I was promptly sick.

"Edith is a fair hand. You will scar, but it shouldn't be bad."

The scars across her face shined in the cracks of light seeping through the shuttered window. "Edith sewed your face up after your accident, didn't she?"

Molly nodded. "She and mother. Father wept."

"Is that why you don't ever leave the ship?" I asked softly.

"No." Molly caressed the wooden wall. "This is my home. The ship is where I belong."

I nodded, though I didn't fully understand her, I could respect her resolve. "He is in Mother's cabin," Molly whispered. "He is very sick. Whatever is in him burns him like a drug. He sweats, he shakes—he needs you, if you'll have him."

I rose shakily. She placed her hand on my good arm to stop me. "If you won't have him, leave him to suffer and mourn. Something so powerful is addictive, but without focus it will be the death of him. You give him focus, I saw him change, but it also consumes him."

She had the same look on her face she had when she was around the lightning. Yes, if anyone understood how power was intoxicating and addictive it would be her. It almost cost her life before, and there was a chance it would again. But she loved it. It was a part of her. Anyone who loved her needed to do more than know it, they needed to understand it and accept it.

To love that damnable man, I needed to understand him. I knew that would come with time. First, I would have to just accept him.

I kept vigil over Nate as he rested. The gentle rocking of the airship was lulling me to sleep so I let myself doze. When I awoke this time, Father Henri was standing over me. My arm ached so badly every move made me grit my teeth. He had his rosary in his hand watching us, carefully passing the beads between his fingers. I shifted on the chair and my accidentally banged on the frame of Nate's bed frame. It brought tears to my eyes. Father Henri handed me a tumbler of wine. "I thought I'd take a moment to check on you. Miss Morgan, Miss Grace Morgan, that is, said you were already looking in on Nathaniel."

"Do you still believe his transformation is a gift, Father, not a curse?" I asked, quietly staring at the man before me.

"I do," he said solemnly. "Were it not for him, many of us would be dead from those creatures, or from a sudden plunge into the sea."

He was right. The thought of falling out of the sky was a terrifying one indeed.

"Well, we can be reasonably sure that it wasn't God that interfered with the construction of the rotunda. I have been thinking of it, I truly believe the gargoyles were offended either that stone was being formed into the rotunda, or by where the stone was being sourced. When I return home, I shall have to look into the matter," Father Henri said with a small smile. "I shall also have to thank Captain Morgan and his crew for their kind assistance. We will be sure to remember his crew in our prayers. If any of the crew was killed, we shall be sure to say a prayer for their soul during mass for one year."

I smiled to myself. That was sure to appeal to a God-fearing man like Captain Morgan. "Be sure to tell him. He will be pleased."

He handed me a book, bound in green cloth, the lettering on the spine nearly faded away. "This is an old tome I had Nathaniel gather for me. It is from my studies when I was a much younger man. The ancient druids had a much different relationship with their animals. They believed in familiars. You see some animals were merely animals, but some animals were something more. They were sacred helpers of man. Guides, companions, protectors. You may find this illuminating considering Nathaniel's current condition."

I nodded and took the book. It had the smell all good libraries shared, the scent of paper and dust and time. "You are a man of God. Isn't this blasphemy?"

"Oh no, my dear. I serve God now because it is my way of serving the people." Father Henri took one more look at Nate, lying senseless on the bed. "I will take my leave, my dear. Take care of Nathaniel if you will."

I nodded and watched him let himself out. "I didn't mean exactly what I said before," I said to Nate when I was sure we were alone. "That is, I meant it, but not like I said it." I paused and set my hand on his arm. This was easier somehow, when he was half-asleep. "I wouldn't be settling for you. As far as reputation goes, I don't care. I don't want anyone else to court me. I don't care who it is, it could be the prince, I have no interest in anyone else."

I couldn't be sure, but I thought I saw his lips turn up in a ghost of a smile.

I vowed right then and there to never need his aid as the monster again. Whatever it did to him was much worse this time, it did not take much to assume that if it kept progressing like it did, the effect might just kill him.

If this was anything like last time, he would awaken ravenous. I went down to the galley to ask Mr. Pierce to make up a tray. If I was lucky, I might be able to get him to make up some of those meat pies Nate was so fond of.

Mr. Pierce did one better. He set me a tray with a meat pie, several pieces of fried potatoes, a fruit tart with strawberries, and a bowl of buttered beets. He passed me a bottle of ale and bade me return if he needed more.

I turned to take the tray, then paused. Captain Morgan seemed to hear about everything that was discussed on his ship, but Mr. Pierce seemed to know more than most about the Lamia. The Lamia was a demon for sure, but thanks to Nate's most recent transfiguration, some of the crew were starting to believe he might have turned into a demon himself.

We were far enough from the Cay that I hoped that my talking to Mr. Pierce would not convince Captain Morgan to turn back to search for the Lamia's lair.

"Mr. Pierce?"

"Hmmm?" He paused cleaning the pan.

"The necklace I traded to Captain Morgan, it was found in the Lamia's lair, but among piles of bones, like she had disposed of it." I was a horrible liar, I hoped he would assume it was the only treasure we had seen there. "Why wouldn't she keep it?"

"Demons never keep closed metal," Mr. Pierce said. "Everyone knows that. If they put on a closed circle they are enslaved and bound to the one who owned it." He set the pan in the rain barrel. "Of course, you have to trick them into putting the circle on themselves or manage to collar one. I'd imagine that would be no small feat."

I nodded, that made sense. Every piece of jewelry I had found in her charnel pit was a closed circle of some sort, rings and necklaces, but nothing else. The rest of the treasure that she kept nearby was all coins, gems, and other gilded items. A collared demon that had to answer to your whim would be an impressive tool indeed.

I thought of Nate in the hold below. I could imagine a collar snapped around his neck, forcing him to do the bidding of whomever held his leash. I loved him, and there was no going back to my old life, I knew that well. Something on the Cay changed the magic within him and it was not a demon. I was not sure if it was subject to the same laws of magic or not, but no one would chain him, no one would collar him. The battle, or maybe my dream, made me realize I had already given him my heart, all of it, freely. I hoped he returned my love, but by his own volition. No one would own Nathaniel Valentine, least of all me.

CHAPTER TWENTY-THREE

THE WHITE CLIFFS of Dover loomed ahead. I had always wanted to visit Dover with my family for holiday, but it was quite an expensive location for a holiday. The cliffs stood as bright and clean as a freshly washed saucer. The chalk from the cliffs was excellent to help settle acid, and sometimes small, hard, clear crystals were found in the chunks of chalk.

"Nate?"

He was up and walking on the deck today. He seemed to finally be fully restored from his adventure battling the gargoyles. He was better off than I, at any rate. My arm throbbed like an infected tooth all day and far into the night, I worried the wound was becoming septic despite my best efforts to keep it clean and well-cared for.

"Hmmm?"

"That's not gargoyles again, right?" I whispered. No need to alarm the crew unless we were sure; after all, the panic I caused over flying fish was still fresh and quite shamefully burned into my memory.

We had been sailing close to the water so Mr. Pierce could restock his stores of fresh fish. In my defense, the splashing and flying was too far over open water to be birds and it sent me almost into hysterics thinking the gargoyles had returned to finish us off and send us crashing into the ocean. It wouldn't have been a problem if Nate hadn't shattered a window and torn out the frame in his bid to gain access into the ship after being trapped in a hanging rope net during the first battle. At the time, Nate's quick thinking kept him from plunging to his death, we would sink like a stone should we go into the water now.

I ran, shrieking through the ship calling for help, rousing everyone from their hammocks and setting the sleeping ship to general chaos. They were none too pleased to find they had been so rudely awakened for mere fish.

Even Nate bounded out of bed, ready to become that massive protective beast should the need arise. Fannie immediately came to my defense—she argued that anyone recently harassed by stone gargoyles would have been a might concerned, and pointed out to the extremely armed, and annoyed crew, that my sharp eyes had averted disaster with the gargoyles initially.

The men remained on edge for the rest of the night. I helped Mr. Pierce to make the crew hot buttered rum, my mother's Christmas recipe, by way of apology. Molly handed me a book she had made of simple, but strange, sea creatures. Each page was skillfully illustrated by her careful hand.

Nate narrowed his eyes, staring out at the cliffs. I saw his knuckles whiten as he clenched the rail. Finally, he turned and brushed past me, mindful of my arm.

"Gracie!" he shouted. "Wyverns off the port!"

"Are they dangerous?" I rushed after him, my boots stamping on the deck.

"Not dangerous, per se, but they are destructive little creatures," Mr. McCabe said. He was loading a canister of aethium and charging the steam cannons.

Grace charged another steam cannon with silver-violet glass balls. Just the sight of them made me feel a bit ill again.

"What do you mean 'destructive'?" I demanded.

"They'll take things just to see how they work. These are little ones. They can tear ropes and cables and try to burst the bladders of the balloon," Mr. Church said.

"Mr. Church, do I hear a bit of admiration in your voice?" I couldn't believe that he sounded fond of yet another creature that seemed both capable, and willing, to send us falling into the sea to drown. My fear of heights, though I had managed to conquer much of it during the encounter with the gargoyles, still seemed quite reasonable

"I'm an engineer, I like to see how things go together." Eli Church loaded a harpoon into the clockwork gun and started turning the dials. They clicked as they wound to full tension. "So do they. I don't believe they're evil, just mischievous."

"The harpoon guns? The cannons?" I pressed.

Nate appeared at my side, taking up another harpoon gun to wind. "They discourage mischief."

"Oh joy." I muttered under my breath. How could they all be so calm over a creature capable of taking the ship down?

I thought the wyverns were some sort of dragon. They only seemed to have back legs, as their front legs were their wings— much like a bat, with wide bones supporting thin fleshy wings. Just a week ago this would have been very strange to me. I would have stared, open-mouthed, at this strange creature. Quite frankly, they were less impressive than the gargoyles, though their lack of murderous intent helped. They were even less impressive than the kraken. Though they caused more concern than flying fish, there was little urgency in preparing for an actual fight. This was more the way Londoners dealt with nuisance pigeons cooing at odd hours outside windows.

The wyverns glided over, occasionally flapping their wings to retain their altitude. They seemed to hover as they cocked reptilian heads, trying to take stock of this strange airship.

The cannons fired, launching glass spheres into the air that sailed by them or smashed into their bodies. One wyvern took three in the chest. They shattered, releasing a violet-silver cloud. The wyvern tumbled, wings over tail, down to the sea, and hit with a splash. The water seemed to revive it. After giving an indignant screech, it took back to the sky.

The remaining wyverns circled and received similar shots for their trouble. Some dove, making harder targets. But all their motion made it hard to get a good look at the airship. After a few more moments of this harassment they decided to return to the cliffs. The airship clearly wasn't worth their trouble.

I released a breath I wasn't aware I was holding. Father Henri had been doing the same. I heard him exhale loudly. He started muttering a prayer of thanks under his breath. I agreed. I planned to do the same, the moment I was safely home.

Home. The thought of it made me positively giddy. If my arm didn't ache so much I would be convinced I was dreaming, maybe I even dreamed the whole adventure. Then I felt Nate's hand on my back just at my belt. If this was a dream, I didn't wish to wake up.

"We'll be in London soon," he had set the gun down after removing the harpoon from the barrel. "You should pack."

"Will you come with me?" I asked, suddenly shy. I had reason to suspect he would. I also had reason to believe he wouldn't. Our adventure had been nothing if not mercurial.

"Yes," he said. "I risked my very life and limb to ensure Cooper didn't harm Miss Theresa. You said you'd let me explain and let me walk you home." He gave a small smile. "I don't think I need explaining to you anymore. Your parents are another matter."

I laughed. "What will Mama say?"

He shrugged. "Either way, hopefully they will let me explain. I'd hate for your reputation to be completely ruined because of me."

"I'm sure it is," I said, grinning. The smile disappeared from his face. I had managed to frustrate him again. I could have kicked myself.

I returned to my berth. Edith had left me the backpack. I had no skirts, but the bustle I made from my burgundy dress would at least cover my rear-end from gawkers. There was nothing I could do about the way my trousers clung to my legs. My mechanical birds, and my spare shirt, and the lightning stones went into the bag. The pouch of jewels from the Lamia's lair was always on my person lest I lose them. I added the Seax in its leather scabbard back to my belt. I divided the simples in the box from the monastery into three piles—the things I planned on taking to my family, the items Father Henri thought would be of use to seal the ley well with Nate, and the potions and salves I planned on leaving with Molly on board the ship to help her care for the crew. It was awkward and slow going, as I was forced to use my right hand only. Unfortunately, there wasn't enough to do. I kept thinking of Nate. Would I ever be able to talk with him without feeling like I offended him or feeling like a complete idiot—without him being near senseless, I mean.

Perhaps this is why men and women married but they spent much of their time in the company of their own gender. Women sewed and gossiped and took tea. Men smoked cigars, drank sherry and port, and discussed whatever it was that men discussed. Then there were women like me: artists, poets, authors, and liberated women. That was the way things were.

I just dearly hoped that being a liberated woman did not mean I would not keep the respect of the man I loved.

London. My beloved London. The rain had set in and from here we saw the wet soot stained streets below. Had it always been this dirty? Had it always been this gray? I was happy to be home. At least I thought I was. Somehow it was much different than I remembered.

Nate was at my side, mindful of my arm bound across my chest. He set his arm around me so when the ship rocked in the storm I didn't bang my elbow against the railing again. It was comforting to lean against his warm bulk. The crew had granted him quite a bit of space since he revealed his transfiguring condition. The crew prepared to tie to the clock tower. How fitting that this was where my adventure started and ended.

Mr. Church set the basket to the winch. Father Henri oversaw the gathering and packing of his luggage and his large box of books into the bottom of the basket, along with quite the selection of weapons Nate chose for the quest. He had a harpoon gun, two spare harpoons, a box of bullets, a huge bag that clanked and was topped with rope, along with his worn backpack. A quick handling revealed that if this is truly where we parted, then I got off light.

Molly looked down at London with disdain. She handed me her book of creatures and a small leather box of lightning stones. I protested to the generous gift. "I will write a new one," she said. "I will write to you. Use care with those—" She motioned to the box. "I don't know how in the world you were blessed enough to have one shatter at just the right time, but I am lucky the Lamia didn't eat you."

"So am I." We embraced. I was pleased to see that this time her embrace was less stiff and more welcoming. She turned and left.

"Tell your mam I was pleased to sail with her daughter," Mr. McCabe said. His voice cracked and he turned away, suddenly very busy with a belaying pin.

Mr. Church gave me a salute with his wrench. I didn't think I had seen it far from his hand during my entire stay on *The Aura*. I nodded back politely.

"I'm glad to know old Tom Plant is at rest, lass," Mr. Pierce said. He had tears in his gray eyes. "I packed you something special for the journey with Nate and Father Henri."

I hugged him and nodded. I didn't have the heart to tell him that I wasn't going with them.

I said the rest of my goodbyes to the crew until I was finally before Captain Morgan. "Did you want paperwork for Nate?" he asked gruffly.

"Because I bought his contract?" I asked.

"That's why," he said, I could see his eyes were wet. The big softy. I never expected to like the old man, let alone come to be so affectionate.

"No, I think I will be fine," I said. He extended his hand to take mine and kissed my knuckles. I stepped into him, wrapping my good arm around him. He gave me a fatherly hug.

"If we can be of service again, please send word," he said with a gruff smile.

"I most definitely will."

CHAPTER TWENTY-FOUR

NATE DESCENDED FIRST with Matt Hines. He sat with the luggage and sent Hines off to secure a coach and driver for hire. I watched them descend onto the city streets that looked up at the clock. I could hear the gears churn and click. I had never been able to hear it from the street below. It was like a heartbeat keeping the city plodding along, doing the same thing day in and day out while people's lives quietly passed them by. They were like ants or bees, working tirelessly towards their goal never wavering, never stopping, heedless of the larger picture, until they were dead. No, bees and ants were industrious. The people milled around unaware of the drudgery they were a part of.

Until recently I was a part of this. My goal was to secure a good match, to advance as high as I could to protect them, then to fall into my place as a wife and, God willing, a mother. Then arrange better matches for my children so they could, in turn, provide for me.

A madness gripped me. I had absolutely no desire to return to London! I wanted to sail away into the sun and beyond the sea with Nate and Captain Morgan and his crew. I wanted to wear boots and trousers and use a long knife. I wanted my own revolver. I wanted my own life, not the one planned out for me.

Nate was calling me. It was time to go. It was only through great effort that I was able to place one foot in front of the other and enter the basket that started my descent back into the life I had before.

"You're quiet," Father Henri said. "Does your arm pain you?"

"Yes," I answered honestly.

He leaned his thin frame against the basket and looked across the horizon. "I do see why this is God's domain. It is so beautiful up here..." He paused expectantly, so I nodded. "It's hard to leave it," he continued.

"That it is."

"Vivian, I was an officer in the French army when I was a young man. A wonderful profession for the third son of a wealthy lord. Then, in 1848, the battle they now call the February Revolution began and King Louis-Philippe was forced to abdicate and flee. I had to make a choice: I could fight for the monarchy I had known my entire life, or I could change."

"Or be killed," I added.

"Perhaps. If I still believed in the monarchy, perhaps it would be something I would be willing to die for. I found I was no longer happy being a part of such a corrupt and spiritually void system. I was unhappy, so I changed."

"It's not that easy," I said softly.

"Why not?" he asked, his eyes never leaving the sky.

I turned to look at him. He stared off at the sky, a look of pure joy on his face. He was unhappy and he changed.

Why not, indeed.

"It's amazing that I would live to see such a thing. An airship that takes me closer to the domain of God." He chuckled. "Technology, not faith, has brought me closer to the Almighty!"

We reached the ground shortly. The bump resulting from the basket hitting the cobblestones sent me stumbling, and I banged my arm on the edge of the basket. "Damn!"

A crowd had gathered to see the airship. Now they gasped at me, my dress, my language. I felt like the far-off Zulu that had been brought back from Africa to be presented to the Queen. I was a foreigner now.

Nate was immediately at my side, wrapping a strong arm around me. It was a good thing, for the pain made my knees weak. He carefully lifted me out of the basket. I felt his heart thrumming under his shirt, sounding quite like the ticking of the clock, but with a faster beat.

I must had scared him. I let him carry me out of the basket and to the waiting carriage. Mr. Hines got back into the basket to return to the ship. I could hear them talking, but didn't care what was said. Safely cradled to Nate, protected from the whispering, and where I could hear his beat of life; this was right where I belonged.

Now if the pain in my arm would just stop.

The carriage drove down the streets until I began to see familiar sites. We passed the square where Mr. Cooper had thrown a rope noose around Nate as Ranger and tried to strangle the life out of him. Sterling's Emporium stood well-lit with electric lights, with the factory behind it. We passed the alley where the Red Hood Society tried to lynch the poor girl, Theresa, until Nate intervened. We passed Hill Street where *Madame Theodora's Tea House* and *The Clockwork Quail* sat in the huge building in the middle of the street. If we took a left here we would pass Mr. Stanton's Shelter for Homeless and Injured Canines and the park across the street. Instead, the carriage rumbled along. I set my forehead against the glass in a very unladylike manner. I wondered if Nate was remembering these sites too. I turned to look at him and he was staring at me. I wasn't sure it was me he was seeing—he had the same queer look he had when staring at dogs, completely consumed in thought.

Father Henri sat across from us with his eyes closed. He also seemed to be consumed in thought, or maybe prayer. It was hard to tell with a priest.

Finally, we turned on to Exeter Street. I saw our sign from here. A harp overlaid with sprigs of herbs. The carriage came to a stop in front of the house, and the footman stepped down to knock on the door. I didn't wait, I opened the door and almost tumbled out onto the street. The footman looked horrified. Ladies didn't wear trousers and boots, and they most certainly didn't open their own carriage doors.

"Take our luggage to the front steps," I commanded him in a voice that sounded stronger than I felt. What if I had caused such a scandal I was no longer welcome at home? Should we have used the servant's entrance in the back? Should I have sent a messenger? Should I have let the footman announce me?

I took a deep breath and raised my hand to ring the bell. The door burst open. My mother stood there, sobbing. She dragged me inside with a cry of delight, kissing my cheeks and my forehead like she did when I was a little girl. Papa was only a few steps behind her.

Papa ignored my strange dress and gathered me up. We all had tears streaming down our faces. Any doubts I had about returning home evaporated like soot into London air.

Mrs. Tabor set to work creating a feast. She generally hated to have a fancy dinner ordered on short notice, but she cried happy tears so much that she had to dab her eyes as she had mother approve her hastily planned, but elaborate, menu for tonight.

Jenny leapt to air out my room and lay a fire in the hearth and in the solar. Papa hastily invited Father Henri and Nate in, after I told him Nate wasn't in the employ of the carriage driver, of course. We all retired to the solar. Mama had left her cards out on the table that sat in front of the bay window.

If Father Henri noticed, he didn't say anything.

"Well, daughter," My father tried his best to sound stern. "I had been told you and a large brown dog were abducted by a flying galleon a month ago. Do you care to explain?"

"No," Nate cut me off. "I wish to explain." Papa and Mama both looked at him. He swallowed hard. "First, your daughter was assisting me in matters of a purely innocent nature but we were set upon by Mr. Cooper and his Red Hood Society. I didn't plan for such an attack, but I was unable to return her to you in a timely manner. I give you my word, her honor was never in jeopardy while in my company, no matter that we were not properly escorted."

I stared at him. Who knew he was capable of such a proper speech?

"I do know, though, that her virtue and my intention must be in question, so I humbly request that you let me explain our absence."

"Where is this coming from?" I whispered to him.

"I practiced it the whole way in the carriage," he whispered back.

Papa nodded. "First, I wish to see the reason my daughter's arm is bound to her side. Jenny, I have a feeling we will be needing several pots of tea. Please have Mrs. Tabor prepare a tray and have her unlock the cellar. I will also be needing a bottle of brandy and several of the good crystal glasses." Jenny bowed and ran to do as she was bid.

We carefully unwrapped my arm. I closed my eyes at the last moment, I didn't want him to tell me the wound was beyond treatment, where amputation of the limb was his only option to save the patient. My mother had my other hand trapped neatly in both of hers, and Nate was holding my shoulder. Given the choice, I found myself longing for Nate's touch alone. He made no move to restrain me but his touch steadied me like nothing else.

Papa took a deep breath. I opened one eye to decipher the sound. He wasn't pleased, but it wasn't the resigned look of nothing could be done. The cut itself was swollen, straining at the stitches, and red—with an oozing crust.

"Breathe, my child," Father Henri reminded me.

I released the breath I had been holding and hastily sucked in another one.

"How did this happen?" Mama asked, staring.

"A gargoyle stabbed me with Mr. McCabe's knife," I said before thinking. She gave me a queer look. "Mr. McCabe says to tell you it was a pleasure to look after your daughter," I added.

She burst into laughter, and father joined in. Some of the tension melted out of the room. I wanted to ask how she knew him but the pain drumming through my arm reminded me this was probably not the best time.

"Lilly," Papa said to my mother. "Please get the supply of fresh bandages out of the cabinet and get the cocaine."

He left me sitting at the dining room table and went downstairs. He returned a few moments later with a bottle of carbolic acid crystals and the box with his burner, mortar and pestle, and basin. I exchanged a look with Nate. He shrugged, but his grip on my shoulder got a bit tighter. I could read him well. This was going to hurt.

Treating the wound ended up hurting more than the actual wound itself. Papa ground the carbolic acid crystals and mixed them with water, making a disinfectant. He put it directly into the wound. I sobbed and gagged against Nate's side as he debrided it, but after that was finished mother coated the wound with cocaine and the process was much easier to bear.

Jenny brought the brandy, which fortified us all through the process. I had a little too much on purpose; it made the story much easier to tell. We left very little out, excluding the nudity of course, and drank so much tea that I lost count of the pots. Every so often the story had to be paused while someone visited the privy house out back.

Then I had to explain about Nate's affliction. There was no way around it. I let him explain the first ley well and the druid site that bound him to

Ranger. I told them of the wonderful dog, and how it saved me on many occasions. I told them of our journey to the ley well in the Molten Cay, and what the voice had said about choosing the form he would keep. It sounded quite ridiculous to me even though I had lived it. I stumbled to explain his monster form. How was I to explain the man I had brought home?

Mama interrupted my stammering. "He's a canithrope. Not a monster."

"What?" Nate and I both stared at her.

"Therianthrope is the ability for human beings to transfigure into animals. Since he is able to turn into a dog, the correct term would be canithrope." Mama said. "It is quite an uncommon gift. I believe that if you were close to your dog at the moment his life was touched by the wild magic in the ley well, he did whatever he could to preserve you and him. You say it was a druid site. The druids were mostly a peaceful, earth-centered religious order. Some orders believed in animals and humans working together. If the site you disturbed was for animal magic or elemental magic, it all fits."

Nate was repeating the word under his breath, testing it. Finally, he nodded.

Mama poured us all another round of tea. Jenny took the empty pot and went to fetch more.

"I'm amazed you discuss it so openly here." Nate shook his head.

"We can trust our household," Mama said simply.

Behind us, Jenny moved through the room like a ghost, lighting the lamps, adding coal to the fires, and replacing empty teapots for fresh. Finally, I set back, story told. I felt strangely light, like the tale had been weighing me down. My hand brushed Nate's beneath the table.

Papa sat back and exchanged a look with Mama. He cleared his throat. "So, I only have one question now," Mama nodded in encouragement. "How long have you been courting my daughter?"

My breath caught in my throat. "What?" I wheeled around to look at him. I thought he might panic or become incensed at the idea.

Nate was sipping brandy. He paused with the glass halfway to his mouth. He set it back down on the table. "Well," he said slowly. "I would say about three weeks."

"What?" I said.

"What?" Jenny squeaked and clasped her hand over her mouth.

"Hmm." Mama gave a little noise.

Papa folded his hands on the tabletop, steepling his fingers. I recognized this look. He had something quite serious to discuss.

"Vivian," Mama said gently. "I do believe we need to go through your dresses." She rose from the table and offered me her hand. It was second nature to obey. After giving him another glance, I stood and followed her up to my bedroom, my mind racing. What had possessed Papa to ask that of Nate? When we told of our adventure we left out me seeing him nude as well as the few kisses we had shared and, of course, me getting drunk on good French wine. Was the way I felt for him written on my face? I had turned to him for comfort while my arm was treated. Perhaps that had given too much away. Below, I could hear the hum of their voices.

"Vivian." Mama sat down on my bed. "There is something different about you." She pulled her cards out of the small pouch at her belt. She offered me the cards.

I took a deep breath. She did this from time to time, needing me to take cards that spoke to me. I often took the cards that just seemed to leap out at me.

This time I took the deck in hand. They felt different this time, like they were humming. My ears were buzzing, and something within me was suddenly very much alive. I took up the deck. It was not the cards that radiated power, it was me. It was like looking through a glass and the world suddenly coming into focus.

I cut the cards, letting my fingers choose the cards I needed, letting my focus guide me. I slid my fingers into the deck and pinned them in place. Then I let the rest of the deck fall. They rained down on the table, leaving me with four cards.

Mama stood, her mouth pursed. I hadn't revealed the cards yet, but she slowly nodded, tears in her eyes. "My daughter," she whispered, pressing her hands to her mouth. "You have now come into your own." She placed her hand over mine, preventing me from turning my hand over to reveal the cards.

"Mr. Valentine first," she whispered. "Because he weighs on your mind."

I turned over the first card. "*The Sun.* That's fortunate union, contentment in marriage." My stomach fluttered.

"Your challenge." Mama looked as excited as I.

I revealed the second card. "*Knight of Staves.*"

She nodded. "Conflict and alienation. I must say you are no stranger to that, my dear. Your father and I have done the best we can to make you strong enough to exist in a world where you can face conflict and come out whole and undamaged." She gave me a sympathetic look. "Your path—you are undecided," she said in a frantic whisper. I had never seen her look this way before. She was possessed with such joy, I could read the cards—the gift had indeed passed from mother to daughter.

I turned the card. I knew what question the focus, the cards, was pulling from my mind. Should I accompany Nate and Father Henri to try to close the ley well? "*Six of Swords*, a pleasant journey."

"If you are going to be traveling in the company of Mr. Valentine it will be a pleasant journey indeed. What awaits you there?"

I turned over the last card. "*Seven of Swords.* That's treason and corruption. Roguery."

We exchanged a look. "I have no desire to commit acts of treason."

"This card doesn't necessarily apply to you. Use care, daughter, you may encounter a very dangerous rogue or a treacherous plot."

When I dropped the cards, the *Ace of Wands* fell face up at my feet. Mama motioned for me to pick it up. "It means a dramatic and unexpected change in position."

I gave nervous laughter. "So, I would be quite happy with Nate should I choose to wed him, but we will be poorly thought of. That is hardly a surprise. My reputation as a well thought of proper lady is quite tarnished, and permanently so, as I reappeared with a roguish gentleman in an airship. Wearing trousers. Something awaits us, something that might result in treason. Either way, my path means we shall be either plunged into poverty when the Lamia's treasure is exhausted, or we shall come in to wealth.

Jenny appeared at my door. "Mr. Harper would like you to join him in the solar for dinner."

Mama watched as I knelt down and gathered up the cards. She handed me the small scrap of hunter green silk she always secured them with. "They are yours now—may they offer you guidance when your life seems adrift." She embraced me fully, like she did when I was a child. I let her.

She finally let go and then stepped back, wiping away tears of happiness. She looked me up and down carefully. "We should dress for dinner."

I nodded.

Nate liked blue. I pulled out my navy velvet dress, the one I was wearing the day I first encountered Mr. Valentine. Mama dressed me herself, waving Jenny off. She brushed and arranged my hair, catching it back with a matching ribbon.

Then it was time to join my father and Nate for dinner. I took a deep breath. The skirts were swirling around my legs, threatening to trip me. Oh, this was ridiculous! I'd had dinner with Mr. Valentine dozens of times, Father Henri several times, and Papa for most of my life. There was nothing that assured me, other than the cards, that Nate might even propose marriage. There was also nothing that assured me that Papa would give his consent. What would we do then? Would we leave in disgrace? Wed in secret? I suddenly couldn't breathe.

I decided to let it happen if it's going to happen but another part of me, something much more reckless and decidedly unladylike, decided then and there that I would not be without him. I loved Nate. In the same realization I knew he loved me. I squared my shoulders and walked into the solar.

Nate was standing at the hearth, examining a glass dome that contained a few carefully preserved roses from my mother and father's wedding. Papa took Mama's hand and gracefully led her off to the dining room where the table had been set.

We were left alone in the solar. My heart was pounding out of my chest.

"That is a beautiful dress," Nate said hesitantly.

"Thank you," I said, giving a small curtsy. His nerves somehow made this easier on me.

"Would you be willing to not go through the waiting? That is, I mean, I know that it's customary for women to wait a year to be courted again if they break an engagement." He turned the color of a beet and looked away, cursing under his breath.

"Why Nate," I stood beside him and placed my hand on his back. "Have we finally found something you can't do?"

He turned around and glared at me. "Marry me. I've never met anyone like you before. I don't want to wait a year. You say you're still a maid— that's good enough for me. Of course, even if you weren't it wouldn't matter much. I mean—" he paused and cleared his throat to stop rambling. "I'd spend the rest of my life taking care of you if you'll let me."

"I accept," I said with a small curtsy. "I will marry you."

He threw his arms around me and crushed me to his chest, trying not to jostle my arm. It hurt, but I didn't care.

"See, I can do that." He growled a very gruff, canine sound into my hair. "I just can't do it all pretty and formal like." He held me tight for a while longer. "I promise your parents will never starve."

"What?" I pulled back to look at him.

"That was one of the reasons you were going to marry Goodwin," he said. "We'll never be rich, I mean like a lord," he added hastily, "But as long as I can work we will have bread."

"You oaf!" I affectionately cuffed his shoulder.

Nate caught my second attempt to cuff his shoulder and turned me aside with the practiced ease of a pugilist. "Of course, we will have to wait until I can afford a ring."

"We don't need you to buy a ring," I said. "We have several from the Lamia's treasure. I'll marry you whenever."

He laughed, "Then you agree to my conditions: a gold ring and you'll never starve."

"I accept." I wrapped my good arm around him, holding him to me again.

"Papa approves?" I asked. He had to approve. If he didn't I would marry him anyway.

"He practically demanded it," Nate chuckled. "Apparently, it's just not done to abduct a young lady and take her off on an adventure without intent to wed—"

We were interrupted when his stomach growled loudly.

"We should sit for supper." I reluctantly let go. He nodded and drained the rest of his glass with one large gulp. He offered his arm and led me into the dining room, where a fine supper awaited us. It had been expertly and swiftly prepared by Mrs. Tabor. My jubilant parents and a priest were in attendance. After the table was set and the fire stoked, I insisted that Mrs. Tabor and Jenny join us as well. It was not my first engagement dinner but the best one I had ever seen.

"Congratulations are in order!" Father Henri said. He raised his glass. "May you share many happy years together and may your union be blessed with strong, healthy children."

We raised our glasses.

Papa drank deeply then he cleared his throat and stood at his position at the head of the table. The smile on his face faded and he squared his shoulders. His lips pursed "Now, as to logistics, Jenny will set the guest room for Father Henri. Nate, you are going to have to sleep in the shop."

Nate nodded. Nothing could dampen the smile on his face.

"So, when will we have a wedding?" Mama asked. "Should we try for spring?"

Later, Mama and Papa went to bed, leaving us to dampen the fire when we were finished, we sat alone in the solar sipping the last of the wine from the decanter. We had moved to the settee. The fire made the room comfortably warm, and I leaned into him drowsily, letting him protect and support my injured arm.

I looked down at my arm swathed in clean white linen. In the morning we would be leaving to close the ley well.

Nate was staring at my arm as well. "I don't like taking you down to the ley well with your arm so mangled."

"Oh," I said with mock anger. "Is this how this shall work, you set the rules?"

"Absolutely," he countered. "No wife of mine shall go gallivanting about in dark tunnels and climbing on rope while wounded." He dragged me against him and kissed me.

I let him.

After a time, he walked me to my room. He bade me goodnight and retired to the shop. Jenny had laid out blankets for him to spend the night on the cold floor, while I slipped into a pre-warmed bed.

I lay there thinking of him. I would rather be sleeping by Nate in a jungle than alone on fancy clean linen sheets. My parents married for love and I was positive that Nate would never deal me away like Byron had. The jewels from the Lamia's lair were worth quite a sum; and best of all, we didn't have to wait for him to be able to afford a ring. I had several we could choose from. I pulled the jewels out and laid them side by side in the moonlight. If carefully invested in something like the railroad, they could even provide indefinitely for my parents old age. Now our only concern was closing the ley well before something awful and unnatural befell my London.

CHAPTER TWENTY-FIVE

THE HOUSE WAS coming alive downstairs. I dressed in clean trousers and a borrowed shirt. It was becoming more comfortable than my gowns and I was sure they would have no place where we were headed. Nate was already in the shop, packing bits and bobs into his battered knapsack, nodding as Papa gave him directions from his ladder and handed over bottles and tins from a shelf. Calvin was staring, caught somewhere between hero worship and extreme annoyance that this man and I were engaged and he had missed out on his chance to court me. Again.

Father Henri was sipping tea at the small round table in the shop and reading the paper, pointing out interesting tidbits as Papa and Nate packed. "Nathaniel, Men have been turning up dead in alleyways by the factory," he crossed himself. "Good lord, your magistrate believes it is some sort of epidemic. He warns all good, honest citizens to avoid walking about alone after dark."

"It is more than some mere epidemic." I said as I tightened my belt over my corset cover. I had to add a new hole to accommodate the Seax at my back but with the leather, long coat at my back no one would notice it. The perfect secret. Ladies enjoyed a scandal. I loved my new blade. "How do I look?"

Nate abandoned his preparations for a moment, "Perfectly prepared for adventure and a hazardous undertaking into the bowels of London."

Father Henri looked up from his tea, "Speaking of which, Lord Sterling has been fined for interfering with public works. Apparently, his factory has dammed up the water flowing under London, forcing the wells on Bromley Street to dry up. The people have to carry water for blocks."

"There's a sewer entrance near there," Nate offered, helpfully

"Then that is where we're headed." I said cheerfully. "Tally-ho!"

Father Henri finished his tea with a hearty gulp and set the cup back down in the saucer with measured care. "Diverting underground water to create electricity to power the factory," he mused to himself. "That I should live to see such a thing. What an age. What an age indeed." He smiled.

Nate seemed just as cheerful to begin an adventure but like all young men, before duty called, he headed off to the kitchen to secure the last provision he was needing before a grand undertaking. Food.

Just as Nate could not leave without being fed, I could not leave without speaking to Papa. The glass bottles tinkled musically as he touched them, working his way thought them, taking inventory and checking their contents. Most of them were new. So many of them had been broken the night our home had been ransacked. The night I left with Nate.

It was a hard thing to realize, for the first time, that I did not need him to keep me safe. I still needed him to love me, to accept that I was different from the woman that left his home months ago. I was still his daughter but different, grown and changed, evolved and always his Vivian but more. Would he be disappointed in the me that sat in the shop now?

I took a deep breath. "I'm sorry I didn't send word. I should have found a way to send a latter. You must have been worried, especially since I left without permission."

Papa froze, his back still to me. The musical clink of the glass bottles stopped. There were so many of them. Clearly, by the look of things they had managed without me. They were hardly on the street. If anything, Calvin had managed to continue to do well as his apprentice, and Jenny and Mrs. Tabor kept the house. Life had continued much as it had when I had been there.

Slowly, Papa climbed down from his ladder. "I'll not pretend we weren't out of our minds with worry when Calvin told us you left the home with Mr. Valentine while we were out with the constables after the shop was ransacked."

I opened my mouth, but he raised a finger to halt me. "The last time you needed my permission to do anything, you were seven years old."

I choked on my remaining tea, "That cannot be true."

He nodded. "It is entirely true. That next summer, you came to us with a family in need of treatment for croup. You assured me that though they could not pay, the father was willing to teach you to ride their ancient plow horse and you would work extra in the gardens to help harvest herbs. It would give him help and not make him feel like he was accepting charity. You reminded your mama and me that it is the responsibility of good men to do everything in their power to assist others but be careful to not strip them of their pride." He fixed me with a look. "Now where would you have gotten an idea like that?"

I smiled, "Something I heard a great father say once."

He rolled his eyes in an exaggerated, comical manner, he remembered too. "You became so adept at brokering deals for anything you wanted, your mama and I was sure we would one day lose you to a band of traveling tinkers."

We shared a laugh. In that moment, I was surely his daughter, any strain I had caused by my sudden disappearance was forgiven. I could breathe again. I remembered the Kirkham family fondly. They all recovered from the croup and their old horse was a kind and gentle introduction to riding. It was far from a fast horse, more a plodding work horse designed for pulling a cart through the streets, or working on their small farm on the outskirts of town, than a pony designed for a ride in the country, but I learned to keep my balance on the massive animal. "Mr. Kirkham said the physician refused to treat them when they couldn't pay so I said you would."

Papa was smiling too, "And I would have, but that day you took it upon yourself to seek out someone who was in need of help and to find something they could offer of themselves so they did not feel like they came seeking aid like a pauper. We tried to teach you compassion and to do what was right. Knowing what is right and acting upon it makes a person, man or woman strong. The moment you learned to be strong you stopped needing our permission, only our guidance." Considering the matter closed he turned back to his counting.

If I stopped needing his permission long ago then how had I managed to become engaged to Byron, a man who treated me with such apathy that I had only now come to realize he caused me misery? Certainly, Papa did not make any great steps to prevent it. I took a deep breath, I wasn't sure I wanted to ask but I needed to know. "Papa, why didn't you advise me against marrying Byron?"

He spared me a glance before returning to his tonics and bottles, "Marrying Byron was never my idea. You had already set your mind. You would not have listened."

I tried to think back on exactly how the engagement transpired. "You said he asked for my hand."

Papa corrected me. "I said he asked my permission to court you. You are the one that agreed. I wasn't even speaking to you." He gave me a sly look. "You were listening in when I was speaking to your mama on the matter."

I hadn't remembered that detail.

Papa continued, "Mr. Byron Goodwin came to the shop in the advice of his physician for treatment on a laceration and tonic for a disagreeable stomach condition."

I laughed, "Both brought on by drinking, no doubt."

Papa let that pass. "He saw you and inquired, believing you to be a servant that he could, ahem, keep company with. I informed him that you were my daughter and he was to treat you respectfully. Four days later, he returned for treatment for a severely contused eye and, over the course of treatment, asked if you were being courted."

I glared at him, I didn't like where this was going, Papa set down the bottle in hand and continued, "You overheard me telling your mama and explained that he was a fine match and that you would be quite fortunate to be courted by Mr. Goodwin."

I did not remember it going that way. The awful thing was, I could see, by some logic, it made sense; Byron would have been a good match on paper. It would have seemed fortunate to be courted by the son of a lord. I would have been able to provide my parents with a comfortable old age and I would not have met Byron by this point, so I would not know him for a cad. "Then why didn't you stop me?"

Papa gave me an indulgent smile, "It is arrogant to believe men own women, but it is the honor of good men to look after their women. Before I could find a tactful way to tell him we would not be accepting his generous offer of marriage, you informed us you would be accepting. You took it into your own mind to marry Byron Goodwin."

Papa leaned across the counter, his face inches from mine. "Your mama and I raised a strong woman, Vivian. We knew you were capable of great things and you knew your mind since you were a young girl. You have a strong mind when you set yourself to a task. The trouble with strong wills is they are set on rushing headlong into trouble, or punishing themselves and there is little anyone can do except love them and hope they realize the error of their way before it is too late."

I swallowed hard my throat was suddenly tight and I couldn't manage more than a whisper, "What would you have done if I realized it was too late, after it was too late?"

Papa smiled, a little twinkle was in his eye. "The man was a drunkard and a gambler, Vivian. I am sure he would have had a little accident. Or one could have been arranged."

The tight feeling was gone. I propped myself up on my elbows like a child. There was no way he was being serious; this from my papa? He is a healer of men. "Papa! Assault and murder? Really?"

We laughed. It felt good to laugh.

Papa suddenly grew very serious. "I have made some very powerful friends by treating their loved ones Vivian, and I have but one daughter. Ahh, here is your young man now."

He was right, Nate had returned. He had been waylaid in the hall by Calvin. I could not hear much, but by the sounds of it, Nate was trying to convince Calvin that I really had fought gargoyles and demons and we had traveled upon a ship that sailed upon the sky.

We left the house just after my wounded arm was wrapped in clean linen for the last time. We didn't wait for Jenny to call a hansom cab, we just stepped out into the cold gray day. Father Henri followed behind us in his brown habit and my papa's best wool coat. Nate and I strode along, the cold and wet were no match for leather, long coats designed for sailors in a lightning storm high above the clouds. I wore no skirts to tangle my legs, no hoop to create a place for me on the crowded footpaths; every bit of space I took up on the street I earned the way a man does as they strode along. My leather boots clicked the cobbled thoroughfare and all the mousey, proper women parted to give me my way. I was one of them once. But no longer.

Nate walked at my side. He offered me his arm.

"I heard you telling Calvin tales of magic and adventure in the hall," I said. "Will you be happy as a married man?"

"Extremely," he said without even a pause.

"I mean won't you miss the Explorer's Society?"

"Why should I?" Nate asked. He stopped walking and turned to look at me. "Are you saying you have no desire to go out into the field again? You will keep me at home under glass?" He laughed and pulled me along to get me walking again. "I assume that you will eventually take over your parent's business, and that Calvin Tabor might open his own shop—though I assume he is giving serious thought to become an adventurer for hire now."

Behind us Father Henri chuckled.

Nate continued, "Will you be content remaining in the shop for years on end, dispensing medicines until your beautiful hair has all gone gray?"

"And toothless, don't forget when I am old I am likely to be toothless," I added with a smile.

He ignored that. "It may be sometime before we are saddled with children. And they will be sent to school before too long. I'm not old enough to retire yet, and I want to go to Zanzibar or Egypt or China. Then when we've seen enough of the world we can retire to the apothecary. You can teach me how to cure boils and sores and upset stomachs."

"Ha!" I could not imagine an individual less suited to learning to cure others. He had a caring heart to be sure, and though there are some men that would be happy with such a sedentary existence, he was hardly one of them.

CHAPTER TWENTY-SIX

WE MADE OUR WAY down Bromley Street to where the foot bridge crossed over where the water had, in times past, surged in the warmer months before meeting up with the Thames. Most respectable people were inside hiding from the cold, wet weather so that and the sulphury fog of another mighty pea-souper on the rise hid our actions well. Nate went first, checking to see that no one was watching then leapt down from the bridge and onto the bank below.

Father Henri went next with a spryness that amazed me. Perhaps his lust for adventure was not sated yet. I hoped that when I was old I moved half as well. "Thank you, Nathaniel."

I looked hastily over my shoulders. Off in the distance, nearly obscured by the fog moving in, a few figures shuffled hunching in their coats and hiding in the chill. I sat on the edge of the bridge and squinted. I could not see the bottom. How could Nate just jump and trust the bottom was there? Well, he just did. The ground had not failed him yet I suppose. I took a deep breath and pushed off.

The ground was closer than I thought. I hit hard and was immediately thankful for the hard-soled riding boots. In a lady's soft shoes, I would have broken an ankle. I half-expected Nate to be there offering me a hand up but he was staring, something else had consumed him entirely and I was forgotten.

The water of the underground stream had indeed been diverted. It carved a great tunnel into the side of the land as though a monster lived there and the resulting entry of the cave loomed like a great dark mouth, warning us away. It made a sharp chill race up my spine. This is the cavern where the man I love was touched by old, wild magic. A magic that was still loose upon the world.

The magic had a scent, hot and sharp, like lightning. Creatures like the Lamia could smell it, and it lured them to set up their homes here. I shuddered again at the thought of a Lamia under London, hunting citizens in the yellow-green pea soup fogs and snatching them out of the shadows. Though London didn't hold the appeal to me it once did, but I still loved too many people who called London home to allow this ley well to draw such a beast to live beneath it. I loved too much of the world to leave anything that would attract those monsters from their own realms to the lands of men.

Without discussion, we followed the dry tunnel for over a mile. Nate led us by flickering torchlight over the smooth rocks in the riverbed. My hard-soled riding boots slipped over the rocks and splashed in small puddles. Every so often, Nate would stop and frown at the wet ground.

"Are we lost?" I finally asked.

"No, these puddles were smaller last time I was here."

"Perhaps the dam is failing," Father Henri said.

"I sincerely hope not," I said. "If I wished to drown I would go swimming in the Thames."

"You can't swim?" Nate asked.

I held up my hand to quiet him, my mind working furiously. If something was wrong with the dam then it would burst, the water would rush through the tunnels of the riverbed, and we would be swept away. I knelt down and touched the water, scooping some of it to my lips. Water that set too long became stale.

"How long ago did the last person drown on Cardigan Street?" I asked, needing Nate to verify what I suspected.

Father Henri had been reading the papers, he would know. "Two nights ago." He confirmed.

Nate turned in a wide circle, taking note of the damp stone walls.

The water wasn't stale, it was fresh. It had filled these puddles within the past few days, and though water dripped lazily from the ceiling, that water had a faint earthen taste from filtering through the ground and along cracks caused by the roots of the trees. This tunnel had been full of fresh water from the rivers that flowed under London.

"Nate, if there is something wrong with the dam it would have burst by now, right?"

"Yep," he said, touching the damp walls.

I felt a chill. "What is between the inlet and this underground river?"

"Cardigan Street and the alley way between Union Court and Ancona Road," Nate said. "And the factory for Sterling's Emporium, of course."

"That's where all those drowning deaths on dry land have taken place." I felt sick.

"What about the burned men in the river?" Nate said after a moment.

"I don't know, I can't think of a fire that burns in water," I said. "But I bet they were related somehow."

"Then Mr. Sterling has been committing crimes against man and God, and mortal sins against his soul," Father Henri said sadly.

"Hang on a minute, doesn't he have that inventor working for him, Geiger someone?" Nate asked.

"Newton Geiger," I said, recalling the newspaper announcement. "He's an inventor and an engineer."

"Shouldn't he know how to build a dam?" Nate asked.

"Perhaps, but not if forced. For all we know Mr. Sterling coerced him into his work."

Nate went a little way ahead and stood at a huge metal door. He had his coat thrown open, and one hand on his hip.

Off to the side, there was a glimmer. I went for a closer look. "What in the world?" It was netting resembling the intricate weaving of a spider web, not the uniform and regular weave of a man-made net. I held my torch under it. It didn't burn, it just glistened like it was made of silver or wire. "This is metal."

"Huh?" Nate was preoccupied with the complicated steel door lock.

"I'm guessing that door wasn't here when you were here last?" I said.

"No." Nate looked around. "No door, no lock." He stopped and turned in a small circle, casting light with his torch in an arc before him. "Someone has been here."

"Spiders have been here."

"What do you mean?"

"Right here." I pointed at the metal web.

Nate looked as though he had just tasted something quite unpleasant. "Just burn it and help me with this door."

"It won't burn," I said. "I already tried. It is some sort of cable or metal thread."

He muttered something under his breath about "girls," and hopped over a few large chunks of stone.

"I hope that disparaging remark wasn't meant for me," I said crossly.

He ignored that and held the torch up beneath the webbing. Just as had happened for me, it didn't burn. I didn't even try to resist informing him of such. He scowled again.

"What do you suppose made it?" I raised my hand and plucked on a strand. It sounded like a harp. The note echoed sweetly through the chamber.

"Don't do that!" Nate whispered furiously.

I scoffed but did as he asked and returned to where he was staring at the door.

"Vivian, I mean it, stop!" he snapped a moment later.

"I didn't do anything," I insisted.

Father Henri held his torch up so the light reflected the webbing. It was vibrating slightly, first one cord then another, creating a beautiful harmony. "Nathaniel, it is not her."

I heard clicking, like a clock winding down double time. The same sound my birds made. Along the webs anchored in the walls, floor, and ceiling, the clicking grew closer and closer.

"Nope!" Nate said quickly, drawing his gun.

"What is the matter with you? Are you going to shoot a spider?" I said as calmly as I could manage, but it was too funny. A big, tough, bold man such as Nathaniel Valentine terrified of spiders. He looked the way I must have when the flying fish struck the airship.

"I don't like spiders. All those legs, its damn unsettling."

Now it was Father Henri's turn to stare at him. "Legs?"

Nate cocked the revolver and held it up and at the ready.

Whatever clicked was large enough to dislodge something behind us. I turned. Spider indeed! It was the size of a cat, with a metal body that reflected the light of the torches. It tapped legs against the strands of the web, eyes made of lenses. The lenses rotated to focus. Small lights embedded on its back changed from green to red.

"Now who made you?" I asked the spider. It clicked at me.

Nate looked like he had fallen off a cliff but had not yet reached the bottom. His jaw was stubbornly set, but his eyes were wide. "For God's sake, Viv, don't take to it!"

Father Henri was trying not to laugh. "I'm not sure if this qualifies as arachnophobia or Chronomentrophobia. That's fear of spiders and fear of clockworks respectively, my dear."

I nodded. The spider made no move to come closer, it just stared with its odd, lens eyes, shifting its focus like it was watching us through a spyglass.

"At any rate, I doubt this thing means us any harm," I said for Nate's benefit. "I'm sure it is someone's invention that has gone exploring, like my birds seeking water."

"Someone set that thing loose upon the city?" Nate was positively horrified.

"Oh honestly, my birds are programmed to act like birds and to maintain each other. I am sure it is nothing more than clever use of fuses and wires."

Nate nodded, but he didn't look convinced. Finally, with great effort, he turned back to the door. Then he turned and stared thoughtfully at me for a moment. He leapt to his feet and pulled me close. With a smile he pulled a pin from my hair.

"And see here, I thought I was going to get a kiss." I smiled.

He turned back and obliged me with a quick peck on the cheek, then he knelt with the pin by a large ornate lock and stabbed the pin into it.

"Do not worry, my dear," Father Henri said with a smile. "He is much more reserved around me. He has always been that way."

There was a *click*. The lock, knife, and pin turned in one smooth movement and the heavy door opened. "Ha!" He pulled the knife and the pin out of the lock. The spider sprang to life and skittered past us. Nate leapt out of the way and gave the thing such a fierce look I half expected it to melt right on the spot.

"Clearly it wanted in," I said with a smile.

"Here we go," Nate breathed.

"'Abandon all hope, ye who enter here,'" I quoted, smiling to myself, and ignoring the looks the two men gave me.

The door opened to a hallway that had been hewn out of the rock itself. Though I didn't know of such matters, I had seen illustrations in the paper of the mines and rock being chipped away or forcibly removed by way of explosion. This channel seemed cut by water. The smooth sides were slick.

The scrabbling thin legs of the mechanical spider faded into the darkness.

"Ladies first," Nate said.

I stared at him, unamused. "You're so gallant." I gave a mock curtsey.

He laughed and went through the door.

"Will you ever cease to surprise me?" I asked, not expecting him to answer.

"Yes," he said in all seriousness. "I can turn into a monster and I'm afraid of spiders. Now you know it all." I couldn't tell if he was joking or not.

"The water would have taken hundreds of years to carve out this path," Father Henri said. "We are probably standing in the very steps that holy druids of old followed to reach their shrine."

"Yeah, the druids, but who else has been here?" Nate muttered.

The door was newly installed. I could imagine some eccentric inventor installing the door as a fail-safe for the rerouted river in case the factory equipment powered by the water had some sort of failure to keep all that water from rushing out.

"My God!" I almost shouted. I nearly dropped the torch on Nate.

Still on edge from our encounter with the spider, Nate leapt about a foot into the air. He glared at me.

"I know what happened!"

"The spider got locked out?" Father Henri said.

"No, the murders. The victims were drowning. Something is wrong with the factory! The water used to flow this way, but they dammed it up to power their machines. What if it breaks? When dams break all that water follows its previous path, and everything in its way is destroyed." I felt positively giddy.

"That would explain the drownings. The influx of water would be swift, but over just as quickly. There would be no trace in the mornings." Father Henri agreed.

"Yes, but why only at night?" Nate said. "The factory runs day and night. There's no reason there would be more water at night. This was being done on purpose. The water is being released when there is less chance of people figuring it out. They're letting the water out to relieve the pressure." Nate said. "Mr. Sterling is murdering people. He's making it look like an accident."

I desperately wanted to find some way this could be all a horrible accident. Sure Mr. Sterling was ambitious, but ambitious enough to kill? To risk the lives of so many people? So many *poor* people. It was rare that nobility thought of the common man as important as they were. I was also starting to suspect Sterling wanted more than just the water to power his machine. I hoped I was wrong.

"He employed Mr. Newton Geiger to build and maintain his machine. I'm sure the spiders maintain the factory. Father Henri is right, this one was clearly waiting to be let back in." I reached out to offer a comforting hand to Nate. "The spider didn't move to harm us."

"I guess so." Nate didn't sound convinced. "Why in God's name did it have to be spiders? Sorry, Father," he hastily added.

Father Henri waved his hand in dismissal.

"With their numerous legs and webs, they can get places other forms could not. I'm sure it is the logical choice," I said, my hand still on his shoulder. "I know, after we seal the ley well we will be sure to ask Mr. Geiger. I'm sure the police will have plenty to say to Mr. Sterling."

CHAPTER TWENTY-SEVEN

I WAS AWARE that we found the ley well even before Nate said we had arrived. There was a lake of molten silver, perhaps four feet in diameter but the same as before—a liquid mirror set in the ground. One end was heavily shadowed, the rock oddly shaped and rough but on the northern end was a monolith made of gray marble, carved with knot work and angular writing and a stone altar in the same stone. There was no marble in London. These pieces had been carefully and purposefully placed. More clockwork spiders, dozens of them, skittered around great domes of copper like enormous kettles that shared a set of wires connecting their great housing and between them held a glowing yellow-green glass canister in the edge of the molten lake. Bellows and pumps whirled away. Having been on *The Lightning Aura* I recognized this for what it was, an apparatus for charging batteries, but much larger than the ones sold by Captain Morgan's crew. The clockwork spiders were charging the batteries with the magic from the ley well.

Two spiders carried a glass canister between them. I watched it disappear up their steel web until all that was visible was the glow of the battery and the blink, blink, blink of the lights upon their backs. They disappeared into a pipe set into the wall. The green- gold was both beautiful and eerie against the warmth of the copper pipe as the light disappeared, their skittering legs scrabbling against the pipe as they hurried away with their precious cargo. New spiders took their place, hooking up a new battery to the kettle chargers and still others set to touching the mirror lake, tasting it with their legs or touching the machinery flashing their lights at each other all the while. They must be communicating. Though I couldn't tell what was being, said they blinked and winked in patterns.

Nate raised the torch over his head. In the silver gleam of the ley well and the reflected torchlight he looked pale. He swallowed hard.

"Is this where it all began?"

I'm not sure why I asked. It was all I could think of, and the silence and faint mechanical whir of the spiders was oppressive.

He nodded dully. "Ranger and I were exploring this site. It had been pointed out to the Explorer's Society head as a hole in the riverbed. One of the trawlers found it while dragging the Thames for anything of value to be resold. Mr. Langton sent me to see if it required further investigation."

"Mr. Langton, the head of the Explorer's Society?" I asked.

He nodded again. "I took Ranger with me."

"You're not the only poor soul that has been here recently," Father Henri said sadly. He was kneeling by a dark form lying in the shadows cast by the marble monolith. He made the sign of the cross over the form.

"Miss Harper, perhaps you should stay back," he called over.

"I have seen dead men before," I said, and joined Nate and Father Henri.

Nate handed the torch over for me to hold. "He's not an explorer. He's some sort of workman." He rolled the man to better arrange limbs that had fallen akimbo.

I could suddenly picture those slack limbs moving under their own power, rising from the ground, and shambling over to us. Perhaps it wasn't the Lamia that enchanted the dead men, maybe the magic of the ley well itself had reanimated the men and set them upon their murderous course and her magical flute merely directed their deadly rampage. I shuddered.

"He was murdered," Nate concluded. "And within the last year. I doubt it is merely water that powers Sterling's factory. He is using ley-magic."

"God be merciful," Father Henri breathed crossing himself. "Are you sure?"

Nate nodded grimly. "Unless he managed to cut his own throat then gather his blood on the druidic altar."

"The ancient pagans who would have used this site believed in ritual sacrifice," Father Henri said, more as a matter of scholarly report than for anything else. "Their notion of sacrifice was generally limited to animals though. Far from a sacrifice of God to save mankind."

"I'm not so sure that animals couldn't sacrifice to save a man," I said.

Ranger. I recognized him from the alternate form Nate took on when he saved me from being assaulted and robbed in the alley, and from resting my hands in his soft, dark, caramel fur. Ranger lay just beyond the torchlight, on his side like he was just sleeping and would spring to his feet in an instant and follow us around the cave.

"I read the book you gave me," I explained. "You said some of the druids believed that animals were helpers, protectors, and partners of man. If something awful happened here it makes sense that Ranger would sacrifice his own life to protect Nate. It would then be a small leap to believe that some part of Ranger melded with Nate and left him a man of both forms."

Nate made a small strangled sound. He knelt by Ranger's side, clearly much more affected by this sight than that of the murdered man.

Father Henri recovered from sounding cross with me. "Based on the information we have from scholars, that would be a reasonable conclusion."

"Ranger loved him so much he tried to protect him with his last breath," I said, placing my hand on Nate's shoulder.

Nate was ignoring us. He buried his hands in the thick fur. So far, Ranger had been immune to the rot that all dead things are subject to. Then again, the murdered man was immune too. It must have something to do with the magic from the site. Nate sniffed hard, wiping his face with the back of his hand, mourning silently in the innocent and shameless way grieving children wept.

"I'm sorry, Nate." I knelt beside him.

"You've got to think me a fool." He sniffed again.

"I think you loved him."

"He was my best friend for a long time. I found him when he was a puppy. We both were young and in need of a friend," Nate explained, fishing a stained handkerchief from his pocket.

"You don't need to explain it to me," I said.

Father Henri had finished his prayers over the fallen man. "I don't suppose we can bring this back with us for a proper burial?"

Nate was still crouching by his best friend looking stunned. "We will send someone for him, I promise. What is your plan, Father?" He asked warily.

"Whatever you bind on earth shall be bound in heaven, and whatever you loose on earth shall be loosed in heaven. That's *Matthew 18.18*," Father Henri said. "You see, Jesus was talking to Peter, but he was referencing closing heaven to the unbelievers and allowing heaven to be accessed by those who are true believers. I think if we believe that the power of belief allows whomever to access this power. If we bind it here we deny him access to it.

"The ivy shall be the barrier; your dog's spirit shall help protect the seal; he shall be the guardian of the keys and make it harder to access. He shall be playing the role of St. Peter. The metal seal will keep the fractured ley line from creating a ley well, and faith will prevent unbelievers from even seeking the magic here. First of all, most people cannot conceive of a system that allows for both magic and religion to coexist. If they do not believe, then they cannot access it."

I was not ready to lose any part of Nate, even if it was only the part of him that was his dog. "How could that be? Isn't Ranger a part of Nate?"

Father Henri took a deep breath, the breath of a man entirely sure of himself, "A soul is hardly a finite thing, Vivian, and love is the most powerful force in all the world. If love makes all things possible, then is the love a dog has for his master any less powerful just because he is a dog?"

Nate gave a grateful breath and for that moment of solace I would be forever in Father Henri's debt.

Father Henri turned to the altar by where Ranger's body lay. "It is my firm belief, based upon my scholarly research and my supreme belief in God's love of us and His desire for all of us to be happy, that God would never remove from Nathaniel one of the few things that make him truly happy."

"Doesn't your church have teachings against these pagan beliefs?" I said.

"Perhaps, but I am also a scholar. I believe there is more in this world than can be explained by science or faith. True reality is a blend of both. My faith gives me strength, but faith as we see it is limited by man's understanding. God understands what we mean as well as what we need, and God will provide."

"Science and faith—I suppose in this modern age we must adjust our thinking," I said hesitantly.

"Hopefully. If not, He will understand that I serve Him as best as I am able and will forgive my fallacies and my occasional trespasses." Father Henri pulled out a small ivy plant wrapped in linen, its roots still enrobed with dark soil.

"If this doesn't work I do believe we may be killed here," I said motioning to the dead man. "He was probably murdered by Lord Sterling when he set up the machinery that is accessing this magic. Tinkering with the ley-magic did Nate no favors the first time."

Father Henri stroked his ivy plant's leaves, "It did neither of you no harm the last time and though I am not a gambling man, I would prefer to look at it through that lens."

I suppose he was right. I would have asked Nate's opinion but he was ignoring us both. He stroked Ranger's fur. It was so strange to see him stroking what I had come to see as his own other self.

"Vivian, be a dear. If you happen to pass first, please put in a good word for me please." Father Henri pushed his glasses up further on his nose and winked at me.

I laughed. It felt good to laugh in here. It pushed back the oppressive darkness.

"Ivy, it is both a guardian and a binding plant. It envelopes things and links them together. It is quite the amazing plant, it can link trees, envelope entire walls, form barriers, and even block out light if given enough time to grow." Father Henri carefully prepared his seedling for its new home.

"Ivy can be so destructive," I said. "It chokes out other plants."

"I prefer to think of it as rather enthusiastic," Father Henri said, smiling at the plant.

Father Henri handed a small silver disk to Nate, and then unpacked his bible and a vial from his small pack. "This holy water should purify the site," he explained to me. "The Vikings had an amazing way of binding. They used runes to create powerful seals. Druidism and the ancient pagan Vikings had a lot in common."

Father Henri set the silver disk etched with runes in the center of the well. He poured the water into the magical pool as he walked around it, chanting. The disk disrupted the perfectly reflective surface. It was such a small thing and yet the intrusion was quite striking. It stirred something violent and primal within me. I had to fight the urge to go retrieve the disk so the ley well could remain a perfect shimmering pool of magic. I knew he was doing what had to be done and yet I could clearly see the other me, the one covered in the dark tarot marks with short, spiky hair nearly leaping out of the mirror lake at me. For a moment, I desperately wanted to stop him, it was like a hook, sharp and deep had grabbed me beneath my breastbone and was yanking me towards the lake.

The holy water pooled, floating like oil on water. The clockwork spiders stopped hovering by the glowing battery and the yellow-green glow faded away. The spiders clicked their metal legs against the rocks and the dark battery. Their little lens eyes whirled and their lights flashed and blinked.

Father Henri chanted on in a wonderful baritone voice, smooth and comforting. "O heavenly Father, Almighty God, we humbly beseech Thee to bless and sanctify this place and all who enter therein and everything else in it, and do Thou vouchsafe to fill it with all good things; grant to this space, O Lord, the abundance of heavenly blessings and from the richness of the earth every substance necessary for life. Bless and sanctify this place and fill it up with Thy mercy. May the angels of Thy light, dwelling within the walk of this place, protect it and those who find themselves therein. Through Christ our Lord. Amen."

He set the sprouted cuttings of the ivy into the cracks where the druidic altar had shattered. Then he returned to his knees, his voice a comforting mumble in the dark as he prayed.

Nate picked up the corpse of his beloved Ranger. I didn't know what to say. The magic had maintained him, like Ranger had just laid himself down to rest before a fire. Nate's eyes shone in the darkness, more than from just the light from the ley well. He knelt and picked up his beloved dog.

"I never got along with people," Nate said. "I got along just fine with him though."

"Oh Nate," I said, setting my hand on his back.

"Always up for an adventure, he was," Nate continued softly.

"I think when he disrupted the battery he sacrificed himself to protect you, and since he loves you so and you love him so much you two became one. I think you carry Ranger with you, now and forever."

Nate gave a wistful smile and set Ranger down on the altar amidst the ivy cuttings.

Father Henri had finished his chanting and his prayers and stood with Nate looking down at Ranger's corpse. "This is not the position of the church, Nathaniel. I have seen many strange things in this life that cannot even be explained by religion unless you count 'The Lord works in mysterious ways.'

"I have seen spirits. Though my faith sustains my soul, knowledge nourishes my mind. Many cultures agree that animals have souls and they can guide people and guard holy sites. I believe as surely as I stand before you now that Ranger will guard this site until the end of time, making sure the ivy binds the site from causing harm and the runes purify the well."

Nate swallowed hard and nodded.

"You know Nathaniel, dogs are special, even to the almighty. A priest can also be known as a shepherd looking after his human flock. But what helps the shepherd look after his flock? The dog. We get along so well because they are the two separate natures of man, God and dog, palindromes to describe man, a being of great power and great loyalty with the ability to protect and to defend; to lead and to follow."

"He was a very good dog," Nate said sadly.

This was no longer a conversation for me. This was between a man and his priest. I could hear them as I turned my attention back to the clockwork spiders.

The clockwork spiders seemed much more sedate, they were no longer blinking at one another. They were watching us. I carefully picked my way around the ley well, the silvery mirror light emanating from it seemed to be fading, slowly but surely and the kettle machine that was charging the batteries was losing power.

I heard the hiss of pistons moving, and the whir and clicking of the clockwork spiders moving in the dark. They seemed sad without the batteries to charge in the ley well. They must be milling about in the darkness, aimlessly wandering. What would happen when they finally exhausted their power supply?

No, they were not aimless, they were headed, *en masse* to the far end of rough-hewn stone. They gathered there where they began blinking again in earnest, first randomly then they began blinking in unison. At first it was beautiful, but it soon filled me with dread. If they were communicating; they were together calling for something.

The darkness itself shifted. One massive light, like a giant shuttered lantern slid open and started rising. The ground beneath my feet trembled slightly. I heard the creak and groan of metal plates moving past one another, pistons hissing, gears turning, and ratchets locking into place. The single yellow light was an eye. A massive eye in the center of a face of a metal man easily seven feet tall.

"Nate," I called, my voice shaking. "How would one fight a giant?" I stumbled backwards over a chunk of broken rock.

"What?" He turned.

The behemoth of a mechanical man had been standing in the shadows. The arms clicked. It was reaching for me. I hit the ground quickly, letting the grasping hand pass over me.

"Nate!"

I dodged. The metal man fixed his single glowing eye upon me, his back to Nate and Father Henri.

"Now darling!" I yelled.

Whatever shock playing across his face was gone. Nate drew his revolver and shot at the behemoth. The bullet pinged off, sending up a shower of sparks peppering me with stinging bits of metal. It startled me more than it hurt.

Out of the corner of my eye I saw Nate rip off his vest and shirt.

Nate growled and dropped into a crouch. The flesh on his bare back swelled and ripped as the canithrope's substantial form tore itself free. His face contorted, tipped towards the sky, nose and jaw elongating with an audible crackling sound like a wood fire. His skull widened, ears lifting, and eye sockets broadening into a canine form.

His gasp of pain turned into a howling challenge. His strong hands widened, splitting the skin for sharp-tipped, black claws. One of his front paws hit the rocky ground. He stiffened and straightened, stretching to the monster's greater height. Hips and thighs morphed into powerful haunches poised to spring.

His dark fur blended with the shadows, his eyes glinted. The snarl echoed. The behemoth tried lifted an arm to smash me into the rocks. He sprang forward, slamming his bulk into the mechanical man. My canithrope slammed his fists into it, claws sending up sparks as he sent a flurry of blows into it.

I edged my way around to the altar where Father Henri was staring, his mouth comically hanging open. "My goodness!" was all he said.

The mechanical man broke through Nate's grip, pinning his arms at his sides. The single glowing eye became brighter and brighter. I grabbed Nate's revolver from where he dropped it. There must be a patron saint of horrendously difficult shots for women with very little experience. I would have to ask Father Henri when this was over.

My first shot missed both Nate and the mechanical man, but the second shot shattered the automaton's eye. It exploded with a burst of light, rocking its head up and back before a beam of hot light shot from its eye. The light hit the ceiling of the small cave, and the impact shook the walls. The floor gave an audible *crack*. I grabbed for Father Henri and pulled him away from the druidic altar in case the fancy knot work carving toppled. I was quite sure it weighed more than a horse and carriage.

Nate wrenched himself free from the metal man's grip. It stumbled around blindly, grasping for Nate. He leapt on top of an outcropping of the rock and threw himself onto the man's shoulders. The metal man whipped back and forth swinging, trying to knock Nate off his back. Nate bit one of the hoses running from the shoulder and down the arm, where a piston moved the massive arms. Black, slick oil sprayed like blood across the cavern. The piston gave a jerky shudder and the mechanical man could no longer straighten his arm.

The oil flowed into the ley well, spreading across the surface like the holy water had, but they danced around each other without mixing. I felt the image quite appropriate, magic, religion, and science dancing around one another creating something beautiful.

More than oil was flowing into the silver pool of the ley well. Water. I followed it back to its source. The altar had cracked again. I saw the glimmer of the water flowing from its cracks. The blast from the automaton's eye had damaged the cavern.

"Nate! The dam!"

Nate didn't acknowledge me. He was quite preoccupied in ripping into the wires and tubes protruding from a now open access port on the back of the mechanical man. It finally managed to get a hold of Nate and flung him over his head and across the cavern. He hit the wall with a solid *thud*, not far from the altar itself.

Nate was back on his feet in a second, scattering the clockwork spiders. It swung that heavy metal fist so fast it whistled through the air. The fist caught Nate below the breastbone. Fortunately, it was a glancing blow. The clockwork man *clicked* and *whirred* as it moved into position to deliver another heavy strike. Nate dodged out of the way, bounding into the near wall then using the power in those burly hind quarters to reverse direction and spring forward, propelling himself into the metal man with an echoing ring.

As the automaton wheeled and spun, I saw the green-gold glow of the battery inside, the same ones that the clockwork spiders were gathering and taking away. The entire side of its chest was crushed—an access panel had broken open and was swinging loose. Nate leapt onto its back, this time attaching himself to the man's head, raining blows down upon it that echoed in the cavern like a gong. The mechanical man raised his remaining arm and grabbed Nate by his neck to pull him off. This time, he had been expecting the automaton's hold and pushed off hard with his back feet, raking him. The blow dented his chest, and his arm creaked and sparked.

The man's arm was now bent at an impossible angle. If the machine had been human, the arm would have been dislocated or broken. This must have been Nate's plan. He bit the joint hard, severing wires and bending gears, and then he slammed his fists into the damaged joint again and again until the metal screamed and the bolts sheered, leaving the arm dangling uselessly at his side.

The battle was all but over. Without arms, the mechanical man spun at the waist and tried to pivot on its feet fighting to keep its balance. Nate ripped open the damaged chest and ripped out handfuls of wires, slick with oil and grease. He followed the wet mess to the ground, sending up a shower of water, tearing and ravaging like a monster gorging on fallen flesh.

The spiders were gathered in a dark corner. They were removing a cover that had been welded into the wall. It was a tunnel. I was fairly sure that we could follow them, but in his present state, mostly due to his size, Nate could not. Either way, we had little choice, the metal man could not fit within the pipe. It could march down the tunnel and follow us to Bromley Street where it might harm the people of London. Therefore, it would not do to leave the way we came.

"Nate!" I cried to get his attention.

He turned towards me, snarling, sides heaving.

"Please." I held a shaking hand out. "Come."

My canithrope crept towards me. "Nate. I know you're in there. You have to change back."

He snarled and gnashed his teeth. He looked over to where the spiders gathered in the corner.

The mechanical man lay belching smoke and steam and a foul oily smell. The battery—its green-gold light was an ominous glow occasionally. The air was full of *clicking* and *whirring*, and all but two spiders focused on the metal cover.

Nate bounded to them, splashing through ankle deep water, and snatched one up in his clawed hands. He tore its legs off and threw them across the cavern. He grabbed another, raised it up to his face and gave a roar that would have frightened any flesh and blood creature to death. The spider's lens eyes whirred and rotated, wholly unconcerned. Nate shattered them with one hammer blow of his fists. The space revealed from the removed spiders revealed a new horror—the spiders were repairing the metal man. They were tinkering with glowing needle-like feet, and legs that rotated into wrenches. They scavenged parts off their fallen comrades. I saw giant gears rotate again and the metal man shuddered, the battery glowing.

I couldn't think of anything else, I shot it.

CHAPTER TWENTY-EIGHT

I WOKE DEAF, my head ringing like I was standing inside Big Ben in the grand tower. The water trickling by my head was cold and had a faint oily taste. Nate was picking me up, gently cradling me to him. I opened my eyes, half expecting to see him still in his beast form. Though I had seen men look worse, it was generally after an evening of bare-knuckle boxing or some other pugilistic pursuit. He was the picture of fatigue, and he grunted as he picked me up, his arms shaking. My revolver was tucked in the front of his belt. His face and hair were covered in grease and oil. He swallowed hard, mouth contorting from the sour taste of the oil.

I had managed to blow myself clear of the ley well, but the dam had sustained damage for water level by the altar was rising; the water Nate was carrying me through reached his thighs. He and Father Henri were slogging through the water towards the pipe in the wall. The spiders had managed to remove the cover and must have retreated inside for they were nowhere to be seen.

We didn't have long until the cavern we were in was full of water, our entrance on the far side was already submerged. The great pipe, first our only choice to escape the great clockwork man that was the final protector of Sterling's battery charging station, was now our only choice for escape, though I suspected Nate was less than thrilled at the prospect of following those clockwork spiders into the dark with no idea where the pipe led.

In moments, the room would be submerged and the tunnel with it. It was a mile or more back to Bromley Street and the outlet to the Thames.

Nate may be able to swim that far, I may be able to make it but Father Henri never would.

I heard a high-pitched ringing in my ears. I was sure I had recovered enough to walk, and the transformation from man to beast and back again was quite taxing on Nate. As much as I would have loved nothing more than to have him carry me out of here, there was still work to be done. "I do believe I can make it from here." Though some of my hearing had returned, I felt as though I was screaming at them from across a great windy cavern.

Nate carefully helped me down from the altar where I had been set and I stood shakily on my feet. I took a few steps towards the altar and turned. From over Nate's shoulder, something glowing blue caught my eye.

Ranger's shadow, blue and ethereal, rose from his body, stood and shook himself. I could hear the slap of his ears as he tossed his broad head. So strange that a ghost should make a sound. The dog looked around at the druidic altar, then at the corpse of the metal man. He leapt on light ghost feet to the altar where I had been laying moments before and sat down, his tail slapping the stone. "Nate, look!" I pointed over his shoulder.

He turned. I felt him take in a sharp breath. "Ranger." He raised his arm slightly to reach out, then paused as though he had reconsidered. My heart ached for him.

Ranger raised his paw and swiped the air, then he laid down on the altar, tail flat, head up, ears erect. He was the new guardian of the ley well. Nothing would interfere with the magic that resided here. Between the binding charm and the ivy, the prayer and the holy water, and the new guardian—this was the safest ley well in the world.

Nate raised his palm. "Stay, boy. You're a very good dog."

The water was rising and with it our torches were lost. We had no choice, we had to get into the tunnel and take our chances with the clockwork spiders and wherever they led. It would be nearly a mile from where we battled the metal giant to the footbridge on Bromley Street, where we had ducked into the tunnel, and though Nate would have no trouble even if the tunnel were to flood, I have never been a strong swimmer and I was sure Father Henri would never make to journey. The copper pipe was ridged within and we followed the clockwork spiders up the gentle slope to their master and to what I assumed would be Sterling's

Emporium of Uncommon Goods for the Common Man. Nate followed Father Henri and me in silence for a while.

I slipped my hand down the neck of my shirt, the key for the birdcage of mechanical birds hung on its gold chain between my breasts. When we managed to stop I would pull the cage out and release *Aureus Lux*. The light from the tiny golden bird would be a welcome addition and Nate would undoubtedly find it more comforting than the cold blinking light of the clockwork spiders. Come to think of it, *Incendium*'s explosion may have been more useful than the revolver in fighting the mechanical man but the ringing in my ears could not be helped now. The only enchanted bird I was sure we didn't need, at least not at the moment, was *Reperio Aquae*—I had quite enough water right now.

We steadily climbed up the ridged pipe, the angle growing very steep. Father Henri huffed and puffed in the lead. He slipped, falling backwards. I hadn't been expecting it and I fell into Nate, sending all three of us into water up to our waists. Nate was shaking now. I longed to wrap him in warm blankets and bring him hot teas and stews until he was restored.

I glanced at him, I could just barely make out his features. No, perhaps strong liquor was more his style, with turtle soup and sherry and a loaf of hot crusty bread. Just the thought of it made my mouth water. I reached out and touched his cheek. I still felt the sticky slickness of the grease, but I could also feel the muscles move as he smiled. He caught my fingers and kissed them before releasing my hand.

My body ached as though I had been beat with a stick. My back was screaming in pain.

Nate dropped his hands on my shoulders. "Are you okay?" he whispered.

"I'm fine," I said, ducking out of his touch and focused on the pipe ahead. I turned my attention back to my grumbling stomach. All I had was my satchel with the bird cage at my side and a few bandages that were near useless now that they were soaked through. Nate's pack had most of our provisions including bottles of ale and a few thick slabs of holiday cake our cook was famous for. They were full of fruit and nuts and heavily fortified with rum. His pack had been left beside the altar along with Father Henri's—"Oh Father Henri, your Bible!"

He turned, puffing. "It is alright, my dear," he said, patting my hand, "I can always replace it. Lives are not so easy to replace. It is merely a representation of my faith, not my faith itself."

The rest of our belongings would be underwater with the ley well as the river flowed again bringing water to the people of Bromley Street and dispersing the magic back into the earth. I could not believe he would dismiss it so readily. "You said you were given that Bible when you left behind your commission to become a priest."

"Yes," He looked sad for a moment. "And I will miss it dearly. But no matter, it served its purpose. I shall get a new one. Were the word of God destroyed so easily then his followers would all be in great trouble."

I suppose he was right, without faith a cross is merely a lump of metal or wood, without faith a bible is merely paper.

The tunnel was getting light. I turned to tell Nate, and he shushed me. He had his head cocked to the side, listening to something we couldn't. Did he retain some of Ranger's senses as a man?

Father Henri carefully picked his way up the tunnel. There was a crack of light ahead. We were standing on the other side of a door. My sigh of relief was twofold—we had managed to find an area that would be safe from the water and full of air- and we had managed to not run into clockwork spiders while in the tunnel. Though I was more relieved for Nate than myself that we had not found more spiders. I found them charming.

As we got closer, we could hear the hum and whine of machinery. I crept past Father Henri. He was bent double catching his breath. Nate was in a similar state, though I was sure it was not the climb that had done him in. His other self, though dreadful and glorious, terrifying and wondrous, was horribly hard on him. It was up to me to figure out exactly where we were, not that I minded; the entire prospect was brilliantly exciting.

I eased the hatch open. We *were* in some sort of factory. Therefore, it must be Sterling's Factory, the one that the inventor, Mr. Geiger built. There were no other factories so close to the wharf, all the other mills and textile plants were further inland. I trusted Nate's innate sense of direction and he was sure of his placement even when there were no landmarks to guide him, after all, it brought us this far.

So, he was the one using the ley-magic. It powered his machines—and he had claimed it was merely the water. I shook my head. Sterling had rerouted the underground river to access the ley well not to use the water.

Not to mention he was slandering the inventor's good name with his plot. Were all high-born men such scoundrels?

The magic might explain the odd deaths. Men didn't drown on dry land. People didn't burn in rivers. But if one added wild magic into the equation, then all things were possible. Though my experience with magic was limited, I did understand that things that couldn't be explained any other way were likely related to magic. But the addition of the massive locked door twisted my stomach into knots. I imagined the machinery charging the large batteries represented a substantial investment and was worth defending but the metal door may not be for keeping meddling adventurers like myself and Nate out. The true purpose of the gigantic metal man may very well have been to defend the ley well from something far more dangerous. As terrifying as she was, I knew with sick certainty the Lamia must not be the most treacherous thing in the world. I shuddered.

The dead men may very well have learned some secret. Or they may have been merely in the way when the pressure behind the dam needed to be relieved as Nate guessed. I wasn't sure which was worse, death by neglect or death by misadventure. Each was just as final. My mind was racing along with the gears of the massive machine before us. Cranks turned driving grimy pistons which in turn pumped shafts up and down in a most obscene manner. The entire apparatus was taller than I was, taller than Nate when he was his other self. It loomed in the room. I had no idea how large the room was as most of it was obscured by the machine and a murky steam like the yellow-green pea soupers of London, but these were not cold— these were more oppressive than the fogs of London, if such a thing were even possible, they were stifling and warm as though produced by lights. I imagined it would be the same lights as the clockwork spiders gleaming off the fumes. At least I hoped it would be the spiders and not an entire army of clockwork men.

The entire contraption dripped foul oil that I could smell as well as taste. My palate was entirely overwhelmed by its mere presence. Small valves hissed and steamed like kettles. I had no desire to touch them, I could feel the heat of them from here. The sound of it all hurt my ringing ears and made them ache deep inside my head. I hoped they were not permanently damaged.

It was beautiful in its own way. It was hypnotic the way it moved, never wavering, always in motion and it nearly made me forget the men in the tunnel. At least there was no need for the mechanical birds now in their cunning little cage. We had light and there was more than enough water back the way we came.

I turned to go back to the men. They would be concerned if I was gone for too long. The machinery was making another noise, this one distinctly different then the even loud hum, something had changed. Something was wrong, and I was not the only person to notice.

"What's happening, Geiger?" A man demanded.

I nearly leapt out of my skin. I thought I was alone.

A second man had a cockney accent; quite the contrast to the educated speech of a wealthy man. "I'm not sure, Mr. Sterling."

The wealthy, educated man was Mr. Sterling. He spoke again, "Then you'd better get your pets to fix it. I have to open tomorrow morning. If the machinery cannot produce the goods then I shall have nothing to sell."

"I will do what I can, Sir," Geiger said, sounding resigned.

Someone grabbed my arm. I nearly shrieked. Nate! He gave me an apologetic smile. I scowled, I would have said something rude but Father Henri was with him. I hated to be startled. "We need to stop him and hold him here until we can summon a constable," I whispered furiously to Nate.

He nodded. "Father Henri, can you sneak around to the factory door and fetch a police man?"

"Of course, I can," Father Henri wheezed. The long, steep climb had done him no favors. I felt sorry for him.

"Maybe you should go get the constable and Father Henri should rest here. I can go speak with Mr. Sterling and keep him on the premises," I offered.

Both men fixed me with a look. "He's murdering people with magic, Vivian. There is no way that I am leaving you here with him." Nate lifted his chin.

I recognized that set jaw—the same look Nate had given before he insisted on taking me home. Damn stubborn male determination!

"I will be fine, my dear," Father Henri said. "Nathaniel, I will return shortly. Take care of Miss Vivian."

We watched him dart as quickly as an old man could, hunched over as if that gave some sort of cover. It would have been comical if we weren't in the factory of a murderer bent on increasing his wealth and family name at all costs. We exchanged a look. Nate placed a finger across my lips before I could protest. "I will go get Sterling. Keep an eye on Mr. Geiger. We may need him to give a statement. He is probably quite unaware of what is happening with his employer."

"You're exhausted," I argued. "Turning into a canithrope drains you. I am surprised you are able to maintain your footing."

He glared at me, annoyed that I pointed out the failing in his hasty plan. "Stay here!" Nate said in a tone that he assumed would be obeyed.

"I most certainly will not," I returned in the same tone. "This is my London, too."

Nate actually rolled his eyes at me. "Just keep an eye on Mr. Geiger, I'll be right back."

I watched Nate circle away in the opposite direction Father Henri had taken. I could either remain here under relatively safe cover or follow along. I had a sudden change of heart. I wanted to call them both back—I didn't want to be here in this loud place of steam and grinding gears and the oily metallic smell of grease that made me want to retch. I was an adventuress now, and I was coming to understand that adventure and excitement went hand in hand with crippling fear.

There was a skittering by my feet. One of the spiders was crawling along on four legs and two others were carrying the broken battery from the mechanical man. One of the spiders had a broken leg, bent backwards, another leg completely missing. The spider deftly navigated around me, leaving a trail of wet claw prints. It headed straight for what I could only assume was Mr. Geiger.

Geiger's head was covered by a newsboy cap. He wore goggles like I had seen in the airship, but these had green lenses. Inventors were the eccentric type, I suppose his strange eye coverings were fitting. His leather apron was full of patch pockets, stained and battered, sporting fluids and burns and the tops of tools poking out of the pockets. He scowled at his machine and listened to the odd sounds coming from it. He was clenching and unclenching his gloved right hand, shaking it and then he would pause and rub the knuckles of that hand between his eyes as though to fend off a headache. Then he turned to a great compressor and bellows and started to fiddle with dials and gages all the while his lips moved as he muttered something lost to the great growl of the room.

The spider waited patiently to be noticed, but Mr. Geiger was too engrossed in tinkering with the side of some sort of huge press to be bothered by the clockwork creation. Perhaps I should just go introduce myself and explain why we were here. I opened my mouth.

"Geiger! I can't find the crates of goods from the machines." Mr. Sterling strode into the room from beyond the steam and the noise.

I dove back to my cover behind boxes of pieces and parts again. I had no desire to be seen by the murderous Mr. Sterling. If they looked over here they would be able to see the slightly open door that led to the pipe that went down to the now flooded lay well. We had neglected to push it closed. I cursed my stupidity.

"The crates are in the office, I asked Lum to move them there myself," Geiger shouted back.

"Forgive me, Newton." Mr. Sterling said, his voice softening. "I spent every penny I had to have you build these machines. My fortune, my family's fortune, depends on it. Forgive me. I find myself anxious."

"Columbus!" Mr. Geiger yelled as though he was calling for a dog.

A hulking man appeared on a raised stairwell. He had been previously hidden by steam and smoke. He set his huge ham-fists on the railing. He would be able to crush it were he so inspired. His ill-fitting, cheap suitcoat was open, revealing a torso like a keg, covered in dirty linen and a green vest. He had a porkpie hat cocked on his head. He looked to be bald beneath. In his teeth he chewed a dark brown cigar, gnawing it to bits, chomping like a street urchin works at a corn cob. He glared.

"Mr. Sterling says he cannot find the crates I had you move."

Columbus pulled the cigar from his mouth and cleared his throat. "I put them in the office, Mr. Sterling, just as Mr. Geiger asked me to."

The huge man and the inventor exchanged a quick look. I caught it, Mr. Sterling did not. I felt a chill race up my spine. Something was very wrong here.

"Ah very good then, Columbus." Mr. Sterling started to climb the stairs to the upper platform.

Geiger shook his head muttering, "Idiot," and returned to his press. He finally noticed the clockwork spider at his feet. He stared for a long moment. He reached down and took the broken battery from the creature. He cursed, and I heard his steps on the floor. I dove and rolled, a skill I had managed a few times before on board the airship, mostly by accident when the storm made the ship toss us about. I landed hard on my shoulder but managed to scuttle into the shadows of a large machine just as Mr. Geiger came into view.

I fought to keep my breath even. Mr. Geiger opened the door the rest of the way. He took a few steps inside and cursed again. He came out and slammed the door. The clockwork spider was following him. He booted it out of the way. It skittered across the floor, righted itself, and returned dutifully to its master.

Geiger snarled in rage, snatched up the spider, and threw it into the huge press. The press slammed closed with a scream of rending metal and the crunch of glass. The leg sticking out twitched, then were still. Poor creature. To serve his master, then to be crushed like that was heartbreaking. Several other spiders appeared out of nowhere and started to pull the press open for the parts of the spider, presumably to repair it.

"Leave it!" Geiger snapped, stalking past. The clockwork spiders fell in step behind him, following like a row of wooden ducks on a string. I let him get ahead of me, then I followed, trying to keep to the shadows.

Geiger stalked by the machinery to a small metal panel in the back wall. He pushed several glowing buttons, the panel flashed blue, then there was a grinding and a rumble. The floor itself shook. The wall split open. It was a massive door, larger than any church door, larger than a castle door. The door opened a few feet, then shuddered and squeaked to a halt.

Geiger snarled again and kicked the door. It made a hollow thud. "Lum!"

Columbus appeared overhead again. I had chosen my hiding place well. "Sir?"

"Lock Sterling up! The dam broke and the factory has lost power. We are moving up the timetable quicker than expected."

"Sir!"

Mr. Geiger slid sideways through the door and disappeared beyond. Where was Nate? I looked around wildly, expecting him to appear or at least be ready to fight with Sterling or the huge thug. Where was Father Henri with the constable, for that matter? This was too much for a simple apothecary's daughter to handle. We needed the police. Whatever this dangerous man was up to was beyond any nefarious plot I could have ever dreamed up. I wasn't a simple apothecary's daughter anymore. A lady would have cowered in the darkness; no, a lady would not even be here. A lady would be hiding in a tea house or a solar waiting for the blustery day to pass or fainting away at the thought of spiders and clockwork men. A lady never would have fought a Lamia or dead men. They were right, we needed the police, but we would make due until they arrived. I would have to make due until Nate managed to discover where I had gone. I just hoped he wouldn't take too long.

I took a few deep breaths to bolster my courage. There was no wisdom in following this man into the darkness, but I couldn't very well stay here. I had to know what he was up to and why he would frame Mr. Sterling for the murders. One thing was certain. I no longer believed that Mr. Sterling's Factory was solely focused on providing uncommon goods at low prices to improve the life of the common man.

I was thankful for the trousers and boots in ways I couldn't even say. I dashed into the darkness after Geiger, shoving my hand into my satchel and into the cage of birds at my side. I may need light where I was headed.

Behind the door, stairs led down into the bowels of the factory. I nearly didn't see them in time. My foot slipped on the first one and it was only tremendous good fortune that my heel caught it before I tumbled down the stairs, breaking my neck.

I crept down the stairs feeling like my whole body was tingling and tense, every drop of water from the gathering steam in the ceiling, every creak made my heart leap into my throat. Above was chaos like a textile factory running at capacity. But this was another thing entirely.

A large, mechanical device sat cranking away looking remarkably like Babbage's Difference Engine I had seen in drawings at the World's Fair a few years back. Several other displays covered with switches and dials blinked and clicked away. It was a flurry of action that was all dwarfed by a great pale mass of shapeless nothing.

The middle of the room was shrouded with sailcloth. It dominated the room, daring anyone to question it, daring anyone to come closer. The sailcloth twitched and wiggled as though something beneath its surface was alive, like maggots crawling beneath swollen, bloated flesh. I could not retch quietly so I shoved my fist into my mouth.

Geiger stared at his machine the way a religious man stares at the chancel. The way a fanatic gazes lovingly up at an idol before he commits blasphemy; the way a madman loves. The boxes would not provide cover for long. Whatever Nate was doing, it was madness to come down here alone. I needed him with me. We should be doing this with a fleet of police at our sides and barring that, at the very least while watching over one another. I ducked and retraced my steps. How in the world had I managed to sneak this far without being seen?

I turned on my toes, still squatting behind a crate searching for my next bit of shadow, and nearly leapt out of my skin.

Lum was standing there, his doltish face twisted somewhere between confusion and annoyance. "And who might you be, Poppet?" Despite the growl there was something soft in his voice.

I think I swallowed my tongue. My mouth was as dry as the sand on Molten Cay.

He glanced from me to the stairs and back again. He opened his mouth and took a deep breath—

Mr. Geiger stormed back from around the panel. "Lum! What the devil is taking you so long?!" Geiger froze. The hammer in his hand lowered slowly, absently. Each word was a punctuated with rage. "Bring. Her."

Columbus visibly paled. His eyes widened. He was caught. I was caught. Whatever he was about to say was lost now. Lum grabbed my upper arm and jerked me to my feet.

Time crawled around us. I could hear his breath in a long rasp, like a file being drawn over metal. I stumbled over his boot and a bit of stone from the ceiling scraped under foot. It plinked noisily along. I could count the turns it bouncing along. Everything was moving slowly, too slowly. Beyond it all, I could feel an image: cups. I tried to count them, but trying to count them was disorienting. There were ten of them, I don't know how I knew, I just did.

No, not ten cups, it was the *Ten of Cups* from the Tarot, super-imposed at the edges of my vision. I could see through it if I really tried to. It was the image one got while waking from a dream, the image that was there and not quite there, reality and surreal. A family rejoiced beneath a rainbow of cups. The tattooed me from the mirror lake had all the suit of cups emblazoned up my left leg beginning with the ace on my foot and the king at my hip. I felt this at my thigh, hot and sharp. It was a warning. The image of cups fractured. No, the family was fractured.

The image was replaced by the *Eight of Swords*, a woman surrounded by swords, hoodwinked and suspended. She couldn't even touch the ground so she couldn't even find her bearings. She believed she was trapped and so trapped she was. Trapped. No choice. No way out. No way out for whom?

I wasn't reading for myself. This only happened when Lum touched me. Was I reading for him? How had I done it? I wasn't sure, but I was sure about one thing: he might not have a choice, his family may be fractured and broken but I was not going to give up without a fight.

Columbus was easily as large as Captain Morgan and Mr. Pierce, and he dragged me down the last few steps as I stumbled along. The world was back to the speed of life. I shook my head to clear the cups and swords. I needed my wits about me.

Mr. Geiger gave me the look one gives a cockroach. "Mr. Baxter, you were hired to protect my inventions from trespassers. All trespassers." He quirked an eyebrow at me. "If her sex is an issue for you, I assure you there are many others for whom that is not a concern."

Lum eased his grip, "Boss, I'm sure this chuckie couldn't wait for the grand opening, that's all."

Newton Geiger wheeled around, his face twisted with rage. He stormed up to me, snarling like a man unhinged. "Who the hell are you?"

"Vivian Harper," I said, raising my chin.

He made an agreeable noise, but the smile on his face didn't reach his eyes. My throat tightened. Lum tightened his grip on my arms. I was a shield but not for him, for something much more precious. The swords around him were easier to see.

"Well now, Miss Harper." Mr. Geiger paced before me, back and forth, on the balls of his feet. I was fairly sure he was going to strike me. "Men bow to lords and kings. How do you present yourself to a God?"

I couldn't have heard him correctly. "Pardon me?"

He slapped me. Hard. If Lum hadn't been holding me up I would have fallen. My arms were now wrenched painfully behind my back. I struggled to my feet, eyes watering and ears ringing.

"You see, Miss Harper, God is dead." He laughed again, triumphant, as if he had been the one to personally murder Him. "Faith and all that superstitious, silly nonsense is beyond the educated man now. God is dead and we killed him. We are the new Gods: men of science and industry and we will remake the world in our image."

He walked towards his machine. On a table lay parts of a mechanical man, an arm not far from a torso, two legs, one missing part of the metal housing so the wires and gears were exposed. The metal man's head was on the table between the legs, unattached. The top of the head was open, exposing a thin shiny board that had several small glass vials attached.

"These fuses hold all the magic the man needs to function. I can even do it on a much larger scale with punch cards." He turned and pulled a stack of square metal plates from his desk. Each had several holes in what I assumed was a specific pattern and sequence.

I scoffed, sounding much bolder than I felt. "You are hardly a God."

"You will be quiet. You are in the presence of genius," he snapped and raised his hand to strike me again. I couldn't help but flinch.

"Welcome to a new age, Miss Harper. Before now, only God could create life. Now, so can I!"

He snapped his fingers, and he was instantly surrounded by his clockwork spiders. They clicked and chittered and blinked at one another. They were not so charming anymore.

Mr. Geiger stood and raised his arms. "Amazing, aren't they? If I gave them the command they would rip you apart. Each has an acetylene torch in one claw. That would turn your pretty little flesh into char steak. And they can talk to one another using Morse's code. With light! Can you imagine, they communicate with one another through light!" He laughed.

Where was Nate?! "You're mad as a hatter," I said.

"If you speak against me again, I will cause you pain," he said with a wicked smile.

I licked my dry lips. I was sure he meant it.

"Now, I don't know how you got in here, but it is actually quite fortunate. You are about to witness the birth of a modern God."

Something moved in the corner of my eye. The ceiling was dotted with small tunnels for his clockwork spiders to move about. Geiger must be used to such movement, for it didn't register to him in the slightest.

"You keep saying that," I said quickly. "A God. It sounds to me that you're really a poor, little man trying desperately to rise above what you actually are."

He bristled and turned. "And what exactly is that?"

Nate was climbing down a large cargo net full of metal pieces and parts. He needed time, time I could give him.

"Nothing," I said softly.

"What?"

"You heard me," I said, louder this time, letting my sweetest smile cross my face. "You are nothing."

He was true to his word. He balled up his fist and slammed it into my stomach. I crumpled to the ground, unable to breathe. Lum let me fall. I sucked in hard, but all that came out was a wheezing sound. If I didn't breathe soon, I knew I was going to die. At this point that was preferable. I thought I had forgotten how to breathe.

"Touch her again and I'll prove to you that you are far from God," Nate's voice rang out. He stood below the cargo net, feet planted and wide. His Seax was in his hand. I had never been so glad to see him.

Lum didn't move for a moment, his dull sunken eyes turned and stared at Nate with his mouth agape.

"Another witness. Wonderful." Geiger rubbed his hands together. "I'm not sure how you got in here. In the future I shall have to make my servants more aggressive. Now as I was saying, to create clockwork life is really nothing special, but to have it know its function and retain it after the clockwork mechanism has run down is a real feat. So far I know of only a few men in the whole world capable of such a wondrous result."

Nate ignored Geiger—Lum had recovered from his shock and the two men were squaring off against one another.

I still struggled to breathe. The whale bones of my corset should have protected me from the punch. How had he hit me so hard?

If Mr. Baxter had any qualms about harming me because I was a woman, Nate was afforded no such consideration. Lum advanced on Nate, his large hands curled into fists. I couldn't wait until Nate transfigured into his other form. Wouldn't they be surprised then; a God, indeed. They were about to see what true power really was.

Geiger was ignoring the men. He pulled a sail cloth cover off of a huge contraption in the center of the room. "You will deal with this, won't you?" He said offhanded to Lum.

He was staring at this new machine like a man possessed. The needle on the large gage in the center just passed from the yellow zone into the edge of the green zone. Much like the copper kettle chargers in the ley well beneath London, there were several rows of sockets to plug the glowing yellow-green canister batteries. All but three slots were already occupied. Two clockwork spiders came from the ceiling with another battery and they fit it into the machine. The needle moved further.

Whatever Mr. Geiger was planning, he was nearly complete. I had a feeling it was more sinister than the metal man on the table.

Demons, undead things and insane inventors, was anything simple anymore? "Mr. Sterling had you do this?"

Mr. Geiger might have forgotten I was there. His shoulders hunched "Sterling was so blinded by his own ambition that he didn't even think twice when I told him I could make him a rich and powerful man. He threw the money at me by the fistful to make his dream come true."

"But you didn't, did you?" I said, forcing myself to stand.

I didn't know exactly what he was doing now, but his machine had a huge collection of batteries charged by the ley well, and I was quite sure I didn't want him activating it.

Behind me, Lum had picked up a length of pipe and swung it at Nate. Nate dodged and rolled to one side, his knife flashing. Why wasn't he changing? Lum's next swing caught Nate behind the knee, knocking both of his feet out from under him and dropping him flat on his back. The air rushed out of him in a *woof*. Change Nate! Now! I need you!

Nate grabbed a wrench from the factory floor and used it to block a blow designed to splatter his head into the floor. Nate rolled, managing to close some of the distance between us.

"Why aren't you changing?" I almost screamed at him.

He was on one knee, panting and gasping. He shook his head. "I can't."

Nate was pale and shaking. He looked on the verge of passing out. He hadn't recovered from the fight with the mechanical man. He snatched my revolver from his belt, raised it, and fired.

Lum cried out and jerked as the bullet caught him in the side. Nate stood.

"You shot me!" Lum stuttered in shock, pressing his hand to his side. He stared at the blood in disbelief.

"You hit me with a pipe," Nate returned evenly.

"Enough!" Geiger snapped. "You men act like primates! Your kind has its uses, but when I am reborn you will be obsolete. Soon you will be useless."

"My kind?" Nate asked.

"Useless?" Lum turned to his boss.

"Idiots with more muscle than brains!" Geiger snapped.

Why were they ignoring the most important thing?! Geiger said 'reborn'! What was he planning? He had to be stopped, his machine had to be stopped. I lunged at Geiger. Both of us hit the floor. There was nothing elegant in it. At least I ended up on top. "Don't let him activate that machine, whatever you do," I screamed.

Nate nodded and turned the gun to the revolving carousel of batteries at the top of the machine. "This is probably going to kill us all," Nate warned. I nodded grimly.

We were all staring. He pulled the trigger. The gun clicked. It clicked again. Damn. He was out of bullets.

My heart sank. Okay. Do this the hard way. I forgot to watch Geiger. He rolled me over him and ended up on top. From the corner of my eye I saw Lum tackle Nate. The gun skittered across the floor.

Geiger grabbed my shoulders. My head cracked against the floor. Bright stars exploded, blinding my vision. I couldn't see but I could feel him. I could smell his breath, hot and smelling like onion and fish. I brought my knee up sharply and slammed my knee into his stomach. He backed off a bit and I kicked hard with both feet.

Geiger caught one foot and flipped me over. I twisted like an eel and curled so I could kick again. He didn't give me another opportunity. Instead my hip hit the ground and pain knifed through me.

He grabbed the shoulder strap of my corset and hauled me to my feet. Beneath the corset, my shirt ripped. My feet left the ground. I tried to kick. I clawed at his arm. My nails were useless and his arm was cold and strong as steel.

Nate called out my name but he and Lum were busy trading punches. Between one man being exhausted post-transformation and one man shot, they were evenly matched. Nate punched Lum hard in the bullet wound and tried to dart past him when Lum doubled over. Lum caught him with a hard slam in the back that left both men on the ground. Despite best intentions, no help was coming.

I made my fingers as straight and stiff as I could and jammed them into his armpit. He hissed in pain and dropped me hard. I landed on my rear. With the same hand he slammed his palm into my chest and threw me aside. I slid across the floor and into the wall. I tasted blood.

"Your primitive weapons are useless. Now witness true power," Geiger said. He removed his apron and shirt. His right arm, from the shoulder down, was encased in metal, shiny and silvery in the dull factory light. No wonder he struck me like a hammer.

I hit the wall hard. My ears were ringing again. I heard music. Wait. I knew that tune.

Primitive or not, I had one more weapon. The satchel at my side. By some miracle, I still had it. I thrust my hand inside. *Aureus Lux* had a swirling pattern. *Reperio Aquae* was smooth and silky to the touch and *Incendium* was rough and angular, nearly sharp. I pulled out a bird. "*Incendium*, Geiger!" I shouted, hurling the bird with all my might.

A glowing red-hot bird streaked across the room heading straight for Geiger. The bird hit him in the face. *Incendium* exploded, sending red hot bits of shrapnel across the room. Geiger screamed in pain. The glass window on the chamber of his machine cracked, sending a spiderweb of cracks across its surface. The charred bits of bird fell to the floor.

For one moment, I thought I had done it. Geiger was no more. I had killed a man. I had stopped whatever he was doing. I saved a city. I was elated. I was going to be sick.

Just meters from me, Nate and Lum were frozen, panting, hanging on each other like exhausted gladiators.

Then Geiger shuddered.

One bloody hand grasped for the machine. Geiger reached for the door. Weakly, I struggled to stand. Nate's arms were clasped tightly around Lum's neck.

Geiger opened a door on his machine and let himself inside, leaving a bloody smear on the door.

The batteries started to spin faster, and their glow became brighter. Nate gave a grunt. Something huge sailed across the factory floor and slammed into the machine.

Geiger screamed. Lum screamed. Nate screamed. I believe I screamed. In fact, the whole world was screaming. I felt something slam into me and knock me onto the ground. The world went black. This is truly how the world was ending, with a shattering *bang* that plunged the world into darkness.

CHAPTER TWENTY-NINE

THE DARKNESS was Nate's long, leather coat. He had managed to throw it over our heads. He carefully pulled it back. The world wasn't plunged into darkness. The world was on fire. I'm not sure which was worse.

We lay side by side on the factory floor. Nate gave me a sly smile and carefully pushed himself up with shaking arms. He turned to give me a hand. Some shrapnel from the explosion had cut into his back, leaving a bloody swath that trickled down his back and legs.

Metal squealed and bent. The clockwork spiders were in a panic. They were exiting through the holes in the walls. I struggled to my feet and turned to see where Lum and Geiger happened to be.

"Why in God's name did you throw the wrench?" I demanded, my eyes stinging from the smoke and heat.

"I learned from the best," Nate yelled over the roaring fire. "When in doubt throw whatever is at hand," He laughed. I stared. The thrashing he received from Lum may have knocked his brains loose.

Banging made us whip around. The machine and its metal chamber were on fire. Geiger was pounding his fists against the sealed door. He was panicked. His metal fist shattered the cracked, glass porthole. He gave a high-pitched keening cry.

Nate darted forward. The flames forced him back. I grabbed his arm before he could try again. A second later the only path to the infinity engine was blocked as a ton of metal, warped and twisted by the heat, came crashing down and bringing with it cargo nets of supplies on fire. Nate started forward, dragging me a step. Geiger gave a shriek, then was silent.

"Nate!" I pointed over to where Lum was struggling to rise.

He didn't think twice. We grabbed Lum's arms and dragged him back from the fire, struggling one inch at a time. Finally, we managed to get Lum to his feet and up the stairs to the secret door in the back wall of the factory.

We could hear shouts of "Fire!" coming from the street beyond the factory doors. The words were our salvation and our ticket out of this damnation. Without speaking, we pushed towards it, dragging Lum with us. I closed my eyes, trying to see the cards I had read for him before. The fractured cups still arched above him but the swords were gone. His eyes rolled back and forth in a stunned sort of way as his world crumbled.

We made it out of Sterling's Emporium of Uncommon Goods for the Common Man accompanied by a cloud of thick, black smoke. It swirled around us and took to the sky, darkening it more than a thousand coal fires. I coughed and choked and leaned heavily against the doorframe sucking in the clean air. In moments, Nate was at my side, his arm wrapped protectively around me. I sagged gratefully against him.

He had managed to set Lum down onto a pile of crates. The large man was now clasping a hand against his side and coughing, same as we were, as we struggled to get the smoke from our lungs. Nate pulled me away from the door; the clatter of trotting horses on cobbled streets and the pinging of a bell cut through the general clamor.

The fire brigade and their carriage drawn by beautiful, white horses came through the crowd and smoke, ringing their bell like heroes of great authority to save the day. The men and women of London gathered to watch the spectacle and some pointed at the three of us, bedraggled and soot stained, a sorry lot we were.

Except, the day had already been saved. They were just cleaning up the mess left behind.

Father Henri had done his job as well. He came trotting along after the fire brigade along with several constables. Mr. Sterling stood there as well, flanked by a policeman, hand half-way to his mouth, watching the factory burn—and with it, his fortune.

CHAPTER THIRTY

AMIDST ALL THE CHAOS, Nate gallantly grabbed a police man and turned Lum over to them. After all we had been through, I knew he was not having Lum arrested but taken to the nearest hospital. He pulled a battered sheaf of papers from his waistcoat and handed them over as well. He must have gathered them from the factory. So that was to explain his absence. I found I didn't care one way or the other what they said. I was too tired to have an opinion on the matter. Then he hailed a cab and helped me inside. The driver cast a wistful look over his shoulder, sad to leave such an intriguing scene.

We returned to my family home on Exeter Street. While most of the people ran to the noise and the hullabaloo to see the great fuss and racket to brighten their dull lives, I had quite enough for the night.

It was strange to know that you saved an entire city, and no one would ever know it. Nate and I both skipped dinner. He stepped out. I assumed it was to report to his contacts in the Explorer's Society about the strange happenings we had participated in the night before. Father Henri went straight to his bed chamber. I was only a hot bath behind him in reporting to my own bed. I fell asleep almost instantly. I never heard what time Nate managed to return.

Mama was waiting for me in the solar the next morning with her sewing, and the previous day's post. "Vivian, a letter came for you while you were out." Mama handed me a thin envelope sealed with a fine seal stamped in black ink. "A clerk from Hartford and Basset's office sent it by yesterday. They wish to speak to you upon your earliest convenience. I recommend after breakfast. That young man of yours is in need of fortification."

Two hours later, fortified with eggs, toast, bacon, and loads of rich coffee, Nathaniel and I made our way across town to the rows of fine offices where the barristers had their work houses. We were both too stiff and sore to attempt the walk, so we took a Hansom cab. A visit to a lawyer was quite an occasion. It must have made an impression upon Nate, as he even shaved for the event.

We finally reached our destination and rang the bell. A junior partner, no older than myself, let us in and bid us wait in a plush office.

"Do you have any idea what this is about?" Nate finally asked me after listening to the *tick*, *tick*, *tick* of the huge standing clock in the corner for far too long. He looked edgy and restless. I shrugged, and though I was sitting patiently with my hands folded neatly in my lap, I kept twisting my engagement ring around my finger. We had decided on the sapphire one.

Finally, a large man in a very expensive wool suit entered and closed the door behind himself. "Miles Callaghan Hartford Jr., Esquire" the man said.

"That is quite a mouthful, if you don't mind me saying so, Mr. Hartford," I returned.

He laughed, his large, round frame shaking. "Yes, I suppose it is, but those of us with impressive family names ought to use them, for nothing else but to honor the men who built them."

"I suppose you are correct." I looked around his garishly colored plush office. "Your letter summoned me. I'm afraid I do not know what this is about."

"Oh, of course." He rang a small silver bell on his massive oaken desk.
A maid appeared at the door and gave a small curtsey. "Sir?"
"Tea?"

At least I knew I wasn't about to be arrested or brought into civil action. If that were the case, I was fairly sure he wouldn't be offering tea. "Ahh, please."

"Brandy for the gentleman?" Mr. Hartford offered Nate.

Nate shrugged. They must have been expecting company, for moments after the order, the maid returned with a tea tray modestly set for one, with more cakes than I could eat by myself.

"First of all, you are Miss Vivian Harper, correct?"

"Yes." I watched the maid pour milk into my cup, followed by strong black tea. So, he was a man who observed the social niceties, but didn't delight in setting out a fine tea. From the scent I knew I was familiar with this blend, fine and strong but of no particular note.

"You are not married are you, my dear?"

"Mr. Valentine is my fiancé," I said, feeling little flutters of pleasure under my bruised breastbone.

"Well, then this concerns you as well, though I suppose indirectly for the time being," Mr. Hartford said to Nate. He handed me a thick sheaf of papers. Before I could open it, he added an unopened letter to the top, this one in an envelope decorated by hand with a small fleur-de-lis and French lilac in the lower right corner.

My Dear Miss Harper,

My husband and I cannot hope to adequately express our thanks for your kind rescue on Molten Cay. As a thank you, I am deeding you one of our small estates in the country. Though it is a villa style, it is adequately furnished and was updated two summers ago. I must confess this home was never to my taste but it is clean, well-maintained, and fashionably appointed, if I do say so myself. You will have to hire your own staff, an arduous task but one I am sure you are equal to. The estate sits on 1200 acres, a small income to be sure but if carefully managed, the home can be kept on that income alone. I wish you continued good fortune and do hope your Mr. Valentine realizes what a treasure he has in you and decides to court you properly. If not, the property is quite the attractive prospect for a proper match.

Your humble servant,

Lady Marie-Laure Rothechild

My hands were shaking. I read the letter three more times, certain I had misread something. Nate noticed, and set down his glass of brandy. I felt his hand on my shoulder as he quickly scanned the letter over my shoulder.

Fortunes did not change this way. A merchant class woman, the daughter of a skilled but simple apothecary engaged to wed a currently homeless member of the Explorer's Society did not go from middle class to a lady overnight. Yet if this letter was to be believed, I was now to be a titled, landed lady with incomes far exceeding anything I might have secured any other way. And I didn't have to marry into the Goodwin family.

Nate swallowed hard. I hoped he understood what this could mean.

"Is this a joke?" I asked, after finding my voice.

"No Ma'am," Mr. Hartford said, a huge smile on his face. "I received this paperwork from Lady Rothechild's lawyer a fortnight ago. The official procedure has already been filed with the offices of land and titles."

I opened the sheaf of papers and rifled through them; inventories, rental agreements, financial statements, and at the bottom the deed to Albion Manor with a heavy wax seal. My breath caught in my throat.

"As her future husband, would you like for your name to be added to the deed, upon provision of marriage, of course?" Mr. Hartford said to Nate.

He looked as stunned as I was. "No," he said, shaking his head.

"Yes," I said at the same time.

Mr. Hartford looked confused—certainly a man wasn't turning down the land and incomes that came with his future bride.

"No," Nate said firmly. "We will revisit this later."

"Do you think you are not going to marry me?" I demanded.

Mr. Hartford chuckled under his breath. I turned in my chair and shot him a look. He, too, lapsed into stunned silence. "Madame…" he began hesitantly.

"Your duty was to inform us of our new estate and the letter from Lady Rothechild, correct?" I said in a manner he clearly wasn't used to from women.

Mr. Hartford nodded. "I do have other appointments this afternoon, but I can leave you my office for a few moments." He gave Nate a look that admonished him to talk some sense into me.

"Vivian, your valor won you this from Lady Rothechild," Nate protested as the door closed.

"You were there, too," I argued.

"Yes, but I ran off with several of the dead men on my tail," he said, lowering his voice.

"You were luring them away," I said.

"Yes, but you fought to protect and defend Lady Rothechild. She is rewarding you, not us. Most definitely not me."

"Do you have reservations about marrying me?" I asked.

"Absolutely not," he said quickly, too quickly.

"You do!" I stared at him.

"No, I don't" He ran his hand through his hair, that absurd habit that always made his hair stand on end like he had been sleeping in a hurricane. So much for his polished look.

"Then what is it?" I demanded.

"This makes you a lady," he said hesitantly.

"And you a gentleman," I said. "Not a peer, of course, but a landed gentleman, an esquire."

"But that's just it, I'm not a gentleman." Nate grabbed my hands in his and set the papers aside. "I can't even afford to purchase you a proper ring. We have to use one from the Lamia's treasure trove."

"Nate. That treasure is as much yours as it is mine." I pulled my hands free and grabbed the sides of his head, forcing him to look at me. "I love you. If you love me too, then none of this matters."

He froze. I could feel the tension melt out of him, and with it any protest. I loved looking into those warm amber eyes, the only feature that seemed to whisper there was something different about him. I had never seen eyes like that before, not in a human anyway. They were Ranger's eyes, and the eyes of the man-dog he could become.

"What?" he suddenly asked, self-conscious.

"What color were your eyes before?"

"Before what?" He looked at me like I had just tried to convince him to commit scandal in the barrister's office.

"Before Ranger and the druid site and everything."

"Blue, why? Are they not now?" He searched the room unsuccessfully for a mirror.

"No, they are not." I smiled.

"You have me at a disadvantage, dear," he said evenly.

"Now, can I have Mr. Hartford add you to the title?" I asked, deftly changing the subject.

"You're really going to marry me?" he asked.

"I am," I said. "Really there is little you can do about it."

"The plight of the married man," he said with a smile. "I had better get used to it then."

"Yes, you better." I kissed him and went to find Mr. Hartford, who was hovering in the hall, no doubt waiting for Mr. Valentine to put his fiancée in her proper place.

We returned home late that night. There was much to do, and though we had all the time in the world, London had become stifling, both from the smoggy air and the completely unenlightened view towards the fairer sex. I wondered how women like Madame Theodora stood the ignorance and judgement as well as she had.

We informed my parents over dinner of our sudden fortune. Mama just smiled. The cards were right, yet again.

CHAPTER THIRTY-ONE

MR. CROSSDALE ACTED as the owner's agent when the Rothechilds were not in residence and assured us he would serve us as well. He took Nathaniel out among the tenants, then they retired to his cottage just beyond the hill where they engaged in all sorts of manly pursuits like cards, cigars, and brandy.

I immediately promoted Mrs. Tabor as our housekeeper in the London Townhouse, a position she had already filled, but now she could command a better salary. Lady Rothechild was correct, the house was smartly furnished it just needed staff, something I meant to immediately remedy. Though I was tempted to just move her and Jenny to Albion Manor, Mama and Papa needed them there for now.

The Rothechilds hadn't been bad landowners, merely absent ones. Papa hired three true apprentices to staff the apothecary with Calvin at their head. He would stay in London while Mama traveled with us to our new home to help me set it up. Papa would join us for his holiday, then Mama would return to London with him. I was quite pleased at the prospect of offering them a relaxing holiday in the country far from the dreary gray of London.

It took a little researching and a few coins in the right hands, then finally a visit to The Crimson Boar to speak to the membership secretary, but soon I found myself traveling to an old but well-kept boarding house on Flint Road. I checked the address again on the small slip of paper, then went inside. The back room on the right, just off the third-floor landing. I took a deep breath then knocked hard on the faded door.

The man who opened the door was numb with amazement. His intelligent, generally witty expression marred with shock. He recovered quickly. A desirable trait in a butler.

"Hiram?"

"Miss Harper?" He stared in disbelief. "I had never expected to see you again in this life, milady."

"I have come to offer you a position," I said as formally as I could.

He blinked hard. "I'm afraid I do not understand. Not that I am not elated at the thought. I was fired from my situation with cause by your former fiancé."

"I am well aware of that. I am also aware that his reason was you speaking against him, in private."

"Miss, I would gladly come work for the Harper family," Hiram said.

"No," I said. "You misunderstand. You will be working for me. I am setting up house in a country estate, and I need a man I can trust as my butler."

He nodded. "Of course, I am glad you found a husband suitable to you, Miss Harper. Might I inquire the gentleman's name?"

"Mr. Nathaniel Valentine," I said. "Though that is not where the fortune and incomes are from. I was gifted an estate for service. I shall be moving my entire family out of London and it falls to me to put a suitable staff in place. I would like you to head that staff."

"Miss Harper," Hiram bit his lip. "I owe you an apology."

"Whatever for?" I asked.

"I should have intervened on your behalf sooner with Mr. Goodwin," he said.

"There is nothing to forgive," I said, and I meant it. "Byron is a sad excuse for a man, and I do hope that he finds a way to be happy and of good cheer with whatever lady he convinces to wed him. He would be better served peddling his name and not meeting the woman until the wedding if he wishes to keep her."

Hiram smiled at that. "I accept the position, Lady Harper."

"Very good." I handed him a card with the address of our new home printed upon it. "I expect you by Saturday, if you please."

Hiram nodded, and I left the boarding house with my head held high. I didn't care who saw me leave the slums, I was too busy securing the future of the people I cared so much for. In the morning, Mama, Nate, and I would be loading all my belongings into the carriage to inspect my new home in the country.

When we first took a carriage up to the manor I was convinced some mistake had been made. The manor was a huge mansion of gray stone, and up one rounded outcropping green vines crept stretching to reach the top to bask in the sun. Stone planters full of orange and pink flowers spilled out like wine pouring from a fountain. Though the front entrance and its set of stone steps leading to a massive oaken door did not have a fully covered entrance where a carriage could pull right up to the door, there was a small outbuilding with a large door designed to hold a carriage and I spied stable doors as we turned. There was a covered porch, a servants' entrance there that could be used in awful weather.

Servants' entrance, listen to me! I looked down at my hands suddenly wishing I had a nicer pair of gloves covering my chipped and torn nails. Nate was not distracted by civility. He stared out the window marveling at the sights. My Mama sat across from me. She had a small smile upon her lips. Now she and Papa able to spend their later years here, in comfort and peace with clean air and the sound of birds rather than rattling carriages clamoring by at all hours provided for by the wealth won in the Lamia's lair that made me smile like a child.

Off one side a large amount of glass glinted in the sun. I hoped it would be a greenhouse. That would make Papa happy. Twelve hundred acres that housed thirteen families. Nate and I would be guardian of them all. It was as daunting as facing another Lamia.

It took less than a week for some of the novelty to wear off. Two sprawling floors; an entrance hall; a glass conservatory full of wonderful green plants; several bedrooms and indoor baths; a grand ballroom, that I was sure we would never use; kitchens and gardens; stables off the back and too many stairways—I was mistress of it all, and I was hopelessly lost.

"Nate!" This was getting ridiculous, having him in the far wing of the manor was proper, but other than the servants, there was no one to gossip and threaten my reputation. I turned down a hallway and almost walked right into a wall.

I cursed in a most unladylike fashion. This was a beautiful home, to be sure—but when one moved from a small-town home to a manor complete with a giant glass conservatory and a great hall, gardens, hunting lands, and an office—it took some getting used to. I wasn't sure whether to envy Lady Rothechild or pity her. She had several of these beautiful manors dotting France, England, and Spain and matching estates in other countries. It was a lot of beautiful homes to decorate and enjoy, but a lot of unique floor plans to learn to navigate. This wall, at the end of a long hallway, was in need of a painting, or a knick-knack of some sort on a fancy table. Lady Rothechild had stylishly appointed this manor house, but she had obviously taken some of her favorite pieces with her in residence. This left a few awkward holes in the decor we would need to fill before we had large parties.

Hiram heard me swear and seemed to appear from thin air. "Did you need anything Ma'am?"

"No, thank you." Then I paused. "Actually, Hiram, do you paint?"

His mouth opened and closed a few times. I seemed to have a knack for posing the strangest questions—questions a lady didn't ask her hired servants. He recovered quickly. "I have painted some, Miss Harper, why would you ask?"

"Because when I came to your home I saw quite a few beautiful paintings—forgive me, but I would assume that even if you had an eye for art, it would hardly be a priority for an unemployed butler. It is either that or you are moonlighting as a forger. If that is the case, perhaps I need to fill your time with more duties."

Hiram had a small smile teasing on the corners of his mouth. "I do paint. I find it diverting."

"Would you paint something for this wall?" I asked. "Something of appropriate size and subject. Nothing of myself please, I can't stomach the notion of running into myself in the middle of the night." The encounter with my other self in the ley well on Molten Cay still haunted my thoughts.

"I would be happy to, though I am sure I could secure something more appropriate in short order." He was trying not to stammer.

"Hiram, you have been given a proper room. I insist on you using it for more than sleeping. I would like to give you a gift of painting supplies and candles. Hopefully, you will honor me in return with your finest work."

He gave a proper bow and nodded. "Ma'am, if you are headed to the conservatory, you will find the stairs down and to the left a more suitable path than through the wall."

I thanked him, grateful for his humor and good will, and went to find my fiancée.

Nate was in the conservatory, staring out the glass windows to the rolling fields that spread out across our new estate.

"You look restless," I said, slipping my arm into his elbow.

He took a long time to answer. "If you had asked me where I would live when I was grown, a manor in the English country-side would not have made the list."

I laughed. "I thought I would have ended up in a large home in Kensington Gardens while Mr. Goodwin spent his time drinking and gambling away his inheritance. We both ended up much better."

He smiled at that. "I suppose you wish to discuss wedding plans again."

"Am I that transparent?" I asked, coyly batting my eyes.

"Well, it is all you wanted to talk about for the past week."

"Actually, I have finished making the decisions," I said. "We will have a modest affair, then a garden party to follow. We can do a nice tea and then a ball. I am sure that after we retire, Hiram could manage the household and the guests."

He gave a wolfish grin when I mentioned retiring. It was becoming quite hard for me to stick to propriety with no one to judge and gossip in a large home all our own.

Hiram walked up to us. "Ma'am" He handed me the day's mail—a cream colored envelope written in Molly Morgan's fine hand. I would know it anywhere, I had read her book on sea creatures almost daily, remembering joyfully our time on board *The Lightning Aura*.

My Dear Vivian,

I have enclosed a gift for you, inspired by your clockwork birds. This is a clockwork mouse. He is equipped with lock picks within his arms, wind him up and set him against the lock. Should he not function correctly please replace the fuse in his back. I hope you enjoy him.

I have also included my schematics for the hydro-ion heater you are so fond of. Hopefully one can be installed within your town-home in London.

We have recently taken in a new crewman. I feel we shall get along well. He is an inventor from London—he is brought his life-savings to purchase a berth on The Lightning Aura. He is studying lightning and how it can be used to better the life of the common man, and he has expressed an interest in my work.

If Nate has not expressed his desire to wed you by now he may need a push in the correct direction. Remind him that Gracie found happiness in an unlikely place.

"I do not need convincing," Nate said. He had been reading over my shoulder again, "My life is here, with the woman I am going to marry."

I smiled and turned to pour him a glass of wine. We had peace here. I would have a husband, a home for my parents but I gained more than that; I traveled into darkness and found myself. Truly a better life was waiting. The trick was being brave enough to seek it. Time for another venture.

My fiancé sat sipping the wine from a glass, the dark bruises from our battle with Geiger for the fate of London still a badge of honor. I was probably much the same. It didn't matter. There was so much more to us both now.

I grabbed the book I placed on the window sill earlier. "What did you say about Zanzibar?"

Nate was frowning at the letter again. "Hmm?"

"You still crave adventure correct? We shall have to visit a bookseller next time we are in London. We do not have a volume on Zanzibar, but Nate, if you are up for an adventure?"

He set the wine glass down, rising from the chair as he did so. A slow smile spread across his face. We spoke the same language now and forever.

I held up the book. "*Empire of the Czar: A Journey Through Eternal Russia.* How do you feel about Russia?"

Nate thrust out his chest protectively. "They are thought to be positively fearsome, Miss Harper. Some days they are an ally of England, other times they are our enemy. It would take a canny traveler indeed to navigate the landscape safely. Do you need your fiancé, a large frightening canithrope, to protect you?"

I laughed and pushed him hard. The air left him in a rush. "Of course not. Haven't you heard? You are engaged to marry a regular adventuress. I fight monsters. I shoot guns, I ride horses. Why, just recently, I have even saved the world. But, I would love the company upon my next grand adventure."

"I am at your command then, Miss Harper," He said taking my hand.

"Tally-Ho; Mr. Valentine, adventure waits for no one!"

ACKNOWEDGMENTS

SPECIAL THANKS to the friends and family that have given me their support, their love, their time and their critiques as I ran down this path. It is all that I ever really wanted to be and thanks to you I am here. Special thank you to Rex, William, Colleen, Dani, Charlie, Aaron, Mel, Stant, and Ellie.

It was an adventure of joy and tears, and one I was blessed to take.

SÖS